Kalev

Kalev

Book I in the Age of the Rephaim Series

By Kenneth Bracker

Knights of Saint George Press

Kalev
Book I in the Age of the Rephaim Series
© 2025 Kenneth Bracker
All rights reserved.

This is a work of historical fiction. While it is inspired by the biblical account of Kalev (Caleb) and the era of the conquest of Canaan, certain characters, events, and dialogue have been imagined or expanded upon for narrative purposes. Scriptural references have been interpreted through the lens of storytelling and literary tradition. Readers are encouraged to refer to the biblical texts for the canonical account.

Published by
Knights of Saint George Press
Charleston, SC

First Printing, 2025

ISBN: 979-8-9992359-0-9 (Paperback) 979-8-9992359-1-6 (digital)
Cover design, interior layout, and typesetting: Knights of Saint George Press
For more information, visit: www.knightsofsaintgeorgepress.com

Printed in the United States of America

Contents

Key Names and Terms

To guide you through this story, here are some important Hebrew names and words you will encounter, along with their traditional spellings and pronunciations. These names carry deep meaning and connection to the ancient land and people. I have chosen to retain many of the Hebrew renderings not for the sake of novelty, but to restore the texture of the world in which these events first unfolded. Language shapes how we perceive time and truth; by hearing the names as they might once have sounded—spoken by prophets, whispered in prayer, etched into memory—we draw nearer to their weight and warmth. To walk these paths with Kalev and his kin is to remember that before they were stories in ink, they were lives lived in dust and fire, under stars, by rivers, and within covenant. The names are part of that world, and by preserving them, I hope to draw you deeper into its breath and bone.

Kalev (כָּלֵב, *pronounced: Kah-LEV*) — Caleb
Also known as **Kalev ben Yefuneh** (כָּלֵב בֶּן יְפֻנֶּה, *pronounced: Kah-LEV ben Yeh-foo-NEH*), meaning "Caleb, son of Jephunneh." A loyal spy and warrior, steadfast in faith and courage, noted among the Israelites for his dark complexion and unwavering spirit. An elder of Judah.

Joshua — "**Yehoshua**" (יְהוֹשֻׁעַ, *pronounced: Yeh-hoh-SHOO-ah*)
While many names in this story are rendered in their Hebrew form to draw you closer to the ancient world and its sounds, the name "Joshua" is kept in its familiar English form. This is not from neglect but intention. Joshua stands as a bridge — a name recognized through generations and across languages, embodying the leader who carries the promise of deliverance and faith. To honor his place in both the story and the hearts of readers, I have chosen to use "Joshua" throughout, even as the land and people speak in the tongue of their ancestors.

Kena'an (כְּנַעַן, *pronounced: Keh-nah-AHN*) — Canaan
The fertile land promised to Avraham's descendants, filled with ancient peoples and many trials.
Kena'ani (singular) in Hebrew is כְּנַעֲנִי (*pronounced: Keh-nah-ah-NEE*) for a male, or Kena'anim (plural) is כְּנַעֲנִים (*pronounced: Keh-nah-ah-NEEM*) for a group of males or mixed group, or כְּנַעֲנִיּוֹת (*pronounced: Keh-nah-ah-nee-YOHT*) for a group of females.

Ivrim (עִבְרִים, *pronounced: Eev-REEM*) — Hebrews (plural)
The collective name for the descendants of Avraham, bound by covenant and promise.

Avraham (אַבְרָהָם, *pronounced: Ahv-rah-HAHM*) — Avraham
The patriarch who obeyed God's call to leave his home and become father of many nations.

Mosheh (מֹשֶׁה, *pronounced: Moh-SHEH*) — Moses
The great prophet and deliverer who led Israel from Egypt and received the Law on Sinai.

Rachav (רָחָב, *pronounced: Rah-CHAHV*) — Rahab
The woman of Jericho whose faith protected Israel's spies and changed her destiny.

Anakim (עֲנָקִים, *pronounced: Ah-nah-KEEM*) — Anakim
A formidable race of giants said to inhabit the land, striking fear in the hearts of Israel.

Refaim (רְפָאִים, *pronounced: Reh-fah-EEM*) — Rephaim
Ancient mighty ones—giants—whose memory haunts the legends of Kena'an.

Shedim (שֵׁדִים, *pronounced: Sheh-DEEM*) — Shedim
Spirits or demons of the ancient world, often feared and whispered about in dark places. The unseen forces opposed to Yahweh's covenant, their shadows lingering over the land.

Nehar ha-Yarden, or "**Yarden**" (נְהַר הַיַּרְדֵּן, *pronounced: Neh-HAHR hah-Yahr-DEHN*) — Jordan River
The Jordan River holds significant religious and geographical importance in the Bible. It marks a boundary, both physical and symbolic, and is the site of several pivotal events, including the crossing of the Israelites into the Promised Land and Jesus' baptism.

Yehudah (יְהוּדָה, *pronounced: Yeh-hoo-DAH*) — Judah
One of the twelve clans of Israel, of which Kalev is eventually the leader and elder.

Chapter One
The Fall of Ai

The sky was copper when the ambush signal rose, a molten veil stretched taut across the heavens, as if the Almighty Himself had forged it in the fires of His wrath. From the ridge line, I saw it—a thick column of black smoke unfurling into the firmament like a serpent, its coils heavy with the weight of judgment. Ai was burning from within, just as Joshua had foretold. The flames devoured rooftops and the north gate, a conflagration kindled not merely by strategy but by the justice of heaven, a purging fire that whispered of ancient verdicts and divine decrees. I turned to the men beside me, my breath sharp in my throat, and gave the signal—two crisp clicks of my tongue, sharp as flint striking stone.

Shields rose, their cedar frames gleaming with bronze rims that caught the dying light. Swords hissed free of leather, their edges honed by the smiths of Gilgal, each blade a prayer forged in bronze. Bows flexed, sinew taut with the promise of retribution. My brothers, my kin—men of Asher, Dan, Naphtali, and Yehudah—stood ready, their eyes alight with a fire not born of mortal will. In that moment, they were no longer mere men. They were Ivrim, sons of the covenant, vessels of a purpose older than the hills we trod. The sun crowned their helmets, and our cries rose like thunder rolling down the slope, a chorus that shook the dust from the stones.

We descended.

Dust exploded beneath our sandals as we poured down the hillside—a wave of sweat and iron, of roaring voices that carried the weight of forty years in the wilderness. The ambush was no longer silent. It had become the voice of retribution, a song of deliverance sung with the clash of bronze and the rhythm of pounding feet. Arrows from the men of Ai hissed overhead—panicked, scattered, loosed by hands that trembled with sudden dread. The men of Ai had turned inward now, their eyes wide with the realization that the first force they had chased into the wilderness was never meant to win. Joshua's column, feigning retreat, had drawn them out, luring them into the open like lambs to the shearer's blade. And we, the hidden blade, rose behind them, unexpected and unforgiving, like death glimpsed in the rearview of a dying god.

They never saw us coming.

And what's more—they never expected we would fight like them.

Joshua had sent us—five thousand men chosen in silence—to the west of Ai under cover of night, threading our way through rock and scrub like smoke on the wind. We bivouacked beneath a tangle of hill and thorn, our breath quiet, our bodies pressed low into the dust of Kena'an. For hours we did not speak. The wind came and went. The stars wheeled overhead. Somewhere below us, the city of Ai still slept, unaware that the hour of its judgment had already begun to count down.

Joshua's plan was bold—like the crossing of the Nehar Ha-Yarden, like the siege of Jericho—but more cunning still. We would not take Ai by might alone. No—this would be a war of patience and precision, a trap laid with a steady hand and triggered at the moment of divine reckoning. From the north, Joshua led the larger host of Israel, twenty five thousand men, to present a direct challenge, plain and visible in the rising light. They came with war cries and banners lifted high, dust rising like smoke behind their march. They came not to win—but to flee.

It was a strange thing, to watch our brethren make a show of cowardice. To watch Joshua, the Spear of the Twelve Clans, whose word could still the sun, feign weakness. But it worked. Ai had tasted victory once before; they remembered how we fled and fell by the sword. Now, seeing Joshua's army arrayed on the heights, they did not hesitate.

"When the king of Ai saw this," the scroll will say, "he and all the men of the city hurried out early in the morning." Not just some—not a raiding party. All the men of Ai poured out through the north gate like water from a breached vessel. And not only Ai, but Bethel too. Every sword, every shield, every spear—gone from the city. They came in haste, eager for another rout, laughing perhaps, their mouths already full of imagined spoils. They rushed to meet Israel in battle on the slopes overlooking the Arabah.

And Joshua let them win.

Our warriors turned their backs, the whole company of them, and fled as if the terror of the Lord had abandoned them. Down the rocky paths they ran, kicking up clouds of dust, their voices raised in mock despair. The men of Ai roared in pursuit, never pausing, never suspecting that they were being led by the nose toward their ruin. They chased with all their strength, with no thought of what lay behind them. They did not know that the city stood naked, exposed, and watched by five thousand silent wolves waiting in the hills.

Then came the sign.

Joshua stopped his retreat and raised his spear—high and still, a blade of iron lifted against the sky. That single movement cracked the silence like thunder. We surged up from the ridge and poured down upon Ai. There were no watchmen. No shouts of alarm. No arrows from the walls. There were no men in the city at all. The north gate gaped wide like the mouth of Sheol.

For we had learned. We had suffered. We had bled already for our arrogance, and the memory of that shame burned hotter than the flames now consuming Ai. This was not our first assault. No, we had dared to strike Ai once before, and we had failed—miserably, wretchedly, as if the Almighty Himself had turned His face from us. Thirty-six men died that day, thirty-six sons of Israel, their blood soaking the dust of these same hills. I saw them fall, struck down by the spears and blades of Ai's defenders, their bodies crumpling like stalks before the scythe. Young men, fathers, brothers—men who had crossed the Nehar Ha-Yarden with songs of victory on their lips, who had seen Jericho's walls collapse at the shout of faith. We had thought no man, no city, no god could stand against us. We had marched on Ai with pride in our hearts, certain that Yahweh's favor was a mantle we could never lose.

But Ai had stopped us.

Ai, small and proud, perched like a hawk on its hill, had routed us. Its warriors, though few, fought with a ferocity that seemed unnatural, as if bolstered by powers unseen. We had sent only a small force—three thousand men, a fraction of our strength—deeming Ai unworthy of our full might. But they had poured from the gate in the North, swift and relentless, driving us back in disarray. I remember the chaos, the cries of the wounded, the dust choking our lungs as we fled. I remember the faces of the fallen, their eyes staring blankly at a sky that offered no mercy. Thirty-six lives snuffed out, not by the might of men alone, but by our own folly.

The truth came later, bitter as gall. Achan, son of Karmi, had sinned in secret. Gold from Jericho, a wedge of forbidden wealth, and a Babylonian mantle—treasures cursed by Yahweh's command to destroy all that was defiled—lay hidden beneath his tent. He had taken what was not his, defying the Holy One who had parted the Nehar Ha-Yarden and toppled Jericho's walls. His rebellion, though unseen by us, was laid bare before the eyes of the Almighty. And because of his sin, the cloud of God's presence withdrew, leaving us exposed, vulnerable, like sheep without a shepherd. Joshua rent his garments and fell on his face before the Ark, his voice a broken plea: Why, O Yahweh, have You brought us to ruin? And the answer came, sharp as a blade: Israel has sinned. Therefore they cannot stand.

The camp was purged. Stone by stone, judgment by judgment, Achan and all his household were swallowed by fire and earth, their sin expiated in the valley of Achor. I stood among the witnesses, my heart heavy, my eyes fixed on the flames. The weight of our failure pressed upon us all, a reminder that the covenant was no light thing, that the God who fought for us demanded holiness as fiercely as He demanded faith. Only then did the cloud of God's silence lift. Only then did the pillar of fire stir once more, its glow a promise renewed.

But Yahweh did not send us blindly into battle again. This time, He gave us a plan—not a march of trumpets and circling priests, not a miracle of crumbling walls, but a strategy born of divine wisdom, a war guided by the hand of the Holy One. Joshua gathered us at dusk, his face weathered but resolute, and spoke of the ambush. A small force would make itself visible to Ai, drawing out their warriors as they had before. Their king, puffed up by his previous triumph, would take the bait, charging into the wilderness with his men, leaving the city vulnerable. And we, the hidden force, would rise from the hills, silent as foxes in the brush, to strike from behind.

The plan unfolded before the moon had set. Joshua led the decoy force, their footsteps loud in the dawn, their banners raised to catch the eye of Ai's watchmen. I led the third division, five thousand strong, creeping through ravines in the dark, our breaths hushed, our sandals wrapped in cloth to muffle the sound. We scaled the hills in silence, our bodies pressed low against the earth, the stars our only witnesses. The cold stung our fingers, the rocks tore at our knees, but we moved as one, bound by the promise of victory. We waited, hidden in the folds of the land, until the signal came—the black smoke rising from Ai, kindled by our scouts who had slipped into the city under cover of night.

Now we descended, a tide of righteous fury. We lit their battle legions on fire with lighted arrows. The fire was not kind, but it was just—a herald of the judgment that had come for the sons of the serpent, the clans of the Anakim who defied the Almighty with their very existence. We could see them now, the men of Ai, turning back from their pursuit of Joshua's force, their faces pale with dread as they realized their city was lost. Their escape was blocked, their ranks trapped between two fronts—Joshua's men wheeling about in the wilderness, and our ambush driving into their flank like a spear through flesh.

They had not seen us coming, for their eyes were blinded by pride, their hearts hardened by the whispers of powers that were not gods. They had thought us broken, scattered by their first victory, unaware that Yahweh had forged us anew in the crucible of our shame. We fought not as men alone, but as the arm of the divine council, the executors of a verdict pronounced before the foundations of the earth. The Anakim, the seed of the watchers, would fall—not by our might, but by the will of the One who drowned their fathers in the flood.

But it was no easy slaughter.

Screams echoed from within their lines, sharp, brittle. I caught one of the men mid-turn. My blade took him at the collarbone, and I felt the crunch, the warmth that came a breath later, and then he folded like clay.

Behind me, my men surged forward, brothers of Asher and Dan and Naphtali, some hardly older than boys, but they fought with the fire of those who knew that to die in Yahweh's war was better than to live under the sons of the serpent. The air was thick with dust and the clamor of bronze, the cries of the faithful rising like a song against the shadowed walls of Ai. We had breached the lines of soldiers.

And the Anakim were waiting within their ranks, we had seen their heads above the front lines.

They stood in the second line, massive and unnatural, like figures carved from old mountain stone. I had heard rumors they still lived—the long-armed kings of Bashan, the forgotten warriors of Rephaim who once ruled the land when the floodwaters receded. Now I saw them with my own eyes. Not as towering as the cedars of

Hebron, perhaps, but this one stood near eight feet, his frame broad as two men, his skin a sickly gray, mottled like stone left too long in a forsaken place. His eyes gleamed with a malice that was not of this world, and his presence seemed to choke the air, as if the very stones of Ai wept at his tread.

He moved—no, lunged—through the smoke like a tree uprooted in anger. His weapon was not of bronze or wood but black iron, a crude blade longer than a man was tall, its edge jagged as if hewn from a nightmare. He swung it sideways, and three of our front ranks scattered, diving to the earth as the iron arc sang above them. The ground shook where the blade struck, gouging a scar in the dust. But none were slain—Yahweh's hand was upon us.

I remembered Hebron.

I remembered the caves.

I remembered the darkness we faced years ago, when Joshua and I had seen the Anakim there—tall as cedars, their voices like grinding stone. The others who went with us lost heart, whispering of giants and doom. But not me. Not Joshua. We had seen the promise of Yahweh, and it burned brighter than fear.

So I did not flinch now.

I drove forward, ducking low as the bronze blade swept over me, its cold breath tugging at the tangled coils that crowned my head, strands snapping free like whispered shadows. The giant's eyes locked on mine, and I saw it then—not flesh or bone alone, but something other, something inhabited. Mosheh had warned us of the shedim, those wandering spirits born of Nephilim blood, drowned in the flood yet clinging still to the earth, seeking vessels to defile. This was no mere man, no simple giant. This was a creature bound to dark power, a servant of the watchers' cursed brood.

"Zabad! Toviah!" I shouted, calling to two of my men. Zabad of Asher, wiry and quick, gripped a spear, his eyes fierce with faith. Toviah of Dan, broad-shouldered and steady as the hills, held a bronze axe. They flanked me, moving as one—brothers in the war against the serpent's seed.

The giant snarled, a sound like boulders cracking in a storm, and charged. His steps shook the earth, dust rising in clouds. I braced my shield, its cedar frame bound in bronze, and gripped my sword, its edge honed by the smiths of Gilgal. He swung the bronze blade again, aiming to cleave me in two. I parried, angling my shield to deflect the blow. The giant's sword slammed into my arm with a force that splintered the shield's edge and drove the amulet tucked against my chest deep into my flesh. That amulet—a final gift from Mosheh—bore the Shema inscribed in ancient Ivrim, the NAME of El Elyon etched with prayer: *"May the faith you hold in the Most High match the power sealed within these words."* It was this blessing, whispered in the wilderness, that guarded my soul from the shadows that claimed others—a silent shield woven of faith and the holy Name.

Zabad darted in from the right, thrusting his spear at the giant's thigh. Not deep, drawing a trickle of dark, viscous blood that smelled of ash and decay. The giant roared and swiped at Zabad with his free hand. He rolled clear, the massive fingers grazing his tunic, tearing a strip of cloth free.

Toviah struck next, swinging his axe at the giant's ankle. The blade sparked against the thickened hide, chipping bone but not felling him. The giant pivoted, faster than his bulk suggested, and brought the bronze blade down. Toviah leapt back, the weapon burying itself in the earth where he had stood, sending a spray of dirt skyward.

I seized the moment. As the giant yanked his blade free, I lunged, slashing at his side.

My sword cut deep, parting the leathery skin, but the wound was shallow for such a beast. He turned, his eyes blazing with that unholy glee, and swung a backhanded blow. I ducked, feeling the air part above me, and rolled to his flank. My shoulder burned from the earlier parry, but the clarity of Sinai surged within me, sharp and unyielding.

"Together!" I called. Zabad and Toviah closed in, their movements a dance of courage. Zabad thrust again, aiming for the giant's knee. The spear sank deeper this time, and the creature staggered, his leg buckling. Toviah hacked at the same leg, his axe biting into the joint. The giant bellowed, a sound that rattled the stones of Ai, and lashed out with his fist. Toviah dodged, but the blow grazed his shoulder, sending him sprawling. He scrambled up, unharmed, his axe still in hand.

I circled to the giant's back, my breath ragged but my resolve unbroken. He was slowing now, his wounded leg dragging, but his strength was far from spent. He whirled, the bronze blade arcing low. I leapt over it, the jagged edge grazing my sandal, and landed in a crouch. Before he could recover, I drove my sword into the soft flesh behind his knee. The blade sank deep, and he roared, stumbling forward.

Zabad struck again, his spear piercing the giant's side. The creature swatted at him, but Zabad was too quick, dancing out of reach. Toviah rejoined us, swinging his axe at the giant's arm. The blade lodged in the forearm, and the giant howled, dropping the bronze weapon. It thudded to the ground, raising a cloud of dust.

"Now!" I shouted. We pressed the attack, a triad bound by faith. I climbed the giant's back, gripping the bristled hide, my sword raised. He thrashed, trying to shake me off, but Zabad and Toviah kept him off balance, jabbing and hacking at his legs. I drove my blade into the base of his neck, where the spine met the skull. The sword met resistance—something dense, not bone, not sinew, but something darker, like bronze sealed in flesh. I leaned my weight into it, and with a sickening give, it split.

A hiss erupted from the wound. Not breath. Not blood. Black vapor, thick and foul, poured out like smoke from a burning tomb. It smelled of rot and copper, of old altars and forbidden rites. The giant screamed—a sound not of this world, a chorus of shrieks like a thousand bats caught in fire. The cry echoed across the valley, chilling the blood of even the men of Ai. The birds fled, and the wind recoiled.

He buckled, falling to one knee, then the other. I clung tight, twisting the blade deeper.

The vapor thickened, stinging my eyes, coiling around us like a serpent. Zabad and Toviah fell back, their faces pale but their resolve unbroken. The giant's body seized, arching backward as if bound by unseen chains. His mouth gaped, and from it came that unholy chorus, a wail of ancient defiance.

Then he went still.

He collapsed forward like a felled oak, the ground shaking with his fall. I rolled clear, gasping, my sword blackened where it had touched the creature's essence. The carcass sizzled where the vapor lingered, skin blistering and splitting.

Zabad and Toviah stood beside me, their breaths heavy, their weapons stained. Behind us, our men surged again, their cries rising as the tide turned. But I saw none of it.

I stood over the fallen giant and whispered words I did not know I remembered:

"the Name rebuke you, ancient one."

The smoke that remained coiled upward like incense—dark and foul—and vanished into the sky.

We stormed the inner regiments.

And there—Yahweh preserve me—stood another.

Not just tall, but wrong. His skin shimmered faintly, like heat over stone. His armor was bone and hide and pieces of skull.

The giant stood a head taller than the tallest of men—twice again as broad—and his skin bore the pallor of old stone, weathered by generations of rot and ruin. His eyes, unblinking, gleamed with a hunger not born of flesh but of something older, something that remembered the verdict of the flood and sought to defy it. I saw one of our men—a young man from Yitzkhakhar, more bravery than wisdom—rush him, spear raised, shouting a cry to Yahweh.

The giant didn't even dodge.

He swung his arm sideways with the weight of a falling tree. It caught the boy mid-leap and sent him tumbling through the air, cartwheeling like a rag caught in the wind. He struck the earth hard, rolling to a stop, dazed but alive, his spear lost in the dust. The boy scrambled back, saved by the grace of the Almighty.

That was when the creature looked at me.

Not past me. Not through me. At me.

And I knew.

This was no mere remnant of old blood. No child of exaggerated bone or luckless parentage. No.

He was inhabited.

Mosheh had spoken of them. The shedim. Disembodied spirits of the giants drowned in the flood, cursed to wander dry places, gasping for flesh to cling to. Hungry, old, and cruel. These were the watchers' bastard brood, twisted beyond even the curse of Adam.

The people of Ai had made a pact sealed in blood—a covenant with powers that rejoiced in the ruin of creation. This was no war against mere men that God had sent us on. This was a war against giants. A war against those who had bound themselves to darkness through bloodlust and child sacrifice. *Eaters of flesh.* Practitioners of abominations so vile they had to be cut from the land like rot from bone.

And now one of them had found a home.

He smiled.

Not like a man. No warmth, no rage. Just that slow, knowing curl of the lip—a predator recognizing another predator, one that had once fallen and now sought to undo the fall with slaughter.

No beast smiles in war.

Only something that remembers a verdict and hopes to reverse it.

I raised my shield, its cedar frame bound in bronze, and gripped my sword, its edge honed by the smiths of Gilgal. The giant came like a landslide, one leg dragging slightly, arms swinging low and wide. He made no war cry—only a deep, guttural groan like stone grinding stone. The earth trembled as he closed the gap between us.

The first blow shattered my shield—splintered it in two and sent me staggering. My shoulder blazed with pain, my left arm dropping uselessly to my side. I tasted blood. But I didn't fall.

I circled left, pain narrowing my vision. He followed, slower now, testing, toying, sniffing the air like a hound. His fingers curled and uncurled, hungry for flesh. His eyes never blinked.

He lunged again. I ducked low, his massive fist whistling over my head, the wind of it ruffling my hair. I rolled beneath his arm, dust clouding my eyes, the ground shuddering beneath his feet. I was behind him now.

I struck high, slicing a shallow cut across the back of his thigh. It should have crippled a man.

He didn't even flinch.

He turned, and his gaze locked mine—there was glee in it now, like a shadow laughing in the firelight. He swung again, a backhanded blow aimed at my chest. I parried with my sword, the blade ringing as it met his forearm, hard as Bronze. The force numbed my hand, but I held firm, twisting away as his other hand clawed at me, missing by a breath.

I danced back, my side burning where my scale armor had grazed my ribs in the roll. My breath was short, ragged. But something in me rose—not fear, not hate, but a clarity I had only ever known at Sinai, when the mountain shook and the voice of Yahweh thundered.

The giant snarled and came again, faster this time, his dragging leg no hindrance. His arms swung in a deadly arc, one after the other, like twin battering rams. I ducked the first, feeling the air part above me. The second I met with my blade, angling it to deflect the blow. The impact jarred my bones, but the sword held. I spun to his flank, slashing at his side. The blade bit shallow, drawing a trickle of dark, viscous blood that smelled of ash and decay.

He roared, more anger than pain, and whirled to face me. His massive hand shot out, fingers splayed to crush. I dropped to one knee, letting his grasp close on empty air, and thrust upward, aiming for the soft flesh beneath his arm. The blade sank deep, and this time he staggered, a low groan escaping his lips.

I yanked the sword free and leapt back. He swung wildly, his balance faltering, and I saw my chance. I darted in, feinting high to draw his guard, then dove low, slashing at the joint of his knee. The blade hit, and his leg buckled. He crashed to one knee, the ground shaking with the impact, his hand catching him as the other clawed at me.

I sidestepped, his fingers grazing my cloak, and sprang onto his back, clinging to the bristled hide and ridged spine. Every breath was a battle as he thrashed, trying to rise. I struck again, driving my sword into the base of his neck.

I leaned my weight into it, and with a sickening give, it split.

A hiss erupted from the wound. Not breath. Not blood.

Black vapor, thick and foul, poured out like smoke from a burning tomb. It smelled of rot and Bronze, of old altars and forbidden rites. It smelled of death.

The giant screamed—truly screamed now—and bucked like a beast in its death throes. I clung tight, blade still buried in his neck. He reached back, his fingers scrabbling for me, but I twisted the sword, driving it deeper. The vapor thickened, coiling around us, stinging my eyes.

His body seized, arching backward as if straining against unseen chains. His mouth opened wide, and from it came not a human voice but a chorus of shrieks—like a thousand bats caught in fire. The sound echoed across the valley, chilling the blood of even the men of Ai. The birds took flight, and the wind itself seemed to recoil.

The giant convulsed once, then went still.

Then the body went still.

It fell forward like a felled tower, and I rolled clear just before the ground shook beneath its final collapse.

I stood, gasping, my sword blackened where it had touched the creature's essence. The carcass sizzled where the black vapor lingered, skin blistering and splitting. Whatever had worn this body like a robe had fled—but not before leaving its mark.

Behind me, our men surged again, their cries rising as the tide turned. But I saw none of it.

I stood over the fallen giant and whispered words I did not know I remembered:

"Return to the dust, shadow of the first rebellion" I said.

The smoke that remained coiled upward like incense—dark and foul—and vanished into the sky.

But there was no time to breathe. The square erupted.

From the eastern valley, a second wave of Ai's defenders surged, their eyes wild and blood-painted. They were not giants—but they fought like they were. Men possessed of a final stand, as if they knew they were already dead and meant to make the weight of their fall crush us.

Yet even as the clash of bronze and the cries of the fallen filled the air, my heart turned to the deeper truth of this war, a truth etched in the words of Mosheh and the visions granted to Joshua beneath the shadow of Sinai. This was no mere conquest of land, no petty squabble over fields and flocks. We fought not against men like ourselves, not against the clans of Edom or Moab, who, though

24

distant kin, were spared by Yahweh's command. No, our blades were raised against the seed of the serpent, the Anakim and their defiled allies, whose cities were strongholds of an ancient rebellion. These were the giant clans, the offspring of the watchers, those fallen ones who had dared to mingle their essence with the daughters of men before the flood. Their progeny, towering and unnatural, had not perished entirely in the deluge. They lingered, a blight upon the earth, their hearts bound to the shedim—disembodied spirits that hungered for flesh and dominion.

The very air of Ai seemed to carry the weight of their corruption, a miasma of dread that clung to the valley and choked the wind. This land was not the dwelling of honest men, but citadels of a people who had bartered their souls for power. The Anakim and their vassals had sealed their pact with powers darker than night, offering the blood of infants and the flesh of their own kin to sate the appetites of their false gods. Our spies had whispered of such horrors—tales of shadowed halls where the innocent were slain, their lives snuffed out to fuel a strength that was not human, their bones defiled in feasts that mocked the Creator's design. These were the abominations that Yahweh had set His face against, and we, His people, were the instruments of His verdict. Not for greed or glory did we march, but to purge the land of this ancient evil, to cast down the thrones of those who defied the Almighty with their very existence.

The men of Ai who fought beside the giants were not mere soldiers, but thralls to a deeper corruption. Their eyes, wild and blood-painted, betrayed a madness born of servitude to the Anakim's lords. They had yoked themselves to the same dark powers, partaking in the rites that sustained the giant clans. Those who had fled Ai's tyranny spoke in trembling voices of nights when the city's fires burned with offerings unholy, when the living were forced to join in the horrors or perish. To fight such men was to fight a shadow cast by a greater darkness, a darkness we were called to banish. Yet we fought with the knowledge that our war was not against all who dwelt in Kena'an. Mosheh had been clear: the clans of men—Edom, Moab, Ammon—were to be spared, their sins those of Adam's line, redeemable by grace. But the giant cities, the strongholds of the Anakim—Hebron, Debir, and now Ai—were bastions of a rebellion older than the flood, a defiance that began when the watchers forsook their station in the divine council.

We were not conquerors, but liberators, bearing the weight of a divine mandate. Our swords sang not for bloodlust, but for justice, for the infants whose voices had been stilled, for the land that groaned under the yoke of the nephilim's heirs. The battlefield was a maelstrom now, dust and sweat and the clang of Bronze, but my soul was anchored by this truth. The men of Ai, though fierce, were pawns in a war that spanned the ages, a conflict between the Almighty and the powers that sought to unmake His creation. And though the giants towered above us, their strength was a lie, a hollow boast sustained by horrors that could not stand before the light of Yahweh's presence.

A horn wailed—ours. The signal from Benjamin's flank. I turned in time to see them faltering, boxed in against a crumbled wall of the outer rim of soldiers. I cursed the men of Ai in the name of God and shouted for half my men to pivot. The ranks of Yehudah followed me. The rest I led myself, charging headlong into the press before they could form a wedge.

The first soldier I struck went down screaming, blood spraying across my face like dye. The second slammed into me with a wooden cudgel, cracking a rib. Pain flashed white, but I clung to my sword with one hand and his hair with the other, dragging him forward and ending him on my knee.

My shield was gone, my breath thin, my hearing ringing. But I could feel the battle like a current now, surging and recoiling all around. We were within Ai, but not yet its masters.

"Forward!" I bellowed. "Push to the center!"

I don't know how many heard my voice. Maybe only a couple dozen. But they followed.

Through splintered carts, over fallen horses, past crumpled men.

We reached the center. And there the ground boiled again.

More Anakim.

These were smaller than the giants near the front lines, but still monstrous—bodies bred for killing, arms like siege weapons. One bore a war-club made from the spine of a bull.

Another had no weapon, just claws like obsidian knives fastened to his fingers by sinew and brass.

But worse—far worse—was the thing that followed them.

A figure wrapped in tattered priestly robes, his face masked in golden bone, carved with sigils that writhed in the flickering torchlight like serpents in a pit. His hands glowed red, not with flame but with a power ancient as the first curse, a malevolence that pulsed like a heartbeat, choking the air with dread. When he spoke, the earth trembled, and the torches flared blue, their flames cowering as if in the presence of something profane. His voice was a rasp, like stone scraped over bone, chanting words that clawed at the soul—words not of men, but of the shedim, the cursed spirits that haunted the dry places, thirsting for flesh to claim.

He raised both hands, and my men froze.

Literally froze.

Mid-step. Mid-shout. Mid-swing. Their bodies seized as though bound by unseen chains, eyes rolling, mouths gaping in silent screams. Reuel, a young warrior of Naphtali, began to lift from the ground, his limbs twitching as if pulled by invisible cords. Blood dripped from his nose, then his ears, a crimson trail staining his ashen face. My brothers—men of Asher, Dan, Yehudah—stood helpless, their shields clattering to the dust, their swords slipping from

27

nerveless fingers. The air grew thick, heavy with the stench of rot and Bronze, the same foulness I had smelled when the first giant fell, a reek that spoke of defilement older than the hills.

I had heard tales of sorcery in the wilderness—whispers of dark rites among the tribes we passed, of powers that lingered in the shadows of Kena'an's hills. But never had I faced such a force. This was not the trickery of men, but Genesis-curse sorcery, Tower of Babel poison, the kindling of Cain's rebellion. This was the power of the Anakim's priests, those who sealed their pacts with the watchers' brood through the blood of infants and the flesh of their own kin, offerings that fed the hunger of the shedim. Ai was no mere city; it was a stronghold of the giant clans, a bastion of those who defied Yahweh with every breath, their lives sustained by horrors that stained the land itself.

Yet as my brothers hung suspended, caught in the priest's vile enchantment, I stood untouched, my feet firm upon the blood-soaked earth. The air pressed against me, thick with the same defiling reek, but it could not bind my limbs nor cloud my heart. I reached instinctively to the amulet Mosheh had placed about my neck in the shadow of Sinai, its weight a steady anchor. His voice echoed in my memory, his hands trembling with the fire of prophecy as he spoke the blessing:

"Yahweh's Name shall be your shield, the Shema your strength."

The amulet, etched with the sacred Name and the words of devotion, burned warm against my chest, a pulse of light against the darkness. The priest's eyes, gleaming with malice, met mine, and I saw his confusion—his power, born of blood and betrayal, faltered before the covenant sealed by Mosheh's faith. In that moment, I remembered: just as at the caves of Hebron, the shedim held no claim over me, for I bore the mark of the Almighty's promise.

I ran at him.

Not because I believed I could reach him. Not because I thought I could live forever. But because no one else could move. Because Reuel, my brother in arms, hung suspended, his life bleeding away with every heartbeat. Because the promise of Yahweh—that not one of His people would perish this day—burned in my soul like a coal from Sinai's fire. I ran screaming, my voice the only fire I had left, and hurled the only weapon I could throw—a broken spear, its shaft splintered, picked up from the dust without thought.

The spear struck the priest in the shoulder, its point hit shallow but true. He staggered, his chant faltering, and for a moment, his glowing hands dimmed. The spell wavered. My men gasped, some collapsing to their knees, others clutching their limbs as if reborn from stone. Reuel fell to the earth, coughing, alive. But the priest's eyes, hidden behind that golden mask, burned with anger. He hissed, a sound like serpents coiling in the dark, and raised one hand again. The air crackled, and I felt my own limbs begin to seize, my steps slowing as if wading through a river of tar.

I ducked low, rolling to avoid an unseen force that tore the ground where I had stood, sending shards of stone skyward. The priest advanced, his robes trailing like smoke, his hands weaving patterns that burned the air with a sickly red glow. I scrambled to my feet, my sword blade still blackened from the giant's essence. He lunged, a claw-like hand reaching for my throat, its radiance searing my skin even from a distance. I parried with my blade, the impact jarring my bones, and twisted away, his fingers grazing my cloak. The fabric smoldered where he touched, the stench of charred linen mingling with the foul air.

He spoke again, his voice a chorus of discordant shrieks, and the ground beneath me buckled, a fissure opening like a maw. I leapt sideways, my sandal catching on a stone, but I regained my balance, my heart pounding with the clarity of desperation. My men, still recovering, shouted warnings, their voices faint through the roar in my ears. I struck at the priest, my sword slashing at his side, but he deflected it with a gesture, the blade glancing off an invisible barrier that sparked like flint. He laughed—a sound like bones grinding in a tomb—and raised both hands, the red glow flaring brighter, a wave of power surging to crush us all.

I darted to his flank, feinting high with my sword to draw his guard, then dove low, aiming for his legs. My blade cut shallow, drawing a trickle of dark, viscous blood that smelled of ash and decay. The priest roared, not in pain but in rage, and swung his arm, a blast of force knocking me back. I hit the ground hard, my breath driven from my lungs, my sword skittering across the stones. He advanced, his mask gleaming with malevolent intent, his hands raised for the final blow. My men cried out, struggling to rise, but the weight of his power held them pinned. Reuel's eyes met mine, wide with terror, and I knew we were lost.

Then, when all hope had fled, a light pierced the darkness, blinding and pure, as if the heavens had torn open.

There, at the center of the valley in the midst of this war, right behind the priest stepped the Angel of the Lord, the Captain of Yahweh's host, His form a vision of glory that no mortal heart could fully bear. He was radiant, clothed in a robe white as lightning, woven with threads that shimmered like the stars over Sinai, each fold aglow with the promise of eternity. His countenance was like the sun at its zenith, yet softened by mercy, His eyes twin flames that pierced through flesh to the soul, seeing all and judging with unerring truth. A sword hung at His side, its hilt blazing with the fire of creation, and the air around Him thrummed with the power that shaped the mountains and bound the seas. The dust at His feet stirred, as if the earth itself bowed, and the shadows fled from His presence like vermin from a flame.

I felt like I was about to fall to my knees, but an unknown strength from within kept me afoot, my heart seized by a terror so profound it was akin to worship, yet woven through it was a love so vast, so tender, that it threatened to unmake me. It was the love of the Almighty, poured out through this divine emissary, a love that had led us through the wilderness, that had parted the Nehar Ha-Yarden, that had promised us this day. My fear was not of death, but of my own unworthiness in the presence of such holiness, yet His gaze held me, steadying my soul with an assurance that spoke of covenant and grace.

He raised a hand, and the priest's sorcery shattered like brittle clay. The red glow vanished, the earth stilled, and my men breathed freely, their strength restored. The priest reeled, hissing in a tongue older than the sons of the serpent, perhaps the very language of the watchers' fall. He turned to flee, but the Angel of the LORD stepped forward, His movement a thunderclap in the silence. With a single gesture, He struck the priest in the chest—not with a weapon, but with the weight of divine authority. The priest screamed, his golden mask splintering, his body writhing as if torn by unseen forces. His robes smoked, his bones glowed briefly beneath his flesh, and then he collapsed, a twisted husk consumed by the fire of holiness.

The Angel of the Lord turned to me, His gaze both merciful and unyielding, a king who had walked the earth before its foundations were laid. "Fear not, Kalev," He said, His voice like the rush of many waters, resonant with the power that spoke the stars into being. "This day, no son of Israel shall fall, for I am with you, and the seed of the serpent shall be crushed beneath the heel of Yahweh's justice."

I opened my mouth to speak. But he turned and was gone into the smoke.

The waves of enemy soldiers began to dissipate. I looked up, and there, walking through the chaos, was Joshua.

He moved with the fury of a storm given flesh, unflinching amid the screams and clashing bronze. His sword remained sheathed, but his hand rose and fell like a master's baton—commanding the rhythm of death. Wherever he pointed, the men followed as if pulled by invisible cords. The enemy's line crumbled beneath his will, the men of Ai's strength folding inward like a dying flame.

Joshua's main force had broken through the final waves of the enemy. Their banners—crimson and blue—fluttered like bloodied flags above the shattered ranks. Men poured into the center of the fray, battered and bloodied, yet unyielding, pressing forward like the relentless tide.

The battlefield was ours—but barely.

Before us stretched the broad valley of the Arabah, a shallow basin nestled between the jagged ridges that cradled the ancient city of Ai. To the south, Bethel crowned its hill—a silent sentinel watching the carnage below. The city of Ai itself lay to the east, its ruined walls smoldering in the morning light. The rocky slopes and terraced fields between the two cities had become a graveyard, littered with the fallen—the thousands who had marched out in arrogance, now sprawled across the hard earth like shattered stones.

Amid the gore and dust, the land bore the scars of war: overturned carts, broken spears, shattered shields gleaming dull beneath the sun. Pools of dark blood seeped into the cracked soil, while vultures circled high above, waiting for the feast.

"Kalev!" Someone called my name.

I turned—half-blind, half-deaf—and saw Hur, son of Miriam, limping toward me, one arm bloodied, the other clutching a sling.

The soldiers of Ai were nearly decimated, the legions of soldiers lay dead on the ground, not a single member of our clans lay with them.

"We've found two temples," he gasped, smoke in his throat and dread in his eyes. "The outer altars are still burning. Though the men of Ai lie slain beyond the north gate, the city still breathes. There are worshipers yet within—priestesses and temple keepers, calling on their gods".

"What altar?" I demanded, though part of me already knew.

He pointed toward the city, where we could see Bethel beyond it, where the smoke thickened and the sky cracked with unnatural thunder.

"The altar of Ba'al," Hur said, his voice barely a whisper, as if naming it might summon its power.

"The city is burning as you ordered" said Zadok, who had come up running and out of breath, "but there is sorcery still at its heart".

My stomach turned.

I had hoped—foolishly—that Ai would be merely a city, another stone in the wall of conquest. But Ai was a throne. A cursed city, its very stones steeped in the blood of the innocent, where the cries of children had echoed for generations, offered to powers that mocked the Creator. This was no war of men alone, but a clash where the battles of earth intersected with the war of heaven and hell, a conflict ordained before the flood, when the watchers fell and their seed defiled the land.

And that war was just waking.

Joshua stepped beside me, silent but watchful, his eyes burning with the fire of unyielding purpose. As the scouts approached, breathless with word from the fronts, he listened. Then, without hesitation, he turned to me—his voice low and steady, like iron drawn from the forge. "Take your men. Bring ruin to the city. Let none survive its shadow. I will follow soon."

I gathered my closest warriors—men proven by battle and bound by trust. Othniel, my kinsman, fierce and tireless; Hur, sun-darkened and scarred, steady as stone; and Reuel, lean and sharp-eyed, forged by fire and near-death. Serach moved like a shadow, his blades swift and sure. Abihud of Dan was a ghost in the fray, pale-eyed and silent. Shammah towered, a storm in bronze, and Avidan, our banner-bearer, stood like a mountain, his presence a steadying force.

We followed Hur through the wreckage, entering the city gate past burning homes and collapsing archways. The air was thick with ash and despair. I stooped to claim a shield lying beside a fallen Kena'ani, its handle still warm. The weight steadied me—a reminder that Yahweh's task was not conquest for glory, but judgment on the Anakim and their thralls, whose sins had poisoned the land promised to Avraham. We slew any living whom we passed that hadn't burned from the fires. We slew all in this city, this clan of giant's, the seed of the Rephaim.

We reached the outer courtyard of the high place, and the smell hit us—sweet, coppery, wrong, like the breath of a tomb opened after centuries. And then the singing began, a sound not in any tongue I knew, yet unmistakably a chorus, low and droning, like wind through a graveyard at midnight. It burrowed into my bones, stirring a dread deeper than battle, colder than the wilderness nights.

We rounded the corner.

There, raised high on a black stone, stood the altar, flanked by two statues with serpent faces, their open mouths gaping as if to swallow the sky. Flames roared from within the altar's maw, casting shadows that danced like specters. Above it stood a priestess—tall, hooded, her face veiled in gold that shimmered with an unholy light. In her hands, she held a dagger carved from black obsidian, its edge gleaming as if it hungered for blood.

She was not alone. Around her knelt six children, no older than ten, their eyes glazed, lips moving in rhythm with the chant, their small bodies swaying under the weight of an unseen power.

Behind the altar towered another figure.

It was not a man. It was not a giant. It was both—and neither.

Its body shimmered like oil and smoke, its form rippling as if it struggled to hold its shape. Its head bore horns, not like any beast's, but twisted and jagged, like antlers grown from something long buried and now risen. Its eyes, twin voids of malice, turned to us as we approached. It saw us. It knew us. And it laughed—a terrible, bubbling sound that filled the courtyard and shook the stone beneath our feet.

Reuel stumbled, his sling slipping from his fingers. One of the boys behind me vomited, his spear clattering to the ground. Even I felt a blade of fear slide into my bones, a terror older than the flood, colder than the grave. My men faltered, their breaths ragged, their courage fraying like a rope stretched too thin. But we were not alone. Yahweh's promise burned within us—no son of Israel would fall this day.

Then the creature spoke, not aloud, but within us, its voice a serpent coiling through my mind. "Kalev, son of Jephunneh," it hissed, each word a wound. "You think yourself Ivrim, but your blood sings of older kin. The Kenizzites, born of the nephilim's line, giants who walked the earth when the stars were young. You betray your own, turning your blade against the clans of these Ivrim. Join us, and reclaim the glory of your true heritage!"

I raised my sword, its weight like a mountain, my heart torn by the accusation. The Kenizzites, my kin, had once dwelt among the giant clans, their strength whispered in tales of old—a cursed legacy I never sought. Yet I was no son of the serpent, no heir to the watchers' rebellion. I belonged now to the God of Avraham, grafted into the covenant of Yahweh by His mercy alone. Still, the creature's words clawed at me, stirring doubts I thought long buried.

The priestess's chant rose like smoke, thick with dread, her face unmasked and gleaming with sweat and paint. Her skin, marked with dark-inked runes and sigils, shimmered in the firelight— symbols twisted in worship of things long cursed. She wore a mantle of animal hides—serpent-scale and jackal fur—draped low about her hips, while her torso remained bare, daubed with sacred ash and inked devotions to the old gods. There was no shame in her—only defiance, as if her exposed flesh was itself an altar. Her form stood both regal and defiled. Her eyes caught mine, wide and wild, and the dagger lifted over the trembling child.

"Kalev!" she cried—no mere voice, but a cry from the pit, a demon wrapped in flesh that knew my name. "You are ours! The blood of the Anakim flows in you—the strength of the Nephilim! Why do you slay your kin? Ai is your home, its power your birthright! Cast down your sword, and we will make you a king among the giants!"

Her words struck like arrows, each one a lie wrapped in truth. The Anakim, the seed of the watchers, had defiled the land with their rites—children slain on unholy fires, their flesh consumed to sate the shedim's hunger. Ai was no home, but a stronghold of abomination, a city where the innocent were sacrificed to powers that mocked the Almighty. I was no traitor to my kin, for my kin were Israel, bound by the covenant of Sinai.

"Forward!" I roared, my voice shattering the suffocating silence. "For the God of Israel!"

The creature's laughter ceased, its horned head tilting as if amused by my defiance. The priestess paused, the dagger trembling in her hand, the children's chanting faltering as their small bodies swayed like reeds in a storm. My men rallied—Hur clutching his sling, lips moving in steady prayer; Reuel, the boy from Naphtali, raising his sling, trembling but defiant; and Serach son of Asher, eyes sharp as a hawk's, stepping forward with sword and buckler ready.

The courtyard exploded into chaos.

From the left, a spear flew—Othniel's, swift and true, striking the priestess's arm, and then grabbing his battle axe he prepared to strike. The spear didn't drive deep, but it was enough to make her stagger. The dagger clattered to the stone, and the children screamed, their voices raw and human again, as if the spell had cracked. The creature snarled, its form rippling like smoke caught in a gust, and lunged—not at us, but at the priestess, its clawed hand seizing her throat. She gasped, her gold veil slipping to reveal a face etched with terror, eyes wide and mortal. Whatever power she wielded, it was not her own. The creature's grip tightened, black veins spreading across her skin like cracks in parched earth. She crumpled, lifeless, and the creature turned its gaze back to us, its antlers casting jagged shadows in the firelight.

"Now," it hissed, its voice a chorus of a thousand graves, "you will kneel."

But we did not kneel.

From the northern archway, a horn blared—Joshua's signal. He and his men now inside the city gate, the ground shook as his main force stormed into the courtyard, their crimson banners snapping in the wind. Bronze clashed against bronze, and the air filled with the guttural cries of Ivrim warriors and the desperate shouts of Ai's last defenders. Joshua himself led them, his face streaked with ash and blood, his eyes burning with a fire that no darkness could quench.

The creature recoiled, its form flickering as if the presence of Yahweh's chosen unnerved it. I seized the moment, charging toward the altar, my sword raised. The creature's claw lashed out, faster than thought, and I ducked, feeling the air scream past my head. My blade struck its leg, biting into something neither flesh nor shadow. It howled, a sound that split the sky, and black ichor sprayed across the stone, hissing where it landed.

I fought my way forward, parrying a claw that sought my chest, the impact jarring my arm. Another swipe came, and I rolled to the side, the creature's talons raking the ground, sending sparks flying. My men pressed in, their spears and swords flashing, but the creature's power held them at bay, a wave of heat and pressure forcing them back. I struck again, my blade slicing across its flank, drawing more ichor that burned the air with its stench.

"Kalev!" Joshua's voice cut through the din. He was at my shoulder now, his sword drawn, its edge gleaming with the reflected flames. "The altar! It anchors them!"

I nodded, understanding instantly. The black slab was no mere stone —it was a door, a conduit for the shedim, the unclean spirits that fed on blood and fear. The serpent statues flanking it pulsed with an unnatural light. Destroy the altar, and we might sever their hold.

But Ai's defenders were not done. From the eastern alleys, a fresh wave of warriors surged, they had come back into the city from the valley, from Bethel, their armor glinting with leather and bone, their faces painted with ash and blood. They were not Anakim, but they fought with a frenzy that spoke of possession, their eyes glowing faintly, like coals in a dying fire. They crashed into Joshua's men, axes and spears flashing, and the courtyard became a maelstrom of bronze and screams.

I pressed toward the altar, Joshua at my side. A warrior lunged at me, his axe aimed for my skull. I parried, the impact numbing my arm, and drove my knee into his gut. He doubled over, and I ended him with a slash to the neck, blood spraying like rain. Joshua dispatched another, his blade moving with the precision of a man who had seen too many battles to falter.

The creature yelled— no, screamed— its form swelling, antlers lengthening until they scraped the courtyard walls—a screech from the depths of Sheol itself— it raised a hand, and the air shimmered, a wave of force slamming into us. My men staggered, some falling to their knees, clutching their heads as blood trickled from their ears. Joshua gripped my arm, his face grim, and pointed to the altar's base, where the flames burned hottest.

"There!" he shouted. "The heart of it!"

I saw it—a glyph carved into the stone, pulsing with red light, its lines twisting like living serpents. It was no Kena'anim rune, no human mark. It was older, from a time when the earth was young and the Nephilim walked freely. I knew again, this was no mere battle for a city. This was a war for the soul of the land, a clash between the God who spoke from the burning bush and the powers that had defied Him since the flood.

We fought on, carving a path through the defenders. A giant of a man loomed before us, smaller than those we had slain, but no less deadly, his war-club studded with obsidian. He swung, and I rolled aside, the club shattering the stone where I'd stood. Joshua struck from the side, his sword slashing the giant's thigh. The creature bellowed, stumbling, and I drove my blade into its chest, feeling the resistance of unnatural flesh. It fell, shaking the ground, and we pressed forward.

The creature at the altar watched, its laughter gone, its eyes narrowing. It raised both hands, and the flames within the altar flared, tongues of fire licking the sky. The serpent statues shuddered, their mouths opening wider, and from within them came a sound—a low, droning hum that made my teeth ache and my vision blur. The children, still kneeling, began to convulse, their small bodies jerking as if pulled by unseen strings.

"Reuel" I shouted, spotting him near the courtyard's edge, his sling swinging in wait, "The statues!"

He understood at once. His sling snapped, and a stone flew, striking one of the serpent statues in the eye. The obsidian cracked, and the statue's hum faltered, its flames dimming. The creature snarled, its form flickering again, and I saw our chance.

"Keep them busy!" I called to my men, pointing to the defenders still pouring from the alleys. They rallied, forming a line to hold the enemy back, their shields raised against a storm of spears and arrows and stones. Joshua and I reached the altar, the heat searing our skin, the glyph's light pulsing faster, as if it sensed our intent.

The creature moved, its claws slashing. Joshua met it, his sword clashing against its shadowy limb, sparks flying like stars in the night. I climbed the altar's steps, my heart pounding, the air thick with the stench of sulfur and death. The glyph was close now, its light blinding, its power pressing against my chest like a physical weight.

I raised my sword, whispering a prayer to Yahweh, and struck.

The blade tore into the stone, and the glyph shattered, fragments flying like glass.

The altar trembled, cracks spreading across its surface, and the flames within died, leaving only smoke. The creature screeched, its form collapsing in on itself, antlers crumbling, body dissolving into a cloud of ash that scattered on the wind.

The courtyard fell silent, save for the gasps of the wounded and the crackle of distant fires. The children slumped, freed from their trance, their sobs echoing in the stillness. Ai's defenders faltered, their possessed madness draining away, and Joshua's men pressed the advantage, driving them back into the alleys.

I climbed down from the altar, my legs trembling beneath me, each step a battle against the exhaustion that clawed at my bones. My rib throbbed where the cudgel had struck in the heat of Ai's fall, a sharp pang that pulsed with every breath, grounding me in the frailty of my flesh. The air was thick with ash, the ground beneath my sandals littered with shattered stone and the blood of the fallen, both Ivrim and Kena'anim. The city was a broken thing, its walls breached, its idols toppled, yet its shadow lingered, a weight that pressed against my soul. Joshua stood amidst the chaos, a solitary figure in the heart of the ruin, his sword lowered, its blade stained dark, his chest heaving as he drew ragged breaths. His crimson cloak, tattered at the hem, hung heavy with dust and blood, yet he stood unbowed, a pillar amid the storm.

I paused, my eyes tracing the man who had become more than a leader to me—Joshua, son of Nun, chosen by Yahweh to guide the sons of Avraham into the land of promise. He was no longer the young Ephraimite I'd known decades ago, when we spied out Kena'an's hills, our hearts afire with faith. Time had carved its mark upon him, his dark hair now streaked with gray, his beard thick but threaded with silver, framing a face weathered by sun and sorrow. His eyes, deep-set and piercing, burned with a fire that no battle could quench, a reflection of the God who had spoken to Mosheh in the flame. They were eyes that had seen the Red Sea part, the manna fall, and the giants of Hebron loom in the torchlit caves—eyes that held both the weight of memory and the certainty of divine purpose. His frame was lean, hardened by years of wandering, his shoulders broad but stooped slightly, as if carrying the burdens of a nation. Scars marred his arms, pale lines crisscrossing sun-darkened skin, each a testament to battles fought and promises kept. His hands, calloused and steady, gripped the sword with a quiet strength, the hands of a shepherd turned warrior, a man who could both tend and slay.

Behind him, two of Joshua's men pressed through the shattered north gate, dragging the king of Ai in chains. He stumbled, limbs jerking against the leather straps, but there was no fear in his eyes—only a venomous hate that gleamed like a blade in the dark. His body, gaunt and wiry, was clad not in royal robes but in crudely stitched animal skins—wolf, lion, and something else, something scaled and unfamiliar, bound together with thongs of sinew. Fetid and rank, the garments clung to him like the death that waited.

He was no giant, but his presence unsettled the air. His limbs were too long, his joints too fluid, his narrow face angular and inhuman. This was the blood of the Rephaim—those ancient ones who walked before the flood, twisted echoes of man and beast, whose children still defiled the land from the shadows. The king's skin bore symbols scorched into his flesh—sigils of unclean power, remnants of rites carried down from the dark valleys and high places forbidden by the Lord. His teeth were filed to points, his tongue forked at the tip. And still, he cursed.

He cursed with every step—guttural, blasphemous oaths in a tongue that reeked of old graves. He spat toward Joshua and the elders, mocked the tribes by name, invoked forgotten gods by syllables meant never to be uttered. "I was crowned by blood," he hissed, his voice like wind through a tomb. "You serve a slave's god. I have feasted on the hearts of children and sung to the watchers in the dark. What is your fire to me?"

Joshua turned then, slowly, the light of burning homes casting shadows like wings behind him. His eyes, clear and sharp beneath his age, settled on the king as if already seeing beyond the dust of time. He spoke not in anger, but with the weight of command—words that echoed with the voice of Sinai. "Keep him at the gate," he said, "Let him watch. But don't kill him yet—not until the city is silent and every last voice has fallen to dust. Then I will deal with him as the Lord has commanded."

And so the king was dragged to the city gate, to the place where his judgment would be written in ash and stone. They tied him beneath the broken archway, where the lintel had split and the fire still hissed through the cracks of the ruined wall. There he stood, tethered like a beast, snarling through cracked lips, as the city burned. The screams of the dying and the roar of collapsing towers were his only court, the flames his throne.

Still he cursed. Still he called out to his unseen masters. But no answer came.
Even the darkness had forsaken him.

Joshua turned, his gaze meeting mine, and for a moment, the chaos of Ai faded—the cries of the wounded, the crackle of distant fires, the stench of blood and smoke. In that glance, we were not warriors, not conquerors, but two old spies, bound by a shared past, men who had stood in Hebron's shadow and lived to fight its giants again. I saw the boy he'd been, defiant before the trembling tribes, proclaiming the land ours when ten others faltered. I saw the leader he'd become, unflinching in the face of Ba'al's altars, his faith a blade that cut through fear. He was no king, no priest, but a servant of Yahweh, he was the Spear of the Twelve Clans, his authority not in crown or robe but in the quiet determination that drew men to follow him into the fire.

"It's not over," he said, his voice low, roughened by the day's shouts, his eyes scanning the smoke-filled sky where clouds churned, their edges tinged with an unnatural green. His words were not a command, but a truth, spoken with the weight of one who had heard the shedim stir, who knew the land's heart was not yet won.

Joshua lifted his eyes to the swirling heavens, where the smoke of Ai joined the clouds like incense rising without direction. The wind carried ash and the scent of burnt cedar, but beneath it stirred something older—a memory, a warning. His lips moved, not in command but in remembrance, and then, as though some echo of Enoch stirred within him, he sang. The words were ancient, older than Torah, passed down in hidden scrolls and whispered by those who remembered the first great rebellion. It was not joy that gave rise to his song, but reverence—the kind that trembles before holy fire and the ruins left behind by giants,

"They rose from the earth, sons of watchers,
Bone and pride bound in flesh of stone.
They lifted blades forged in the fire of forbidden stars,
And made war upon the innocent.
But El Elyon beheld their wickedness,
And sent the scribe of heaven to proclaim judgment.

Armoni fell, and Gilgam wept in chains.
The flood did not cleanse them,
But the deep swallowed their breath.
Now their seed trembles,
For Israel walks with the flame of God,
And even the mountains bow."

I nodded, my throat tightened, knowing he was right. The altar was broken, its obsidian shards scattered, the creature that had laughed with a thousand voices gone, its ashes scattered on the wind. Yet Ai was not fully ours. The temple Hur had spoken of, the throne of Ba'al in the north quarter, still stood, its black stones a defiant scar against the sky. Beyond it, in the lands we had yet to conquer—Hebron, the hill country, the plains of the south—other powers waited, their presence a whisper in the wind. Shedim, the unclean spirits of the Nephilim, hungered for flesh and dominion. Sorcerers, wielding rites older than Babel, wove curses in hidden groves. The remnants of the Nephilim's blood, the Anakim and their kin, guarded altars soaked in centuries of sacrifice. The land was Yahweh's by promise, but its shadows fought with a ferocity that tested even Joshua's fire.

He stepped closer, his sword sheathed now, his hand resting briefly on my shoulder, a gesture of brotherhood forged in the wilderness. "We've faced worse," he said, a faint smile tugging at his lips, though his eyes remained vigilant, scanning the ruins for any sign of lingering threat. "Hebron was but the beginning, Kalev. Yahweh's hand is on us still."

I met his gaze, drawing strength from the man who had stood with me when the tribes wavered, when the ten spies' fear nearly broke our people. "His hand has never left us," I said, my voice steadier now, the pain in my rib a reminder of battles won.

"But the giants we face now—they're not just flesh, Joshua. The shedim know our names."

His smile faded, replaced by a grim resolve, his hand falling from my shoulder to rest on his sword's hilt. "Let them know us," he said, his voice a low growl, the voice of a man who had seen Yahweh's fire consume Egypt's might. "They'll learn to fear the God who sent us."

The moment passed, the chaos of Ai pressing in again—the shouts of our men securing the streets, the groans of the wounded, the acrid bite of smoke in the air. Joshua turned, his cloak snapping in the wind, and began issuing orders, his voice cutting through the din, steady and sure. I watched him, this leader of Avraham's seed, a man who bore the weight of a nation yet walked as if carried by the hand of God. He was not flawless—his temper could flare, his patience thin when doubt lingered too long—but his faith was a rock, unshaken by giants or gods. In him, I saw the promise of the land, not yet fully claimed, but closer with every step he took.

I steadied myself, the trembling in my legs easing, the ache in my rib a dull companion. The temple of Ba'al waited, its altars calling, and beyond it, Hebron loomed, its caves a memory and a challenge. Joshua and I, two old spies, would face them together, as we had before, armed with a faith that had outlasted years of desert wandering. The land remembered us, and we remembered it, our swords ready, our hearts bound to the God who had promised it all.

We gathered our men, and moved north. The streets of Ai were a labyrinth of fire and ruin, collapsed walls and burning beams blocking our path. The smell of blood and charred flesh clung to us, and the thunder in the sky grew louder, as if the heavens themselves were watching.

The main temple loomed ahead, its black stone walls carved with the twisted forms of Ba'al and his many consorts, their vacant eyes seeming to follow our every step. Serpents coiled across nearly every surface—etched in stone, wrapped around columns, leering from archways. The singing had ceased, but the air still pulsed with a dark rhythm, a low hum that made my teeth ache and the hairs on my arms rise.

The courtyard gate yawned open. Beyond it stood the altar—a monolith of basalt, ancient and dark, its surface soaked with generations of blood. Twin braziers flanked it, their green flames licking the sky like the breath of some hidden beast.

But no priests waited. No giants. No guards. Only silence—thick, unnatural, wrong.

Joshua raised his hand to halt the line. "Kalev," he said, voice steady as ever, "you and I will enter first. Choose your best to hold the rear."

Without pause, I turned to Othniel. He met my eyes and nodded—my kin in blood and battle, the warrior I trusted above all. "Hold the line behind us," I said. "Take twelve—no more. The passage is tight. If it narrows, we'll need your bronze close but not crowded."

He nodded again, wordless. There was no need for speeches between men who had fought through fire together.

And with that, Joshua and I stepped forward, into the belly of the temple where gods of stone once demanded the blood of children —and where today, if the Lord willed it, those gods would fall silent forever

The air grew colder as we entered, the green flames casting eerie shadows. The altar was not empty. At its center lay a pile of bones—human, animal, and something else, their shapes twisted, unnatural. And above them, suspended in the air, was a sphere of black light, pulsing like a heart. Crafted through the stone so that the sun's light was intercepted and made to be a dark presence.

"It's a seal," Joshua whispered, his voice tight.

I remembered Mosheh' warnings, his tales of the shedim and their hunger for the earth. This was no mere altar. It was a gateway, a breach between the seen and the unseen, and we had walked straight into its heart.

Before we could act, the sphere of light pulsed, and the air tore open. From the rift stepped a figure—not a giant, not a man, but something clad in armor of molten bronze, its face a featureless mask. It carried no weapon, but its presence was a weapon, its very existence a violation of the world Yahweh had made.

Joshua moved first, his sword slashing at the figure's chest. The blade sparked against the armor, leaving no mark. The figure raised a hand, and Joshua flew backward, slamming into the courtyard wall with a sickening crunch. I shouted his name, charging, my sword aimed for the figure's neck. It turned, its mask reflecting my face, and a force like a tidal wave struck me, hurling me to the ground.

My vision swam, pain radiating from every bone. The figure advanced, its steps shaking the earth, and I knew we could not fight this alone. But then I heard it—a voice, clear and strong, cutting through the darkness.

"The Name is my strength and my shield!" It was Phineas, I had not seen him all day, the son of Eleazar the high priest. Phineas a Levite, fought in prayer and psalm. He held up his hands and called upon the Name to defeat this foe,

Beside him was Othniel and Reuel at the temple's entrance. Othniel's axe ready to kill. Reuel's arm in fluid motion ready to hurl his weapon of stone. Othniel, broad-shouldered and still growing into his frame, he cut the figure of a young lion—warm bronze skin catching the sickly green light of the braziers, wiry hair damp with sweat, and a full beard just beginning to assert itself along his jaw. His eyes were steady, calculating—always watching, always weighing. Behind him, the rest of our men chanted, their voices rising, a song of defiance and faith, ancient as the wilderness and sharper flint. They called up the Name to defeat this foe.

The figure before the altar paused, looking at Phineas, with each word our priest chanted, it was like a dagger cutting at the face of this wretched foe. Then—snap—Reuel loosed his sling, and the stone struck true, hitting the soft crevice of its head. As the creature's neck snapped backward, a fleeting gap in its armor appeared. Othniel, swift as a hart, hurled his axe like thunder. It flew, spun over and over, and then landed with a thud deep in the folds of its chest. The creature screamed. Othniel's battle axe lodged deeply in its being.

Joshua, now risen, his bronze sword gleaming with the fire of righteousness, unleashed a piercing strike upon the glowing sphere above the altar. A spiderweb of cracks raced across its surface, and the air itself seemed to flinch, the force of his strike was so great against the sphere it knocked Joshua backwards.

The rift flickered, and the figure staggered, its armor dimming. I scrambled to my feet, grabbing a fallen spear, and hurled it at the sphere. It landed, and the black light shattered, the rift collapsing with a sound like a thousand screams. The figure vanished, its armor crumbling to dust, and the green flames in the braziers died.

Joshua rose, blood streaming from a gash on his forehead, but his eyes were clear. "The temple is ours," he said, his voice steady. "Burn it."

We set to work, tearing down the altar, smashing the braziers, and setting fire to the cursed stones. The flames roared, consuming the temple, and the thunder in the sky answered. Ai was broken, its power shattered, but the war was far from over.

As we left, I thought of Hebron, of the giants we had seen forty years ago, and the promise Yahweh had made. The land was ours, but its shadows would fight to the last. And we, the dogs of the desert, would meet them, sword in hand, until the earth was clean.

The city of Ai was a corpse, its bones of stone shattered, its flesh of timber and thatch reduced to ash that swirled in the dawn's gray light. I stood atop a crumbled gatehouse, my sandals crunching on charred fragments—bone, bronze, and the brittle remnants of idols that had screamed as they burned. The air was thick, a suffocating veil of smoke and decay that clawed at my throat, carrying the stench of blood, and something fouler, older, like the exhalation of a god long banished but not forgotten. Below, the streets were gashed with ruin, walls toppled into heaps of rubble, doorways gaping like the mouths of the dead. Crimson mud pooled where blood had soaked the dust, streaking the sandals of my men as they moved through the wreckage, their faces hollow, their spears clutched as if the shadows might yet rise, making sure none were left living.

The battle was won, yet victory was a bitter weight. We had slain the giants, their massive bodies sprawled across the city like felled cedars, their blood black and viscous, hissing where it spilled. The priests of Ba'al were dead, their altars smashed, their fires quenched by Ivrim blades and Yahweh's wrath. But the air pulsed with a residue of their power, a lingering malice that pressed against my chest, whispering of wars older than Kena'an. My rib ached from the cudgel's blow in the battle, each breath a sharp reminder of the cost, but it was not the pain that troubled me. It was the eyes of my men—young warriors, some barely bearded, their gazes haunted not by death but by what they had seen. The Anakim, the shedim, the creature at the altar—they were not mere enemies. They were a violation of the world Yahweh had made.

I descended from the gatehouse, my sandals slipping on ash-slick stone, and walked among the ruins. The city was a labyrinth of loss, its markets silent, its homes gutted, their roofs collapsed into smoldering heaps. A child's sandal lay abandoned in the street, its leather scorched, and I turned away, my jaw tight. We had spared none, as Yahweh commanded, but the weight of such judgment was a burden even the righteous could not escape. My men worked in pairs, salvaging what could be cleansed—bronze blades, untainted grain—

while others making sure none of the enemy were left alive, their movements mechanical, their voices muted.

Near the outer temple's ruins, where the altar had stood, I saw a young soldier from the tribe of Benjamin—no older than eighteen, his tunic stained with blood that was not his own—kneeling in the debris. His hands trembled as he held a relic, turning it over in the dim light. I approached, my shadow falling across him, and he flinched, dropping the object. It was a mask, carved from bone, its surface smooth as polished stone, its eyeholes empty but seeming to watch. Glyphs were etched along its edges, Nephilim runes like those I'd seen in Hebron's caves so many years ago, their curves and angles unnatural, pulsing with a faint green light that made my skin crawl. The boy stared at it, his breath shallow, his fingers hovering as if drawn to touch it again.

"Kalev," he whispered, his voice barely audible, "what were they?"

I crouched beside him, my knees creaking, and picked up the mask. It was cold, heavier than it should have been, as if it held the weight of the souls it had consumed. The glyphs seemed to move, a trick of the light or something worse, and a whisper brushed my mind—soft, insidious, urging me to wear it, to see through its eyes. I hurled it to the ground, shattering it against a jagged stone, and the boy gasped, scrambling back. The fragments lay still, their light fading, but the air hummed with a faint dissonance, like a chord struck on a broken lyre.

I did not answer his question. I could not. My silence was a wall, built of memories too raw to speak—Hebron, the caves, the giants' silhouettes in the torchlight, their voices like grinding stone. I saw them now, as clear as if I stood there again, their eyes glowing like embers, their presence a weight that had nearly broken me. The boy watched, waiting, but I stood, my hand on his shoulder, and gestured for him to rise.   "Keep moving," I said, my voice rougher than I meant. He nodded, his eyes still fixed on the shards, and hurried to join the others.

I walked on, the city's ruins stretching before me like a battlefield of the soul. Near a collapsed wall, I found another relic—a bronze amulet, its surface etched with a serpent coiled around a horned figure, its eyes inlaid with obsidian that gleamed like wet blood. I kicked it into a pyre, the flames flaring as they consumed it, and the smoke curled upward, blacker than the rest. My men watched, their faces pale, and I saw their fear—not of me, but of what such things meant. Ai was not just a city; it was a throne, a seat of powers that had ruled before the flood, and we had torn it down. But the land was vast, and other thrones waited.

A shout broke my reverie. Near the northern gate, a warrior held up another find—a tablet, like the mask, carved from bone and etched with glyphs. I strode toward him, my heart pounding, and took it from his hands. It was larger than the boy's, its surface slick with a residue that smelled of copper and decay. The runes were deeper, their lines sharper, and they pulsed with a light that seemed to draw the eye, to promise secrets if only I would look closer. My fingers tightened, the urge to keep it strong, but I remembered the caves, the whispers, the weight of Yahweh's promise. I raised the tablet high and smashed it against a stone, the fragments scattering like teeth, the light dying with a hiss.

The warrior stared, his brow furrowed beneath the smear of ash and blood, his question unspoken but writ plain in his eyes. I met his gaze and spoke, not in rebuke, but with the quiet weight of command, "Gather the spoil and the flocks. Leave none living, but take what Adonai has granted. The city is fallen." He gave a short nod, turned, and barked to the others. Men fanned out through the streets, slipping through alleyways like shadows, their footsteps soft over scorched earth. The cries of the dying had faded to silence, yet a heaviness clung to the air—as though Ai itself resisted its end.

Smoke swelled upward in twisting pillars, thick and black, borne of pitch and cedar wood and the broken bones of towers. The fires we had set did not burn clean. They roared with a kind of wrath, as though something within the city burned beyond wood and stone —something ancient and unrepentant. I stood alone among the ruin, my spear planted in the dust, the blood on my arms already drying. The spoil would be divided later—flocks and gold, bronze and scarlet —lawfully ours by Yahweh's decree. But no man lingered with joy.

I turned down a narrow lane where the earth was cracked with heat and the stones still bled firelight. Then the lane opened and I saw him—Joshua standing beneath the scorched arch of the gate. The king of Ai lay before him, dead and shackled, impaled upon a rough-hewn pole driven into the earth. Joshua's sword was sheathed at his side. He looked neither triumphant nor weary—just resolved. The dying light passed over the king's body, and men straightened the pole until it stood erect.

A hush fell and all eyes turned to Joshua. His voice cut clear through the silence, low and immutable as stone: "Leave him here. Let his body stand until eventide." I saw the king's lips were curled in a death's rictus. Watching that, I understood the judgement of Yahweh woven into this final act.

His body hung crooked on the wood, the hides of lion and wolf clinging like shamed trophies to a frame too wicked for burial. The scaled pelt of some desert serpent still wrapped his shoulder, a mockery of armor, as if the beasts themselves had once sworn allegiance to his reign of blood. Flies gathered like priesthood around his eyes. The wind stirred the remnants of his mane, yet no breath stirred in him now—only the heavy silence of a cursed throne broken. Even the vultures waited, as if reluctant to feast on a thing so steeped in defilement.

The rest of the day the king remained there—an object lesson to the fallen city's heart. And when the sun's edge touched the horizon, Joshua spoke again: "Take him down, and cast him at the threshold of this gate. Pile stones upon him—let all see the heap."

I helped, using broken masonry from the ruined wall, as the last of the flames guttered out beneath the scorched beams of the city gate. Around me, five thousand of Joshua's warriors—bloodied, wearied, and solemn—heaved stone upon stone in silence. The heap rose steadily, until it stood fifteen cubits high, a towering monument of ruin above the lifeless king of Ai.

Then, as the last light died, I surveyed the ruin-littered street—columns toppled like idols, braziers hissing their final embers, and the charred skeleton of Ai's temple crouched in the shadows beyond.

The king was gone from sight, but his judgment remained—entombed in stone, mortared into memory. And as twilight deepened, I felt the weight of what had passed, and what would stand until the end of days. To this day the pile of stones still stands where we buried the king of Ai.

The men passed by, some clutching sacks of silver, others leading bleating goats still trembling from the flames. None spoke of the darker relics, none took the evil amulets of Ai or the scarabs from Egypt that littered the ground. We had learned from Jericho what came of taking what was not given by Yahweh. Ai had offered its spoils, and Yahweh permitted them. But not all spoils are gifts. Some are lures. Some are chains.

The fire blazed higher behind me, wind tugging at my cloak, and the smell of charred stone and death clung to every breath. I thought I heard voices in the wind—not speech, but murmurings, low and cold. I closed my eyes, and in my heart I prayed the psalm Mosheh taught us: "Let God arise, let His enemies be scattered; let those who hate Him flee before His face."

Even in victory, the land groaned.

Ai was ours. Its walls, its gate, its treasures—all taken beneath the sign of the Name. But as I turned away, the ruin loomed behind me, as though watching, waiting. There are places where death does not sleep. And some fires, even when they die, still whisper in the ash.

I turned from the hill, my sword heavy at my side, my heart heavier still. The boy's question echoed in my mind—what were they?—and I had no answer, only memories of Hebron, of giants and caves and a promise that had carried me through many years. The land was Yahweh's, but it was also a battlefield, its soil soaked with the blood of gods and men. As I rejoined my men, the wind rose, carrying the ash of Ai southward, toward the hills, toward Hebron, where the true war waited.

The sun had dropped low, casting bronze fire across the wreckage of Ai, and as I made my way down the ridge, the voices of the camp began to rise—low murmurs, the clang of arms, the distant call of shepherds corralling their flocks. But one voice stood apart, steady and raw like a string pulled taut against the ache of memory. A young man, seated near the remnants of a ruined terebinth, sang alone—his voice neither bold nor trained, but shaped by the dust of the wilderness and the weight of a hundred battles he had not fought but still carried in his bones. The song was one I had heard in fragments among the elders, a refrain from before the flood, from scrolls sealed and hidden by those who feared the knowledge they carried. *The Lament of Gilgamesh's Line*, it would later be called—a hymn of warning and witness, sung in the twilight where shadows of old evils still crept,

"I saw them fall—the sons of shadow,
Stretched high like cedars but hollow at the root.
Their names were mighty: Gilgamesh, Mahway, the left-handed
Repha.
But they fell not by strength,
They fell by covenant.
The seed of Avraham marched with fire in their breath,
And the hosts of the Holy One encamped around them.

The watchers hid their faces,
And the Nephilim fled into wind and earth.
Ai is smoke,
But Israel stands,
For Yahweh is terrible in battle."

Chapter Two
The Caves of Hebron

The wind blew over the hills like a whisper of ghosts, and the scent it carried reminded me of fear. Not the sharp, stinging kind men know in battle—but the long, slow fear that rots a man from the inside. I'd smelled it once before, long ago, the first time we walked into the land. Before we called it ours. Long before the battle of Ai. Back when we were just shadows on the edge of Kena'an, twelve spies sent to peer into a place dripping with both honey and horror.

We were young then, or so the others seemed, their steps light, their eyes bright with dreams of a land promised by Yahweh, their hearts untested by the weight of years or the shadow of giants. I was older now, my years carved not merely by time but by a life forged far from the tents of Yehudah, in a world apart from the tribes of Israel. I am Kalev, son of Jephunneh the Kenizzite, born in the sun-scorched lands of the south, where the earth is red as blood and rivers flow only in the memories of elders. My skin is dark, kissed by the fierce sun of the land my fathers called home—a place of vast deserts and hidden springs, beyond the borders of what the tribes knew, though later tongues would name it for distant peoples. I was not of Israel's blood, not born of Avraham's seed, but grafted into their covenant by faith and fire, a stranger made kin through the will of the God who sees all.

My people, the Kenizzites, were wanderers, traders, warriors, pitching their tents where the stars burned brightest, their songs older than the stones of Kena'an, their stories woven with the winds of the southern wastes. As a youth, I came to the Ivrims, drawn by tales of a God who shattered Egypt's chains, who parted a sea for His people, who spoke in fire and cloud on a mountain trembling with His voice. I stood among them, my skin dark as night, my hands calloused from spear and plow, my voice carrying the cadence of a tongue not theirs, its rhythms shaped by the deserts of my birth. I swore allegiance to Yahweh, to Mosheh , to the promise of a land I had never seen, but trust was a slow flame, kindled only through deeds, not lineage. I was tolerated, my name whispered with caution rather than kinship, my place among the tribes a fragile thread.

Yet it was the Pascha, the Passover, the meal of liberation, that bound me to Israel's heart. In the wilderness, under a sky ablaze with stars, I partook of the lamb's flesh, its blood a seal of the covenant, its taste a vow of faith. The Pascha was no mere feast, but a sacred act, a rite that marked me as one of Yahweh's own, no longer a stranger but a son of the promise. With the bitter herbs on my tongue and the unleavened bread in my hands, I stood before the tribes, my dark skin gleaming in the firelight, and ate as they ate, my heart joined to theirs by the God who delivered us from Egypt. Mosheh watched, his eyes seeing beyond my foreign birth, and when he laid his hand upon me, declaring,

"He has a different spirit in him," his voice was a seal, binding me to Yehudah's line, though some still glanced askance, measuring the outsider in their midst.

Now, after the battle of Ai, my mind drifted, back many years, back when I was not yet "Kalev the Giantkiller," I was not yet the man who would face the Anakim and live, whose name would echo in the hills of Kena'an. I was only "Kalev," a Kenizzite among Israelites, my place earned through faith, through the Pascha's blood, through the fire that burned in my soul for a God who saw no boundary in His call.

Even now, as I walked the hills of Ai, sword in hand, the weight of those early days clung to me—the eyes that followed, the whispers that questioned my right to stand among Ya'akov's sons. My skin, black as the night over the southern deserts, marked me as other, a son of distant lands woven into the tapestry of Israel. Yet it was that same spirit, born under foreign stars, kindled by the Pascha's covenant, that strengthened me against the giants, that kept my heart steady when others faltered.

In the wilderness, the Pascha had been my entry, my adoption into the clan of Avraham's heirs. Each year, as we ate the lamb and retold the story of deliverance, I felt the bond deepen, the mistrust of the tribes softening. My dark hands broke the bread, my voice joined the songs of exodus, and I became more than a Kenizzite—I became a warrior of Yahweh, chosen to claim a land not my own by birth, but mine by divine decree. That meal, shared in the dust of Sinai, was my forge, shaping me for the battles ahead, for the giants whose shadows loomed in Hebron, for the promise that burned brighter than fear. I was older, yes, but not weary—my fire came from a God who called me from the sands, who sealed me with the Pascha's blood, who made me a brother to Israel and a foe to its enemies.

The first time I saw the hills of Hebron, I nearly turned back. Not because I feared them—but because I feared what was buried within. The land was ancient. Older than our wandering. Older than Avraham. The stones there did not simply sit in the earth; they brooded. Carved altars left by men long dead, names scratched into rock in a script older than Babel. And the fruit—we found clusters of grapes so large they bowed the shoulders of two men.

There were twelve of us sent to scout the land of Kena'an, each man chosen from a tribe of Israel, our names bound to the covenant of Yahweh. I remember their faces, etched with hope as we set out, their eyes bright with dreams of a land flowing with milk and honey. They walked with a swagger, as if the hills were already ours, as if the promise was a scroll already unrolled. But that was a delusion, a veil over their hearts. They believed scouting was a mere ritual, that we would return with tales of bounty, and Mosheh would lift his staff, parting the walls of Kena'an as he had the sea. Yet the land was no passive prize; it watched us, its stones heavy with memory, its shadows whispering of powers older than our fathers' tents.

We moved cautiously, threading along rugged mountain trails, avoiding the open roads where dust could betray our steps. Villages dotted the valleys below, their smoke rising like offerings to unseen gods, their herds grazing under the watchful eyes of shepherds. We steered clear, our cloaks drawn tight, our voices low, knowing a single misstep could end us. The air was thick with the scent of wild thyme and dust, the sun a relentless weight on our shoulders. Joshua, son of Nun, walked beside me, his gaze steady, his sword a quiet promise. I felt the land pulse beneath my sandals, its ancient heart stirring as we drew near to the ancient place.

When we reached Hebron, the air changed, growing heavier, as if the hills themselves held their breath. We could not avoid what awaited us there—Sheshai, Talmai, Ahiman, the sons of Anak, giants whose names were whispered in fear even among the children of the land. There were no tales spun by fireside, no bedtime story to thrill children. They were real, and their presence was a wound in the world.

We first saw them from a ridge, crouching low among the scrub and stone, our breaths shallow, our hands gripping spears and slings. Below, near the entrance of a great tomb carved into the hillside, they labored, their forms towering against the dusk. They moved massive stones, each the size of an altar, with an ease that mocked human strength, their hands like stone themselves, their shadows stretching long and dark. At first, I doubted my eyes, thinking the sun's glare or the wine we'd shared the night before had tricked me. But no—their reality was undeniable. They stood like cedars, their shoulders broad as ox yokes, their height a defiance of the earth's limits. One of them, Talmai, laughed, a low, rumbling sound that we felt in the ground beneath us, a tremor that shook the pebbles at our feet. Their armor was not of Kena'anim make, but older, forged of dark bronze, etched with spirals and shapes that seemed to bleed, eyes that stared without blinking, runes that pulsed with a sickly light.

The sight broke something in the others. I saw it in the faces of my fellow spies—Shammua's eyes wide, Shaphat's jaw trembling, Igal's hand clutching his cloak as if it could shield him. They were men of Israel, chosen by Mosheh , yet the Anakim's shadow stripped them bare, exposing hearts unready for the promise's cost. That night, we pitched tents in a hidden hollow, far from Hebron's gaze, our camp shrouded in silence. None dared light a fire, fearing the Rephaim' eyes would find us in the dark. The air was cold, the stars sharp, and the men's whispers were a tide of dread

"They're too strong," Palti muttered, his voice barely above the wind.

"We're like grasshoppers to them," Nahbi added, his hands shaking as he clutched his spear.

Joshua and I sat apart, our backs to a boulder, our eyes on the horizon where Hebron's hills loomed

"We can take them," Joshua said, his voice low but firm, his faith in Yahweh a flame that no shadow could quench. "The Lord who broke Egypt is with us. These giants are bread for us."

I nodded, my heart stirred by his words, though the memory of those towering forms gnawed at me,

"Yahweh has promised this land," I said, my voice steady, a Kenizzite's resolve grafted into Yehudah's covenant. "Their size is nothing to Him who parted the sea. We will stand where others fall."

The others heard us, their faces pale in the moonlight, their eyes hollow with fear. They looked at us as if we were already dead, their courage crumbling like dry clay.

"You're mad," Ammiel whispered, his voice a hiss. "Did you see their armor? Their strength? We'll be crushed."

The murmurs grew, a chorus of doubt, and by dawn, ten of them had fled, slipping away under cover of darkness, their footprints a trail of betrayal back to the camp of Israel.

Only Joshua, son of Nun, and I, remained, our hearts bound to the promise, our eyes fixed on Hebron's shadow.

We lingered near the cave in Hebron for days, creeping closer, our steps silent, our cloaks blending with the dust and stone. We watched the Anakim from hidden clefts, noting their movements, their strength, their rituals. They gathered at the tomb's mouth, chanting in a tongue that grated like stone on stone, their voices summoning something unseen, the air shimmering as if the shedim stirred. We saw them drag a calf to an altar, its blood spilling black in the moonlight, the runes on their armor glowing as they raised their hands to the sky. The land remembered them, and they remembered it, guardians of a cursed legacy we were called to break.

That night, as Joshua slept in our hidden camp near the caves, I awoke with a start, my heart hammering as if struck by an unseen fist, each beat a thunder that echoed in my bones. The air was thick, oppressive, as if the night itself had grown claws, the stars veiled by a shadow that was not cloud but alive, pulsing with malice. A chill slithered over my skin, not the crisp bite of the desert, but a cold older than stone, older than the graves of the earth, a cold that whispered my name with a lover's intimacy. My limbs trembled, my throat tightened, and a primal dread coiled in my gut, urging me to flee, to bury myself in the dust and pray the darkness passed me by. My breath came in shallow gasps, tasting of ash and decay, and my vision blurred as if the world itself wavered under the weight of an unseen gaze.

I rose, my hand clutching my dagger, its hilt slick with sweat, the blade trembling in my grip as if it sensed what I could not yet name. Compelled by a force I could neither resist nor understand, I stepped beyond the camp's edge, drawn to the darkness where the caves loomed, their mouths gaping like the jaws of forgotten gods, carved into the hillside we had watched that day. The Anakim's presence lingered in my mind—their towering forms, their dark bronze armor etched with runes that pulsed with sickly light, their laughter shaking the earth. Now, in the hollow of a twisted olive tree, its branches gnarled as if writhing in eternal agony, a form took shape —not flesh, but smoke and malice, its edges fraying like a tattered shroud torn by unseen winds.

Its eyes were coals in a dying fire, smoldering with a light that pierced my soul, stripping away courage until I stood bare, a boy beneath the gaze of eternity. It was a shedim, a spirit of the nephilim, its presence a weight that pressed against my ribs, threatening to crack them, to crush the breath from my lungs. My knees buckled, and I gripped a jagged rock to steady myself, my fingers bleeding where the stone cut into my palm. Fear clawed at my heart, not merely of death, but of being known, of being claimed by a past I had never lived, a heritage I thought severed. My vision swam, and a scream lodged in my throat, stifled by the terror that this spirit saw me as its own.

"Kalev, son of Jephunneh," it whispered, its voice a blade sliding through my thoughts, sharp and cold, yet seductive, like a promise laced with venom that burned and beguiled. "Your blood sings of the ancient ones, the Kenizzites, born of the giant clans who strode the earth when the stars were yet unformed. You are no stranger to us, child of the nephilim's line, heir to the strength that shook the heavens. Why do you skulk in the shadows, yoked to these frail sons of Adam, these Ivrim who cling to a desert god's fleeting whims? You have seen the Anakim, felt the pulse of their power. Have you come to return to your people, to claim the birthright that flows in your veins? Cast off this covenant of dust, and we will raise you as a lord among the giants, your name carved in the stones of eternity, your might a song that echoes beyond the flood."

Its words were a tide, surging against the roots of my soul, stirring visions I had never seen—towering figures wreathed in dark bronze, their hands dripping with the blood of forbidden rites, their laughter a storm that shattered mountains. My Kenizzite heritage, a chain I thought broken, tightened around me, each link forged in the sins of the watchers who defied the divine council. My dagger slipped from my grasp, clattering to the ground, and I clutched my head, my nails digging into my scalp as visions of Nephilim thrones and blood-soaked altars flooded my mind. I saw myself as the shedim saw me—a traitor, a Kenizzite who had forsaken the might of his kin for the fleeting promise of a foreign god. My heart faltered, the temptation a siren's call, offering power, belonging, a place among the giants whose shadows had haunted me since dusk.

The shedim's eyes flared, and its form swelled, tendrils of smoke coiling toward me like serpents, their touch a promise of dominion and ruin,

"You cannot escape your blood, Kalev," it hissed, its voice now a chorus, a thousand graves speaking as one. "The Ivrim will fall, their god's light snuffed out by the strength of the nephilim. Join us, and you will stand when the earth burns, a king among the sons of the watchers. Deny us, and you will be dust, your name forgotten, your soul a feast for the dry places."

My vision darkened, my knees struck the earth, and I gasped, the weight of the shedim's presence crushing my spirit. I was a child again, small and frail, standing before a legacy I could neither claim nor fully reject. The temptation gnawed at me, a whisper that my Kenizzite blood might yet find a home among the Anakim, that I might wield their power and rewrite my fate. My hands shook, my breath a ragged sob, and I felt the shedim's tendrils brush my soul, cold and hungry, ready to claim me.

Then, a rustle broke the silence, and Joshua stirred, his eyes snapping open as if roused by a divine call. He rose, his form a silhouette against the dim starlight, standing tall, his face alight with a fire that no darkness could quench. "Kalev!" he called, his voice a clarion, cutting through the shedim's whispers like a blade through mist. He stood firm beside me, his hands raised. He looked at me, wondering, puzzled at what stood before us.

Suddenly, he seized my hand and pressed it against the band at my arm—the one my father gave me before he died, with the Name etched in bronze and the Shema carved like flame into its face. It gleamed in the moonlight, a relic of blood and blessing. Then, lifting his hands to heaven, he began to pray—a torrent of faith unleashed, invoking Yahweh's name with the fervor of one who had stood before the burning bush.

"O Sovereign of Hosts, shield Your servant! Break the chains of the serpent's seed, and let Your light cast upon my brother!!"

The shedim recoiled, its coals dimming, its form fracturing as Joshua's prayer rose, a flame that burned brighter than the spirit's malice. The warmth of Yahweh's covenant kindled within me, faint at first, then blazing, a fire born of the God who had called me from the shadows of my past. I staggered to my feet, my fear a storm but my soul anchored by Joshua's faith and the truth of the Almighty's promise. I faced the spirit, my voice trembling yet resolute, and spoke words that rose unbidden, rooted in the scrolls of the sons of light, a war cry against the darkness: "By the might of Yahweh, the Eternal King of Israel, I stand, and you are cast down! The Lord of Hosts has decreed your ruin, His arm raised against the nephilim's thrones. His covenant endures, and His enemies are as chaff before the wind of His glory!"

The shedim shrieked, a sound that split the night, its form shattering like glass, its coals extinguished as it dissolved into the darkness, leaving a chill that seeped into my bones, a haunting echo that would linger through the years. Joshua's hand steadied me, his eyes fierce with the assurance of victory, he had fought beside me in this unseen battle. Yahweh's hand shielded me, His promise a bulwark against the shedim's lies, and I stood, trembling but unbroken, under the watchful stars, the caves of Hebron a silent witness to the war that had begun within me.

As the shedim's sounds faded into the night, leaving only the whisper of the desert wind, Joshua's hand remained firm on my shoulder, his touch an anchor against the chill that lingered in my soul. We stood in the shadow of the caves, the stars above us sharp as spears, and his eyes, fierce with the fire of faith, met mine.

As dawn broke over the rugged folds of Hebron, we trod softly from the caves, each step a whispered prayer that the Anakim would not trace our path. Joshua, his cloak stirred by the morning's breath, turned to me, his eyes like flint struck with fire,

"Kalev," he said, his voice a low chord woven with the weight of Sinai's call, "what vision held you in the dark of the caves last night?"

My heart staggered, besieged by the memory of shadowed forms—shedim, their voices hissing like coals in a dying flame, their eyes agleam with malice older than the earth. I gripped the bronze band at my arm, its etched Name warm against my skin, the cord wrapped thrice around with oil-dark leather. "Spirits, my lord," I said, my words rough-hewn, "foul and formless, speaking my name as if to claim it. They wove tales of my blood, of a Kenizzite shadow I cannot fully flee."

Joshua's brow furrowed, and he paused, his gaze searching mine. "Shedim?" he murmured, as if tasting the word. "I saw no such powers, Kalev, only the flicker of the moon and the weight of the Anakim's threat. Yet your eyes..." He stepped closer, his voice softening to a cadence of wonder, "They see what mine do not. Yahweh has opened your sight to the unseen, a gift rare and perilous, born of the blessing of God sealed upon you."

I stood, the weight of his words kindling a fire within, though my heart still quaked at the memory of the shedim's malice, "My lord," I said, my voice steadying as I clutched Mosheh's amulet, its warmth a seal of truth, "if Yahweh has granted me eyes to see the unseen, I tremble at its burden. Yet I trust His hand, for the Name upon me is stronger than the shadows that hunt." My gaze lifted to the hills, and I felt the spark of His promise stir my soul.

"The land is ours, Kalev, not because of our strength, but because the Lord who parted the sea has spoken. The Anakim, the shedim, the altars of blood—they will fall, for no power can stand against the Holy One of Israel."

The silence returned, heavy and reverent, the kind that falls not after danger, but after deliverance. Joshua stepped a pace away, eyes raised toward the jagged rim of Hebron's hills. The wind stirred his mantle like unseen fingers, and light caught the edge of his brow as though the desert itself dared not speak while he prayed. Then he began to sing—not in the tuneful chant of the Levites, nor in the rough ballads of our marching men, but in a cadence older than Mosheh, older than Sinai, the words falling like stones into deep water. I had heard such language only once before, from an elder who muttered it in dreams—words said to be taken from the writings of Enoch himself.

"Gilgamesh fell like a cedar,
And Og like a stone from heaven's sling.
Arakiel howled from his pit,
And Azazel covered his face.
They boasted in the old days:
'We are the lords of earth and sky.'
But the flood swallowed their laughter,
And Enoch wrote their shame on stone.
Now only dust bears their names,
And their seed turns to ash at the name of El Shaddai."

His words were a balm, a fire that burned away the shadow of doubt, and I felt our bond tighten, two sons of the promise standing against the darkness,

"Together," I said, my voice steadier now, "we will see Kena'an bow to Yahweh's will."

Joshua nodded, his hand clasping mine, a vow sealed under the rising sun. "Together," he echoed, "for the God who delivered us from Egypt will deliver this land into our hands." The caves of Hebron stood silent, their menace dimmed by the flame of our faith, rekindled and unyielding. One day I would return and seize the land of Hebron from the evil that binds it.

When we left the land, we carried a cluster of grapes, so vast it took both Joshua and me to bear it, slung between us on a pole, its weight a testament to the land's bounty and its burden. Each fruit gleamed in the sunlight, heavy with juice, a sign of Yahweh's promise, yet also a reminder of the giants who guarded such riches.

The memory of the Anakim seared my mind, their towering forms and bronze-clad armor a scar that lingered, vivid and raw, even years later. We had slipped past their notice, our stealth a gift from Yahweh, who cloaked us in the shadows of the hills, but their presence haunted us, a specter that followed through the rugged trails. The land was no passive prize; it watched us, its heart ancient and unyielding, its stones whispering of powers that defied the God we served. We were but two men, chosen to face its giants, armed only with a promise that burned fiercer than fear, a flame kindled by the covenant we carried.

We returned to the camp of Israel at Kadesh-Barnea after forty days of scouting the land, the grapes swaying between us, their size drawing gasps from the tribes gathered in the wilderness. Mosheh, the prophet of Yahweh, stood before us, his frame stooped by years yet towering with the authority of one who had spoken face-to-face with God. His beard was white as the snows of Sinai, his eyes deep pools of wisdom and sorrow, reflecting the weight of leading a stiff-necked people. His hands, gnarled from wielding the staff that parted seas and struck rock, reached out to touch the grapes, their richness a sign of the land he would never enter. To me, a Kenizzite grafted into Yehudah's line, Mosheh was more than a leader—he was the voice of Yahweh, the man who bore the law in his heart, who stood in the gap when Israel faltered. His presence was a fire, holy and unyielding, and when he looked upon us, his gaze saw not just Kalev, the outsider with skin dark as the southern night, but a son of the covenant, sealed by the Pascha's blood,

"Well done," he said, his voice low, resonant with the weight of prophecy, and I felt the honor of serving under such a man, whose every word echoed the God who called us.

Yet the report the other spies brought was bitter. Their courage broken by the Anakim's shadow, spoke poison, their voices trembling with tales of giants and walls, of a land that devoured its inhabitants. The tribes wailed, their faith crumbling, but Joshua and I stood firm, our hearts joined by the prophet's charge and Yahweh's promise. Mosheh listened, to the faithless, his face heavy with grief, and I knew he saw the cost of their fear—a generation doomed to wander.

I stepped forward then, my voice steady, my gaze unflinching,

"The land is good," I said, and the murmurs fell still beneath the authority that laced my words, "Exceedingly good. A land flowing with milk and honey, just as Yahweh promised. If He delights in us, He will bring us into it. Do not fear the Anakim of the land—their protection is gone, and Yahweh is with us."

A stillness cloaked the camp, as if the winds of the wilderness held their breath, and the clans, gathered beneath the shadow of the Almighty's promise, hung upon my words. I spoke of the Anakim's might, yet declared the land ours by Yahweh's decree. Mosheh's gaze, sharp as the flint of Sinai, never wavered from me. In his eyes, aglow with the fire of visions past, I glimpsed a knowing deeper than words

— A prophet's certainty stirred my soul. It was not mere approval, but recognition—profound and unyielding—as though he saw in me the elder I had become.

Still, the people refused to hear Joshua and I. Instead they listened to the ten spies who defied us. The cries of the clans rose, harsh with rebellion, until the glory of Yahweh appeared at the Tent of Meeting, a radiance that silenced all. The judgment came swift and sure: the faithless would not enter. They would turn back to the wilderness, their bones destined for dust.

But we—Joshua and I—we were marked. Not by our own strength, but by the Spirit who stirred us to stand when others fled. Mosheh turned to us then, his voice low, for our ears alone: "You will see it. You will cross over. And you, Joshua... you will lead them."

It was not triumph we felt in that moment, but awe. The land was promised, but first came fire, sand, and waiting. The burden of the future rested on our shoulders, and we bore it—not for ourselves, but for the children of those who wept that day, that they might walk in freedom where their fathers refused.

Yet the weight of that day did not end with the judgment's echo. The people's grumbling, their faithlessness woven like thorns through their hearts, had sown a deeper curse. The camp at Kadesh-Barnea became a crucible, where the rebellion of the ten spies—Shammua, Shaphat, Igal, and the rest—ignited a fire that consumed a generation. Their words, "We are like grasshoppers in their sight," had not merely sown fear but defied the Almighty who had parted the Red Sea and fed them manna from heaven. The tribes, swayed by their trembling voices, wept through the night, their cries a chorus of unbelief, accusing Yahweh of leading them to slaughter,

"Would that we had died in Egypt!" they wailed, their hearts turning back to the chains they had left behind. Yahweh's verdict, spoken through Mosheh, was a blade of divine justice, sharp and unyielding,

"As you have spoken in My ears, so I will do to you," He declared, His voice a storm that shook the Tent of Meeting, "Your bodies shall fall in this wilderness, all who were numbered from twenty years and upward, who grumbled against Me. You shall not enter the land I swore to give you, save Kalev, son of Jephunneh, and Joshua, son of Nun."

The promise was not revoked, but delayed, stretched across more decades of wandering, a pilgrimage of penance through fire, sand, and starlit desolation. For every day we had spied out the land —forty days—so the faithless would bear their guilt for forty years, one year for each day, until the generation that doubted perished, their bones bleaching under the desert sun.

Scarcely had seven dawns passed since Mosheh's voice, an oracle heavy with the Almighty's decree, rang out among the clans, when a shadow fell upon the ten spies. A wasting sickness seized them, swift and merciless, as if the very breath of their doubt had kindled Yahweh's wrath. Their eyes grew dim, their limbs faltered, and one by one they crumbled to the dust, their whispers of fear silenced beneath the weight of divine judgment. The camp stood hushed, the air thick with the echo of their folly, a solemn testament to the covenant that bound Israel to the One who sees all.

For Joshua and me, the judgment was both mercy and burden. We were spared, marked by our faith in the God who had called us to Hebron's shadow, yet we grew older under the weight of waiting. Our hair grayed, our limbs hardened by years of leading a people prone to stumble, yet our hearts burned still with the vision of Kena'an's hills, its rivers flowing with the milk of promise, its fields heavy with the honey of Yahweh's word. We watched the children of the faithless grow, their eyes unclouded by the fears of their fathers, their hands untainted by the stones once raised against us. These were the ones we would lead, the generation destined to cross the Nehar

Ha-Yarden, to face the Anakim and their shedim-haunted strongholds, to claim the land where giants guarded a cursed legacy.

The wilderness years were not idle. We walked circuits through the desert, from Kadesh to the Red Sea, from Paran to the borders of Edom, each step a lesson in trust, each dawn a reminder of Yahweh's faithfulness. Mosheh taught us the Law, his voice a beacon in the dust, and we learned to lean on the pillar of cloud by day, the pillar of fire by night. The Anakim's shadow lingered in our dreams, their towering forms a challenge we would face when the time was fulfilled, but we knew the God who had broken Egypt's chains would break their bronze as well. Joshua's faith grew fiercer, a flame that kindled mine, and together we bore the promise, not as young men, but as elders seasoned by trial, our eyes fixed on a horizon we would yet reach.

The forty years were a forge, shaping us, refining us, until the day came when the last of the faithless fell, and the children of Israel stood ready. Kalev, son of Jephunneh, and Joshua, son of Nun, now older, our faces etched with the lines of waiting, turned our faces toward Kena'an, the land of giants and glory, knowing Yahweh's word would not fail.

Now, we had returned to the land of God's promise. The forty years of judgement over. Yet now our tribe was bereft of the prophet who had led us. Mosheh , the man of God, was gone, his life ended on Nebo's peak, his eyes having seen the land of promise but his feet never touching its soil. The weight of his absence was a stone in my heart, a lament that shadowed every trail we trod. I, felt it keenly—his voice, resonant with Yahweh's fire, no longer called us to courage; his staff, which had parted seas and struck water from rock, lay still, passed to Joshua's hands, which would soon once again stretch forth the power to still the sun.

Mosheh had been our guide, our intercessor, the one who stood between Israel's doubt and Yahweh's wrath, whose face glowed with the glory of the Most High. He had seen me, a dark-skinned stranger from the southern deserts, and named me kin, sealing me to Yehudah through the Pascha's blood, declaring my spirit different, my faith a flame to rival Israel's sons.

Before we stood at the Yarden's edge, before our great Prophet passed to Avraham's bosom, the shadow of the Amalekites had crossed our path, a scourge that tested Israel's resolve and marked our journey with blood and fire. In the wilderness, when we were yet a fledgling nation, newly freed from Egypt's chains, the Amalekites struck at Rephidim, preying upon our weary, straggling kin with a cruelty that reeked of the serpent's seed.

They were no ordinary men, but the blood-stained offspring of giants—the brood of Anak, distant heirs of the Nephilim. Though their stature had waned, their savagery had not. These were a people who defied the laws of Yahweh and hunted His chosen with blades forged in hatred older than Sinai. Their rites were abominations: children burned upon stone altars, and the flesh of men consumed in secret feasts beneath the moon. Mosheh, upheld by the hands of Aaron and Hur, called upon the strength of the Most High, and Joshua—then still young and untried—led our warriors to drive them back. That day Yahweh's judgment fell like fire, and the victory was sealed with an altar named Yahweh- Nissi—a banner against the darkness. It burned in our memory like a living flame: a sign that no enemy, however monstrous, could stand before the God who shattered the gods of Egypt.

But the Amalekites' shadow lingered, their hatred undimmed. After the spies' rebellion at edge of Kena'an, when the faithless tribes recoiled from Kena'an's giants, a remnant of Israel, stung by Yahweh's judgment, defied Mosheh's counsel and marched unbidden against the hill country. The Amalekites, joined by other Kena'ani, fell upon them like wolves, smiting them as far as Hormah, a slaughter born of our own presumption. That defeat was a bitter wound, a lesson carved in the dust of our shame: without Yahweh's presence, our strength was as chaff before the wind. Yet even in judgment, the Almighty spared Joshua and I, our faith a shield against the wilderness's despair. Years later, as we circled through the wastes, the Amalekites' raids persisted, their ambushes a thorn in our side, their alliance with darker powers—whispered to echo the Anakim's pacts —stirring the shedim that haunted Kena'an's hills.

When Mosheh ascended Nebo, his final charge to Joshua was clear: remember Amalek's evil, and blot out their name under heaven. Thus, as we turned toward Kena'an, older now, our bodies hardened by forty years of trial in the desert, we carried not only the promise of the land but the memory of Amalek's defiance—a prelude to the greater war against the Nephilim's heirs that awaited us in the land ahead.

But before he vanished from our sight, the prophet called me to him, alone beneath the shadow of the mountain. His eyes, dim with age but bright with fire. Without a word, he brought forth a flask of sacred oil and poured it upon me—not only my head, but my hands, my chest, my feet, until I was marked from crown to sole. "Let every part of you be set apart," he said, voice low with the gravity of farewell. Around my neck he placed a small amulet, bound with cords of crimson and blue, carved with the words of the Shema. He pressed it to my chest, fingers trembling. "Hear, O Yisra'el," he whispered, "and may this word shield you when blade and shield fail. May it burn in you like fire, and shine in the dark like the pillar once did." He blessed it with a prayer known only to prophets, and kissed my brow as the oil dried beneath the desert wind.

That was the last time I saw him. He had sealed me with oil, with word, with memory. And I carried them all as we crossed the Yarden, toward flame and conquest and the reckoning of giants.

Chapter Three
In the Shadow of Jericho

Now, in the days that followed our clan edged closer to Jericho, the city's walls jutting into the sky like the bones of some defiant beast, high and ancient, thick with pride. Behind them, fear brewed like smoke in a sealed vessel. The people of the city surely had heard of our coming—of the sea that split, of the kings we had already broken. But now they watched, silent, from behind stone and bronze.

Joshua was no longer the young Ephraimite whose eyes first blazed with the daring of youth when he spied upon Hebron. Now he was a seasoned warrior, anointed by Yahweh, the sword raised in the name of heaven, commander of a people forged by wilderness and covenant. The mantle of Mosheh rested on his shoulders not like a burden, but like armor, and the words of the prophet still echoed in his every breath. He led not with his own strength, but with the voice that once thundered from Sinai.

And I, the son of Jephunneh, the outsider grafted into Yehudah, had not let the years dull my resolve. My limbs bore the weight of many seasons, but my heart still burned with the same fire that once carried me into Hebron's shadow, past the sons of Anak. Joshua, who had stood with me in the wilderness when all others trembled, now stood over Israel as its head—commander, prophet, and shepherd. From his tent he summoned me, and with solemn words and eyes like flint, he gave the charge. *Go,*

"Take your most trusted, and scout out the city" he ordered me, in front of the Temple of Meeting, before all the elders. And so I chose Othniel, my kin, my companion. But before we went, Joshua spoke to me again, away from the others, quieter than before, as though the voice of the Lord still lingered in his breath,

"There is a reason I place this charge upon you Kalev: there may yet be those within the city who hears the Name," he said. "Those whose heart is ready to turn from the idols, who no longer drink the lies of the Nephilim. Mercy goes where swords cannot."

I saw the look in his eye—not only of conquest, but of remembrance—he remembered who I was, the blood from which I was born, and whom the Lord had grafted in among Yehudah. If I, born of a shattered clan, could be called friend of God, could not even one from Jericho yet turn and live? This, too, was our task: to find the listening ears amid stone walls, to see if any spark was lit. We would search the city—not in doubt, but in faith. To prepare the blow before the trumpet's blast.

The sun slipped behind the western heights, spilling gold across the plain and igniting the heavens. Jericho's walls rose in the distance—mute, immense, and defiant of Yahweh's word. We moved like shadows, cloaked and quiet, slipping through the murmuring outer court of the city as travelers, unnoticed by the sentries. Our waterskins were dry, our sandals worn, but the charge of heaven was upon us.

We carried more than our own lives into that city—we bore the weight of a promise made to Avraham, to Mosheh, to every child of the covenant whose bones lay buried beneath the desert sands. We would enter Jericho not as scouts of uncertainty, but as witnesses of judgment and mercy. And though the city's walls reached toward heaven, we knew they would soon fall at the voice of Yahweh.

We dressed as traders, our cloaks patched and dusty, our faces smudged with earth to mask the desert's mark on our skin. I bore a sack of barley, its weight a flimsy disguise for the sword hidden beneath my tunic, its blade a quiet promise against the city's threat. Othniel carried a bundle of dried figs, his dagger strapped to his thigh, his steps measured but alert, his faith a shield no wall could pierce. The city gates stood open, their bronze hinges catching the fading light, but the guards were lax, slouched against the walls, their spears propped like afterthoughts. Their laughter was slurred, their breath heavy with wine, and they barely glanced at us as we passed, our heads bowed, our movements deliberate, as if we moved with Jericho's pulse. Yet my heart pounded, the land's ancient gaze upon us, and I knew this city, like Hebron, remembered those who dared its secrets.

Getting in was easy, a stroke of grace that felt too clean, too fragile, and I felt a prickle on my neck, the kind that warns of eyes unseen. Jericho's streets were a labyrinth, a writhing maze of narrow, twisting alleys carved between mud-brick walls that seemed to lean inward, as if the city itself conspired to trap those who dared its depths. The air was thick, a stifling blend of baked bread from clay ovens, the acrid sweat of laborers, and the faint, coppery tang of blood seeping from the market's butcher stalls, where flies buzzed in frenzied clouds. But beneath these mortal scents lurked something darker—a cloying, sickly sweetness, like incense burned for gods who demanded more than worship. The city was a living thing, its pulse a cacophony of voices: merchants haggling over pomegranates and bronze, children shouting as they chased one another through the dust, the clatter of carts grinding over uneven stone, their wheels creaking under the weight of goods or offerings for the temples. Othniel and I moved swiftly, cloaked as traders, our sandals silent on the packed earth, keeping to the shadows where the sun's dying light could not betray us. We slipped behind ovens, their heat radiating through the dusk, their embers glowing like the eyes of serpents coiled in the dark, watching, waiting.

The city's architecture was a testament to its ancient defiance, its mud-brick houses pressed so close their walls shared secrets, their flat roofs cluttered with drying herbs, stacks of flax, and clay jars sealed with wax, their contents hidden but potent. Windows were small, dark slits, some veiled with linen, others bare, their emptiness watchful, as if the houses themselves were spies for the gods of Kena'an. The streets were alive with movement, but it was not the orderly bustle of a city at peace. There was a fever to Jericho, a restless hunger that pulsed through its veins, fed by the pagan rites that defined its soul. As we moved, I caught glimpses of the city's idolatry —crude idols of Ba'al and Asherah poles perched in doorways, their stone faces smeared with oil and blood, their eyes hollow but seeming to follow us. Serpents were everywhere, carved into lintels, painted on walls, their sinuous forms coiling around clay altars where offerings of grain and flesh smoldered, the smoke curling upward like prayers to a sky that offered no answer.

The pagan heart of Jericho beat loudest in its people, their lives steeped in a worship that was both fervent and grotesque. Men and women moved through the streets with a casual disregard for modesty, their bodies often bare or draped in sheer linens that left little hidden, a reflection of the city's cultic rites where nudity was not shame but devotion. Priestesses of Asherah, their hair adorned with beads and bones, danced in small squares, their movements fluid, their skin glistening with sweat and oil, their chants rising in a low, hypnotic drone that made my skin crawl. Men joined them, their torsos painted with ash and ochre, their eyes glazed, as if the spirits they invoked had already taken hold. These were not mere dances, but rituals, offerings to gods who thrived on flesh and frenzy, and I saw the marks of their worship—scars on arms, brands of serpents and stars, tokens of vows made in blood. Phalluses adorned many of the buildings, even strung around the necks of children.

We ducked beneath a line of linen hung across an alley, its fabric brushing our shoulders, its scent earthy and damp, mingling with the incense that drifted from a nearby shrine. The shrine was small, tucked between houses, its altar carved with images of Ba'al, his horned head crowned with a crescent moon, his hands gripping a thunderbolt and a serpent. A clay bowl at its base held the remnants of a sacrifice—bones, small and delicate, too small for livestock, and I turned away, my stomach churning, the truth of Jericho's bloodlust a shadow I could not escape. Mosheh had spoken of such places, where the Nephilim's legacy lingered, where the shedim fed on the lives of children, their cries a currency for power. I gripped my cloak tighter, the sword beneath it a cold comfort, and grazed Othniel's arm, a silent signal to stay calm, his eyes betrayed the same unease.

The city's temples loomed over the streets, their walls higher, their stones smoother, adorned with lotus flowers, friezes of serpents their mouths open, as if devouring the offerings brought daily. The largest temple, dedicated to Ba'al, stood at the city's heart, its entrance flanked by twin pillars carved with eyes that seemed to watch, their pupils inlaid with obsidian that glinted in the torchlight. Priests in robes of dyed wool moved through the crowd, their faces masked with clay, their hands stained red, carrying bowls of blood or bundles of herbs to burn on the altars within. The air around the temple was heavy, thick with the stench of burning flesh and the low hum of chants, a sound that burrowed into my bones, promising horrors I could not yet name.

The market of Jericho was a furnace of color and sound. Perfumed smoke drifted from brass censers swaying in the hands of temple girls; vendors shouted the glories of their wares—fresh dates from the Yarden groves, linen dyed with Tyrian purple, fish glistening on woven mats, still flinching with the last throes of life. Drums pulsed from the temple quarter. Bronze clanged on bronze. Above it all, the high sun glared down through the gauze of incense and dust.

I kept my hood low, my face shadowed. Beside me, Othniel walked with the confident step of a trader, his eyes calm, always watching. We passed beneath a great awning where merchants sat on carpets, hawking lapis from the mountains, and carnelian in tiny bowls like pomegranate seeds. A priestess brushed past us in silk so sheer it was more whisper than fabric, her hair braided with disks of gold. Her perfume clung to the air like fog.

"Don't speak" I whispered without moving my lips, "Too many ears."

We made our way to a stand where a man with skin like weathered leather and a beard streaked gray with age was arranging oil jars into a pyramid. His cart bore the insignia of Shechem—three interlocked mountains cut into the wood.

"From the north?" I asked in Akkadian, letting the foreign tongue fall from my mouth with casual effort.

He looked up sharply, squinting beneath his turban. "Shechem. Good eyes. I have pressed olives from the Hill Country. No better oil east of the Sea" his gaze sharpened. "And you, strangers—where do you hail from? Your accent is not of this city."

I exchanged a quick glance with Othniel, "From the southern hills, near Hebron," I replied, careful to sound sure but unassuming. "We seek passage to trade—spices and copper from the desert caravans."

The shopkeeper's eyes narrowed slightly as he measured us with a cautious gaze, though a faint, wary smile touched his lips, "Desert traders, you say? Bold folk to wander here, especially with the Ivriam clan so near. This city is tense—whispers reach even these walls of their god's wrath." He reached beneath his stall and lifted a clay jar, the scent of fresh olive oil rising. "For travelers such as yourselves—pressed this very morning from the hills of Shechem. May Dagon watch over your steps.

I bent to pick up a jar and sniffed, "You've come far. What do you make of this city? Any word on the new king?"

The man gave a snort and spat into the dust. "King? Bah. He's a boy, fat with wine and dreams. Built a new altar to Dagon last week and parades through the streets as if Ba'al himself called him to rule. No sense. His father would've never opened the city gate to trade with the hill tribes he didn't trust. The king talks often of the clans from the desert, he fears them"

Othniel stepped forward and lowered his voice. "The desert clans.. you've heard of them stirring?"

The man narrowed his eyes. "You mean the stories? The Ivrim?"

I said nothing, letting the silence stretch. He looked around once, then leaned closer, his voice a whisper. "They say a swarm of them came out of the desert like hornets. Took two Amorite kings east of the river. Now they camp in the plains of Shittim. My cousin's caravan saw them with his own eyes—fires like stars across the land, and a great black tent in the center. They follow a god who rides on thunder."

Othniel feigned amusement. "Sounds like tavern talk."

The man shrugged. "Talk travels fast when it carries fear." He paused, then added, "But I'll tell you this—people are afraid. There are soldiers at every gate. Even the temple guards are armed now, not just for show. Look across the square, the king has posted guards everywhere"

Behind us, a woman laughed too loudly, and across the way we saw two men with bronze collars leaned against a pillar, their eyes resting a little too long on us. One gestured faintly with his chin. The other adjusted his grip on his spear.

The shopkeeper was in mid sentence when we abruptly took our leave, hastening to leave before our ruse was discovered by the palace guard.

I touched Othniel's elbow, "Move" I whispered.

We turned from the stall, slipping into the flow of the crowd. I glanced back once—the merchant had vanished behind his cart, suddenly preoccupied with his jars. We pressed deeper into the market's underbelly, where the wares grew cheaper and the people warier. Chickens flapped in cages. A beggar with no legs dragged himself after us on a board with wheels, muttering words I didn't know.

A group of women passed, balancing clay pots on their heads, their eyes darting toward us, then away. I caught the barest flicker of recognition—was it my accent? My posture?

We walked through a crooked archway, past a perfumery thick with myrrh and crushed lilac, and into a narrow lane where the stone walls rose close on either side. The noise of the market fell behind like a dropped curtain. Only the hiss of wind between the walls remained.

"Too many eyes," I said, "That merchant sold us. Or warned someone."

"I think so as well."

Othniel's jaw clenched, his eyes scanning the crowded street ahead.

A boy, no older than ten, darted suddenly across the narrow lane, his skin streaked with soot and dust, a rough linen sash tied low around his waist. He froze as he caught sight of us. His sharp eyes flicked over our cloaks, then caught the glint of something slipping free beneath the hem of my robe—a worn leather cord, braided and inscribed with Ivrim script, a talisman of prayer and blessing I wore close but tried to keep hidden, lest it draw unwanted attention.

For a moment, his gaze locked on that faint symbol, an unspoken recognition flickering in his eyes. My hand instinctively moved to cover it, but the boy's mouth parted in a silent gasp before he bolted, his bare feet pattering hard against the stones as he vanished into the crowd. The noise of the market swallowed his flight, but the weight of his knowing glance lingered—an invisible mark that we were seen, and no longer safe

My breath caught.

"The boy," Othniel said, his voice barely audible, his eyes scanning the alley's end, where torchlight flickered from a broader street, "We need refuge, now. We'll never make it to the city gate"

I nodded, my heart pounding, the weight of our mission a stone in my chest. The city was a trap, its streets designed to confuse, to ensnare, and we were marked—our cloaks too new, our steps too careful, our eyes too alert. We turned another corner, the alley darkening, the torchlight fading, replaced by the glow of oil lamps hung from ropes above. The air grew thicker, heavy with the scent of myrrh and the faint, copper tang of blood, and I saw another altar, this one in a little niche, its stone blackened, its surface slick with offerings. A figurine of Asherah stood atop it, her curves exaggerated, her eyes painted red, a serpent coiled around her feet, its fangs bared. A small skull, no larger than a child's, rested at its base, and I looked away, the city's cannibalistic hunger a truth too raw, too vile, where the Nephilim's blood ran deep, where the shedim demanded sacrifice, their altars fed by the innocent. Jericho was no mere city; it was a throne, a seat of powers that had defied Yahweh since the flood, their worship a cycle of blood and lust that stained the land. I saw it in the people—men with brands of serpents on their chests, women with necklaces of bone, their eyes empty, as if the gods they served had hollowed them out. A man stumbled past, his tunic open, his body painted with ash, chanting softly, his words a plea to Ba'al for strength, for victory, for blood. A woman followed, her robe sheer, her movements slow, her laughter a lure for those who sought her trade, her trade a ritual in itself, a surrender to the city's gods.

We slipped into a narrower alley, the walls closing in, the air damp with the breath of the city's underbelly. The sounds of the market faded, replaced by the soft creak of shutters, the low moan of a flute from a hidden courtyard, the whisper of voices offering pleasures or prayers. The city's religion was not just in its temples, but in its veins, its streets a stage for rites that blurred worship and depravity. I saw a group of youths, their bodies entirely bare, their skin painted in gold, young men and and young women, dancing in a circle around a fire, before an idol of Asherah, their blades flashing, blood dripping from gashes they'd made on their arms, spilling out onto the stones as they chanted to the old goddess of fertility. Around them men, women and children passed by amidst their daily routine, as if the sight of idolatry and orgy was simply normal fair in this city of abomination.

The air shimmered, as if the shedim were near, drawn by the offering, and I felt a chill, the city's hunger a presence I could not shake. The footsteps grew louder, soft but deliberate, not the stumble of a drunk or the shuffle of a beggar, but the tread of hunters. I glanced back, seeing shadows move, torches flickering, and my pulse quickened, the city's noose tightening. The boy's flight had roused them, guards or priests or worse, their voices low, their intent clear. We were not traders, not of Jericho, and the city knew it, its gods whispering our names, its streets a snare for the unwary. Othniel's body tensed besides me, his eyes blazing with urgency, and we moved faster, the alley twisting, the walls pressing close, their serpents watching, their eyes unblinking, as Jericho's pagan heart beat louder, hungry for our blood.

"We need cover," Othniel whispered, his voice low, his eyes scanning the alley's end, where torchlight flickered from a broader street. "We can't outrun them, not here."

I nodded, my mind racing, the sack of barley heavy on my shoulder,

"A tavern, a market—somewhere we can blend," I said, my voice barely audible over the distant hum of the city, "But we're marked. They know we're not theirs."

We moved faster, the alley twisting, the air growing thicker with the stench of refuse and smoke. A woman's laughter echoed from a doorway, high and brittle, and I caught a glimpse of her silhouette, her robe clinging to her form, her hair unbound. The city was a predator, its streets a trap, and we were prey, our trader's guise unraveling with each step. We reached a small square, its edges lined with stalls, their awnings sagging under the weight of goods—pottery, woven baskets, slabs of salted meat. Merchants called out, their voices competing, but their eyes followed us, sharp and suspicious, and I felt the boy's gaze, hidden somewhere in the crowd, tracking us like a hawk.

Othniel paused, his gaze fixed on a narrow street leading toward the city's outer wall. "There," he said, his voice urgent. "The wall—it's less guarded, fewer eyes. We find a house, a trader, someone who'll take coin for silence."

I nodded in agreement, but doubt gnawed at me. Jericho was no friend to strangers, and coin could buy betrayal as easily as refuge. We slipped into the street, the walls rising high, their bricks blackened by years of smoke and sacrifice. The torchlight faded, the shadows deepening, and the sounds of the market grew distant, replaced by the soft creak of wooden shutters and the occasional bark of a dog. The footsteps followed, closer now, joined by voices—low, gruff, the guards roused from their wine, their spears no longer props but weapons. I glanced back, seeing shadows move, and my hand tightened on the sword beneath my cloak.

We turned another corner, the street ending at the base of the city's outer wall, its stones massive, unyielding, a testament to Jericho's defiance. A stone stair wound upward, its steps worn smooth, leading to a passage carved into the wall itself, a warren of homes built between the stones, their entrances hidden in shadow. My heart pounded, the footsteps louder, the guards' voices sharp with purpose. "They're here," one growled, his spear scraping the stone, and I knew we had moments before they closed in.

Then I saw her.

She stood at the stair's base, her figure framed by the faint glow of a torch above, her presence a sudden stillness in the city's chaos. She wasn't dressed as a priestess, nor a housewife, but her clothes—rough-spun, clinging to her form—hinted at a life lived on the edge of respectability. Her hair was dark, unbound, falling in waves that caught the torchlight, and her eyes were sharp, glinting like obsidian, taking us in with a glance that saw too much. She leaned against the wall, her posture casual, but her stance was coiled, ready to move, to strike, to vanish.

"Ivrim," she said, her voice low, carrying over the alley's hum, her gaze flicking from me to Othniel. "You're running from guards. Come."

I froze, my hand on my sword beneath my cloak, the word 'Ivrim' a blade that cut through our disguise. Othniel's eyes narrowed, his dagger half-drawn, but her smile—faint, almost amused—disarmed us, if only for a moment,

"How do you know us?" he asked, his voice rough, the sack upon his back slipping slightly, his shoulder aching.

She stepped closer, her scent—jasmine and something wilder, like the desert after rain—filling the air, her eyes never leaving mine. "I know strangers when I see them, and you're no traders," she said, her tone nonchalant, a prostitute's ease with men who hid their truths. "Your cloaks are wrong, your steps too careful. And the guards —" she glanced down the alley, where torchlight flickered, the footsteps louder—"they're not chasing shadows. You need a door, and I have one. Unless you'd rather fight?"

Othniel's hand relaxed, but his voice was firm, testing her. "What's your price?"

Her laugh was soft, a melody that belied the danger, her eyes glinting with a mix of cunning and weariness. "Everything has a price in Jericho, I will reveal mine in time" she said, her voice teasing but firm, "Now we must hide you".

She stepped back, her robe swaying, and gestured toward the stair's shadowed mouth, her posture a blend of urgency and nonchalance, as if leading strangers through Jericho's underbelly was merely another night's work, "Follow close," she whispered, her voice low, cutting through the alley's hum, "The city's awake, and it doesn't like strangers."

Othniel and I exchanged a glance, his hand on his dagger, my sword heavy beneath my cloak. The guards' footsteps echoed, closer now, their torches casting jagged light on the walls, and I felt the city's pulse quicken, its jaws tightening. We moved, our sandals silent on the worn stone, trailing her up the twisting stair, its steps slick with damp and grit. The passage was narrow, the air thick with the scent of smoke and decay, the walls etched with faint carvings—serpents, eyes, runes that seemed to pulse in the torchlight's flicker. Doors lined the way, some barred, others ajar, leaking whispers of laughter or low chants, the city's heart beating in every shadowed nook.

She moved like a shadow, her steps sure, her head turning to scan the darkness, her hand brushing the wall as if reading its secrets. The stair climbed higher, winding into the city's outer wall, a warren of passages where the outcast thrived—prostitutes, thieves, those who lived between the stones, their lives a reckoning of Jericho's gods and goddesses. The air grew colder, the torchlight fading, replaced by the faint glow of oil lamps hung from ropes, their flames trembling in the draft. Below, the guards' voices grew louder, their spears scraping stone, and I heard a shout—"They're near!"—sharp with purpose, sending a jolt through my chest.

We reached a landing, a small platform where the passage split, one path leading deeper into the wall, the other descending to a street below. She paused, her eyes narrowing, her hand raised to silence us. Footsteps echoed from the lower path, not the guards but someone else, their gait uneven, their breath heavy with wine. A figure stumbled into view—a man, broad-shouldered, his tunic open, his beard matted with sweat and ash. His eyes, bleary but sharp, caught us in the dim light, and he froze, his hand gripping a clay jug that sloshed as he swayed.

"Foreigners," he slurred, his voice thick, his gaze flicking from Othniel to me, then to her, "Rabaha, who are these men with you?" To me he said, "You're not... not of Jericho. Traders, eh? Or something else?" His eyes narrowed, suspicion cutting through the wine's haze, and I felt the weight of our mission teeter, the city's noose tightening. My hand moved to my sword, Othniel's stance shifting, ready to strike, but she stepped forward, her presence a sudden blaze in the gloom.

"Zimri," she said, her voice smooth, a purr that wrapped around the man like a spell. She moved closer, her robe clinging to her form, her smile slow and deliberate, the smile of a woman who knew her trade, "You're out late, and drunker than last time. These are my guests—traders from the south, here for my... company." Her tone was teasing, her hand brushing his arm, her fingers lingering just long enough to draw his gaze from us. "You wouldn't ruin my night, would you?"

Zimri blinked, his suspicion wavering, his eyes tracing her form, the wine dulling his edge. "Rabaha," he mumbled, a grin spreading, sloppy but eager. "Always the charmer. But I saw 'em— cloaks too new, eyes too sharp. They're not traders, are they?" His voice hardened, his hand tightening on the jug, and I tensed, the guards' footsteps echoing below, closer now, their torches painting the stair's mouth with light.

She laughed, a sound like water over stones, bright but dangerous, and stepped closer, her body a shield between us and Zimri, "Oh, Zimri, you see spies everywhere when you've had too much," she said, her voice low, intimate, her hand sliding to his chest, her fingers tracing the edge of his tunic, "They're paying customers, like you, and they're generous. You wouldn't begrudge me a night's coin, would you? Besides—" she leaned in, her lips near his ear, her voice a whisper that carried a prostitute's promise—"come see me tomorrow, and I'll make it worth your while. Just you and me, no interruptions."

Zimri's grin widened, his suspicion crumbling under her touch, his eyes glazing with desire, "Tomorrow, then," he said, his voice thick, his hand reaching for her, but she slipped back, her smile never faltering, her eyes sharp as a blade.

"Tomorrow," she agreed, her tone firm, guiding him toward the lower path. "Go home, Zimri. Sleep it off. The guards are out, and you don't want trouble."

He nodded, swaying, and stumbled down the stair, his jug sloshing, his laughter fading into the night. She turned to us, her smile gone, her eyes blazing with urgency. "Move," she hissed, leading us into the darker passage, the guards' voices now less muffled, their torches too close. We followed, our breaths shallow, the passage narrowing, its walls slick with moisture, its air heavy with the stench of incense and blood, the city's rites seeping through every stone.

The path twisted, branching into smaller tunnels, a maze within the wall where the daughter of the night navigated with ease, her steps silent, her robe a faint shadow ahead. We passed a doorway, its linen curtain parted, revealing a dimly lit room where a husband and wife lay close on a woven mat, their forms entwined, their movements practiced, a quiet intimacy as common in Jericho's homes as in the tents of Avraham's kin. The air was warm, heavy with the scent of olive oil and fresh-baked bread, a fleeting glimpse of ordinary life amid Jericho's pulse. Nearby, their children stirred on shared bedding, their laughter vibrating the walls over some game they enjoyed, the closeness of family a simple fact of life, unremarkable to me where such moments passed without notice everywhere, yet a small home alter to Asherah stood against the wall and a clay pot of oil burned. The idol, with engorged female curves carved in pale terebinth wood, gleamed faintly under the flickering flame, its form both alluring and unsettling, a goddess wrought by Kena'anim hands to cradle the hopes of the living and the fears of the dead. Her eyes, mere slits beneath a brow adorned with crescent moons, seemed to watch, unyielding, as if the spirit of the grove beyond Nehar ha-Yarden lingered within her grain. Her breasts, full and rounded, promised fertility to the fields and wombs of Jericho, while her hips, broad and unapologetic, anchored her to the earth, a mother eternal amidst the dust of the Kena'an plain. A garland of dried figs and myrtle leaves hung about her neck, offerings from hands that tilled the soil and baked the bread, hands that knew the rhythm of seedtime and harvest.

I paused, my gaze caught by the idol's mute presence, its power woven into the very warp and weft of this house, this city. The daughter of the night glanced back at me, her eyes sharp as flint, as if to warn that Asherah's gaze brooked no doubt, no wavering, and she hastened me to keep following. In that moment, the laughter of the children faded, and the walls of Jericho seemed to lean closer, heavy with the weight of a thousand such altars, a thousand such flames, burning for the Lady of the Groves whose name was whispered from the river to the sea.

We slipped past another door, this one leaking the low moan of a flute, the scent of myrrh, the soft clink of coins—her world, where survival was a dance with danger.

The passage opened to another stair, steeper, its steps crumbling, leading higher into the wall's heart. The guards' voices faded, but the city's pulse remained, its hunger a presence that followed us, its gods whispering through the stones. She paused at a landing, her hand on a scarred wooden door, its hinges rusted, its surface etched with a faint serpent rune, "Here," she whispered, pushing it open, the creak loud in the silence.

The room was small, its air thick with the scent of flax and dried herbs, the walls draped with coarse linen that swayed in the draft from a single window. A clay lamp flickered on a low table, casting shadows that danced like specters across the uneven bricks. Bundles of flax were stacked in a corner, their fibers catching the light, and a loom stood half-finished, its threads taut and tangled. The floor was packed earth, scattered with straw, and a narrow pallet lay against one wall, its blanket worn but clean. Two small pairs of sandals, child-sized, sat neatly by the door, their leather cracked from use, and I felt a pang, wondering at the lives tied to this place. Against the wall, half-hidden by a fold of linen, stood a small Asherah idol, its wooden form—carved with exaggerated rounded curves—gleaming faintly in the lamplight, its presence a quiet, yet ominous, pulse in the room.

The door shifted on its worn hinges and she barred it with a wooden beam, her movements swift, practiced, as if she'd shielded this space from prying eyes countless times. Inside, an older woman stood—her features strikingly similar to those of the younger woman who'd guided us here. Her eyes, heavy with the fatigue of long nights and harder days, held a quiet strength. Rough hands moved gently as she gathered the two small children clinging to her skirts, their breath uneven with restless wakefulness. The single room was tight, shadows pooling in every corner—bare stone for a floor, a low pallet piled with rough linen, and a small brazier still faintly glowing.

Her voice was calm but firm, a voice accustomed to command, "Mother, the children must be laid down. Take them to the far corner, where the shadows are soft. They need their rest."

The woman blinked, lips pressed thin, "Again so soon, daughter?" she said, annoyance in her voice, she folded the children into her arms, "Men come. You cannot always say no?"

Her eyes narrowed just slightly—sharp as flint, but tempered by habit, "Tonight is no trade for coin, mother, do as you're told."

The older woman sighed, but her hands moved obediently, settling the children on a worn mat near the wall. She hushed them with soft lullabies, their eyes drifting shut, though the air in the room hung taut with unspoken questions. Settling into the corner, she clutched her small loom, her gaze fixed on us—more from habit than curiosity.

The woman of the night stood still, watching us with measured poise. Her beauty was a blade, honed by years of surviving a city that devoured the weak—hair falling in dark waves, framing eyes like polished obsidian, sharp enough to cut through lies. Her voice, low and honeyed, carried the weight of one who knew the cost of every word.

"You were bold to linger in the market, Ivrims," she said, her tone cautious, the daughter of Ba'al's acknowledgment of the danger we'd courted.

"The guards were close—why risk Jericho's jaws after I marked you as strangers?" She asked

Othniel's grip tightened on his dagger, his knuckles pale, his eyes narrow as he studied her, his silence a shield. I rested my hand on my sword's hilt, my voice steady, shaped by the customs of the Ivrims, "We are travelers, seeking only passage," I said, my words careful, a Kenizzite's measured response to a woman whose home was both refuge and risk, "We thank you for your aid, but we mean no harm to you or yours."

Her lips curved, a faint smile that held no trust, her eyes flicking to the alcove where her children and mother lay, their breaths soft in the dimness, "Travelers don't skulk through alleys with swords hidden under cloaks," she said, a knowing gaze at the weapons we thought were hidden, her voice soft but pointed, stepping closer, her scent—jasmine and desert wind—mingling with the room's warmth, "I knew you in the market, Ivrims, your steps too careful, your eyes too keen. Why come here, to a city that hunts your kind?"

I studied her, the weight of her knowledge unsettling, her presence like a flame in the dim room, "The man outside, Zimri, called you 'Rabaha,'" I said, my voice steady, probing. "Is that what we should call you?"

She tilted her head, her dark hair catching the lamplight, her smile deepening, as if the question stirred a private jest, "I am Rabaha, daughter of Hanan," she said, stepping closer, her scent—jasmine and something wilder, like the wind after a storm—filling the small space, "My name means 'broad' or 'open' in our tongue, a hope my father gave me, for a life unbound by these walls. Some call me daughter of the dragon, my father, Hanan, his name, spoke of mercy, though little of it thrives in Jericho's streets. Names are but breath when gods clash, yet they carry what we make of them."

I stood taller, looking down upon her, my eyes locked on her with a blend of wariness and regard, "Rachav is your name in our tongue. Names are sacred among our people," I said, my voice steady, resonant with the traditions of the Ivrims, forged in the wilderness under Yahweh's covenant, "I am Kalev son of Jephunneh, of the tribe of Yehudah, servant of Yahweh, sent to scout the land He has sworn to give us."

Othniel stepped forward, his stance firm, and he spoke in the manner of our fathers,

"I am Othniel, son of Kenaz, of the tribe of Yehudah—husband to Acsah, sister of Kalev, and bound by blood and oath to the house of Jephunneh"

Rachav's eyes flickered, weighing our words, her bracelet of red cord glinting as she crossed her arms. "Kalev son of Jephunneh... Othniel son of Kenaz," she said slowly, tasting the names, her tone thoughtful—a mother's mind measuring the weight of strangers in her home. "Not mere spies. Sons of promise. Your God's hand is upon you, isn't it? That's why the priests of Ba'al tremble, why the giants' shadows grow long." She paused, her gaze lingering on me, a spark of recognition kindling in her eyes. "Your names will echo, I wager, when Jericho's walls fall.""

Othniel's voice was steady but guarded. "Why help us, Rachav? What do you gain?"

Her smile faded, and for a moment, her eyes flickered with something raw—fear, perhaps, or longing, "This city is a cage," she said, her voice dropping to a whisper. "Its walls keep us in as much as they keep others out. The kings, the priests, the giants—they rule by fear, and I've seen what fear does." She glanced toward the corner of the room, where two small pairs of sandals rested by the door, their leather cracked from use, and then she looked at the Asherah idol before us and her eyes filled with hate,

"The goddess of this city has never answered my cries, only bound me to nights of shame, my body a coin for men who take without giving. I'd rather my children live in a world where your God's fire burns away the shadows than one where they grow up bowing to monsters, and be slaves to defilement"

I shifted, the mention of children grounding the moment, making her more human, yet no less formidable. "You believe our God will win?" I asked, my tone skeptical, though her words stirred something in me—a spark of hope, or recognition.

She laughed, a sound like water over stones, sharp and clear, "I believe in what I see, Kalev, son of Jephunneh. I hear of a people who broke Egypt's spine, who walked through a sea, who carry a fire that makes our priests tremble. I see you, and him—" she nodded at Othniel, her eyes lingering, weighing him—"and I see men who don't flinch at evil."

Othniel's jaw tightened, but a flicker of respect crossed his face. "You're bold, Rachav," he said, his voice softer now, testing her. "But boldness isn't faith. Why risk your life, your children's lives, for strangers?"

She folded her arms, the motion drawing her robe aside just enough to catch the lamplight on a cord at her wrist—braided red, like blood let from a covenant, its threads worn smooth with wear and meaning. "Faith?" she echoed, her voice edged with dry humor. "I am no priestess, Othniel, son of Kenaz. I have knelt at no altar but necessity. I've weathered the gods of this city, the whims of its kings, and the hunger of its streets. And I've learned to smell a storm long before it breaks. Your God—He is no idol of stone. He is wind and fire. A tempest. And I—I would rather cling to the whirlwind than be crushed beneath it."

She took a step closer, the shadows rising like witnesses behind her. Her voice dropped, low and urgent, "But I am not a fool. I know what's coming. I want a vow. If your God truly gives you this city—then spare me. Spare my mother, my brothers, the children who sleep beneath my roof. That is the price I ask, and more than fair."

She paused, her eyes gleaming dark beneath the wavering lamplight. "This city is cursed. A place of blood. The cries of the innocent rise from its stones, but no one listens. Do you know what happens in the high places? What abomination festers in the temple of Ba'al? They do not just kill our children there—they burn them, eat them, call it sacred. I have seen it. I have smelled the flesh."

Her voice faltered, then steadied again, "The gods of Jericho are devourers. I would rather cast my lot with the God who thunders from Sinai."

I studied her, seeing the bronze beneath her beauty, the cunning that had kept her alive in a city of predators. She was no mere harlot, as some would later call her; she was a survivor, a mother, a strategist playing a game older than Jericho's walls. "And if we fail?" I asked, my voice low, testing her resolve.

Her eyes met mine, unflinching. "You won't," she said, her certainty a blade that cut through doubt. "I've seen the Rephaim, Kalev son of Jephunneh. I've heard their voices, felt the ground shake when they walk. They're strong, but they're afraid. Your God is coming, and they know it."

The room fell silent, the lamp's flame flickering, casting her shadow across the wall, tall and steady. I spoke, the weight of command in my voice, "You have our word," I said. "When Jericho falls, you and all who shelter beneath your roof will be spared."

She exhaled, a faint tremor in her breath, the only sign of vulnerability. As if the weight of a thousand lifetimes fell from her being. Finally, after what seemed like an eternity of silence, she spoke,

"Good," she said, turning to a shelf, pulling down a clay jug, "Then drink with me, as friends not foe." She brought the wine—sharp and sweet—the clay pot worn smooth by years of use. Her fingers brushed mine as she poured, warm and deliberate.

"To survival," she toasted, her smile returning, a mix of defiance and charm.

Rachav set the jug on the table and paused, her sharp eyes catching the flicker of wariness in Othniel's glance. Her lips curved faintly, as if she'd already anticipated our hesitation.

"You're Ivrim," she said, her voice low, remembering our brush in the market. "Your God shuns what's poured for Ba'al or Asherah, yes? This wine's mine—bartered from a desert merchant, kept for my own table. No priest ever touched it, nor was it spilled before an altar."

Her gaze drifted to the Asherah idol in the corner, its wooden curves aglow in the clay lamp's trembling light. With a sudden, solemn resolution, she drew a sharp breath and spat at the idol, a sacred defiance that seemed to still the air itself. Her eyes blazed, as if a veil had torn, casting off the chains of Jericho's gods in a single, unyielding act.

I met Othniel's eyes across the table, both of us weighing her words and action against the covenant we bore. As sons of Avraham, we were bound to guard against the defilement of pagan rites—a lesson hammered into us in the wilderness, where Yahweh's law made us a people apart. But her words rang true. She was no temple devotee, but a woman who survived by wit and barter, her trade far removed from incense and idols. And in this house, trust—however cautious—was the price of survival.

I reach for the cup and spoke,

"Blessed art Thou, Yahweh Elohei Yisrael, who bringest forth the fruit of the vine and guidest the feet of Thy servants through lands not their own. As Avraham was received in strange tents and offered bread without knowing the hearts of men, so we receive this cup with eyes fixed upon Thee. Let not our lips be stained with false worship, nor our hearts turn from Thy covenant. But if this house be counted righteous in Thy sight, then let this wine be as a seal of mercy between Thy servants and the woman who has given us shelter beneath her roof. In the shadow of the walls of Jericho, may Thy hand be our shield, and Thy truth our deliverance".

We drank, the wine warming my throat, easing the knot of tension in my chest, its sharp, sweet tang a fleeting comfort in the dim room. Rachav sat, her movements fluid as a dancer's, her rough-spun robe catching the lamplight as she settled across from us. She spoke of Jericho, her voice a low melody, weaving tales of a city teetering on the edge—its markets buzzing with trade yet shadowed by fear, its people whispering of the Ivrims who had shattered Pharaoh's might.

"The city's alive with rumors," she said, her tone rich with a survivor's insight, "of a people led by fire, who walked through a sea, who carry a God's wrath in their bones."

Her gaze hardened, her fingers tracing the edge of the cup, the scarlet cord wrapped around her wrist glinting like a warning, "The priests of Ba'al burn their offerings, begging the gods and goddess to protect them from your God" she continued, her voice dropping, laced with bitterness, "And the giants—those Anakim from Hebron— they come, demanding tribute: grain, gold, the blood of our children. Many call them gods, but I see abominations, relics of a cursed age."

She leaned forward, her eyes burning with a mother's defiance, "They act like gods, striding through our streets, their voices shaking the earth, their armor etched with runes that pulse with unholy light. The people kneel, but in their hearts, they loathe them, hating the chains of fear they forge."

Othniel listened, his eyes sharp, absorbing every word, but I saw the way he watched her, wary but intrigued, "You speak like you've fought them," he said, his tone probing.

Rachav's laugh was sharp, edged with pain, a sound that carried the weight of years spent outwitting Jericho's cruelties, "I fight every day, Othniel son of Kenaz," she said, her voice low, resonant with a Kena'anim's defiance, "Not with swords, as you do, but with words, with lies, with keeping my children's bellies filled in a city that devours its own. Your blades will clash with giants, but my battle is to draw breath in this cage of stone." She glanced at the small sandals by the door, her expression softening, her eyes tracing the cracked leather as if it held her children's dreams, "My boy, Aram, seven summers old, speaks of being a trader, of crossing seas for spices and silks. My girl, Lirah, five, sings to the stars, believing they sing back. They are my heart, the reason I risk all."

I nodded, seeing her not merely as an ally, but as a mother, her love a flame fiercer than the fear that stalked Jericho's streets,

"They are blessed to have such a protector," I said, my voice quieter than intended, shaped by the Ivrim reverence for those who guard life against darkness, yet mindful of speaking to someone of the house of Ba'al whose gods differed from ours. Rachav's smile was genuine, a fleeting breach in her guarded demeanor, making her both more perilous and more human, a woman who walked the edge of survival with unyielding purpose. Her eyes softened for a moment, like a desert flower caught in the shadow of a passing storm, before hardening again, her strength a shield.

"Blessed?" she said, her tone wry, almost mocking, a woman of the land's skepticism of such lofty words, "In Jericho, blessings are as fleeting as rain. My Aram dreams of far lands, but this city would sooner grind his hopes to dust. Lirah's songs are sweet, but the priests of Ba'al would silence her, offer her voice to their altars."

She set the wine jug down, the clay clinking softly against the table, and leaned back, her fingers tracing the edge of her red cord bracelet, its blood-hued strands glinting in the lamplight, "They're not blessed—they're bound, like me, in a place that chews dreams and spits out bones. But they're mine, and I'll hew a path for them, even if I must walk through the fires of your God or mine."

The room fell silent, the lamp's flame flickering, casting shadows that seemed to coil around Rachav's words, her defiance a spark in the dimness. I watched her, the weight of her decision settling over me, a mother's love clashing with the city's hunger, her faith in survival a mirror to our own covenant with Yahweh. Othniel's gaze lingered on the sleeping figures in the alcove—Aram, Lirah, and their grandmother, their breaths soft, unaware of the peril we brought to their door. The air grew heavier, the city's pulse a distant thrum through the walls, and my thoughts turned back to the shadows I'd seen in Hebron, the giants whose presence had marked me.

Othniel leaned forward, his voice breaking the silence like a stone cast into still water, carrying us from Rachav's children to the ancient terror that bound our fates, he had been listening intently to all she had spoken, especially about the Rephaim,

"You know much," he said, his tone cautious, testing her, "Kalev and our chieftain Joshua saw the sons of Anak—Sheshai, Talmai, Ahiman. They were no mere men, taller than cedars, their armor etched with signs older than Kena'an. Their voices shook the earth, and their presence... it was like standing before something not meant for this world."

Rachav nodded, her expression darkening, her fingers tightening around her scarlet corded bracelet, "The Anakim," she said, her voice steady but laced with a mother's fervor, "They're not just giants, are they? They're something else, something left over from a time before the flood. In Jericho, the priests call them the Rephaim, the shades of the Nephilim, born when the Watchers fell, when angels took daughters of men and spawned a race that defied your God."I leaned forward, my hands clasped, the wine souring in my throat.

"You know of the Watchers?" I asked, my voice low, the weight of her words stirring memories of Elidad's tales by the campfire, of the Nephilim's blood running through the land, "How? Do the priests of Ba'al speak of such things openly."

Her laugh was sharp, like a stone struck against flint, but her eyes were distant, as if seeing a past she'd buried deep, "I listen, Kalev. I've always listened. The priests of Ba'al worship their idols, and they fear the old stories, the ones whispered in the dark. The Watchers, the bene ha'elohim, came before the flood, possessing kings who mated with women, teaching men forbidden things—war, sorcery, the crafting of weapons that cut deeper than bronze. Their children were the Nephilim, giants who ruled the earth, whose hunger broke the world. When the waters came, most drowned, but their spirits—the shedim—lingered, seeking new bodies, new thrones."

Othniel's jaw tightened, his gaze fixed on her, his voice steady but urgent. "And you think the Anakim are their heirs? Not just men grown tall, but vessels for these spirits?"

Rachav stood, her movements fluid, crossing to the window where the night pressed against the city's walls, "I know they are," she said, her voice dropping to a whisper, her silhouette framed by moonlight. "Last year, when they came to Jericho. demanding tribute —grain, gold, the blood of our firstborn. Their armor was black bronze, forged in no human fire, etched with runes that pulsed like living things, signs that made my skin crawl, like the altars in the hills. They didn't walk like men; they moved like storms, their steps shaking the ground, their voices low, like the rumble of a cave collapsing."

She turned, her eyes burning with a mother's defiance, "I hid Aram and Lirah on the roof, told them to be silent as death. My boy clutched his sister, his eyes wide, her songs silenced by fear. My mother stood at the door, a knife in her sleeve, ready to die if they came for them. I hid in the square, and I watched the priests of Ba'al kneel before them, offering sacrifices, chanting to appease the shedim they claimed lived in those giants' bones. They took what they wanted and left, but the city hasn't slept easy since."

I felt a chill, her words echoing the weight of Hebron's caves, where we'd seen the Anakim's power, their presence a violation of the world Yahweh had made

"You believe they're possessed?" I asked, my voice rough, the thought of shedim stirring a dread older than my years. "That the spirits of the Nephilim live in them?"

Rachav returned to the table, sitting, her hands clasped, her bracelet glinting like a warning. "I believe what I see, the Anakim aren't just tall—they're wrong. Their eyes don't blink like men's; they glow, like something else is looking through them. Their strength isn't human; I saw one lift a stone altar, as big as this room, and set it down like a child's toy. The priests say the shedim give them power, that the old gods, the elohim who fell, still speak through them, demanding worship, blood, dominion."

Othniel leaned forward, his voice intense, his eyes searching hers. "And yet you defy them, Rachav, you hide us, knowing what they are, what they can do. Why? What makes you think our God can stand against such powers?"

Her smile was faint, almost sad, but her voice was flint, "Because your God isn't like theirs, Othniel. The elohim of Kena'an, the old gods, they're petty, hungry, they desire the flesh of children bound to their altars, their blood. Your God—Yahweh, you call Him— He's different. He broke Egypt, parted the sea, led you through the wilderness with fire and cloud. Some of our priests here whisper of Him, say He's the Most High, the one who judged the Watchers, who drowned the Nephilim. If He's coming for this land, I want my children on His side, not the giants'."

There was a pause, then her voice softened, curling like smoke into the silence. "Word reaches us, even through the walls. We hear things. Stories. Of men who walked dry shod through the Sea of Reeds while Pharaoh's army drowned screaming behind them. They say Egypt's king wears the sun on his brow and calls himself the son of Ra. In this city, we speak of him like a god—his name a curse and a prayer in the same breath. But your God broke him. Crushed his chariots in the deep and shamed the might of the two lands."

She looked at me then, not as a harlot, not as a traitor, but as a mother who had chosen a path for her children, for her family, for life and not death,

"I have seen blood poured on altars while the Rephaim chant in tongues not meant for this world. I have heard children scream beneath the high places. And I've wondered if the heavens sleep. But then you came—men of dust and breath—bearing the Name. You've seen the giants and lived. That means something. Your God is no idol cast in wood or clay, or bronze. He fights."

Othniel nodded, a flicker of respect in his eyes, but his voice was firm, seeking clarity. "You say the shedim are in them, Rachav. How do they endure? What keeps them bound to this world?"

She exhaled, her fingers tracing the scarlet corded bracelet again, as if drawing strength from its red fibers, "The altars," she said, her voice low, heavy with truth. "In Hebron, in the hills, there are places older than Jericho, stones carved with runes, soaked in blood for centuries. The priests say the shedim are tied to them, that the giants guard them, feed them with sacrifices—children, mostly, or warriors who defy the old gods. The Anakim are their vessels, their hands in this world, but the altars are their roots. Where the terebinth trees are tall. Destroy them, and the shedim weaken, the giants fall. In Ugarit are the secret writings, that tell of the enchantments men must do to summon the power of the shedim"

I felt a spark, a clarity that cut through the dread. "You know where these altars are?" I asked, my voice sharp.

Rachav's face was sly, filled with solemnity beyond her years, "I know enough, Kalev. There's one in Hebron, near the caves, by the groves of terebinth trees, guarded by the sons of Anak. Others are scattered, hidden, always groves of trees, but the priests talk when they drink and lay in my bed....and I listen. If you want the giants, you'll need to burn those altars, break their hold. Sacrifice to your God in those places. Sanctify the terebinth trees and rid the land of the spirits. But it won't be easy—the shedim know you're coming, and they're not just spirits. They're angry and ferocious."

I stood, my shadow long in the lamplight, my voice resolute, "Then we'll face them. Our God is greater than the shedim, greater than the Watchers who fell. But we need you to stand with us, to trust us when we return."

She rose, meeting his gaze, her posture unyielding, a mother's strength in every line. "I trust what I see, Kalev son of Jephunneh. You and Othniel, you're not just men—you're marked, chosen. I'll stand with you, for my children, for a world where they don't hide from giants. But don't underestimate the Anakim. They're not just flesh—they're a memory of a world that burned, and they want it back."

The lamp flickered, its flame nearly spent, and the room seemed to close in, the weight of her words a leather strap linking us to Hebron, to the war that waited. We stood, the conversation a pact, Rachav's eyes a beacon in the dark, her children's future a fire that burned brighter than fear.

Rachav arose and turned slowly, the lamplight brushing her skin in gold. As she moved along side the windowsill, her robe slipped from her shoulders and fell to the ground, baring her form in full—unveiled, unashamed, a silhouette carved against the night. Her smile was slow, inviting, honed in the hidden places of Jericho. The light caught upon the darker flushes of her skin, soft peaks rising in the cool air, exposed and unashamed—like the bud of a flower opening beneath a moonlit sky,

"Come, it is late now. My children sleep with my mother" she said.

Her voice lowered to a hush, rich as dusk. She stepped nearer, her body un-shrouded, not raw but resolute—a woman who knew the weight of being seen. The scent of jasmine and wind-blown myrrh clung to her like memory,

"Both of you, come to my bed. I know ways to ease a man's burdens. No coin, no vows—only a moment's peace before the storm. Let this be our covenant, sealed in flesh. That our oaths to each other be final."

Othniel's gaze flicked to me, his eyes wide with a flicker of shock, his hand tightening on the hilt of his dagger beneath his cloak as if to anchor himself against her words.

I did not flinch, though I felt the weight of the moment settle on me like scale armor. My hand moved instinctively to my chest, fingers brushing the edge of the amulet, then pausing over another small pendant hidden beneath my cloak, I spoke, my voice was quiet, but it rang like bronze striking stone,

"We do not seal covenants in the way of this city, Rachav," I said, meeting her gaze without wavering, "But you have shown us mercy, and mercy must be returned. There is a vow more enduring than flesh, and I make it now before the face of Yahweh."

Othniel stood beside me, silent as a blade in its sheath, his presence sure as the ground beneath my feet. I nodded, steadying myself despite the heat of her presence.

"Your heart is fierce, Rachav, and we are grateful," I said, the words shaped by the weight of an Ivrim's vow. "But we are bound to Yahweh's law. We seek no comfort, only your help in fulfilling His promise."

I reached beneath my robe and drew out the token Mosheh had given me in the shadow of Nebo, still strung to the leather cord he'd fastened with his own hands. Though not old, it already bore the sheen of sweat, dust, and prayer. The bronze amulet, etched with ancient letters, caught the lamplight like the edge of a blade—its words a shield, its memory a fire I dared not forget.

"This was given to me by Mosheh—our prophet, our shepherd in the fire and wind," I said, unclasping it from my neck, "The Name is upon it. The Shema is written inside. It has hung over my heart in battle, in hunger, in the long silence of waiting. It has been blessed. It's protected me in battle and against the dark arts of the enemy. It will mark this house—not with the rites of this city, but with the covenant of the One who brought us out."

I pressed the amulet into her palm, my fingers closing gently over hers, then lifted my other hand to her forehead. My touch was steady and solemn, not the gesture of a soldier but of one who carried a vow.

"By the Name upon this token, and by the God of our fathers —Avraham, Yitzhak, and Ya'akov—I seal this vow between us," I said.

The weight of my hand was a quiet benediction, binding not only promise but protection. Rachav bowed her head slightly, receiving it without flinching, like one who understood the cost such words carried.

"Keep this momentarily," I told her. "Not as payment, but as a sign. As long as you bear it, I will not forget you. And the God of Israel, who sees in secret, will see you. And when this oath is fulfilled to you and your family, return the amulet to me, that you might know my word is true."

Rachav's fingers tightened around the amulet, her breath still for a moment, as if catching the echo of a distant call. She looked up, the lamplight catching her eyes—dark, unblinking, now softened with a glimmer of awe. The offer she had made, her body bared in full beneath the flickering glow, now felt like a soul laid open, touched by a purpose beyond Jericho's walls. A quiet shame stirred—not a wound, but the dawning weight of dignity, drawing her toward a people not her own. Suddenly aware of her nakedness, as if seen anew by eyes beyond the room, she bent with graceful reverence and lifted her robe from the earth. Draping it over her shoulders, she shielded not just her form but a heart turning from the gods of stone, stepping into the shadow of a greater covenant.

"Your God must be true," she said, her voice low, tinged with a daughter of the house of Ba'al's newfound reverence, "Men of Jericho would not turn from such an offer, but you hold fast to His ways. It strengthens my heart to believe in your God, who forges such loyalty." Her gaze held ours, a mother's hope mingling with a strategist's mind, her faith in our God emboldened by our stand.

I nodded once, "Perhaps you are already one of us. One day soon you will eat of the pascha meal and join our clan."

Rachav's breath caught, and for a moment her eyes shimmered—not with fear, but with the weight of belonging long delayed. She turned from us then, as though looking into some invisible past, into the hills of childhood, into the rhythm of woven chants sung by mothers and sisters on rooftops during spring harvest. Her fingers brushed the edge of the table, almost absently, and when she spoke again, it was not in the voice of a harlot, nor of a broker of secrets, but as a daughter of a land learning to hope.

She sang—not loudly, not for us, but for the air, for the stones of Jericho, for her unborn future:

"Rain and barley, figs in the basket,
Give them to the brave, to the blood-marked men.
My roof is yours, my gate is yours,
For the wind has told me:
Your God is the storm that answers.
Where you pass, the earth trembles,
Let me not be like the stalks trampled underfoot—
Take me up like firstfruits, O sons of the fire-cloud."

A silence bloomed between us, not of shame or fear, but of something deeper. Trust, quietly born. A covenant sealed, not in flesh, but in faith.

Outside, the wind whispered of walls and war. But within that room, the God of Israel had begun to write a new story—in the heart of a harlot, and through the hand of a spy.

The lamp flickered, its flame guttering, casting jagged shadows across the walls, the air growing heavier with the scent of flax and herbs, now tinged with the faint tang of smoke drifting from the city beyond. Before I could respond, a sound pierced the silence— a low, rhythmic thud, like sandals on stone, growing louder, closer, echoing through the passage outside. Rachav's head snapped toward the door, her body tensing, her hand darting to a knife hidden beneath her robe, its blade glinting in the dim light. Her face hardened, the mask of the seductress gone, replaced by a mother's instinct to protect.

"Guards," she whispered, her voice a hiss, her eyes darting to the alcove where Aram, Lirah, and her mother slept soundly on woven mats, their forms barely visible in the shadows. "Stay silent, or we're all dead."

Othniel and I froze, our hands on our weapons, our breaths shallow, the room's walls seeming to close in like the caves of Hebron. The thudding grew louder, joined by voices—gruff, slurred with wine, but sharp with intent. "Check the wall-houses!" one barked, his words muffled but urgent, the wooden beam of the door rattling as a fist pounded against it. The air thickened, the city's hunger pressing through the stones, and I felt the weight of our mission teeter, the guards' pursuit a thread unraveling our disguise.

Rachav moved with the speed of a desert cat, she grabbed a knife from the table it vanishing into her sleeve, her face transforming —calm, almost bored, a mask of innocence that chilled me with its precision. She gestured toward the roof, her eyes blazing with urgency,

"Up, now," she mouthed, pointing to a narrow ladder behind the loom, its rungs worn but sturdy, "hide under the flax."

We obeyed, slipping silently across the packed earth floor, climbing into the darkness where bundles of flax awaited, their earthy scent a shield as we burrowed beneath them, the fibers scratching our skin, the shadows swallowing us whole.

A soft whimper broke the silence below, and I froze, my heart lurching. In the alcove, the sleeping figures stirred—Aram and Lirah, Rachav's children, and their grandmother, awakened by the guards' pounding,

"Mama?" Lirah's small voice trembled, barely audible, and Rachav's head snapped toward them, her mask faltering for a moment, a mother's fear flickering in her eyes. She crossed to the alcove in two swift steps, kneeling beside the mats, her voice low and soothing, a stark contrast to the tension in the air.

"Hush, my star," she whispered, brushing Lirah's hair from her face, her hand steady despite the thudding at the door. "It's just noisy men, nothing more. Stay quiet, and sleep will come again."

Aram, his eyes wide, clutched his blanket, his voice a whisper. "Are they giants, Mama?"

"No, sweet one," Rachav said, her tone firm but gentle, a mother's strength shielding them. "Just guards, and I'll send them away. Stay with Nana, and be still." She glanced at her mother, an older woman with gray-streaked hair, who nodded, her arms encircling the children, her face lined with quiet concern.

"Keep them silent, Mother," Rachav murmured, her voice urgent but soft. "No matter what you hear."

Her mother's eyes met hers, a shared understanding passing between them. "Go, child," she whispered. "Do what you must."

Rachav stood, her mask returning, and moved to the door, her steps unhurried, her voice rising, smooth as oil, to answer the guards' clamor. "Who's there? It's late, and you've woken my children. What do you want?"

The pounding came again, harder, the door groaning under the force. "Open the door, Rabaha!" a guard growled, his voice close, his shadow looming through the crack beneath the door. "We heard of men on these streets—strangers, cloaked. Ivrims, maybe. Open, or we'll break it down!"

From the roof, hidden beneath the flax, my heart pounded, my grip tightening on my sword. Beside me, I felt Othniel's tension—a subtle shift in his breath, fingers twitching near his blade. I laid a steadying hand on his shoulder, meeting his eyes with mine, "God be with us", I whispered. He nodded in agreement.

Below, Rachav didn't flinch. Her smile was faint, almost amused, as she leaned against the door, her voice dropping to a purr, laced with a prostitute's charm.

"Ivrims? In my house? You've been at the wine again, Terah. I know your voice, and I know you well, many a day you've enjoyed my embrace. I'd know if strangers were here—I don't let just anyone past my door." She paused, her tone teasing, dangerous. "Unless you're here to pay for my time, but not tonight—my bed's cold, and my children need me."

Laughter broke out among the guards, rough and easy, realizing their leader was a frequent client of this daughter of Ba'al, but the voice of Terah cut through, colder now. "Enough games, woman. We're coming in. Step aside, or your brats will answer for it."

Rachav's fingers twitched, her body coiled like a spring, but her voice remained firm, commanding. "Wait," she said, her tone sharp, a mother protecting her own. "You want to search? Fine. But you'll find nothing, and you'll owe me for disturbing my family. Let me unbar the door—unless you'd rather break it and face the king's wrath for harassing a woman who pays her taxes."

A murmur passed among the guards, their shadows shifting, and I held my breath, the flax's fibers stifling, the tension thick as smoke. Rachav glanced toward the alcove, ensuring her children were still, then moved to the door, her hands steady as she lifted the beam. The door creaked open, and the guards' sandals thudded on the floor, their voices loud, their spears clinking against armor,

"Where are they, Rabaha?" Terah demanded, his tone sharp. "We tracked them here—two men, cloaked, seen near the gate."

Rachav stood her ground, her voice calm but edged with mockery. "You tracked shadows, Terah, oh great captain of the king's guard. I've been here all night, weaving, tending my children and mother. Look around—do you see cloaks? Weapons? Men?" She gestured to the room, her arm sweeping toward the alcove where Aram, Lirah, and her mother sat huddled, their eyes wide but silent, the grandmother's arms tight around them. "Or are you here to scare my boy and girl, who've done nothing but sleep?"

Terah's eyes narrowed, his gaze raking the room, lingering on the children and the old woman, then moving to the loom, the table, the shadows. "Check everything," he ordered, and the guards fanned out, their sandals scuffing the earth floor, clay pots clinking as they shifted them, linen curtains rustling as they prodded. One guard, younger, his face flushed with wine, stepped closer to Rachav, his spear lowered, his eyes gleaming with a different hunger. "Maybe you're hiding more than men, Rabaha," he said, his voice low, suggestive. "What's a night with you worth, eh?"

Rachav's smile was a blade, her charm a weapon honed in Jericho's streets. She stepped closer, her robe clinging to her form, her voice dropping to a sultry whisper that carried a practiced tone beneath it. "Oh, Jair," she said, her voice teasing, recognizing him also as a past customer. "You know my price, but not tonight—my children are awake, and my bed's for sleeping, not for you," she leaned in, her eyes locking with his, her words soft but firm, "Come tomorrow, when the sun's high and my family's fed. I'll make it worth your coin, but now? Leave us be, or the king hears of your heavy hand."

Jair hesitated, his grin faltering, caught by her charm. He nodded, stepping back, muttering, "Tomorrow...," his voice trailing thick with thwarted desire, his resolve for the search dissipating. Rachav's laugh was soft, triumphant, as she guided him toward the door, her presence a shield for her family and us.

Another guard who had climbed the ladder to the roof, was an arms length from where we lay hiding, his spear scraping the wood, his shadow falling across the loom below, "What's up here?" he growled, his breath reeking of wine, his sandals creaking the rungs. I pressed deeper into the flax, Othniel beside me, his breath steady but his hand on his dagger, the fibers scratching our skin, the darkness our only ally.

"Flax," Rachav said, her voice sharp, following him up, her steps light but commanding. "For weaving, for trade. You think I hide men in my work? Go ahead, stab it, ruin my livelihood. The king will love hearing how you damaged what is his."

The guard paused, his shadow looming, and I held my breath, the memory of Hebron's giants flashing in my mind, their eyes like embers in the dark. He cursed, prodded the flax with his spear, the point grazing inches from my side, then descended, the ladder creaking under his weight. "Nothing here," he muttered, and Rachav's voice followed, smooth as oil,

"Told you. Now get out, before you wake my children further. They've had enough nightmares without your spears."

The guards muttered, their sandals retreating, the door slamming shut with a thud. Silence fell, heavy and tense, broken only by Lirah's soft whimper from the alcove, quickly hushed by her grandmother. We waited, the flax's weight pressing against us, the night's cold seeping into our bones. When the moon was high, Rachav's shadow appeared, her face calm but her eyes alert as she pulled back the stalks. "You're safe," she said, "you must leave the city now, climb down the wall, and don't look back." she said.

But we didn't move, not yet. I stood, my face lit by the moonlight, my expression earnest as I clasped her hand, my grip firm but gentle,

"We will remember you, Rachav," I said, my voice steady, a vow. "When we come for Jericho, you and your family will be spared. But you must be ready. The thunder of our God will bring down the walls of this city"

Her eyes narrowed, her hand trembling in mine, her voice edged with caution,

"Ready how? Your army will march, your God will strike. What can I do against falling walls and giants?"

I released her hand gently, my gaze unwavering, my words carrying the weight of an Ivrim bound to Yahweh's covenant,

"When you hear the trumpets, when the walls tremble under the breath of our God, tie this red cord in your window," I said, drawing the scarlet cord from her wrist with care, its fibers vivid as blood against my calloused palm. I held it forth, the cord catching the lamplight, a beacon in the dim room, "Keep your family within—your children, your mother, all you claim as kin. No one in this house, marked by this cord, will be harmed. Our men will know it, and Yahweh, Lord of Hosts, He will see it and He will honor it."

I paused, eyes lifting to the heavens. This was the first time in my life—though it would not be the last—that my mouth spoke, but it was not I who spoke. A power beyond my own filled me, a breath from the Presence that moves over the waters, stirring my heart and shaping my words. My voice softened yet rang with a strength not mine alone, resonant as if called forth by the Almighty Himself. Holding the cord aloft, I raised my other hand, fingers tracing the air in a gesture of consecration, echoing the ancient rites of the wilderness where Mosheh had blessed the people.

"O Yahweh, God of Avraham, Yitzhak, and Ya'akov, who parted the sea and broke the chains of Egypt, hear my plea," I prayed, my words woven with the language of our fathers, rich with the imagery of covenant and redemption, "Let this scarlet cord be a sign, as the blood of the lamb upon the doorposts in Egypt, a seal of Your mercy upon this house. May it stand as a banner of Your promise, a thread of salvation woven by Your hand, guarding Rachav, daughter of Hanan, and her kin from the sword of Your judgment. As You spared Your people in the Passover, so spare those beneath this cord, for they have turned to You in faith."

The room seemed to still, the lamp's flame steadying, as if the air itself bore witness to the prayer. My voice grew stronger, my eyes fixed on the cord, its scarlet strands a symbol of life amidst Jericho's doom, "By Your name, Yahweh, let this cord be hallowed, a mark of Your covenant extended to this woman who has sheltered Your servants. Let it shine as a flame in the darkness, guiding our warriors to spare this house, a beacon of Your grace amidst the fall of idols."

I lowered the cord, placing it gently in Rachav's hands, my fingers brushing hers, my gaze unwavering, "Bind it in your window when the hour comes, and trust in the God who sees you."

Rachav's breath caught, her eyes wide, the cord trembling slightly in her grasp, as if the weight of the prayer had imbued it with a sacred power. She nodded, her expression a mix of awe and grace, a mother grasping the promise of a God she had only heard in whispers,

"And when the walls fall?" she asked, her voice soft, a mother's fear and concern, "If the giants come, if the city burns?"

"They will fall," I said, my voice unwavering, my eyes burning with the fire of one who has seen Yahweh's hand, "The giants, the kings, the walls—they're nothing before our God. But you must trust us, Rachav. Stay in this house, keep the cord in the window, and no sword will touch you."

She nodded, her jaw tight, her eyes searching his, then mine, "I trust you," she said, her voice low, a pact sealed, "But trust is a rare coin in this city of defilement, I pray you haven't spent it lightly."

Rachav stood at the window, the scarlet cord now in her hands, its vibrant fibers glowing faintly against her palm, a fragile thread of hope woven into the shadows of Jericho's doom. "When you return to shatter this city," she said, her voice steady, resolute, a mother's plea laced with a survivor's hope, "remember me, and those I hold dear." Her eyes held ours, fierce yet vulnerable, a woman who had staked her life and her children's on a God she had only glimpsed through our words.

She moved to a corner of the room, retrieving a coiled rope, its fibers rough but strong, and secured it to a beam near the window, letting it fall into the darkness beyond the city's wall. The night was thick, the moon a sliver casting pale light on the stones below, Jericho's walls looming like silent sentinels. Othniel and I approached the window, our cloaks heavy with the dust of the city, our hearts heavier with the weight of her trust. I gripped the rope, its coarse texture biting into my palms, and glanced back at Rachav, her silhouette framed against the lamplight, a beacon in the gloom. Her face—those obsidian eyes, that voice like honey and bronze, the memory of her children seared itself into my mind, a vow I would carry beyond these walls.

Othniel went first, his movements sure, his form descending into the shadows, the rope taut under his weight. I followed, my hands burning as I slid down, the city's walls towering above, their stones cold and unyielding, etched with the faint runes of forgotten gods. The descent was slow, each shift of the rope a reminder of the peril we left behind and the promise we carried forward. Rachav's words echoed in my heart—"remember me"—a charge as binding as the covenant we served. The land was watching, its ancient pulse thrumming through the hills, and so was she, a Kena'anim who had wagered everything on Yahweh, a God she had never seen but chose to believe.

We reached the ground, the rope swaying above, and melted into the darkness, the city's glow fading behind us. Neither of us spoke, the silence a cloak as we moved through the hills, the memory of Rachav's face a light that did not dim. Her eyes, her voice, the quiet strength of a mother who defied her city's gods—these lingered, a testament to a faith that mirrored our own.

After three nights hidden in the hills, Othniel and I returned to the camp of Israel, our sandals heavy with the dust of Jericho's paths. The wilderness stretched before us, a sea of tents shimmering in the morning haze, the banners of the tribes rippling like promises in the breeze. Our spirits burned with the weight of what we had seen— walls rising like fortresses of pride, unyielding as the giants who guarded them, yet pierced by a single scarlet cord, a fragile thread woven into destiny's loom. In the shadow of those walls, within the dim glow of a harlot's house, a covenant had been forged, not in the ways of Kena'anim, but in the mercy of a woman who dared to spit at the gods of the city and bind her fate to ours.

The memory of Rachav lingers, not as a vapor that fades, but as a flame kindled in the heart of Yehudah. Her eyes, once sharp with the art of desire, had softened under the lamplight, her voice a hush that carried defiance and hope. Her robe had fallen, baring her soul as much as her flesh, only to rise again in reverence, as if she glimpsed the shadow of Yahweh's hand. When the trumpets sounded and Jericho's walls crumbled under the breath of our God, His promise held fast. Rachav and her kin—her mother, her children, all she claimed—emerged from the ruin, marked by the cord's blood-red sign, a beacon spared amidst the storm.

She came to us, to the clan of Yehudah, not as a stranger but as one reborn. With quiet grace, she pressed the amulet into my hand, returning the same small token I had seen her clutch in that lamplit room, its weight now a seal of trust unbroken. Her fingers, once trembling with the fear of giants, now bore the scarlet cord about her wrist, a vow she wore until her final breath. And as I stand here, gazing across the wilderness toward the banks of Nehar ha-Yarden, I see her still—not the harlot of Jericho, but Rachav, woven into the clan of Yehudah, her courage a thread that binds us to the eternal promise of Yahweh, Lord of Hosts.

Now the people looked to Joshua not as a young spy, but as their chieftain—the Spear of Israel, Yahweh's chosen successor, the man whom Mosheh laid hands upon before he climbed Nebo's heights and vanished into the mystery of God. They looked to me, not as the man who was black as night, but the lion of Yehudah, the great elder who stood alongside the Spear of Israel and leads the people into the promises of God. No longer were we underlings but we were the sons of promise. The seed of giants in Jericho was destroyed, crushed under the weight of its walls; but a prostitute who had professed faith truer than princes, now partook of the promises of Avraham.

Chapter Four
Veil of Smoke And Shadow

Jericho was a distant memory, the dust of its fall long settled in the corners of my mind. The dream had passed; the present pressed in like smoke. The battle against the city of Ai was Joshua's second great victory.

The Ivrim camp sprawled across the plains beyond Ai's smoldering ruins, a patchwork of tents stitched together by firelight under a sky heavy with storm clouds. I walked through its heart, my sandals sinking into mud churned by a thousand feet, the air thick with the tang of blood and the acrid bite of smoke. The sounds of our people surrounded me—mothers keening for sons lost in battle, warriors sharpening blades with rhythmic scrapes, priests chanting low as they burned relics salvaged from Ai's cursed altars, their flames casting shadows that danced like specters. Exhaustion hung over the camp, a weight heavier than the ash that drifted from the city, and every face I passed bore the marks of war—eyes hollow, cheeks streaked with dirt, lips pressed tight against the memories of giants and unholy fires.

My rib throbbed, a dull ache from the cudgel's blow in Ai, but I kept my stride steady, nodding to the men who met my gaze. They were of Yehudah, Asher, Dan—tribes bound by blood and covenant, yet strained by what we'd seen. A young warrior, his arm bandaged, offered me a skin of water, and I took it, drinking deeply, the coolness a fleeting relief against the heat of memory. He said nothing, but his eyes lingered, as if seeking assurance I could not give. I handed the skin back and moved on, the weight of their unspoken questions a burden I carried alongside my sword.

The camp was alive, yet it felt like a breath held, a pause before the next plunge into the unknown. Tents sagged under the damp, their canvas patched and faded, while children darted between them, their laughter sharp and fleeting, swallowed by the low hum of mourning. A group of women knelt by a fire, weaving bandages from torn cloth, their hands steady but their faces etched with grief. Nearby, a priest swung a censer, its smoke curling upward, heavy with myrrh and the faint, sour tang of unclean things burning— amulets, idols, fragments of bone etched with runes. The air shimmered where the smoke rose, as if the spirits bound to those relics fought to linger, and I quickened my pace, my hand brushing the hilt of my sword.

I found Joshua near the camp's center, standing outside his tent, its crimson and blue standard drooping in the still air. He was speaking to a knot of elders, their beards gray, their staffs planted in the mud, their voices low but urgent. His cloak was stained with ash, the hem frayed, yet he stood tall, his gestures sharp, shaping the future with every word. His presence was a fire, steady and unyielding, and the elders leaned toward him, drawn like moths to a flame. When he saw me, his face softened, the lines around his eyes easing, and he raised a hand, dismissing the others with a nod. They shuffled away, casting glances my way, their murmurs fading into the camp's din.

"Kalev," Joshua said, his voice warm, roughened by days of command. He stepped forward, and we embraced—a brief but deep bond of decades, sealed with a brotherly kiss no battle could sever. His grip was firm, his scent a mix of sweat, smoke, and the leather of his armor, and for a moment, we were not warriors, not conquerors— just two men who had seen Hebron and lived.

"You look like the caves haunt you still," he said, pulling back, his eyes searching mine.

I managed a grim smile, my rib protesting as I straightened. "They may never leave me, Joshua. Nor the promise, thank God."

He laughed then—not loud, but with the breath of wonder, like a man tasting hope again,

"But hear this, my brother—we lost no one today! Not a single soul. Not like before." His voice softened, reverent. "Not one of the sons of Israel fell. Thirty-six bled into the dust when we first climbed Ai's slopes. But against Ai? Not a drop. The hand of Yahweh was with us."

I lifted my eyes to the darkened sky, a silent prayer swelling within me,

"Truly, Yahweh is our shield and strength, the keeper of life in the face of death. His mercy walks before us like a blazing light—undaunted, unbroken" I said.

We sat on a bench of rough-hewn cedar, its surface scarred by years of campaign, the firelight casting shadows that flickered across his face. He was older now, his hair streaked with gray, his hands calloused from sword and staff, but his eyes burned with the fire of a man chosen by Yahweh. We spoke of Ai, of the giants' fall, of the altar's shattering, but my words turned to the unease that gnawed at my soul, a shadow deeper than the battle's toll

"We are fighting more than men my lord" I said, my voice low, the camp's noise a distant hum, "Not just men, not just giants. The tablet, the mask—something knows us, something older than this land."

He leaned forward, his elbows on his knees, his gaze piercing the fire's heart. "Mosheh warned us," he said, his voice steady, each word deliberate, "The land is defiled, Kalev, given to the shedim, to powers that should have drowned in the flood. They cling to it, to the altars, to the blood of the innocent. These are eaters of the dead. But Yahweh is greater. He told Mosheh , 'I will drive them out before you.' Do you trust that?"

I nodded, though doubt coiled in my chest, cold as the mask's touch. The tablet's glyphs, the creature's laughter, the pit of slain warriors in the hills—they were not mere foes, but signs of a war beyond flesh, a clash of heavens and hells. Joshua's faith was a rock, but mine was stone worn by years of seeing what should not be. I thought of Hebron, of the giants' eyes, of the shedim, of Rachav's warning in Jericho, her voice like honey and tempered bronze, promising truths we were not ready to hear.

He clapped my shoulder, his grip a lifeline, "Rest, my friend," he said, his tone softening. "The hills wait for us, and they will test us. But we are not alone."

I met his gaze, seeing the boy who had stood with me before the camp all those years ago, defying the ten spies' fear, proclaiming the land ours. That fire was still there, tempered by time but unquenched, and it steadied me, if only for a moment

"You quote Mosheh like he stands here," I said, a faint smile tugging at my lips.

Joshua's eyes gleamed, "He does, in every word Yahweh spoke. And so do you, Kalev, in every step you take toward the promise."

We sat in silence, the fire crackling, its sparks rising like prayers into the darkening sky. The camp pulsed around us, a living thing, wounded but defiant. A woman's voice rose in a lament, high and piercing, joined by others, their song weaving through the tents, a thread of sorrow and strength. Nearby, a group of warriors laughed, their voices rough, sharing a tale of battle, but even their mirth carried an edge, as if they laughed to keep the dark at bay. The priests' chants grew louder, the smoke from

Their fires thickened, glowing like stubborn embers struggling against the gathering night. I saw a young warrior lurking in the shadows—Othniel, son of Kenaz. His face was sharp with hunger, his eyes hungry for the path ahead. I marked him quietly, sensing a destiny in his silence, but I said nothing.

Joshua stood, his cloak heavy around him as the camp's chatter dimmed under the weight of his presence. I rose alongside him,

"In two days, we march," Joshua said, his voice steady and sure. "We will assemble at Mount Ebal. Return to me in the morning and we will discuss the march, tonight is time for men, women and children to rejoice."

His eyes caught the firelight, a fleeting spark of warmth kindling within them as he spoke of women, a reminder that life was not forged solely in battle's forge but in the softer embers of love, of children, of legacies woven through the tribes of Ivrim. His countenance softened, no longer the unyielding commander but a man glimpsing the promise of a land where hearts, not just swords, would endure.

I nodded, but the name struck deep—Mount Ebal. The memory of Hebron weighed on me like a stone—its dark caves, the shadows where giants had marked me, and the fears I had faced and overcome. Only now did my heart turn fully homeward. I had kept her from my thoughts throughout the battle, afraid that even a glimpse of longing would make me falter. My wife and children whom I loved more than life itself only now began to flood my entire being, now that the battle against Ai was complete.

"Not yet," I whispered, barely audible, more to myself than to Joshua, though my mind was already walking the torchlit quiet of our tent, to Azubah waiting there for me. Joshua's hand found my arm, a brother's grip, firm and steady—a final bond before he turned back toward his own tent, his silhouette steady in the flickering firelight.

I lingered, letting the camp's restless life wash over me. The air had grown colder, the storm clouds gathering with an unnatural green tint along their edges, flickering faintly in the firelight. The priests' sacred flame flared higher, consuming a shard of bone that hissed as it burned. A shiver ran through me—not from the chill, but from knowing. This land was Yahweh's, yes—but it was also a battlefield. Its soil soaked with the blood of gods and men. Its shadows alive with powers older than memory, powers that whispered my name in the dark.

I turned from the fire, the weight of my sword heavy at my side, and walked slowly into the night. The call of the hills was a summons I could not deny.

Night cloaked the tents of Israel, spread wide across the plains beyond Ai's smoldering ruins. The stars had vanished behind thick storm clouds heavy with rain's promise. We had returned from the battle, Joshua's army still exulting in the hard-won triumph over Ai's giants and cursed altars—our swords stained with the blood of victory.

The camp thrummed with the noise of families reunited: children's laughter, women's songs, the low murmur of priests purifying the spoils. Yet in the midst of it all, my thoughts were not with the celebration, but with her—Azubah, my wife. Her presence was a beacon in the clamor, a balm for my aching ribs, still sore from the cudgel's blow. Her touch, her relief, her quiet beauty were stronger medicine than any salve.

The firelight flickered across the warriors' faces. Young men, some barely bearded, their cheeks streaked with ash and sweat; older men, their scars like maps of wars fought and survived. I leaned back against a weathered stump, the memory of Ai's giants pressing down heavier than the sword at my side.

The men spoke quietly, their voices thick with fear and bravado, weaving tales to make sense of the horrors we'd faced. The giants, the altar crowned with smoking horns, the terrible creature that moved like a shadow—they were no mere enemies.

They were riddles, puzzles whose answers lay buried in the fireside stories of the camp.

"They're cursed men," a young warrior whispered, clutching his spear as if it could hold back the dark. "Struck down by Yahweh for sins we dare not name, twisted into monsters for their defiance."

His name was Gilead, from Dan. His eyes shone like twin embers, wide with awe and dread.

"They eat men," a boy whispered, no older than sixteen, his voice barely audible. "In Ai, in the first battle, I saw one tear a man's arm clean off, like a wolf with a lamb." His hands shook, spilling wine into the dirt, and the others leaned closer, their breaths held, as if his fear were contagious.

"That's nothing," another countered, his voice loud, forced, trying to drown the boy's terror. "I heard they drink blood, like the priests of Ba'al, and their bones are stone, unbreakable. The flesh of children is what they want most of all." He was of Naphtali, his beard sparse, his bravado thin, and his words drew more laughter, but it was brittle, breaking under the night's weight.

I stirred, the stump digging into my back, and the men's eyes turned to me, expectant—as if I alone could name what lurked beyond their fears, as if my scars spoke of knowledge they lacked. The silence stretched, heavy and waiting, a question unspoken but understood: *What are we truly facing?* But before I could speak, Elidad chieftain of the Benjamin clan spoke, his silhouette sharp against the firelight, his face lined like cracked clay, his eyes deep with seeing what others forgot. The chatter died, the men leaning forward, their shadows pooling like ink.

"Listen," Elidad said, his voice low, rough as the desert wind. "You speak of giants, of curses and monsters, but you know little of the truth. The Nephilim's blood still runs deep—in the Anakim, in the Rephaim, in the shadows of this land. They are no mere men, nor beasts, but the sons of the fallen—born when elohim defied Yahweh and sowed their seed among the earth's daughters through possessing the kings of this land."

He paused, his gaze sweeping the circle of soldiers, and the firelight flickered as if drawing breath with his words.

"In the first battle at Ai, thirty-six of our own fell. Not for lack of courage, but because of sin among us—disobedience to Yahweh's command. Achan took what was forbidden, and his betrayal brought death upon the camp. Our loss was a lesson carved in blood: the Lord demands purity if we are to claim His promise."

Elidad's eyes burned bright, reflecting the flames. "But today, not one man died. No blood stained the dust. Why? Because we followed Yahweh's law to the letter, because our hearts were united in obedience. The Angel of the LORD moved among us—shattering giants, toppling altars, and guarding every step."

He lowered his voice to a reverent hush. "We are the people of Israel, bound by Yahweh's covenant, called to purge this land of its cursed seed and claim the inheritance promised to Avraham."

As Elidad's words faded, a low chant rose from the heart of the camp, drawing my gaze toward the Tabernacle, its linen curtains glowing faintly under the clouded sky. The Levite priests had begun the evening prayers, their voices a solemn cadence that wove through the tents like a sacred thread, calling the tribes to worship. I rose, my hands brushing the dust from my cloak, and moved toward the gathering, the campfire's tales yielding to the liturgy of thanksgiving for Ai's victory. The camp stirred, men and women emerging from their tents, their faces lit by torchlight, drawn to the Tabernacle where the presence of Yahweh dwelt. Children trailed behind, their footsteps light, their whispers and soft laughter a gentle undercurrent, weaving through the crowd like streams around stones, their presence a reminder of the life we fought for.

The Levites stood before the altar, their white linen robes shimmering, their heads bowed as they kindled the evening incense, its fragrant smoke rising in curling tendrils, a sweet offering to Yahweh, ascending like the prayers of His people. The scent of myrrh and frankincense mingled with the camp's cooking fires, filling the air with a holy weight, a reminder of the covenant sealed in the wilderness. Their chants, rich and resonant, echoed the psalms of our fathers, praising the God who had delivered us from Egypt and now from Ai's giants,

"Blessed be Yahweh, who gives strength to His people," they sang, their voices rising and falling in a rhythm that stirred my soul, drawing me into the mystery of worship.

The men gathered on one side, silent and still, heads bowed beneath the flickering torchlight, swords sheathed but never far from reach. Across the courtyard, separated by distance and the unspoken customs that governed our people, the women assembled. I could not cross the line tonight—not while prayer held us in its quiet grip—but my eyes sought her among the cluster of veiled figures, and there she was, Azubah's presence was a soft beacon: small, yet somehow radiant in the muted glow, her dark hair wrapped modestly beneath her shawl, olive skin catching the firelight with a warmth that made my chest tighten. She stood close to Iru and Elah, our sons, who fidgeted like all boys their age, caught between reverence and restless youth. Their eyes flickered between the altar and their mother's steady gaze, learning the rhythms of worship under her gentle watch. I could not see her face clearly, only glimpses—an outline here, the curve of a shoulder there—but those moments were enough. Enough to fill the ache in my heart until I could leave this sacred space and take her hand in mine, safe in the knowledge that, for all the battles fought, this was the place where our family's true strength lay.

The high priest, his breastplate glinting with the twelve stones of Israel's tribes, raised his hands, his voice a clarion call. "Give thanks to Yahweh, for He has broken the gates of Ai, cast down the Anakim, and delivered His people!"

The crowd murmured assent, a soft wave of "Y'hi" rippling through the assembly, the children's voices joining faintly, their small forms darting between tents, chasing shadows but pausing to watch the smoke rise. The incense ascended, a visible prayer, curling toward the heavens, its fragrance a plea for mercy, a song of victory, a shield against the shedim that haunted the land.

As the Levites sang, their words spun a mantle of praise and supplication, recounting Yahweh's mighty acts—the sea parted, the manna given, the giants felled.

The camp was a living altar, each heart turned to the God who had led us, each breath a vow to claim the land. I stood, my rib aching, my dark hands lifted, my voice joining the silent prayer of my people, thanking Yahweh for Ai, for Azubah's embrace, for the promise that burned brighter than the storm clouds above.

As the Levites' chants softened, their incense smoke rising like a whispered prayer, I turned from the Tabernacle, its linen glow fading under the clouded sky. The jackal's howl pierced the distance, a call from the wild beyond our tents, but my heart yearned for home, where Azubah and our sons, Iru and Elah, awaited. The clans of Israel, sprawled across the plains, thrummed with the quiet of families settling after Ai's victory, the air rich with the scent of smoldering cookfires and the faint tang of the day's offerings. I wove through the tents of Yehudah, their goat-hair canopies rustling in the breeze, my rib aching from the battle's cudgel, my soul lifted by the liturgy's promise and the hope of Azubah's embrace.

Chapter Five
The Embrace Beyond the Sword

The path to our tent was worn and familiar, laid out in the same sacred order wherever our Ivrim tribes pitched camp, lit by the soft gleam of clay lamps and the low hush of mothers murmuring lullabies. I had thought to walk back with Azubah who might still be among the women in prayer, her small figure luminous in the torchlight, but she had slipped away early, quiet as the wind passing through pomegranate leaves.

At the entrance of our tent, I paused. My fingers brushed the carved letters upon the Shema — the doorpost marked with the Name — and I pressed a kiss to my finger, a silent *baruch Hashem* rising from within me. The tent flap hung open, warm light spilling through like oil. A small flame danced in a clay bowl on a low table, casting soft shadows across woven mats. The air was fragrant with *mor*, sweet myrrh Azubah must have kindled before I came, the scent curling like a prayer through the stillness — a sanctuary set apart from the ruin of Ai, a place made ready for peace, for nearness, for love..

She stood small—no taller than a young olive sapling, slender and resilient against the desert wind. Her frame was delicate yet unyielding, a breath of beauty whose presence filled the space like a song. Her hair, dark as the midnight over my southern deserts, flowed in gentle waves, catching the firelight like polished ebony, framing a face of quiet strength. Her eyes, deep as the wells of Kadesh, shimmered with a knowing warmth, their almond shape holding both tenderness and resolve—a mother's gaze that had borne our sons, Iru and Elah, into a world of promise and peril. Her skin a warm olive kissed by the sun of Kena'an, glowed with a radiance that rivaled the camp's flames, its smoothness a contrast to my own dark, weathered hands, blackened by the fierce sun of my homeland. Her nose, finely curved, and her lips, full and soft, spoke of a beauty that endured the trials of a warrior's wife, her cheeks flushed with the relief of my return.

When I stepped into our tent, she greeted me with a lightness that lifted the weight from my shoulders. Without hesitation, she sprang into my arms, her embrace fierce and warm—an anchor in the storm. Her breath came in soft prayers of thanks to Yahweh for sparing me from the enemy's wrath. Tears glimmered on her cheeks, but they were not of sorrow—they shone with joy, relief, and love.

"You live," she whispered, her voice a tender song that wrapped around my heart. Her fingers, gentle and sure, traced the scar on my cheek as if to claim it as part of our story—a testament to the battles we had faced together. She clung to me tightly, unwilling to let go. The strength of her embrace spoke of the passion she carried.

Our sons, Iru and Elah, ran to me, each throwing their arms around my legs, their young eyes alight with a hunger to know, to understand the man who was their father—eager to hear the tale of the battle against Ai, as every boy would. But Azubah, with quiet authority, gathered them close and led them to their mats. Her gaze met mine, deep and unwavering, silently urging me to rest—to save the stories, the weight of Ai's horrors, for another time.

"Tomorrow, boys," she said softly but firmly, "tomorrow your father will tell you his tale."

She turned back to me, her smile steady and sure, the warmth of a thousand promises shining in her eyes, "I left prayer early to get them ready—for us," she said, her voice low and rich with intention, "When I saw you praying, my heart longed to run to you." She paused, then asked quietly, "Will you give them the words, Kalev?"

Her question hung in the air, more than a request—an invitation, a bond, a shared future. I nodded, feeling the quiet strength of her love as fiercely as the sword at my side.

Iru stood tall for his size, clutching a woven reed doll under his arm like a warrior's blade at rest. Beside him, Elah wrapped his woolen cover around his shoulders, eyes wide and solemn, the flicker of the fire reflected in his gaze. As a family, we all faced the direction of the Tabernacle, its sacred presence veiled in the distance — that mysterious heart of the camp, where the Ark rested beneath folds of linen and the hovering flame of Yahweh.

Inside the tent, just beyond the flap, an olive oil lamp flickered gently, its glow spreading like soft breath across the canvas walls and catching the edges of a wooden carving I had shaped long ago in the wilderness. One of our servant girls—Mihlat, barely twelve—stepped carefully over the mats and lifted it in her small hands. Reverent, though she hadn't been taught to be, she carried it to the doorpost, where it always rested for the night. The carving, smooth acacia etched with the ancient letters of the Name, bore the mark of Eleazar's blessing. It had watched over many camps. It was our guard through the dark.

Scraps of blue and scarlet thread had been bound around its base, signs drawn from priestly garments, reminders of a covenant we had not inherited by blood but entered by vow—through blood, through wilderness, through fire. The doorframe of the tent itself still held the stain of an older blood, a small piece, now barely visible to anyone but me. It had come from Egypt, long before the Red Sea ever parted. Some now call such a thing a mezuzah. I call it what it was: sacred. It was given to me by my father.

Our second servant girl, Tirata, just thirteen, was already spreading out the woven linen beside the boys' sleeping mats. Her eyes moved often toward Azubah, measuring her pace against the quiet, practiced rhythm of my wife. Both girls had come to us before Jericho, when the walls came down and the smoke had not yet cleared. They had no mothers to return to, and no kin who called for them. Their clan, a small group of Amalekites wandering in the desert were killed by Rephaim even before we arrived. We gave them new names, and a home, and a place near our sons. And we'd chosen to keep them.

Azubah stirred the fire pit gently, the soft hiss of coals folding beneath the crackling bark. The boys' sandals were flung near the flap, still carrying the dust of a day half-spent in swordplay and tree-climbing. Iru and Elah were already flopped across their mats, their tunics damp with sweat, their faces pink from sun and running. They smelled of campfire, earth, and wind—my sons, loud and full of breath, with hearts too large for their frames.

I stepped between them and placed a hand on each of their heads. Under my palms, I felt the living weight of them—warm, tired, safe.

"Shema Yisrael," I said, voice steady. "Adonai Eloheinu, Adonai Echad."

Their lips moved at once. "Baruch shem kevod malchuto le'olam va'ed."

Mihlat, who had just settled near the entrance, whispered the words alongside us. Tirata joined softly, halting in pronunciation but trying. Born of other gods, now learning the words of the One.

"You shall love the LORD your God," I continued, brushing Iru's brow, "with all your heart, and with all your soul, and with all your strength."

They waited for the rest. They always did.

So I spoke the commandments again—the words Mosheh had given us, words to carry in our hearts and bind on our doorways, words for walking, for resting, for rising, for sleeping. And then I gave them words that were mine.

"You are sons of the covenant," I whispered. "The giants still roam the hills, and the false gods still prowl behind trees and stone, but Yahweh is not like them. He does not forget. He does not fall. His arm scatters kings like dry straw, and His hand can cradle your dreams without breaking them."

Iru's eyelids dipped. Elah's breath deepened, his small arm curling across his chest.

I leaned lower, resting my brow against theirs.

"The same God who crushed the walls of Ai," I murmured, "walks beside you now. Even in dreams, He does not leave."

Their breathing slowed, settling into the rhythm I knew so well—one I'd learned in the dark of Sinai, in the hush of battle, in the silence after the trumpet's blast.

Tirata moved again, gently covering them with a woven cloth. She adjusted the folds over Iru's shoulder with the same care Azubah used to show when they were infants. Mihlat placed a small clay token between the mats, its edge marked with the ancient sign of El Shaddai, a whisper of the covenant. She adjusted it with care, as though setting a seal upon their dreams, then watched their faces, reading them like scripture..

Azubah stood behind me. I turned and met her gaze.

"For a moment," I said, "I forgot there was anything left but war."

She crossed the tent and placed her hand over mine, "Then remember," she said.

"There is still peace."

With a motion of her hand, she signaled to Tirata, who gave a short bow and settled beside the boys' mats. Mihlat nestled beside her. Neither of them was sleepy, not yet—but they knew how to keep still, how to be present, and how not to be noticed.

The lamp's glow softened the tent's shadows, and the scent of myrrh hung like incense before the Ark — sweet, earthy, lingering — as though holiness had settled over our home like dew on the morning grass. I drew her close, my arms encircling the one for whom I had fought and returned, and the ache of battle, the cries of the slain, the dust of Ai, all faded in the hush of her breath. She had prepared this space with quiet reverence — guiding Iru and Elah to rest, smoothing their blankets, setting the flame low, steeping the air in a fragrance that called not to memory but to peace. The desert outside may have still echoed with the sounds of marching men and distant grief, but here in this small dwelling, we had built a place of remembrance, not of death, but of love sustained.

We lay beside one another on the woven mats, the flicker of the lamp dancing across the walls like the fire that had once burned atop Sinai. Her head found its place beside mine, our hands entwined, our breaths finding rhythm once more. I traced the braid at the edge of her garment — scarlet thread wound with blue — a sign of devotion and a reminder of covenant, both ancient and our own. Her touch quieted the tremor in me that battle had stirred. In her presence, I did not need to be a warrior, only a man who had returned home. She whispered no words, yet everything in her stillness spoke — of longing fulfilled, of love weathered and unwavering, of sacred nearness restored.

Outside, the wind moved softly through the camp, brushing against the tent flaps like a blessing. Inside, we rested — not just in body, but in soul — as if Yahweh Himself had drawn a curtain between us and the noise of the world. In the hush of that night, beneath the covering of goat's wool and heaven's favor, we remembered who we were: not only those who endured the fight, but those who had been given back to one another by the mercy of the One who sees. Our love, sealed not by words but by presence, lingered in that sacred stillness — a union unshaken by sword or fire, born again in the quiet aftermath of deliverance.

And there, in the soft hush of the tent, she turned to me — not in haste, but in welcome. As husband and wife, we came together not to escape the world's pain, but to answer it with life. No words passed between us, only breath, only nearness, only the deep knowing that flesh was never meant to be far from covenant. We were no longer alone. In love, we remembered Eden. In her arms, I remembered peace. And beneath the shadow of Yahweh's presence, our bodies wove a prayer too ancient for speech.

Chapter Six

The Stillness Before the Ascent

The early sun beamed into our tent, its golden rays slipping through the woven seams, casting a soft glow across the mats. Azubah stirred beside me, the woolen blanket sliding down, revealing the gentle curves of her body, a reminder of her beauty that stirred my heart with thanks to Yahweh. Her eyes fluttered open, dark and deep as the wells of Kadesh, twinkling in the morning light as she smiled,

"Last night was beautiful, my beloved," she said, her voice a melody, her gaze warm with the memory of our closeness. She leaned up, stretching her small frame, her dark hair spilling like a river, then glanced toward the corner where the servant girls and our boys lay, their young forms curled under blankets, their breaths soft in the quiet,

"Are the boys still sleeping?" she asked, less a question for their slumber than a spark to kindle our dawn. She nestled closer, her head resting against my shoulder, her arm draping across my chest, fingers tracing the scars of battles long fought, a tender dance across my weathered skin,

"The morning is still ours, come claim me again in passion's fervent heat" she whispered, her breath warm against my neck, a glint of delight in her hushed tone, beckoning me once more tot he fire of her embrace.

I laughed softly, my heart stirred by her nearness, and drew her close again,

"Your desire burns like a flame unquenched my beloved! As the hart longs for streams of water, so my soul longs for you, my dove," I whispered, my fingers tracing the curve of her hairline. Her warmth beckoned me to stay, and everything in me wanted to. I kissed her gently, my lips brushing the place just above her brow,

"But Joshua has summoned me — an early council, I must not tarry long."

I began to stir from the bed, but her hands slid up my chest, drawing me back with the gentlest insistence, her lips already parting in reply,

"Let the sun delay its rising," she said, her breath warm against my neck, and then in a low whisper, "Let the council wait. This morning, let your strength be for me. This morning you are mine. This hour, you are mine—not the lion, but the man who fills my heart."

I closed my eyes at her words, the longing stirring deep, fierce and aching. I wanted her — not in haste, but in the fullness of love, in the peace she had kindled with myrrh and silence. For a moment, I hesitated, the weight of her hand on mine almost enough to make me forget the burden of command.

"Ahavat chayai," I breathed. "Love of my life. If it were mine to give, I would give you this whole day, the night after, and every day until my last.

Azubah searched my face, her eyes both tender and strong, the way only a woman who has waited through war can be,

"I love you, Kalev," she said, her voice soft but steady — a vow not made in youth, but in fire, "Yesterday, while you fought at Ai, I stood with the women. We sang the Psalms of Deliverance, lit the oil and flax outside our tents, offered up our fear to the One who sees. And when I saw your shadow returning, my knees gave way from the weight of the waiting."

She pressed her hand to my chest, over the place where my heart still raced with the nearness of her, "Is Joshua calling the men to assemble for war?"

I cupped her cheek, brushing her temple with my thumb. "Not to battle," I said, my voice low. "Not yet. He said we will gather at the foot of Mt. Ebal, calling all the clans to gather breath and give thanks.

But his heart is already facing the hills — he sees what others do not. And if Yahweh speaks, I will be ready to listen."

"Then now," Azubah murmured, her eyes softening with a quiet fire and a slight smile forming, "let us hold this moment, for Yahweh has granted us this breath of peace."

Her fingers tightened in mine, a vow woven in touch, and in the hush of the tent's embrace, her lips found mine again, slow and searching, and I kissed her in return—not out of farewell, but of promise. Just as I settled back onto the mat beside her, pulling Azubah's body into mine, Iru and Elah stirred awake, their small voices threading through the tent. I laughed, a hushed and knowing sound, as if the dawn itself were teasing us with its little heralds.

The soft light of morning crept through the tent's flap, and Azubah's eyes flickered toward the shadowed corner where Mihlat was silently yawning herself, and with a single fluid tilt of her head Azubah summoned the attention of the servant girl, her gaze soft but commanding, and the young girl knowingly glided forward to hush the boys with gentle whispers. Turning back to me, Azubah's breath wove with mine, a quiet tide, and in the shelter of the dawn's first glow, and deep beneath the woven cloaks that hid us, we surrendered anew to the silent song of our entwined hearts—undaunted by the nearness of little limbs and sleepy murmurs, for a family's tent held many lives, and love was no exile from its warmth.

The tents of Yehudah stretched in orderly rows, their goat-hair canopies taut against the morning breeze, each a home to families bound by the covenant. Smoke rose from countless fires, women kneeling to grind barley into flour, their pestles rhythmic against stone mortars, their voices weaving songs of Miriam's triumph at the sea. Azubah joined them soon, though a little later than she normally would, the older women looking at her with knowing smiles on their faces. Her small frame moving with purpose, her hair bound in a linen scarf, her hands deft as she kneaded dough for flatbread, her laughter mingling with the other women's as they shared tales of children and battles. Her beauty drew eyes, yet her strength held them—her quick smile, her steady gaze, her voice that could hush a quarrel or soothe a child's cry.

Soon our sons, Iru, eight summers old, and Elah, six, darted through the camp, their bare feet kicking up dust, their shouts joining the chorus of children playing among the tents. Iru, wiry and bold, led a game of chase, his dark eyes—Azubah's eyes—gleaming with mischief, while Elah, stockier, followed, his laughter a bell in the morning air. They wove between women carrying water jars, their clay balanced on shoulders, and men tending goats, their bleats a constant hum. I watched them, my heart swelling, yet tempered by the memory of Ai's giants, knowing the land we claimed was not yet safe for their dreams.

The camp was a hive of purpose, each tribe contributing to the rhythm of survival. Men of Levi, their linen robes marked with the sanctity of their calling, moved among the tents, overseeing the purification of spoils from Ai—bronze blades, woven cloth, untainted grain—sprinkling them with water and salt, their prayers a low chant to cleanse what had touched Ba'al's altars. Elders of Yehudah, their beards gray, gathered near the central fires, their voices rising in council, debating the path to Mount Ebal, where Joshua would lead us to renew the covenant. I, a Kenizzite grafted into their tribe, joined them briefly, my dark complexion a quiet contrast to their sun-browned faces, my words weighed for the battles ahead, my thoughts drifting to Azubah's steady hand in our tent.

Women wove linen on looms staked in the open, their fingers nimble, their chatter a soft counterpoint to the men's debates. Azubah, her scarf slipping to reveal a lock of dark hair, worked beside them, preparing the morning meal, her voice guiding younger female servants with a patience that belied her warrior's heart. She glanced at me, her eyes catching mine, a silent question—Are you whole?—

and I nodded, her presence a tether amidst the camp's clamor. Children ran past, some carrying sticks as mock spears, reenacting Ai's fall, their shouts a blend of joy and awe at their fathers' valor. The scent of baking bread mingled with the tang of roasting goat, the morning meal taking shape as families gathered around low tables of woven reeds.

After listening to a few of the men talking for a moment, I returned to our tent, where Azubah had set out flatbread, dates, and a clay bowl of curdled milk, her hands brushing mine as she passed me a portion.

"Eat, Kalev," she said, her voice soft but firm, her eyes tracing the bruise on my rib. "The giants are dead, but you must live to face the next."

I smiled, her care a warmth that rivaled the sun, my dark fingers breaking the bread, its crust crisp against my calluses.

The camp's rhythm pulsed beyond our tent. Shepherds led flocks to graze on the plains' edge, their staffs tapping the earth, their dogs barking at stray lambs. Blacksmiths hammered bronze, sparks flying, crafting spearheads for the battles to come, their anvils ringing like bells. Young men trained with slings, their stones whistling through the air, their laughter mingling with the grunts of effort, preparing for the wars Yahweh had promised. Women dyed wool in vats of indigo and madder, their hands stained, their songs praising the God who had delivered Ai into our hands.

The Levites' presence was a constant thread, their chants drifting from the Tabernacle, where morning offerings were made— lambs slain, their blood sprinkled, their fat burned as a sweet savor to Yahweh. The smoke rose, a gray plume against the sky, a reminder of the covenant that bound us, its scent mingling with the camp's life. I saw Iru pause, watching the priests who passed by, his young face solemn, always learning the ways of worship, while Elah, clutching his ram, mimicked their gestures, a child's heart drawn to the sacred.

Azubah sat beside me, her small frame pressed close, her beauty a quiet fire that burned through the camp's chaos,

"The men speak of giants," she said, her voice low, her eyes searching mine. "But you saw more, didn't you? In Ai, like when you were in Hebron."

I nodded, the weight of her gaze pulling truth from me,

"The shedim stir, Azubah," I said, my voice rough, the memory of Ai's creature sharp. "But Yahweh is greater. He gave us Ai, and He'll give us the land."

Her hand found mine, her fingers warm, her strength a mirror to my own, a mother and wife who faced the same shadows I did.

Iru and Elah had joined us, their faces flushed, their stories tumbling out, and Azubah's laughter, bright as a desert spring, filled the tent. I sat among my family, my heart anchored by their love, yet my thoughts drifted to the horizon, to Joshua's summon for a morning council. I rose, and kissing Azubah, her deep eyes holding mine with a quiet strength, a silent prayer for my return. The morning air was crisp, the camp stirring under a sky still heavy with clouds, and I stepped from the tent, my sandals soft on the dew-damp earth, drawn to the council that awaited in Joshua's presence.

The tents of Israel sprawled across the plains and I wove through the camp, my rib a dull ache from yesterday's cudgel, my heart stirred by the rhythm of my people, yet quickened by the weight of Joshua's call. The journey to Mount Ebal, a name etched in Mosheh's Torah, loomed in whispers—a sacred place near Shechem, where Avraham had first built an altar to Yahweh, marking the land as promised.

Joshua's tent stood at the camp's heart, its crimson and blue standard fluttering like a banner of hope under Adonai's hand. Larger than most, its goat-hair walls were stretched wide, the entrance framed by two warriors of Ephraim, their spears catching the morning sun, eyes sharp but yielding as I approached. Pausing briefly, I pressed my hand to the Shema on the doorpost of the tent—an unspoken prayer and quiet homage—before stepping forward. The scent of cedar and olive oil drifted from within, a faint echo of the Tabernacle's sanctity. The guards nodded, parting to let me pass into the dim interior, where shadows danced in the glow of a single clay lamp.

The tent was spare, its woven mats strewn with scrolls of hide, the words of Mosheh etched in dark ink, a testament to the law that bound us. Joshua sat cross-legged, his gray-streaked hair bound back, his beard thick, his eyes burning with the fire of a man who had seen Yahweh's wonders. His crimson cloak, frayed from Ai's battle, draped his shoulders, and his hands, scarred from sword and staff, rested on his knees, steady yet heavy with a leader's burden. Beside him sat Eleazar, the high priest, his linen robe pristine, his breastplate glinting with the twelve stones of Israel, his face calm but etched with the gravity of his office. Two elders of Yehudah, their beards white as winter, flanked them, their staffs leaning against the tent's wall, their silence a weight of expectation.

"Shalom, Kalev," Joshua said, his voice low, resonant, tempered by the bond we'd forged in Hebron's caves, a brotherhood sealed by giants and faith. "Sit, my friend. We have much to weigh."

I lowered myself to the mat, my heart quickening, the air thick with their gazes. Eleazar's eyes, sharp as a seer's, seemed to probe my soul, while the elders' nods around us were cautious, acknowledging my valor at Ai but always testing me. The lamp's flame flickered, its myrrh-scented oil weaving a quiet sanctity, and I waited, my hands clasped, sensing a moment that would shape our path.

Joshua leaned forward, his voice steady but laced with the weight of yesterday's battle. "Ai's fall was a mighty work of Yahweh," he said, his eyes meeting mine, a spark of shared memory. "The giants are dust, their altars broken, thanks to your courage, Kalev, and the strength of Yehudah's sons. Yet the land stirs, its shadows unquiet.

What did you see in Ai's heart, my brother? Tell us blessed Elder of Yehudah whom He has bestowed the sight"

I paused, the memory of the creature with horns of smoke flashing in my mind, its laughter a wound still raw,

"More than giants," I said, my voice low, measured. "The shedim were there, Joshua, in the altar's flame, in the madness that turned men to slaughter. We struck them down, but their whisper lingers, a hunger that knows our names."

Eleazar's brow furrowed, his fingers tracing the edge of his breastplate, his voice soft yet piercing. "The shedim are old, Kalev, bound to the land since the flood, when the Nephilim's blood defiled the earth. Ai's victory is a sign, but the covenant must be renewed to purge their hold. We are not merely warriors, but a holy nation, set apart by Adonai's torah."

Joshua nodded, his gaze distant, as if seeing beyond the tent's walls,

"Mosheh, spoke of a place for such renewal," he said, his voice softening, a leader reflecting on a prophet's legacy. "Near Shechem, where Avraham built an altar to Yahweh, where the promise of this land first took root. There, between Mount Ebal and Mount Gerizim—the twin heights that cradle covenant—we will stand to bind ourselves to Adonai's will."

I felt the weight of his words, the name Shechem stirring memories of Torah scrolls read in the wilderness—Ebal, the mount of cursing, Gerizim, the mount of blessing, a sacred act to seal our fidelity,

"Avraham's altar," I said, my voice low, reverent, "marked the land as Yahweh's, a seed we now reap. To stand there is to walk in his faith, to claim what was sworn."

Joshua's eyes met mine, a spark of approval, but his brow creased, a man wrestling with a nation's soul,

144

"More than a walk, Kalev. It is a vow, a *hesed* between Yahweh and His people. The battle at Ai showed His might, but the land's heart is not yet ours. The Anakim linger, the shedim whisper, and the nations watch. We must renew the covenant, write the law upon stones, and chant the blessings and curses as one body."

Eleazar's voice rose, a priest's cadence rich with the Tabernacle's sanctity,

"The renewal is a living encounter, Kalev, not mere rite. It is the torah made flesh, a path to life through obedience. At Ebal, we stand between curse and blessing, sanctified for Adonai's purpose, a light amidst Kena'an's idols. As Avraham offered his heart, so we offer ours, binding Israel to the Most High."

I nodded, the vision stirring my soul—a nation not just of warriors, but of priests, knit to Yahweh's eternal will, a foretaste of the glory chanted in the psalms, where His people might dwell in His presence. Shechem, where Avraham's faith took root, was a sacred call, urging us to purge the shedim's shadow and claim the promise.

"When do we march?" I asked, my voice steady, though my heart quickened at the task.

Joshua's gaze softened, a leader sharing a burden with a friend,

"At dawn, we move," he said, his voice firm. "Two days, perhaps three, through hills that test our strength. The Levites will carry the ark out in front, all the clans, the women and children with us, for all Israel must stand at Ebal. I need you, Kalev, to lead Yehudah's men, to guard our path, to stand with me as I build the altar."

My chest tightened, the honor heavy, yet my faith burned bright,

"I will lead," I said, my words a vow, "as Yahweh strengthens me."

Eleazar's eyes gleamed, his voice a quiet chant,

"*Baruch atah*, Kalev, for you shall stand with Yehudah, a witness to Adonai's covenant. The law will endure, the land will know His name."

The elders murmured assent, their staffs tapping the earth, a sign of unity, though their eyes held questions for the trials ahead. Joshua stood, his hand on my shoulder, his grip a bond of brotherhood,

"Go, rest," he said, his voice softer now, "Tell Azubah, for she will bear this journey's hope with you."

I rose, the lamp's glow fading, the tent's shadows deepening, my heart alight with purpose. To stand at Ebal, where Avraham's altar rose, to renew the covenant that bound us—this was a calling greater than Ai's fall. I stepped into the dawn, the camp stirring, the air alive with the bleat of goats and the chant of prayers. Azubah waited, her love my anchor, and I knew this march would test us, drawing us closer to Yahweh's promise, to the land where His glory would dwell.

Chapter Seven
In the Company of Twelve Banners

The dust had not yet settled on Ai's ruins before we were on the move again. Three days only had passed, the stones of the fallen city still smoked in the sun, yet the trumpets sounded, and the tribes stirred like a river breaking free of stone. There was no rest, no turning back.

The sun crept over the eastern hills, its pale light stretching like fingers across the valley floor, gilding the rocks and torn tents with a false calm. The camp stirred in waves—first the shepherd boys, coaxing restless goats from sleep; then the women, stoking embers and rolling up mats with the swift rhythm of those who had packed and repacked a thousand times; and finally the warriors, their armor clinking like distant chimes in the cold dawn.

I stood at the edge of our tent, shoulders stiff beneath the weight of the past days, but thankful for three days rest, and having spent it with those who I loved. I watched as Azubah and the servant girls folded our woven cloaks into neat squares. She did not look up, but her hands moved with practiced certainty, her brow serene, though I knew the strain that constant moving always beset upon the mother of a home. Our sons carried bundles to the caravan carts—Iru with exaggerated seriousness, Elah flitting behind like a moth drawn to motion. They did not yet know what it meant to carry the burden of memory.

Joshua's word had come swiftly. We would not linger in Ai. Mount Ebal awaited us—a holy task, one Mosheh had spoken of long before my bones ached like this, when I was still young and fierce and foolish enough to think the land would fall easily.
We were not fleeing Ai, but neither were we lingering to celebrate. There was no time.

There never was.

I tightened the strap on my satchel and turned back toward the others. Already the tribes were moving out in their order— Yehudah at the front, Reuven and Gad to the left and right, Levi moving through the ranks like veins through the body. The Ark would follow at the center, veiled in linen and reverence, the priests solemn in their sandals, their voices lifting in soft songs.

As we began the ascent from the valley, the stones of Ai behind us, I felt the weight of silence settle in. Not the silence of grief —that had passed—but the silence of something unfinished, a waiting. It coiled in my chest like a sleeping serpent.

I had not spoken of the horrors of Ai or the shedim that I had seen. Nor of the glyphs on the broken altar. Nor of the chill that crept into my bones when Elidad named the Nephilim out loud. Some had gone on pretending it was finished, but I knew better. That kind of evil does not die in fire. It waits. It waits beneath the earth, in dark places, where bones remember the shape of old rebellions.

The path twisted through narrow passes and broad meadows, the land rising steadily. Ebal and Gerizim would meet us soon—two ancient brothers of stone, watching over the promise and the curse.

Azubah walked beside me for part of the way, our sons drifting ahead with the other children. She didn't speak at first. Just the rhythm of her steps beside mine, steady and grounding, like the hum of the earth beneath our sandals. Around us, the caravan creaked forward—oxen lowing, children murmuring, the occasional bark of a shepherd calling out to a stubborn goat—but between the two of us there was quiet.

At last she said, "You've been quiet."

"There's much to hold," I replied.

She nodded, accepting the half-truth. "I saw you before sunrise," she said softly,   "Standing outside the tent with your arms hands raised in *tefillah*. I wanted to run to you. But I knew it wasn't for me."

"No," I said, my voice rough. "It was for Him. To ask His blessing on the days to come."

A silence passed between us, not awkward but full. Like water in a deep well, still and echoing. There are moments between husband and wife where words only dilute what is already understood. Still, she glanced sideways at me, her eyes narrowing against the sun,

"You do that when the weight's too much. You stand until it lifts."

"Sometimes it doesn't," I said.

She reached out and brushed her fingers against mine, a fleeting touch that spoke more than a hundred embraces,

"Even if it doesn't," she said, "you always persevere. That's what I've always loved about you. Not your strength—though you're as strong as the cedars of Bashan—but that you bend, and you rise."

I let out a dry breath that might have been a laugh. "You didn't always see me that way."

She smiled, eyes tracing the dust-choked path ahead,

"No. At first, you were just the loud Kenizzite who never knew when to stop talking."

"You weren't impressed by my stories?" I asked, mock-wounded.

"You told me you once killed a lion with your bare hands," she said, arching a brow.

"I did," I said, placing a hand on my chest.

"You failed to mention it had been dead for three days when you found it."

We both laughed then, and for a moment the miles felt shorter.

"But you were brave," she continued, her voice quieter, "And stubborn. And you looked at me like I wasn't just Eleazar's daughter or a name on a marriage list. You saw me."

"I saw you long before you saw me," I said. "I remember you at the spring in the wilderness, singing to your sisters. Your hair was tangled with wind and your voice was too loud, but I thought—I'd follow that voice through any desert."

She gave me a look,

"You said nothing for weeks" she said.

"I was afraid."

"You?"

"I was afraid your father would kill me before you ever smiled at me."

"My father liked you."

"Eventually."

"Well," she said, lifting her chin, "you proved yourself. Carrying water jugs. Mending the goat pens."

I chuckled, "You made me mend them twice. The second time was for a tear that wasn't there."

"I wanted to see if you'd complain."

"I nearly did."

"But you didn't."

"Because I wanted your father to see what I already knew," I said, more serious now, "That I belong among your people. That I would not break faith. That I wasn't just following Mosheh, but following the God of Mosheh."

Her hand found mine again, this time holding it longer, "You could have walked away. After Sinai. After the grumblings, after the rebellions."

"I had no homeland to return to," I said. "My kin were already fading. The fire in the wilderness stripped everything false from me. All that was left was what I couldn't explain—but couldn't deny. Yahweh is the One. The only. And I wanted to serve Him. And you... you showed me how to live that."

She looked down then, as if shy all over again,

"I didn't think we'd grow old together."

"We haven't yet," I said, grinning.

150

"No," she agreed, "But we've survived long enough to see a generation rise from the dust of the old."

Her voice trembled slightly, and I knew she was thinking of those we had buried in the sand. Friends. Parents. Brothers.

"I used to fear we'd never make it into the land," she said.

"I didn't," I said simply.

She glanced at me, surprised.

"I saw the giants," I went on. "I saw them with my own eyes. Tall as trees, cruel as serpents. And yet when I looked at them, I saw their bones already scattered. Because He had spoken. And when Yahweh speaks, the earth shifts."

Azubah walked in silence a while, the sun glinting off her veil. When she spoke again, her voice was low and reverent.

"I've always wondered why He chose you. A Kenizzite. A man from beyond the camp. You and Joshua—only the two of you were kept alive for this."

"I've asked myself the same," I admitted.

"And what do you think?"

I looked toward the horizon, where Ebal's outline rose like a sleeping beast,

"Because I believed Him. When others feared the darkness, I feared His absence. That's what kept me faithful—not courage, not tribal loyalty. Just fear of being where He is not."

She tightened her grip on my hand,

"Then don't let the silence trouble you. If He is testing you, it's not because you're forsaken. It's because you're still His."

I nodded, not trusting myself to speak. The wind rose as we crested a hill, and below us the road unfurled like a scar through the land. Still miles to go. Still work to be done. But with her beside me, and the memory of Sinai burning in my heart, I walked on. And though the sky was silent, my soul was not alone.

Hours passed. The sun rose higher, and the sweat beneath our tunics clung like shame. Dust filled our mouths, our lungs. But the march continued, unbroken. A people on pilgrimage, not conquest. This road was older than our swords.

At midday, we rested beneath terebinth trees, their wide arms giving us momentary relief. I drank deeply, the water cool and tasting of stone. Beside me, a Levite sang a psalm under his breath, the melody rising like incense,

"He will not let your foot be moved; He who keeps you will not slumber".

I closed my eyes.

Sinai came back to me then—not in full color, but in the shiver of memory. The fire on the mountain, the smoke that blotted out the sky, the trumpet blast that shook our bones and made the earth moan. I had been young, terrified, half-convinced the mountain itself would collapse and swallow us whole. And yet I had stood there, trembling with the rest, when Yahweh spoke. I had seen the elders ascend into the clouds with Mosheh. I had watched the sky burn.

And I remembered thinking, This is the God who speaks through flame and shadow. This is the God who remembers His promises.

That day, I had become something different—not just a man of Kenazite blood grafted into Yehudah's branch, but a witness. Not because I understood the covenant, but because I had stood under its weight.

The others—most of them—were long dead now. The generation that grumbled, that feared the giants more than they feared Yahweh. Only Joshua and I remained, walking relics of a vow sworn in fire and carried through wilderness.

I opened my eyes to the rustle of movement. Joshua was approaching.

He sat beside me, his eyes scanning the horizon. We didn't speak right away.

That was Joshua's way. He let silence speak first, and only when it was spent did he speak himself.

"Gerizim will greet us by sunset," he said.

"And Ebal with its shadow," I murmured.

He looked at me sideways. "You remember Mosheh' command?"

I nodded, "Half shall stand on one mountain to bless. The other to curse. An altar built of uncut stones. The Law written plainly for all to see."

"Even now, I hear his voice when I close my eyes," Joshua said. "I see the fire in his eyes. Do you?"

"Yes," I said. "But I also see the smoke. And the bull. And the broken tablets."

Joshua's jaw tightened, "Then you know why we must be swift. There is still defilement in the land. Not just in the soil, but in us. We carry Egypt in our bones."

He rose then and extended his hand. I took it, and the strength in his grasp reminded me—not of battle or conquest—but of Sinai. Not the thunder or the fire, but the man who had climbed into it while the rest of us trembled below. He pulled me close, and we kissed as brothers do when words are too small for what has been endured together.

The camp stirred around us. Ropes were unfastened, fires stamped out, and the long procession began again—oxen creaking, feet stirring dust, mothers calling to children. As we fell into step once more, the rhythm of our people on the move returned to me like a heartbeat—ancient and persistent.

But something in me had shifted.

The road to Ebal would not be merely one of stones and ritual. It would be a reckoning. A dividing line drawn in covenant fire—

between who we had been and who we must become. And somewhere beyond the smoke of sacrifice and the echo of blessings and curses, Hebron still waited for me. The land of giants. The place I had once entered with trembling knees and returned from with fire in my chest.

But my mind drifted further still—past Hebron, past Ai, even past Jericho's fallen walls—to a different mountain burned into the soul of every son of Israel....back to Mount Sinai.

I was much younger then. Not yet a husband. Not yet a father. Still new among the tribes—foreign in tongue, but burning with the same hunger they carried. I had seen the sea part and close again, seen the bread fall from heaven, and yet nothing had marked me like Sinai.

Even now, four decades later, I could still feel it—the trembling earth, the black cloud veined with lightning, the voice that split the sky. I had stood among thousands, my face in the dust, heart pounding as the mountain shook. And above us, one man went up alone.

He did not flinch.

We watched Mosheh disappear into that holy fire, and in his absence, our hearts failed. We demanded a god we could see, and Aaron gave us what we wanted—shaped in gold, born of fear.

Even now, I remembered the sound of those tablets breaking, the cry in Mosheh' voice when he came down. I remembered the sickness in my gut, knowing we had betrayed the One who had pulled us from Egypt.

And I remembered the choice that followed—when the Levites drew swords not against the nations, but against their own kin.

Sinai was not just covenant.

It was judgment.

It was mercy burning in wrath.

And now, as we journeyed again—toward another mountain, another covenant, another altar—I could not help but wonder what in us had changed. Or if we were only older. More weary. Still dragging Egypt behind us like a corpse that refused to be buried.

Azubah walked a few paces ahead, her veil catching the breeze. I watched her and knew that the boy I was at Sinai—furious, foreign, uncertain—would not have known what to do with such a woman. But Yahweh had not shaped me only for Ebal. He had shaped me through wilderness and flame, through silence and smoke, through the long ache of waiting. And now, at the edge of fulfillment, I could feel the old fire stirring once more. Not the fire of conquest—but the fire of remembrance.

The giants lay ahead. The promise beckoned.

But first—was Mount Sinai.

Even now, the name burns on the tongue, bitter and bright.

And as we walked, the past returned—not as a dream, but as a voice. I heard the mountain again. I saw the gold. And I remembered.

Chapter Eight
When Covenant Cracked Like Stone.

The clan had only just crossed the sea then—its walls of water still haunted my dreams, rushing and rising like beasts awakened. The Egyptians had drowned, yes, but the chains did not break as cleanly as we told ourselves. Slavery had soaked too deep. It stained our thoughts, our habits, the way we feared.

It was four decades ago, I was a child when the clan of Israel set up camp at the foot of Mount Sinai. A stranger among the tribes, grafted in by mercy and fire. My father Jephunneh was a Kenizzite, of Edomite blood. My family had wandered north when famine struck the hill country, drawn not to Egypt, but to the promises whispered among Avraham's descendants. My father heard the words of Mosheh and believed. As a child I saw the fire by night and knew it was the only true light. When the sea broke open before us, I crossed over with them—not just across water, but into something older, truer.

We reached the mountain with hearts still racing from deliverance. Sinai rose before us like a blade stabbed into the earth, dark and terrible and holy. No one approached it lightly. No animal, no foot, no hand touched it without death trailing close behind. We camped at its base, three days trembling while the sky bruised black above us and thunder rolled like the growl of something immense and unseen.

Then He descended—the glory of God came down from above.

It was not sunlight nor storm. It was a presence that filled the mountain, split it from within. Fire surged up its flanks, smoke coiled into the heavens, and a sound like shofars filled the air, though no man blew them. We were undone. Every man dropped to his knees, face pressed into the stones. Some wept. Some wailed. Others shouted for it to stop, but no one ran. There was nowhere to go that God would not find.

Mosheh alone went up.

He did not flinch. He vanished into that holy storm, a shepherd drawn by the voice that had once burned in a bush. And for forty days, we waited.

At first, there was hope.

But hope without faith is short-lived.

The days passed. No word from Mosheh. No sign. The fire raged on the mountain, but we told ourselves maybe it had consumed him. Maybe we were alone now. Abandoned. And so we turned again to what we knew: gods of our own making.

It shames me still. Even now, my stomach turns at the memory of the bull—gold hammered by trembling hands, born not of reverence but panic. I did not dance around it, I was but a youngling — a few years past my entrance into the tent of men—but many of our neighbors did. Many had only left the gods of Ba'al but a fortnight earlier in Egypt when they were adopted into the various clans, and I watched, silent, horrified, frozen in the moment of betrayal. The people had crossed a line, and they knew it. The mountain still burned, but they chose to look away.

The air at Sinai had grown thick with something other than smoke. It was not just the fear of abandonment that drove them to the bull. There was a pull, a whisper in the dark places of the camp, like the voices I would later hear in the ashes of Ai. Those unseen powers that linger in the crevices of creation—had not been silent. The bull was no mere statue. It was a gate, a summons. The people thought they were crafting a god to lead them, but instead they were opening a door to something ancient, ravenous and evil.

I saw it in the way they danced. It was not joy. It was frenzy. Men and women, faces flushed, eyes wide and unseeing, moved as if pulled by strings. The air pulsed with a rhythm that was not music—

low, guttural, like the heartbeat of something vast and buried. The firelight warped their shadows into grotesque forms—horned, writhing, as if possessed by a will not their own. The priests of Egypt had taught them this, and the old gods of Kena'an whispered it still. The bull gleamed, its gold catching the flames, and I swear I saw its eyes move, just once, as if something looked through it.

I stood apart, my small heart pounding, barely tall enough to see over the crowd. Joshua was beside me, just as young, we had joined the tent of men together not long before Sinai, his eyes wide with the same fear and wonder. We were young, yet the fire on the mountain had marked us, its glow a truth we felt in our bones. The golden bull gleamed, its worship a lie, a theft, a mockery of the God who had parted the sea. The dancers moved in frenzy, their shadows twisting into shapes that made my skin prickle. I wanted to cry out, to hide, but the weight of the moment held me still. The people were not just dancing—they were giving themselves to powers I could not name, powers that made the air feel heavy, wrong.

I had joined Israel before that betrayal, not by blood but by my parents' oath. Not long before Sinai, in the shadow of Egypt's ruin, we had partaken of the Pascha meal, and I tasted the lamb's flesh, as all in the household must. The blood's stain lingered in my heart, a vow sealed in my soul. My mother, an Egyptian slave, sitting with the tribe of Yehudah, our adopted kin, would later remind me of that night— the bitter herbs that burned the tongue, the unleavened bread that crumbled in the hand, the wine sharp with deliverance—binding us, even me, to the covenant, grafted into the promise of Avraham.

My father, a Kenizzite from Edom's hills, having come to Egypt during famine as a slave, he'd forsaken the gods of his fathers, drawn to the promise of Avraham, and inspired by the teachings of Mosheh. And it was on the night that the Angel of the Lord slay the son of Ra, my family partook of the sacred meal, we tasted of the lamb's flesh, and we were then bound to the covenant and grafted into Israel. The Law was not yet given, but the Pascha was its prelude, a vow that we would walk with this people, under this God, no matter the cost.

The camp at Mount Sinai sprawled like a living thing, a tangle of tents and fires beneath the mountain's unyielding gaze. Dust hung in the air, stirred by the restless feet of thousands, mingling with the smoke of countless altars. Day and night, the mountain burned, its fire a beacon that never dimmed, its smoke curling into a sky that seemed too small to hold it. The thunder rolled on, now distant, now near, like the breath of a god who had not yet turned away. We were a people caught between wonder and dread, tethered to a presence we could neither grasp nor flee.

I walked among the tents of Yehudah, my heart heavy with the Pascha's vow. The camp was alive with sound: the bleating of goats, the laughter of children chasing one another through the narrow paths, the low chants of elders reciting the stories of Avraham and Yitzhak. Women knelt by grindstones, their hands turning wheat to flour, while men drove stakes to tighten sagging tents against the desert wind. Everywhere, life pulsed—raw, unpolished, human. Yet beneath it, something darker stirred, a restlessness that grew with each day Mosheh did not return.

The incense never ceased. Every morning, as the sun breached the horizon, the priests of Levi kindled fires on the altars. The air grew thick with the aroma of spice and myrrh. These were not mere rituals but feasts of communion, supposed to bind us to Yahweh and to one another.

Yet not all altars of incense then were pure. At the foot of Sinai, in the shadows of the camp, away from the faithful priests' watchful eyes, forbidden fires burned. I saw them at dusk, flickering among the tents of those who had not fully forsaken Egypt's gods. Strange symbols marked their stones—spirals and eyes, carved with tools that glinted in the firelight. These were the amulets of the old ways, not the seals of Yahweh's covenant but charms to appease the spirits of the Nile or the gods of the hills. I remembered them from tales my father told of his childhood in Edom, where my father used to wear a bronze pendant etched with a serpent, whispering prayers to powers I now knew were false. Here, some still clung to such things: beads of bone, stones inscribed with forbidden names, hidden beneath tunics or buried under tent flaps. These were demonic amulets that were believed could ward off the desert's dangers or the mountain's wrath. They were wrong.

Yahweh had given us amulets of His own, though they were not mere charms but commands. The elders spoke of the physical signs we would one day bind to our hands and foreheads, words of the covenant to guard our hearts. Even now, we carried His name in our songs, His promise in our stories. I touched the woven cord around my wrist, a simple band dyed red with the memory of the Pascha lamb. It was no idol, no spell, but a reminder: I was His, grafted in, chosen not by blood but by faith. Yet the forbidden amulets whispered to others, their allure as old as the serpent's voice in the garden.

The camp was a crucible, and in Mosheh's absence, it began to crack. The days stretched on—ten, twenty, thirty—and the fire on the mountain showed no sign of fading. Some said Mosheh was dead, consumed by the blaze. Others whispered he had abandoned us, leaving us to the mercy of a God too vast, too holy. Fear bred doubt, and doubt bred rebellion. I saw it in the eyes of the men who lingered too long by the forbidden altars, in the hushed voices of women trading charms for grain. The Pascha had bound us, but not all hearts were steadfast.

I kept to the tents of Yehudah, my small hand clutching my mother's, where the elders taught the ways of Yahweh. At night, we gathered around fires, the stars sharp above us, and spoke of the promises given to Avraham. Joshua, my friend in faith, was often there, though young, his face was already lit by the flames, his young voice echoing his father's as he spoke of the sea's parting. He did not waver, even as the camp grew restless, "Yahweh is with us," his father would say, his eyes fixed on the mountain. "Mosheh will return." Joshua would reply.

I clung to those words, whispered to me by my mother as well. Once an Egyptian slave, now a daughter of the Most High. But the camp's shadows gnawed at my heart. I was a Kenizzite, an outsider by birth, my parents wanderers from Edom's hills and Egypt's streets. Some days when doubt overcame me, I would ask: did I belong here, among these tribes, under this God? It was always the memory of the pascha meal, its bitter herbs would quiet the doubt.

At the foot of Sinai, the forbidden altars grew bolder. One evening, as my father walked with me along the camp's edge, I saw a gathering near the tents of Dan. A fire burned low, its light catching the glint of gold. Men and women stood in a circle, their voices chanting in a tongue I did not know. At the center was a stone, carved with glyphs that seemed to writhe in the flickering light. A woman held a clay figure, its form twisted, half-man, half-beast. She poured oil over it, and the flames flared, casting shadows that danced like living things. I felt a chill, not from the night air but from something deeper, older—unseen powers lurking in the crevices of creation. This was no mere charm. It was worship, a summons to forces that fed on fear. I buried my face in my father's shoulder, my heart pounding, too young to speak but old enough to feel the wrongness.

I did not turn away alone—my father did also, his steps quick, his voice low as he muttered prayers to Yahweh. He wanted to overturn their altar, I could tell, but he was one man, and the camp was vast. Instead, he brought me to Joshua's father, Nun, by the central altar, where the priests prepared the evening incense. The scent of myrrh filled the air, and the faithful Levites chanted still changed Yahweh's names. Nun stood apart, Joshua at his side, the boy's eyes on the mountain. My father told Nun what we had seen, his voice hushed.

Nun nodded, his jaw tight, and said to my father,

"They forget the sea. They forget the fire" he said.

"They forget the plagues, they forget our deliverance" my father replied.

Joshua looked up, his small face fierce, and I knew he felt it too —the cost of turning away. The incense offerings were our anchor. At dawn, as the priests kindled spices on the altars, my parents brought me to the gathering to pray to the One True God, my young heart steadied by the sweet smoke of prayer curling skyward. The fragrance of frankincense and myrrh filled the air, a reminder that Yahweh was not distant but near, a God who dwelt in the rising fumes. We shared unleavened bread, its taste dry but holy, our voices raised in thanks. It was not like the offerings of Edom, where my father said the gods demanded blood and left the people empty. Here, the incense was a bond, a foretaste of the promised land. I stood with Yehudah, my adopted kin, the Pascha's memory burning in my soul, renewing the vow in my young bones.

But the rebellion grew. The whispers became shouts, the forbidden altars multiplied. By the fortieth day, the camp was a tinderbox. I woke to the sound of hammers, the ringing clash of bronze on anvil, my mother's face full of sadness. My father, Jephunneh, led us to a clearing near the tents of Reuven, following the noise. A crowd had gathered, their faces flushed with a strange fervor. At the center stood Aharon, Mosheh's brother, his hands raised. Before him was a pile of gold—earrings, bracelets, amulets melted from Egypt's spoils. Men fed the fire, their tools shaping something I could not yet see. The air was thick, not with the sweet scent of incense but with something sour, copper, alive.

My father's face filled with righteous fury and I saw Joshua nearby, beside his father Nun. Our eyes met, two young men caught in a storm we could not name. I felt it—the presence of unseen powers drawing near. The gold took shape, hammered into a the form of a bull, its eyes hollow, its surface gleaming like a false dawn, its horn the very shape of evil, its nostrils demanding incense to smell.

The people shouted, their voices raw, and Aharon proclaimed: "This is your god, O Israel, who brought you out of Egypt!" The words pierced me, cutting through the fire on the mountain. Men and women had brought with them newly formed Asherah's formed of clay and wood and they venerated them in the shadow of the golden bull. Kissing their evil gods, something that we all knew was defiance against the one true God.

And then, the dance began—not joy but madness. Men and women moved as if possessed, their bodies swaying to a rhythm not of this world. The firelight twisted their shadows into shapes that were not human—horned, clawed, flickering with a life of their own. The air pulsed, low and guttural, like the heartbeat of something vast and buried. The golden bull gleamed, and I swear I saw its nostrils move, as it breathed in the incense burned before it. This was not worship but surrender, a gate opened to powers that fed on betrayal. I was sickened.

Their voices hissed beneath the chants, a laughter older than the desert.

I clung close to father, my hand on the red cord at my wrist, tied there by my mother to recall the Pascha and our covenant. Joshua was still, his small hands tightened in a fist. We did not dance. We did not bow. This bull was a lie, a mockery of the God who had spoken. I wanted to cry out, to silence the chants, but I was too young, the moment too vast. The people were offering themselves to powers they could not name.

The bull was a test, a temptation my parents to return to Egypt and Edom's gods, to the amulets my father had forsaken. Yet we would not yield. I touched the cord, its red thread a lifeline. "El Elyon," I whispered, my voice a child's squeak, lost in the din, "I am yours."

The camp spun around me, a whirl of fire and shadow.

The mountain still burned, its light a rebuke to the bull's false glow. I clung to that light, to the Pascha, to the covenant that made me whole. The camp was breaking, but I would not break with it. Not by blood, but by oath. Not by my strength, but by the fire that never dies. The mountain loomed, its fire a silent judge, its smoke weaving patterns no man could read. And by that fortieth day, the camp's rebellion had reached a crescendo, its worst center being the tribe of Dan.

The Danites were like my family—outsiders, woven into the tribes of Israel not by birth but by choice. My mother told me tales, whispered over meals, of how, in Yosef's days, when Israel dwelt in Egypt's shadow, a band of Sea Peoples had come. They were wanderers, men of the waves, their ships carved with serpents' heads, their tongues sharp with the salt of distant shores. The elders called them *Pelishtim*. They had settled among the Ivrims in Goshen, trading oars for plows, their sea gods for Avraham's promise. Like my parents, they had partaken of the Pascha, their hands stained with the lamb's blood, their hearts sworn to Yahweh. But unlike us, their oath was shallow, a veneer over hearts that still longed for the deeps.

My father joined Yehudah in Egypt not long before the Angel of the Lord descended upon the house of Pharaoh, but the Danites were already joined to the children of Avraham, long before my father came into the clans. Many years prior, the Egyptians defeated the Sea Peoples, and their descendants were made slaves just like the clans of Israel in Goshen.

Now the tents of the Danites were at the camp's edge, their voices carrying the sea's cadence. I knew them by their walk—lithe, restless, as if the ground rocked like a ship. I knew them by their eyes, always glancing westward, as if the waves called.

And here at the foot of Mount Sinai their unfaithfulness was a wound in the camp's heart. The golden bull was not their doing alone —Reuven and others joined—but the Danites were its spark. I had seen them in the clearing, their hands swift with the hammer, their chants the loudest. They were the least faithful, the most wicked, their hearts untamed by the fire that delivered us. Even now, with Egypt's chains broken, they clung to their old gods, their altars hidden but ever-burning.

Days earlier, my father took me toward their tents, driven to understand. The camp was a maze, its paths winding through goatskins and woven reeds. The air was thick with the scent of incense, the chatter of merchants bartering grain mingling with children's laughter. We passed Levi's altars, where priests cast spices into the flames, their voices raised in praise. Families gathered, sharing unleavened bread, their unity a fragile shield against the camp's unrest.

The Danite shelters were unlike Yehudah's—smaller, patched with salt-scented hides, adorned with shells and bones that clinked in the wind. Men sat in circles, their skin weathered by sun and sea, their beards trimmed short, marking them apart. They spoke in low tones, their words clipped, rolling like waves. I saw amulets at their necks— not covenant cords but charms of bone and bronze, etched with fish and serpents, worn as if Yahweh's fire were a tale for babes.

My father approached a man he knew, Dagonis, son of Baalor, a Danite elder whose voice carried weight. His name echoed Dagon, the sea god, and his father's name called to Baal, Kena'an's storm lord. Dagonis sat by a fire, sharpening a blade with a whetstone, his eyes narrow. His tunic was edged with blue thread, a nod to the sea, and a pendant hung at his chest, carved with a coiled fish. My father greeted him, his voice steady but guarded, as I stood close.

"Dagonis, the mountain still burns," my father said, nodding toward Sinai's glow. "Mosheh will return."

Dagonis did not look up, his stone scraping with a tide's rhythm, "Mosheh is gone, Kenizzite," he said, his voice low, laced with a coastal lilt. "The fire is a storm, nothing more. We need gods we can touch."

His words were sharp, cold. My father knelt, keeping me near, the fire between us. "You ate the Pascha," he said. "You crossed the sea. You saw the fire lead us. Was that not enough?"

Dagonis's lips curled, not a smile but a grimace, "The sea is vast, Kenizzite. It gives, it takes. We know its ways. Your god demands too much, speaks too little. In Egypt, we learned to bargain with the powers." He tapped the pendant, its fish gleaming. "This keeps the deeps at bay."

I felt a chill, my small hand tightening on my father's. The Danites were like us, grafted in, their oath sworn in Egypt's shadow. Yet where my parents clung to the Pascha, the Danites kept one foot in the sea. So quickly they gave up faithfulness to the one true God and fell back to their gods, the spirits of wave and storm, powers they thought they could tame with charms and oil. I saw it in Dagonis' eyes—a restlessness, a hunger for the old ways, as if the camp were a cage and the mountain a chain.

"You are Danite now," my father said, his voice firm. "The Pascha bound you. The lamb's blood spared you. Why turn back?"

Dagonis laughed, a sound like breaking waves, "We are Dan, sons of the sea. We joined your tribes for survival, your God has abandoned us. The Pascha was a meal, nothing more. Blood washes off." He leaned forward, his blade still, "You're no different, Kenizzite. Your Edom blood sings of the hills, not this desert. Why pretend?"

167

His words struck my father, and I felt his hand tense. We were strangers, grafted in, our Kenizzite roots a shadow we could not outrun. Yet the Pascha had changed us.

"I chose Yahweh," my father said, his voice steady. "Not for survival, but for truth. The sea is vast, Dagonis, but it drowns. The fire saves."

Dagonis snorted, returning to his blade. "We'll see, Kenizzite. When you see that Mosheh never returns, we'll have our gods."

We left him, my heart troubled. The Danite tents buzzed—men carving charms, women weaving nets as if for fishing, children playing with shells. Their speech was quick, their laughter sharp, but beneath it was defiance. They were Israel, yet not, their hearts divided, their altars secret. My father paused by a man, Yamir, younger than Dagonis, pouring oil over a stone etched with a wave's shape. His name called to Yam, the sea god who wrestled the heavens. My father spoke, his shadow over him, as I watched.

"Yamir," my father said, "the priests offer incense to El Elyon. Join us. The gathering is for all the clans."

Yamir looked up, his eyes bright but guarded. "Incense?" he said, his voice carrying the coastal lilt, "We know offerings, Kenizzite. The sea demands oil, smoke, sometimes blood. Your god asks for spices, but what's the difference? Power is power."

He held up the stone, its wave glinting, "This brings luck. Your altars don't."

My father knelt, his voice low, as I clung to his side, "The sea's power failed in Egypt. Yahweh parted it. The Angel of the Lord spared you, not your charms. Why trust what drowned the Egyptians?"

Yamir shrugged, tracing the stone, "The sea is home. We Danites don't forget. Your god's fire is too hot, too far. We need what we can hold." He tossed the stone, catching it with a grin, "You're like us, Kenizzite. Wanderers. Why chain yourselves to this?"

My father stood, his heart heavy, and led me away. The Danites were our mirror, their grafted status like ours. Yet where we embraced the covenant, they endured it. Their unfaithfulness was not just rebellion but a clinging to the sea's dark embrace. They were the most wicked, their charms a mockery of the fire that led us. The mountain's glow was a beacon in my soul, even as a child. The camp's fracture widened. The golden bull's shadow grew, its worship a fever.

Now, as an old man, my bones ache with the weight of years, but the memory of that day at Sinai burns brighter than the mountain's fire. As we returned to the main camp where the golden bull gleamed. The sight of that wickedness, the sound of it, the stench of it—they carved themselves into my soul, a scar that shaped me, a warning that bound me to Yahweh forever. As a child, I felt the terror of unseen powers; as a man, I know their name—demons, summoned by betrayal, feasting on Israel's fall. That memory, more than any other, solidified my oath, not by my Kenizzite blood but by the Pascha's vow, to serve the God who parted the sea.

It was the fortieth day since Mosheh had left us.

We'd left the Danite tents, their charms and oils still sour in my nose, my father's face grim as he led me back through the camp's maze. The air was heavy, not with the sweet frankincense of the priests' altars but with a cloying heat, like breath from a furnace. The mountain loomed, its fire a silent rebuke, its smoke twisting into shapes no child could name but all could fear. We reached the main clearing, where the golden bull stood, its form a mockery of life. The firelight caught its curves, making it shimmer like a false sun, its hollow eyes staring as if alive. Men and women thronged around it, their faces flushed, their eyes unseeing. Aharon, Mosheh's brother, stood nearby, his hands still, his gaze distant, as if he too were caught in the spell. The people had brought their gold—rings, bracelets, amulets from Egypt's spoils—and now it was a god, a lie forged by their own hands. I clung close to my father, my heart pounding, sensing even then that this was not worship but a wound, a tear in the covenant that had bound us.

They ate and drank, but not the unleavened bread of the Pascha. Tables groaned with food—grain pilfered from stores, dates and figs from the desert, wine that was looted from Egypt's cellars. The scent was not holy but greedy, thick with fermentation and waste. Men tore at the food with stained hands, their laughter slurred, their mouths dripping. Women poured wine, their voices shrill, their movements loose, as if the ground swayed beneath them. This was no sacred meal, no echo of the lamb that spared us. It was a feast for the flesh, a communion with powers that fed on chaos.

The music began, a sound that still haunts me. Drums pounded, their rhythm deep and relentless, like the heartbeat of the earth itself. Flutes wailed, their notes sharp, twisting into melodies that made my skin prickle. Men struck lyres, their strings humming with a fevered urgency. The Danites were there, their sea-born chants rising above the rest, their voices laced with the cadence of waves. Dagonis, his fish pendant glinting, beat a drum, his eyes wild. Yamir, his wave-stone tucked away, swayed with a flute, his grin a blade. Their music was not praise but a summons, a call to spirits older than the desert, hungrier than the sea.

The dance followed, and it was no dance of joy. Men and women moved as if pulled by strings, their bodies jerking, spinning, collapsing in heaps only to rise again.

I saw a woman, her hair unbound, her robed loosed, pour oil over the bull, its surface hissing as the flames flared. The smoke was sharp, not like the priests' frankincense but acrid, laced with spices I could not name, curling into shapes that made me hide my face in my father's tunic. As a man, I know now what I felt then—the air was thick with the shedim, unseen powers drawn by the gate this idol opened, their laughter a hiss beneath the chants.

And yes, there was more—things a young man who was very much still a boy saw but could not grasp, things my older heart names with sorrow. The dance grew wilder, bodies pressing close, hands grasping, voices moaning. Couples slipped into the shadows beyond the firelight, their forms entwined, their movements urgent, hidden but not secret. Others stayed in the open, their embraces bold, their laughter a mockery of love. The Ivrim word for their "play"—*tzachak*—carried a weight I later learned, a hint of flesh offered not to Yahweh but to gods who demanded it. In Kena'an, in Egypt, such rites were common, fertility cults that bound men to demons through the body's surrender. Here, at Sinai, Israel fell into that trap, their covenant forgotten, their Pascha defiled.

I was too young to name it, but I felt the wrongness. My father's body tightened, his breath sharp, his eyes fierce with a pain I now understand. He had forsaken Edom's gods, their altars, their rites, to join Israel. He had eaten the Pascha, bound us to Yahweh, and now he saw his people—our people—betray that vow. I felt his heart break, this moment changing him, and it marked me too. As a child, I sensed the bull was a lie; as a man, I know it was a door to death, a communion with powers that enslave.

My father turned us away, but not before I saw Joshua, standing by Nun, his father, at the crowd's edge. His small face ghastly pale, his eyes wide, but fierce, like mine. We did not dance, we did not bow. Nun's jaw was tight, his stance a shield for Joshua, as my father's was for me. They spoke no words, but their eyes met us, a silent vow to hold fast.

We fled to Yehudah's tents, the camp's madness fading behind us. The priests' false altars still burned behind us, their incense rising. My mother waited, her face filled with tears, her hands pulling me close. She whispered of the Pascha, of the blood that spared us, of the God who led us through the sea. Her words were a balm, a reminder that Yahweh was not the bull, not the shadows, not the powers that hissed in the dark. My father stood, his hands raised in prayer, his voice low, reminding us of the covenant we had sworn.

That night, as I lay in the tent, the camp's din a dull roar, I dreamed of the bull, its eyes alive, its shadows reaching. I woke crying, my mother's arms around me, her voice singing of Yahweh's fire. As a child, I feared those shadows; as a man, I know them for what they were—shedim…demons, lured by Israel's betrayal.

Those memories, seared into me at Sinai, shaped my faithfulness. I was Kalev, a Kenizzite, grafted into Israel not by blood but by the Pascha's oath. The golden bull showed me the cost of turning away—the feasting, the dancing, the rites that bound men to demons. It showed me what my father's gods might have been, what I might have become. But the Pascha, the incense, the mountain's fire —they held me fast. As a spy in Kena'an, as a warrior against the Amalekites, I carried that memory, a shield against the idols that whispered still.

The Danites, with their charms and chants, were but a shadow of that day. Their sea gods, their oils, their defiance—they echoed the bull's madness, a warning I heeded. Joshua, too, bore that scar, his faith as fierce as mine. We were young then, but Yahweh marked us, bound us to His covenant. The sea could not claim us, nor the hills of Edom, nor the gods of Kena'an. We waited for Mosheh, for the fire, for the God who called us.

Finally, the mountain shook.

A sound like shofars, though none were blown, rolled down from Sinai's peak. The camp's noise faltered, heads turning, eyes squinting against a light that was not the sun. Mosheh descended, a figure of fire, his form wreathed in glory that hurt to behold. His face glowed, as if the mountain's flame had seeped into his skin, his eyes like burning coals, his robes shimmering with a radiance that made the bull's gold seem dull. He was no mere man but an angel of Yahweh, a prophet bearing the weight of God's word.

172

In his hands, two tablets gleamed, their words carved by the divine finger, a covenant now betrayed.

I stared, my breath caught, my youthful form pressed tight against my father,

"Abba," I whispered, "is that Yahweh?"

He shook his head, his voice low, "It is Mosheh, touched by Him. See, Kalev, the fire of God."

The crowd parted, some falling to their knees, others shrinking back. The dancers slowed, their frenzy broken by the light. Aharon stood by the bull, his face pale, his hands trembling. Mosheh's gaze fell on him, and the air crackled, as if the mountain itself held its breath,

"Aharon!" Mosheh's voice was thunder, yet laced with grief. "What have you done? This people, redeemed by Yahweh, delivered by His hand—why have you led them to this shame?"

Aharon stammered, his voice weak, his eyes darting,

"Mosheh, do not be angry. The people—they were afraid. They said you were gone, that we needed gods to lead us. I took their gold, threw it in the fire, and this beast came out!"

His words were a child's excuse, a lie that hung heavy in the air. I felt my father's grip tighten, his breath sharp,

"He speaks as if blameless," he muttered to Nun, who stood nearby, Joshua in his arms. "Yet he stood by as they defiled the covenant."

Nun nodded, his jaw tight, "The Pascha bound us, Jephunneh. This—" he gestured to the bull, its fire still burning—"this is death."

Mosheh's face darkened, his light flaring. He raised the tablets, and with a cry that shook my bones, he hurled them to the ground. They shattered, their fragments glinting like broken stars, a mirror of Israel's broken vow. The crowd gasped, some weeping, others shouting, but the dancers resumed, their madness unquenched. Men and women swayed, their bodies entwined, their chants rising, as if

173

the bull could shield them from the fire in Mosheh's eyes. The air pulsed, the unseen powers hissing louder, their shadows writhing in the smoke.

Mosheh turned to the bull, his voice a blade,

"This is no god! You have forsaken Yahweh, who parted the sea, who fed you manna, who called you His own!"

He seized the idol, its gold hot as flame, and cast it into the fire. The bronze hissed, melting into a shapeless mass, its eyes dimming, its power broken. He ground it to dust, scattering it into the water, a judgment on their sin. I watched, my child's heart pounding, knowing even then that this was justice, though it tore at me.

But the rebellion did not cease. The dancers pressed closer, their voices defiant, their bodies swaying in the shadows. Couples slipped into the dark pretending that none saw them, their embraces a mockery of the covenant, their rites a communion with powers that fed on flesh. The elders, who had led this sin, stood unrepentant, their wood and clay idols gleaming, their eyes wild. The camp was a furnace, its corruption a curse on the land, a stain that threatened us all. I felt it, a weight that made me cling to Jephunneh, my red cord a lifeline.

Mosheh climbed a rise, his light blazing, his voice like a shofar,

"Who is for Yahweh? Come to me!"

The words cut through the din, a call not to Mosheh but to the God who had redeemed us. The camp froze, eyes turning, hearts trembling. From the tents of Levi, men surged forward, their faces fierce, their hands gripping staffs and blades. At their head was Eleazar, a Levite elder, his voice ringing as he reached Mosheh's side.

"We are for Yahweh!" Eleazar cried, his eyes burning with zeal. "The covenant is broken, the land defiled. Speak, Mosheh—what must we do?"

Mosheh's gaze swept the camp, his light dimming with sorrow,

"The unrepentant harden their hearts. They choose death over life, demons over Yahweh. Go, Levites, through the camp. Those who refuse to turn, who cling to this sin, must be removed, lest the curse consume us all."

Eleazar hesitated, his voice low,

"Mosheh, they are our brothers, our kin. Must it come to this?"

Mosheh's face softened, but his voice was firm,

"It is not my will, Eleazar, but Yahweh's justice. The Angel of the LORD spared us, but they spit upon the meal that preserved us. The land cries out, the covenant bleeds. Act, or we all perish."

I felt my father's breath catch, his hand shielding me, "Kalev," he whispered, "this is the cost of betrayal. Remember it always."

Nun stood beside us, with Joshua close, his voice a murmur. "Yahweh is holy. We cannot stand with the bull."

The Levites moved, their blades flashing in the firelight. The camp erupted—screams, shouts, the clash of bronze. Some fell to their knees, weeping, begging for mercy, and Mosheh's intercession to spare them, but others, hardened in rebellion, fought back, their chants defiant, their eyes wild with the bull's madness. The Danites were among them, Dagonis and Yamir wielding staffs, their sea-chants a mockery. Three thousand fell that day, their bodies a grim harvest, their blood a cleansing of the camp's curse. I hid my face, the sounds searing my soul, a young man's terror that became an older man's foundation.

Mosheh stood apart, his light unwavering, his hands raised in prayer,

"Yahweh, forgive Your people," he pleaded, his voice breaking. "They are stiff-necked, but they are Yours. Spare them, for Avraham's sake, for the covenant's promise."

The air shifted, the unseen powers retreating, their hisses fading. The camp grew still, the survivors weeping, the Levites bloodied but steadfast.

Eleazar returned, his blade stained, his face ashen,

"It is done," he said, his voice hollow. "The unrepentant are gone. The land is clean, but at what cost?"

Mosheh placed a hand on his shoulder, his light softening, "You have chosen Yahweh, Eleazar. Your tribe is His priesthood now, a holy guard for Israel. The cost is great, but the covenant endures."

I watched, my heart trembling. The Levites' zeal, Mosheh's fire —they were Yahweh's justice, His mercy. The bull's worship had opened a gate to demons, but Mosheh closed it, his light a beacon, his intercession a shield. Back then I saw only the glow, the blood, the sorrow; as a man, I now see the truth—that Yahweh's holiness demands purity, that His love spares the repentant.

My father led me back to Yehudah's tents, my mother's arms waiting. Joshua and Nun were there, their faces solemn, "The LORD holds us," Nun said, his voice steady,   "We are Israel, Jephunneh, even now."

My father nodded, his eyes on the mountain,

"Kalev will remember," he said.   "He will know Yahweh's fire, not the bull's lie."

That day shaped me. The golden bull's madness, its feasts, its dances, its rites—they showed me the abyss of idolatry, the shedim that lurk in betrayal. But Mosheh's light, the Levites' blades, the incense's sweet rise—they showed me Yahweh's truth. I was Kalev, a Kenizzite, grafted by the Pascha, bound by my parents' oath. The sea could not claim me, nor Edom's hills, nor Egypt's gods. I carried that memory to Kena'an, to Hebron, a shield against all idols.

The mountain burned, its fire a promise. I clung to that fire, to the Pascha, to the covenant that made me whole. The camp was cleansed, but I was forged. Not by blood, but by oath. Not by my strength, but by the fire that never dies.

The memory of Sinai lingers like smoke on the wind—neither sharp nor distant, but folded deep into the marrow. I carry it quietly, a shadow and a flame both, felt more than spoken. Before me now, Mount Ebal rises solemn and still, its slopes etched by time and witness. Across the valley, Gerizim watches, silent as the covenant we are about to renew. Azubah walks beside me, her presence steady and soft, eyes reflecting a hope I have not dared to name. Iru and Elah cling close, their small hands seeking comfort in mine as the camp stirs with murmurs and prayers. The victory at Ai still hums beneath our feet, a reminder that Yahweh's hand moves among us, though the path is never without trial. Here, at this ancient altar, something old and new will meet—promise, judgment, and the unyielding call to faith.

The journey from Ai was swift, our hearts buoyed by the ruin of Kena'an's walls. The camp moved as one, a river of tents and voices, threading through the hills and wilderness. Dust rose beneath our feet, mingling with the scent of myrrh from the priests' censers, a sweeter air than Sinai's sour betrayal. Children laughed, chasing goats along the paths, while elders chanted Avraham's tales. Azubah sang, her voice a melody that steadied me, her hands weaving nets for our sons' games as we walked. Iru and Elah ran ahead, their shouts echoing, their small cords—red, like mine—glinting in the sun. The Danites trailed, their sea-born gait unchanged, even after the judgment all those years ago at Sinai. Yet even they could not dim our joy, for Ai's fall was Yahweh's hand, a sign that Kena'an was ours.

Chapter Nine
The Blessings and the Curses

When we arrived at the Mount Ebal's summit, Joshua and his men built an altar, his form steady, his voice a clarion as he directed the altar's building. No bronze touched the stones, each rough and unhewn, as Mosheh had commanded long ago. When it was finished the Levites kindled incense, its fragrance rising like a prayer, many sacrifices were made, and then the tribes divided: half the people stood in front of Ebal, the other half Gerizim, their faces turned to the valley where the Levites would chant the Law's blessings and curses.

I paused on Ebal's slope, Azubah at my side, our sons tugging at our tunics. The camp sprawled below, a sea of tents catching the sun, their colors vivid against the dust. Iru pointed to the altar, his voice high,

"Father, is this like Sinai?" Elah echoed, "Will the mountain burn with fire and smoke?" I knelt, my hands on their shoulders, my heart swelling. "Not like Sinai, my son. This is joy, not sorrow. Yahweh renews His promise here."

Azubah's hand touched my arm, her eyes searching mine. "Kalev, you speak of Sinai often, but I was not born then. What shadow does it cast, even now, when Ai's victory lights our way?"

I drew her close, the camp's hum fading as I spoke, my voice low, woven with memory,

"Azubah, my heart, Sinai was a wound. I was young when the bull rose, its gold a lie, its worship a gate to demons. Men danced, their shadows horned, their voices wild. Women poured oil, their chants a mockery. Couples vanished into the dark, their rites a defilement of the Pascha that bound us. My father, Jephunneh, shielded me, but I felt the air thicken, the unseen powers hissing. Mosheh descended, his face like fire, his tablets shattered, and three

179

thousand fell by the Levites' blades. That day scarred me, but it forged me too—for Yahweh's light outshone the bull's deceit."

Her breath caught, her hand tightening, "Such darkness, Kalev. How did you, so small, hold fast?"

I smiled, my fingers tracing the red cord at my wrist, its thread worn but strong. "The Pascha, Azubah. Its blood spared us, its meal bound us. My parents ate it, as did I, as all twelve clans must. That vow held me, even then. Each year as you and I and our children partake of it—it is still a lifeblood to me that strengthens my inner being. Here, at Ebal, that fire burns anew, not in judgment but in promise."

She glanced at Joshua, the Spear of the twelve clans, his form commanding as he raised a stone, plaster coating it for the Law's words, "He leads as Mosheh did," she said softly, "But Ai's victory—Kalev, it fills me with hope. The walls fell, the kings fled. Was it not Yahweh's hand?"

I nodded, the memory of Ai's ruin vivid,

"It was, my love. The ambush, the smoke, the clash of spears—Ai crumbled as Jericho did. I fought beside Joshua, my sword heavy but sure in every strike, Yehudah's men at my back. The altars of the Kena'an, their glyphs pulsing with dark power, we shattered them, their whispers silenced. Yahweh gave us the land, a taste of the promise Avraham walked. Now, at Ebal, we seal it—not with blood, but with the Law's voice."

And then, after a long pause I shared with her the wonder of Ai, "I saw the Angel of the LORD, at Ai, in the midst of the battle," Azubah tensed, realizing the sacredness of such a thing, "He was beauty itself, and when He spoke, I both coiled in fear and love. He upheld me, and promised that none of our clan would die. He fought alongside us" I said.

She slid her hand within mine, her eyes moist with thankfulness to the One True God, and then ever so gently she squeezed my grip and spoke, "Surely God is faithful to His people, surely God will remember us unto the ages of ages."

Iru tugged my tunic, eyes wide with wonder, "Father, did you kill a king?"

Elah's voice followed, laced with excitement and mischief, "Did he wear a crown? Did you fight giants too?"

I hesitated, the weight of memory pressing down—a shadow over the triumph.

The giants. The darkness in Ai was more than stone and flesh. It was the evil of spirits, curses woven into the land and blood. "Giants…" I murmured, not meeting their eyes at first. "Yes, I faced them."

Iru's breath caught. "What were they like?"

I swallowed hard,

"Not like men. Their height, their strength—only part of the terror. It was their eyes, hollow and burning, that chilled my soul. And worse—there were things in Ai no sword could cut. Spirits that whispered lies, tried to bend our hearts with fear."

A grizzled warrior from our traveling clan stepped closer, voice low but proud, "A giant? You should know, your father—Kalev ben Yefuneh,, is now called Kalev the Giant Killer. He struck down more than one, standing firm where others faltered. His blade is a sign of Yahweh's power."

I cast a glance around, feeling the weight of their awe and the unspoken dread,

"They were not merely giants of flesh, but of shadow and curse. I do not speak lightly of them" I said.

Iru's eyes shone with both fear and admiration, "Did you ever want to run father?"

I smiled faintly, though the memory was bitter,

"Fear is a part of battle. But Yahweh's strength carries us beyond it."

Azubah's firm hand grounding me, "Our sons must hear truth —both the victory and the cost."

I nodded slowly

"At Sinai, I learned of Yahweh's justice—the bull's sin, the Levites' blades. But here at Ebal, the covenant will be renewed. The land is given, but so too is the struggle. Iru, Elah, you will walk paths shadowed and bright. Know that the promise is not without its trials."

She smiled softly, "You are no longer a wanderer, Kalev. You are Yehudah's own—rooted and grafted by faith. I see it in your eyes —the fire of Sinai and the steady hope of this day. Our sons will see it too."

I drew her into my arms, the camp's clamor a distant hum, "Azubah, you are my joy, my anchor. You were not at Sinai, but you carry its promise. When I fought at Ai, your prayers held me. Here, at Ebal, your love binds me. We stand as one, for Yahweh, for our sons, for the land."

Her eyes glistened, her voice a whisper,

"I prayed, Kalev, as the battle raged. I saw the smoke from Ai, feared the Kena'anim' gods. But you returned, and now we stand here, whole. What of tomorrow? Will more battles come?"

I kissed her brow, my heart steady, "They will, my love. Kena'an's kings still breathe, their altars linger. But Joshua leads, and Yahweh's fire goes before us. Today, we renew the covenant, and tomorrow, we walk in its strength. Iru and Elah will see it—a land flowing with milk and honey, as Mosheh promised."

Suddenly, in the distance the shofar sounded—a ram's horn, curved and ancient, its cry tearing through the morning stillness like a blade of fire. It was the sound of summoning, the voice of covenant calling us to order. All fell silent. Joshua stepped forward, his presence a calming breeze upon the multitude assembled before him.

Two Levite priests stepped forward, solemn and steady, bearing the tablets of stone they had brought from the Ark. They placed them into Joshua's hands, and the weight of the covenant seemed to rest on all our shoulders. Behind them came five more Levites, cradling the parchment scrolls of the Law. They moved like threads through the sea of men, women, and children—winding their way tribe by tribe, ascending and descending the slopes of Gerizim and Ebal. Each scroll was carried with care, encased in in cedar for protection, they processed through the midst of the people so that every tribe might witness the law of the living covenant. They did not walk in haste, but their priestly procession were measured steps, their path a woven liturgy through the gathered nation.

And as they passed, those of us standing near leaned in to kiss the scrolls, our lips brushing the cedar cases that carried the sacred words—the Law of Mosheh, living still among us. Not all could reach, but those within the sweep of the procession gave their reverence, each kiss a vow renewed, each breath a prayer unspoken. The holy law of the covenant was venerated not in haste but in awe.

Among the crowd, Azubah moved no closer than custom allowed, yet as one Levite priest passed near, she discreetly reached out, her fingers brushing the fringe of his robe. It was said that such a touch carried blessing, and none who saw it thought to question—for her eyes were full of the same devotion we all bore, fixed not on the man, but on the holiness he bore upon his shoulders.

Other Levites stood in the valley, their censers swinging in measured rhythm, incense rising in delicate veils, a fragrant offering to the unseen presence.

Finally, after the procession came to an end, all the Levites assembled at the altar and our chieftain spoke, the Spear of the Twelve Clans,

"Shema, O Israel!" Joshua cried, his hands lifted high, the stone tablets gleaming in the morning light, a priest standing before him holding the parchment of the law in front of him to read,

"This day, we renew the covenant of Yahweh—who brought us from Egypt, who gave us Ai, who gives us this land! Hear, O Israel!" Joshua cried, his hands raised, the Law's stones gleaming, "This day, we renew the covenant of Yahweh, who brought us from Egypt, who gave us Ai, who gives us this land!!"

The tribes answered, their voices a thunder.

"In the days of old," Joshua began, his voice steady as the mountain itself, "our fathers stood trembling before the mighty hand of Yahweh, when He descended in fire upon Sinai's peak. The covenant was given then—laws inscribed by the very finger of God, words to shape a holy people."

A hush settled over the valley—a sea of faces still as stone. Elders cloaked in wool, mothers with infants pressed to their breasts, children like Iru and Elah wide-eyed with awe. I felt Azubah's hand tighten around mine, her own life begun after Sinai's shame. The memory burned in me still—my father's arms about me as Mosheh shattered the golden bull, as Levite blades swept the camp clean. But here, on this day, no idols cast shadows. Only the promise of Kena'an shimmered before us, sealed in Ai's flame.

"But the covenant is no dead scroll, no faded memory etched on brittle parchment," Joshua continued, his voice rising like a shofar over the assembly. "It lives—here—in the breath of our obedience, in the marrow of our days." He kissed each piece of stone and then raised the tablets high once again. Sunlight illuminated the carved words, the cloud-filtered sky hanging thick with frankincense and flame, "Today we do not stand as slaves from Egypt, nor as wanderers of the waste, but as heirs of Yahweh's promise—keepers of His law, builders of His kingdom. Each of you has been cut into the covenant, you and all your children partake of the pascha meal every year"

Joshua's voice was focused, sharpened like a drawn blade,

184

"Hear, O Israel, the words that bind us. If you obey Yahweh your God, and walk in His ways, then all these blessings shall come upon you and overtake you."

Eleazar lifted his staff, his face lined like the wilderness paths he had walked.

"Blessed be he who walks in Yahweh's ways!" he cried, his voice a golden thread woven into the air.

From Mount Gerizim came the answering thunder—Shimon, Levi, Yehudah, Yitzhakhar, Yosef, and Binyamin roared as one: "Blessed!"

One by one, the elders rose, their names called, each proclaiming blessings before his tribe. Their words echoed across the valley:

"Blessed is he who keeps the commandments of Yahweh!"

And the people answered, "Blessed!"

Each response struck like a bell tolling for the soul. The people did not merely speak—they pledged. They did not simply hear—they bore the weight of the words.

Across the valley, on Mount Gerizim, the blessings rang out in turn.

"Blessed be the womb that bears life, the hands that give freely, the heart that remembers the covenant!"

"Blessed!"

The tribes stood between the twin peaks—Ebal and Gerizim— the blessings surrounding them like fire and cloud. No man could say he had not heard. No child would forget this day. The valley shook with the rhythm of call and reply. It was a liturgy of fire and stone. Iru mimicked me, his small fist raised, his voice thin but clear, "Blessed!" He shouted.

But then came the weight of warning. Eleazar's tone deepened,

"Cursed is the one who carves an idol, who mocks father and mother, who sheds the blood of the innocent."

From Mount Ebal, the tribes of Reuven, Gad, Asher, Zevulun, Dan, and Naftali responded with fierce unity, "Cursed!"

Iru pulled at my robe, "Papa," he whispered, his eyes wide, "why do they curse?"

I knelt beside him, "To warn," I said quietly, "so that no one forgets. A curse is not spoken in hate, but in grief—for what may come if we turn away."

His brow furrowed, "But I like the blessings better."

I smiled and drew him near, "So do I, little warrior. May Yahweh keep you always on the path where blessings dwell."

The chanting of the Levites surged across the valley, "Cursed be the man who sets up a carved idol!"

And from the gathered tribes at Mount Ebal the response: "Cursed!"

"Cursed be he who perverts the justice due to the sojourner, the fatherless, and the widow!"

"Cursed!" They yelled.

My gaze shifted to Ebal's shadowed line. Among them stood the Danites—no longer adorned with sea-born amulets, their defiance subdued. Their fathers had danced at Sinai, conjuring spirits from the dark. I had seen it, even as a child. Today, they stood among the faithful.

"Do you see them?" I murmured to Azubah. "Their fear? Their hope? Once they called upon what slithered unseen. Can they forget?"

She leaned close, her voice dusk-soft.

"They may stumble, but the Law binds us all. You fought at Ai, broke their altars of shadow. This day is new. Iru and Elah will know only this light."

Her words settled over me like balm. I looked to our sons—Elah resting against her side, Iru still mimicking the chants, his heart open and bright.

"For them," I said, "may it always be so."

Joshua stepped forward, the stone tablets in his grasp. His voice rang with the weight of ages,

"This is the covenant of Yahweh," he declared, "given to Mosheh, sealed in blood, remembered in fire. These are the words that will shape our children and guard this land."

He turned to the altar, where the stones gleamed. The Levites stood flanking him, incense drifting like a veil into heaven. The tribes fell silent.

"You shall have no other gods before Me…"

The command struck like flint on my soul. Even now, so many years beyond Sinai, I heard the cry of the golden bull. That idol's laughter—mocking, inhuman—rattled in memory, only now silenced by truth.

Joshua read on. Each command a hammer: Honor the Sabbath. Do not kill. Do not bear false witness. Do not covet. Stone by stone the Law built its tower within me again, not a tower of pride, but of remembrance.

Azubah's voice came soft at my side, firm as braided linen, "They will carry this, Kalev. Not the scar of Sinai, but the vow of Ebal. You have given them that."

I said nothing at first. My gaze followed the curling smoke, higher and higher, as if seeking again that unseen mountain where the Holy One dwells.

At length I answered, "This is what I dreamed of when the bull danced and the swords of Levi fell. Not the madness. Not the stain. But this—the Twelve Clans whole, covenant-bound, our sons free."

She placed her hand on mine, and I felt again the weight of the red cord on my wrist. A sign of deliverance. A thread in a greater story.

"The land will test them," I said. "As it tested us."

"They will not be alone," she replied. "You are of Yehudah now, Kalev—by choice, by blood, by faith. They will remember."

The reading continued. Joshua's voice did not falter, nor did the people's response.

I turned toward my sons. Elah had gone quiet, watching, his fingers wrapped about a small stone he had picked from the valley floor. Iru stood solemn, lips moving with the chants, his small brow furrowed in fierce resolve. They were listening—not just with ears, but with heart.

As the last words were spoken, Joshua lifted the stone tablets again and held them before the altar,

"Choose this day whom you will serve," he cried, the wind catching his cloak. "Whether the gods your fathers served beyond the River, or the gods of Kena'an, in whose land you now dwell. But as for me and my house—" he struck his chest—"we will serve Yahweh!"

A tremor passed through the people. Then came the cry—not from one tribe, nor from the Levites alone—but from all of the Twelve Clans, as with one voice.

"We will serve Yahweh!"

Their shout shook the valley. The very ground of Ebal seemed to stir beneath our feet.

Eleazar stepped forward, raising his censer, "Yahweh is our God!" he declared, the smoke of incense and sacrifice mingling.

Joshua's eyes found mine across the crowd. His eyes betrayed his own wonder and delight in this moment. It seemed like a dream that we stood here, assembled before Yahweh, all the people, a covenant renewed. After all we had gone through, and all that we'd seen. He stepped down from the altar, his face aglow, not with fire, but with purpose, the liturgy was nearly done. The tablets of stone were being placed back inside the Ark by the Levites. The sacred scrolls of the Torah back in their tents.

While we waited for the Levites to return to finish the liturgy, Joshua came and stood next to me and my family,

"We saw the bull," he said quietly, when he reached me, "We saw the flame that burned, but did not cleanse."

"We did," I answered. "And I see now what it meant. This—this is the fire that does not consume. The fire that makes whole."

Eleazar joined us, his robes smelling of the sweet aroma of incense, "The Law is written now—on stone, on scroll, and in the hearts of your children. We carry Sinai's wound, Kalev," and as he looked out at the Twelve Clans, he said, "They will carry its healing."

I looked to Elah who still held his pebble as if it were a sacred thing. I saw Iru murmuring one of the blessings under his breath, tuneless but true. My heart swelled.

"They will not forget," I said.

Azubah stepped closer, her voice soft as fleece, "This day is theirs, Kalev. As you told of Sinai, they will tell of Ebal."

Joshua then walked back and faced the Ark of the Covenant, he knelt and prostrated before it, kissing the ground. He did this seven times and all of the tribes kneeled and followed him as one. I knelt beside my wife and sons, the red cord warm against my skin, the altar's smoke rising like a promise. We each kissed the sacred ground at the foot of Mount Ebal. Seven times we venerated the land where Yahweh renewed the covenant with His people. Sinai had scarred me. Ai had tested me. But Mount Ebal—Ebal had renewed me.

Then the final Shofar was blown, the liturgy was over.

We rose. The smoke drifted and thinned, but the Law stood unmoved. The stones bore witness. The sky bore witness. And the land… the land would now await our faithfulness.

As we began to descend from the mountains, Azubah's voice broke the silence, light as birdsong,

"What now, Kalev? Hebron's hills? Or rest beside a vineyard?"

I smiled, not with mirth, but with hope, "Hebron, Azubah. Vines will grow there for our sons. The place where I faced the shedim, and God withheld me, we will one day plant our fields and offer sacrifice to Him. But first—battles yet remain. The land is not won."

She nodded, "Then lead on, my Kenizzite. I will follow, as I followed to Ebal."

We walked on. The sun dipped behind Gerizim, casting long shadows down the valley. But the fire in my chest burned steady.

Not by my hand would the land be claimed, but by the covenant written this day.

Not by sword, but by faith.

Not by strength, but by the voice of Yahweh, who called me from the wilderness to this place.

We found our place among the campfires, Azubah kneeling to set out cloth and bread. Iru held a portion of lamb with reverence, the bone still warm in his hand. Elah chewed solemnly, his brow furrowed in a mimicry of thought. Around us, voices lifted—not in chant now, but in laughter, in song, in blessing.

The tribes feasted, not in haste like the Pascha of Egypt, but in joy—present, full, unafraid. Reuven passed wine to Zevulun, while Naftali shared fruit with Asher. No clan held back; no family stood apart. Beneath the twilight sky, the Twelve Clans became one body—fed by the sacrifice, bound by the Word.

The elders spoke softly as they ate, recalling Sinai, recalling Egypt, and remembering those who had fallen along the way. But none lingered long in sorrow.

This was not the grief of wilderness, nor the mourning of sin. It was the stillness that follows obedience, the peace that grows in the soil of vows kept.

Even the Danites, long wary, had unshuttered their hearts. I saw them seated beside Gad and Levi, eating from the same fire. A wonder, and a mercy.

I leaned back beside Azubah, the flames reflected in her eyes. The children nestled between us, drowsy with meat and warmth.

"This is what I longed for," I said, voice hushed as night fell, "a feast with no fear, a table where all of Israel eats as one."

She looked at me, the covenant's echo in her smile, "And still, the land waits."

"Yes," I said, my gaze turning eastward, toward the hills of Hebron. "But the seed is planted."

And so the fire burned low. The valley hummed with the fullness of evening—crickets in the grasses, the murmur of prayer, the last laughter of children. The altar smoldered behind us, its stones blackened, its witness sure.

Night clothed the mountains, and we lay beneath the stars, wrapped not in fear but in faith. The covenant had been spoken. The feast had been shared. The land listened.

And in the silence, Yahweh watched.

Chapter Ten
The Weight of Mercy's Blade

The first light bled over the hills, slow and golden and the horizon bathed in a light that was both tender and unyielding, as if Yahweh Himself had etched His covenant into the stones once again. The air was fragrant with the scent of incense, its cedar and myrrh tendrils rising from the altar, mingled with the morning offering—a lamb of the *tamid*, its blood poured out, its flesh joined by flour kissed with oil and a libation that caught the first light, a daily plea for atonement as Mosheh's Law commanded. The echoes of the tribes' voices still hung in the valley—shouts of *Y'hi* that had shaken the earth, a chorus woven into the smoke that curled heavenward. We stood at the mountain's base, a nation forged anew, our hearts raw from the weight of the Law read aloud, our bodies weary from the labor of stone and the solemnity of service. The covenant renewal had been no mere ritual; it was a blade sharpened, a bond sealed in blood and fire, a reminder that we were not merely wanderers but the sword of the Almighty, called to carve His promise into the heart of Kena'an.

I stood among my kin, my cloak still dusted with the ash of the altar, the scent of incense clinging faintly to its folds. My eyes lifted to the slopes above, where Joshua had led us with solemn purpose to carve the words of Torah into the very bones of the mountain. Ebal and Gerizim stood like twin witnesses, their silence weightier than a thousand voices. The stones still shone with morning dew, as if creation itself had wept with joy. The night before had been a balm—laughter rising with the smoke of roasted lamb, children chasing sparks beneath the stars, songs echoing the names of Avraham and Mosheh. It was the celebration of covenant renewed, of tribes gathered not merely by blood, but by promise. Family and clan, stranger and native-born, all united beneath the wings of the

Almighty. And yet, even in joy, the coming day loomed. The time for feasting had passed. War now stirred beyond the hills.

Now, as the tribes were dispersed to their tents and clans, the camp buzzed with a restless energy, a murmur of purpose tempered by exhaustion. The children played among the stones, their laughter a fragile thread against the weight of what lay ahead.

The elders gathered in knots, their voices low, their gazes turning westward, where the hills of Kena'an rose like the spines of a slumbering beast, guarding the strongholds of the Anakim and their defiled kin.

The war council convened at midday, beneath a canopy of woven goat-hair stretched between acacia poles, its shadow a respite from the sun's unyielding gaze. Joshua, son of Nun, stood at the center, his face etched with the lines of a man who had carried a nation through decades of sand and fire. His eyes, sharp as flint, held a fire that no wilderness could quench, a faith forged in the shadow of Mosheh and tempered by the caves of Hebron. Beside him stood Eleazar, the high priest, his linen ephod gleaming, the Urim and Thummim at his breast a silent promise of Yahweh's guidance. Phineas, Eleazar's son, was there too, his staff steady, his zeal a flame that had once pierced the heart of rebellion at Peor his prayers would fight alongside us. Othniel, my kinsman from the Kenizzites, leaned against a spear, his youth belying the strength that would one day judge Israel.

We were a council bound by covenant, yet each carried scars—some of flesh, others of spirit—from the long road to this moment.

I took my place at Joshua's right, my heart heavy with the memory of Ai's fall, the black vapor of the shedim, the altar's flames that had consumed the innocent.

"Speak, men of Israel," he said, his gaze sweeping the scouts who stood before us, their cloaks stained with the dust of Kena'an's trails, "What word do you bring from the land?"

The lead scout, a wiry man of Benjamin named Zadok, stepped forward, his eyes darting as if the shadows of the hills followed him still, "The cities of Kena'an stir, my lord," he said, his voice low, taut with urgency, "From Gibeon to Shalem, from Lachish to Debir, the Kena'anim muster their strength. Their kings forge alliances, their forges burn day and night, crafting spears and shields. We heard whispers of the Anakim rousing in the south, their war drums echoing in the valleys of Hebron. They speak of blood-oaths, of altars fed with the lives of their young, of powers that answer their cries with fire and shadow."

A rustle of unease rippled through the council, and Phineas's hand closed like a trap, silent and sharp, his jaw set like stone. Othniel's eyes met mine, a silent question passing from him—could the nephilim's heirs withstand the God who had toppled Jericho, and Ai?

Eleazar's fingers brushed the ephod, his lips moving in silent prayer, seeking the Urim's light. I felt the weight of Zadok's words, a chill that echoed the shedim's hiss at Hebron, the priestess's plea at Ai. The Kena'anim were not mere men; their cities were strongholds of the watchers' brood, their rites a defiance of the Almighty, sealed in the blood of infants and the flesh of their kin. This was no war for land alone, but a clash of thrones, where the divine council's verdict met the serpent's rebellion.

Another scout, a man of Yitzhakhar named Eliab, spoke, his voice steadier but no less grave, "The people of Kena'an fear us, yet their fear drives them to madness. They have heard of Jericho's walls, crumbled by a shout, of Ai's gates consumed by fire. Their spies watch our camp, their runners carry tales of our numbers, our faith. But they trust in their giants, in their dark pacts, believing they will shield them from Yahweh's wrath."

Joshua's eyes narrowed, his hand resting on the hilt of his sword—the very blade that had struck down Ai's defenders. "They trust in lies," he said, his voice a low thunder. "The God who parted the Nehar ha-Yarden will break their altars, as He broke Egypt's gods. But we must be wise as serpents, steadfast as stone. Son of Jephunneh, my Chief—what counsel do you offer?"

He looked to me. A stillness held the circle—not the hush of fear, but the silence of men who knew the weight of coming war. The morning light filtered through the seams of the tent, cool and clear, touching the edge of Joshua's brow like a crown forged from the sun itself. No one spoke. Not yet.

He had grown into this—this quiet authority that did not need to be declared. It wasn't the sword at his side, nor the way men rose when he entered. It was something deeper, something hewn through trial. I remembered the first battle against Ai—the defeat, when the camp was sick with shame and our strength had turned to dust. Others blamed the spies, or the warriors, or even the silence of heaven. But Joshua... Joshua tore his robes and fell to the ground— not in display, but in longing. He had waited, not for men, but for God to speak.

And when the answer came—when the sin was exposed and burned from among us—he rose. Not with bitterness, but with determination. I remember the march back to Ai: the plan drawn like threads through a loom, each line tightened by his hand. The feint, the retreat, the stillness of his raised arm above the ridge—he held it aloft until the last defender fell. That day, the mantle passed. Not by ceremony, but by blood and fire.

Now he stood at the heart of our council, listening, commanding without a word. The man who once waited for Mosheh now gathered warriors and elders with a single glance.

I drew a breath to speak—but paused. Not from doubt, but from reverence. Let the others continue to speak. The morning carried enough weight without my hastening to fill it. With each passing year, I had come to know that true strength lies not in being first to speak,

196

but in waiting—listening deeply—and choosing to speak only when the hearts of the men are truly ready to hear.

Othniel was the first to break the silence, his voice edged with zeal, "Let us strike now, before their alliances harden. The Anakim are few, their cities scattered. We have Yahweh's promise—no gate shall stand before us."

Phineas shook his head. His tone was calm, but firm, "Wisdom bids us wait—to scout their movements, to test their strength. The Nephilim's power lies not in numbers, but in the darkness they call upon. We must seek Yahweh's voice before we march."

Eleazar lifted a hand, his eyes distant, as if peering into the unseen, "The Urim will guide us, but the heart of Israel must be pure. No sin, no hidden rebellion, can abide in our camp, lest we falter as we did at Ai. Let us seek the Almighty's face, that His will be clear."

I felt their words stir within me, a tension between action and patience, judgment and mercy. My thoughts turned to Rachav, the harlot of Jericho, whose faith had spared her house, an outsider woven into Israel's story. Was this not the mystery of Yahweh's heart —that even in Kena'an's shadow, grace could find a foothold? Yet the Anakim's crimes—children slain, flesh consumed in rites defiled— demanded justice, a verdict older than the flood. My Kenizzite blood, a whisper of their legacy, tugged at me, a reminder of the shedim's temptation, the priestess's cry. Could mercy ever extend to such as these, or was my blade called only to strike?

Finally, after all had spoken, I stepped forward. The eyes of warriors, elders, and priests turned to me—not as they would to Joshua, but still with weight. I was the last to speak, and so I bore the sum of their words within me. My voice came steady, though the storm beneath my ribs had not stilled.

"Yahweh has spared Edom, Moab, and the sons of Ammon— men of Adam's line, kin to us through the breath of the same dust. They are fallen, yes, but redeemable by grace. They bear the image, however marred. But the Anakim..." I let the name hang like ash in the air, "The Anakim are another matter."

Faces around me hardened, eyes narrowing at memories unspoken. "They are not simply enemies. They are the sons of rebellion, the heirs of the Nephilim—those who made league with the Watchers and drank deep of the poison in that ancient well. Their cities are thrones of defiance. Their altars, carved with blood and shadow, mock the Most High. Their priests call to things that crouch behind the veil, and the veil grows thin when they chant. You know it. You've felt it."

I saw Othniel's jaw tighten. Phineas, ever measured, gave a slight nod.

"But let us not forget Ai," I said, and my voice dropped low. "Let us remember how we stood amid the smoke of our own failure. It was not our sword that delivered us—it was the hand of the Lord. He revealed our hidden sin. He burned the rot from among us, and then—only then—He gave us victory. We do not war by numbers. We do not win by might. We follow the pillar and the flame. And we strike only when the Ark goes before us."

I paused, not for effect, but because the memory caught in my throat.

"We will scout, yes. We will pray. And we will sharpen every blade and bind every sandal. But we must not delay His purpose. When the trumpet sounds, we move. Not before. Not behind. But with Him. For it is not by our strength that we take the land, but by the word that thundered from Sinai and split the river's heart."

I let the silence breathe, the weight of the moment settling on every brow.

"We go not to slaughter the sons of Adam, nor to erase the children of Eve. This is not vengeance. This is not conquest. It is judgment. And we are not the judges—only the sword in Yahweh's hand. We wage war not against nations, but against a blight older than Babel, older than Mizraim. The seed of the watchers yet walks among the hills—the sons of Azazel, the cursed bloodlines that drink from the old defilements, who build altars of bone and feast on the flesh of innocence. Their cities reek of abomination. Their shadows fall long across the land. This is a holy war—not of man against man—but of light against what should not be."

I turned slowly, my eyes meeting those of the council one by one—Phineas with his brow set like stone, Othniel with fire yet forming in his thoughts, and Joshua, whose silence was the measure of every word.

"And yet," I said, my voice lowering, gentling as a stream finds the still waters, "we must also be ready—for mercy. Ready for the stranger who kneels before the Ark. Ready for the son of Anak who weeps before the Tabernacle. The God of Israel is mighty to save —even from the line of the Rephaim, even from the house of the serpent. I should know."

A hush fell—not from hesitation, but from the reckoning that comes when truth and mystery walk hand in hand,

"For Yahweh is no respecter of blood, or color, or past. He calls whom He calls. And when He calls, He makes new. He shatters chains. He severs legacies. He carves sons of dust into sons of promise."

I stepped back then. No one spoke. No one needed to. The stillness that followed was not silence—it was awe, and it bore the scent of holiness.

A breath passed through the tent—then the sound of feet, deliberate and firm, striking the earth like distant thunder. Some stamped once, others twice, a rhythm not rehearsed yet somehow ancient. The butt of a staff struck stone. Another followed. A low murmur rose, not of dissent but assent—deep, wordless, and full of weight. Heads bowed, jaws set, eyes met across the council ring. No cheers, no shouts. Just the solemn chorus of men who knew truth when they heard it and were steadied by its telling. The fire was not needed now; the heat came from within. In that moment, unity was not declared—it was felt.

I turned to look at Joshua, and he met my gaze and nodded—once, but it carried the weight of years. A silent affirmation passed between us, forged long ago beneath the oaks of Hebron, tested in the furnace of the wilderness, and tempered now in the nearing blaze of war. His eyes, steady as ever, held something deeper than approval. They held memory. Brotherhood. Covenant.

"Well spoken, Elder of Yehudah," he said at last, his voice neither loud nor soft, but steady—the kind of voice men followed into fire, "The words you have spoken bear the weight of truth, and the wisdom of one who has not only seen much, but endured much. You are not merely my chief in battle—you are my elder in faith."

He turned to the others, his mantle falling about his shoulders like a king's robe, though no crown adorned him but obedience.

"We will seek Yahweh's counsel," Joshua declared, his voice rising like the wind over the ridges, "but we will not shrink from the fight. The land is ours—not by spear or sword, not by cunning or strength—but by the Word of the Almighty, who rides upon the storm and speaks from fire."

A murmur of assent stirred among the circle. Phineas inclined his head, the tautness in his jaw now given over to grim resolve. Othniel's brow furrowed in thought, but he struck his spear against the earth once in quiet agreement. Eleazar, high priest and guardian of the Ark, lifted his hand in blessing, lips moving in silent prayer. Even the younger men—the runners, the shield bearers, the watchers at the gate—stood a little taller, as if the bones of their fathers stirred in their blood.

Then Joshua turned back to me, and his voice softened—not in weakness, but in grace, "And we will show mercy," he said, "to those who repent. Even to the seed of the Rephaim. Even to a creature such as giant who once defied heaven, if he should fall to his knees and turn his face toward the God of Avraham."

His gaze swept the council once more.

"Let it be known among our people: the sword is drawn, yes— but the hand that holds it longs to heal. The God who broke Egypt for our sake also spared Rachav the harlot for her faith. And He will not withhold redemption from any man—or beast—who turns from darkness and bends the knee before the Ark."

The war council dispersed like embers scattered from a fire, each man carrying a spark of purpose sharpened by the weight of the task ahead. The canopy's shadow lingered over us, a fleeting sanctuary as voices faded and footsteps stirred the dust. Eleazar adjusted his ephod, his eyes distant, as if the Urim whispered still. Othniel clasped Phineas's arm, their words low, a murmur of strategy and zeal.

I lingered a moment longer, my gaze meeting Joshua's across the circle of stools and spears. His face, weathered by wilderness and war, softened with a brother's warmth, not a commander's command,

"Kalev," he said, stepping close, his voice low, resonant with the timbre of Hebron's caves. "Your heart speaks what mine cannot always find words for. Yahweh has bound us, you and I, for this hour." His hand gripped my shoulder, not with the formality of a leader, but with the weight of a friend who had faced the shedim's shadow beside me.

I nodded, my throat tight with the honor of his trust. "Always, Joshua," I replied, my voice a vow. "For the God who delivered us, and for you."

He smiled, a rare flicker of light in his storm-gray eyes, then turned as Phineas approached, his spear gleaming. "Stay, Phineas," Joshua said. "The clans bring disputes—quarrels over flocks, boundaries, debts. We will judge as Yahweh commands, that no discord festers among us." Eleazar joined them, his presence a pillar of priestly authority, and I knew the day's burdens would fall to them, as judges in the stead of Mosheh. I slipped away unseen, craving one last breath of stillness before the clash of voices and the weight of judgment returned.

Chapter Eleven
The Scarlet Cord and the Sword

I stepped from the canopy into the early sunlight, the air crisp with the promise of a new day. The valley shimmered with the scattered homes of our clans, as if stars had fallen to rest— tents shifting in the breeze— their colors—crimson, indigo, ochre—vivid against the earth. The mingling scents of ash from morning fires, oil from polished shields, sweat from warriors' drills, and myrrh from the Levites' incense wove a song of life, of a people poised between covenant and conquest. The hum of voices rose, a chorus of purpose, as Israel prepared for the war that loomed like a storm over Kena'an's hills.

As I walked through the camp, the title Elder of Yehudah hung about me like a mantle, unasked yet undeniable. Many bowed to me as I passed, their eyes alight with respect, while children paused their games, small hands raised in mimicry of warriors' salutes. A young man of Gad, his face flushed with effort, recited Deuteronomy's words, his voice stumbling over a phrase. I paused, my hand resting lightly on his shoulder. "Shema Yisrael," I corrected gently, "not shama. The Lord our God is one." He flushed deeper, nodding, and I smiled, my heart warmed by the Torah carried on his tongue, as vital as the sword at my belt.

I walked past scribes copying the Law on parchment, their quills scratching like the whispers of Sinai, past mothers teaching their sons to knot slings, their hands steady, their voices firm with the courage of those who bore warriors. Levites tuned lyres, their strings humming psalms that would rise with the evening star. The camp was alive, a heartbeat of faith and readiness, yet beneath it pulsed a question—could we stand against the Anakim, whose altars reeked of blood and shadow?

I paused at a shaded tent near the camp's edge, drawn by the sound of laughter—bright, unguarded, a melody of children and a woman's voice. The flap parted, and Rachav emerged, transformed since Jericho's fall. Her indigo tunic, modest yet rich, a thread of red cord braided through her dark hair, a sign of a past redeemed, not forgotten. Her face, once taut with fear, now glowed with a peace that spoke of Yahweh's mercy. She was no longer the harlot of the wall, but a daughter of Israel, grafted into the covenant as surely as I, a Kenizzite, had been.

"Kalev!" Rachav called, her voice warm as the dawn, her arms opening as if to embrace a brother long absent, "Come, sit. The day is too fair for such a warrior's frown." Her laughter was a balm, a melody that softened the edges of war, and I stepped into the tent's shade. Nearby, her son Aram, sharpened a stick with a flint knife, his talk of crossing seas for spices and silks a trader's dream born of his mother's tales. Lirah, his sister, wove reeds into a basket, her fingers deft, her quiet song a whisper of Jericho's lost walls. Rachav's husband, Salmon of Yehudah, was absent, training scouts in the hills, a quiet man whose faith had seen beyond her past to the woman Yahweh had made her. They had only married a couple weeks prior, it was thought best to integrate Rachav into a clan immediately. Azubah, my wife, forged a bond between our families, a thread of grace woven into the chaos of war.

We sat beneath an olive tree, its branches heavy with unripe fruit, their green a promise of harvests yet to come. Rachav offered pomegranates and barley cakes, their sweetness a fleeting peace amid the camp's restless hum. Her eyes, sharp with memory, held mine, seeing past the warrior to the man who carried Hebron's shadow.

"You carry Hebron's weight still," she said, her voice soft but piercing, like a blade that cuts to heal. "I saw it in your eyes at Jericho —fear, yes, but faith stronger than stone. You have both, Kalev, yet the darkness gnaws at you."

I nodded, the shedim's hiss at Hebron, the priestess's cry at Ai, stirring within me like embers in a dying fire. "The Anakim haunt me," I admitted, my voice low, the words heavy with truth. "Their strength, their darkness. Their blood calls to mine, though I am Israel's now. Yet Yahweh has brought us this far."

Rachav leaned forward, her gaze steady as the hills, "The people of Kena'an do not fear your swords, Kalev, nor your numbers, nor even your giants' blood. They fear your God….." She paused, "my God" she said, each word slowly, as though merely saying it aloud was a delight too great to express.

She continued, "In Jericho, at night, men whispered His name —the God unknown, the God with no name—and their hearts quaked. Their gods—Baal, Moloch, Dagon—are hungry, never holy. They demand blood, flesh, the cries of the innocent, but they give no peace. Your God speaks, and walls fall. He breathes, and the shedim flee. I saw it, Kalev, when the scarlet cord hung in my window, when the earth shook and my city crumbled. I knew then that no power in Kena'an could stand against Him."

Her words struck deep, a prophetess's witness cloaked in a mother's voice, her Kena'ani past lending weight to her truth. "You were one of them," I said, my voice a question and a confession. "You knew their ways, their fears. How did you choose to trust the spies, to risk all for a God you did not know?"

She smiled, a flicker of sorrow and triumph. "I did not know Him, not as you do, not as your beloved wife Azubah teaches me. But I heard the tales—of a sea parted, of Egypt's gods broken, of a people led by fire and cloud. In Jericho, the priests of Baal burned children to appease their god, their screams a weight I carried in my dreams. I was a harlot, Kalev, bound to their world, yet my heart longed for something true. When you came I saw in your eyes a hope I had never known. I chose it, not for myself alone, but for Aram and Lirah, that they might live free of Moloch's shadow."

I glanced at Aram, his knife pausing as he listened, his young face marked by a cunning and a boy's wonder. Lirah's song faltered, her eyes on her mother.

"You are the clan of Yehudah now," I said, my voice thick with awe, I looked at the children, "All of you are, as I am, though my blood whispers of the nephilim."

Rachav's eyes softened, her fingers resting lightly on the red cord braided into her hair. "It was you, Kalev, who brought us together beneath the stars—one quiet evening as the camp settled after the day's toil. You saw the loneliness in my gaze, the weight I carried from Jericho's fall, and without ceremony, you led me to Azubah's tent. She welcomed me as if I had always belonged, sharing her firelight, her songs of Miriam, the prayers that bind us to Yahweh's covenant. Azubah did not ask of my past, only offered me a place beside her, a hand to hold when the memories became too much. I am Kena'ani by birth, yes, but Yahweh has made me His own, just as He made you. We are not so different—you and I—both outsiders called to carry His promise."

Her words stirred the memory of Hebron's shedim, its temptation to reclaim my Kenizzite heritage, and the priestess at Ai, her plea that I was Anakim still,

"The Kena'anim call me traitor," I said, my voice low, "as they once called you. Their gods—their rites—sicken me, yet their blood runs in my veins. How do you bear it, Rachav, knowing what you were, what you might have been?"

She reached across, her hand resting lightly on mine, a gesture of kinship, "I bear it because Yahweh's mercy is wider than our past. In Jericho, I was nothing—a woman of the wall, despised yet used. But He saw me, Kalev, as He saw you, a Kenizzite among Yehudah's sons. The Anakim's rites—children slain, flesh consumed—are a mockery of His holiness, but they cannot claim you unless you let them. You fight not against your blood, but for the God who redeems it. Trust Him, as I did when I hung the cord, when I stepped from ruin into Israel's camp."

I exhaled, her words a lantern in the fog of doubt. My thoughts turned, drawn away to the war council I'd just left,

"You know this land better than many," I said, watching the firelight catch the amber in her eyes. "What of the cities stirring in the hills—Lachish, Debir... Gibeon? What do you know of them?"

Rachav's gaze sharpened, her Kena'ani past rising like a blade drawn from water. She had heard many things in Jericho—from the lips of traders who lingered too long, whose stories were murmured in the dark of her room, tangled with breath and lies. It was a past she did not always care to recall. She did not answer at once,

"Lachish is proud. Debir hungers for vengeance. But Gibeon..." she paused, tasting the name like something bitter. "Gibeon is not cruel—but they are clever. Traders. Word-weavers. They fear death more than they cherish truth. In Jericho, their merchants came often—smiling, flattering, never meaning half of what they said. Their bargains were soft on the tongue and sharp in the hand. If they come to you, Kalev, they will not come with swords drawn. They will come wrapped in humility, speaking peace. But beneath the olive branch, they will hide a net."

I nodded my thanks, then paused at the tent's entrance, the words I meant to speak caught between gratitude and the quiet press of something heavier. In so short a time, she had become dear to Azubah and me—a friend not born of years, but of fire and trust.

As the moment stretched between us, she filled the space with gentle words, her hand touched her belly, a protective gesture, "I have not even told Salmon yet but I believe I am with child," she said, her voice tender but sure, "I know it will be a boy."

I met her gaze not sure what to say, but a smile on my face expressed my joy at all God had done for her, and all the promises that awaited. Her eyes brightened, and a faint smile touched her lips, "Yes," she whispered, "it will be a boy, and I will name him Boaz"

I waited for her to speak, "Boaz means strength—sure and steadfast. A place of refuge. It is like the mighty oak that shelters those who seek shade, the rock that stands unyielding against the storm" she said.

She paused, her fingers tracing invisible patterns on her womb, "In this harsh land, I pray he will be a refuge to the weary, a man whose feet are firmly planted even when the winds rage. A name that carries hope."

I nodded slowly, the weight of her prayer sinking deep into my heart. "A fitting name," I said. "May Yahweh grant him such strength—and more."

The irony was not lost on me—that from the harlot of Jericho, from the very city whose walls had fallen before our God, would come a son whose name meant steadfast refuge.

"Do you fear for him?" I asked quietly, my gaze steady on her two other children playing nearby, "In these times, a child of promise is also a child of danger."

Her eyes darkened, the flicker of past shadows crossing her face. "I do. Every day. But the God of Israel is a shield to the broken, a sword to the unjust. He has called me away from death and despair into this strange new life. I trust His hand will protect Boaz, just as He protected me. And I trust in you, Kalev—your strength, your honor. He will need men like you when he walks the earth."

I swallowed hard, touched by her faith and courage. "He will have women like you too," I said softly, "women whose prayers rise like incense before the throne. Azubah, you, and all who have trust in Yahweh—your legacy will shape this land long after we are gone."

A quiet settled between us, a fragile peace woven through the tent's air. Then she looked up, her gaze sharp but kind. "Tell me, Kalev, how does your heart carry the burden of this war? You have seen so much, borne the weight of command. Does your spirit grow weary?"

I considered her question, the distant echoes of battle drumming in my veins. "There are moments," I admitted, "when the night feels endless, when the faces of the fallen haunt the silence. But then I remember why we fight—not for conquest, but for a promise older than the stones beneath our feet. For a future where children like Boaz can grow without fear. That gives me strength."

She nodded, reaching out to squeeze my hand. "We carry that promise together. The Lord is binding unlikely threads into something enduring—giants and harlots, warriors and women, all drawn by His covenant."

Then she added, almost as an afterthought, yet with a spark in her eye, "And this child within me... I don't know why, Kalev, but I feel there will be something in him that echoes long after we are gone. Perhaps through him, someone great will rise."

I felt a surge of hope, the burden lighter somehow. "I will guard that hope," I promised. "For you, for Azubah, for all of the Twelve Clans."

Her smile was soft but fierce. "And I will pray for the day when Boaz can stand among your warriors, not as a child of shadow, but as a beacon of the covenant's mercy."

As I stepped back toward the council's hall, the image of that name—Boaz—lingered in my mind. Strength. Refuge. A promise whispered into the night, carried on the breath of a mother's hope, destined to root deep in the soil of this land.

Chapter Twelve
The Weighing of Words

The sun arched toward its zenith as I retraced my steps to the war council's canopy, its light weaving through the dust of the camp's ceaseless pulse. Rachav's words—Boaz, a refuge—burned in my chest, a flame of hope tempered by caution.

Beneath the canopy, the air was heavy with the echo of judgment. Joshua sat at the center, his face carved with the weariness of a man who had sifted the clans' disputes—flocks strayed, debts disputed, a widow's plea for justice. Eleazar stood beside him, his ephod's gems catching the light, the Urim and Thummim silent after the morning's deliberations. Othniel gripped his spear, his eyes fierce, his zeal a fire unquenched by hours of debate. Phineas, leaned on his staff, his young face thoughtful, as if tracing the threads of Yahweh's will. The elders of Reuven, Gad, and Manasseh lingered, their voices low, their hands clasped in weary accord.

Joshua rose as I entered, his storm-gray eyes lifting from the earth to meet mine with a brother's warmth. His mouth pulled into something between a smirk and a sigh. "Kalev," he said, his voice resonant, carrying the weight of Hebron's caves, "I gave you the morning. I hoped the silence might give you strength again. But I see by your eyes that it gave you more than that."

I said nothing of Rachav, nor of the quiet moment between walls not my own. But he saw it, as he always did, as if we shared the same breath.

"I knew you'd return before the sun reached its peak," Joshua continued. "Even giants need rest. But the quarrels of the clans wait for no one. Come—your counsel is needed now, great Elder of Yehudah."

He placed a hand on my arm—not in reproach, but in recognition. That silent language forged between wilderness and war, where words failed but trust endured.

I sighed inwardly, my jaw tightening as I took my place beside Joshua. His eyes told me all—no rest since the smoke of Ai cleared, no peace since the trumpet blast that felled the ramparts. The blade may have slept, but the burdens of judgment did not.

The first dispute was already upon us before I could draw breath. A man from Zebulun rose, his tunic torn at the collar in a show of grief, though his eyes flashed more with spite than sorrow. "My ox was taken by Reuven's herdsmen," he barked. "It was yoked to my cart before dawn and gone by midday. Witnesses saw it driven toward the Wadi Fara"

From across the gathering, a Reuvenite elder stood, arms crossed, unimpressed. "Lies. The beast wandered and your tongue worse."

Joshua raised his hand, and both men fell silent. I studied the Zebulunite's face—grimy with travel, streaked with dust and self-righteous fire—and the Reuvenite, calm but coiled like a resting viper. A shepherd's quarrel. A man's pride wounded more than his flock. Yet we sat here, judges of such things, hours into the weight of it.

"Do you have proof, its neckband perhaps?" I asked. "Or witness of its yoke when last seen?"

The man hesitated, fumbling with a scrap of leather—a faint mark burned into it, the sigil of his house. It was not conclusive. The Reuvenite spat into the dust.

Phineas shifted beside me, muttering under his breath. "We slay kings and dash idols, and now we arbitrate oxen."

Eleazar leaned toward Joshua. "Shall I cast the Urim?"

Joshua nodded wearily. "Do so. Let Yahweh's judgment speak."

Eleazar reached into his breastplate and cast the Urim, his eyes intent—yet no light shone, no answer came. He sighed, lowering his hand.

Joshua's voice was steady but tinged with gravity. "No word today. Let justice be judged by eyes of flesh and hearts of men."

So we judged. The ox was returned, but the Zebulunite was fined a measure of grain for slander. He grumbled, but withdrew. The Reuvenite bowed, but the satisfaction on his face soured my stomach.

Then came two women—both from Benjamin, both veiled, both trembling with fervor. One clutched a bronze amulet, its surface etched with a tribal blessing, its cord frayed from generations of hands, while the other accused her of stealing it from her tent during the night, claiming it as her family's sacred heirloom.

"Her brother fell in the first battle of Ai," the accuser hissed, her voice sharp as a flint blade. "She has no kin left to claim it. She took it from my hearth, where it hung as my father's legacy, a blessing for our line!"

"She lies!" the other cried, her hands tightening around the amulet, her eyes blazing beneath her veil. "My mother passed it to me before Ai's fire, a token of Yahweh's mercy to our house. This widow covets what was entrusted to my care!"

The amulet gleamed faintly in the tent's dim light, its inscription—a prayer for protection, carved in the script of the wilderness—seeming to pulse with the weight of their words. Joshua closed his eyes, the toll of these disputes drawing lines across his face like the scars of Kena'an's hills. I remembered the stones at Ai—the burnt gate, the twisted remains of altars, the silent witness of blood spilled when Achan's sin brought defeat. How strange that such fire should be followed by this—a clash of bronze and blessing, honor turned to litigation in the shadow of covenant renewal.

I took a step forward, my voice low but firm, "Show the amulet." A Levite obeyed, taking it gently from the woman's grasp and holding it aloft, its cord swaying like a pendulum in the council's gaze.

The elders leaned closer, their murmurs a ripple of curiosity, their eyes tracing the artifact's worn edges. Phineas's staff shifted, his zeal tempered by the weight of judgment, while Othniel, my kinsman, studied the amulet with a furrowed brow, as if seeking truth in its ancient lines. Eleazar, the high priest, brushed his ephod, his lips moving silently, perhaps invoking the Urim's light, though no divine word came.

"Speak your claims plainly," Joshua said, his voice weary yet steady, a commander sifting truth from passion. "This amulet is no mere trinket—it bears a blessing, a mark of covenant. Who has the right to it?"

The accuser stepped forward, her veil trembling with her breath. "My father carved it in the wilderness, when Mosheh led us under the cloud. It was his, passed to my brother, who bore it into Ai's first battle. He fell there, struck down when Yahweh turned from us. I am his last kin, and it is mine by right. She stole it, thinking none would challenge a widow's greed!"

The other woman's voice rose, sharp with defiance. "Her brother's death is no claim! My mother, a daughter of Benjamin, received it from her father, who blessed our house with it before we crossed the Yarden. She gave it to me before Ai burned, a sign of Yahweh's favor restored. This woman's grief has twisted her mind—she sees my treasure and calls it hers!"

The council stirred, voices clashing like bronze in a forge. I felt the weight of their words, the amulet a symbol of more than inheritance—of identity, of survival in a land where the Anakim's shadow loomed. My Kenizzite blood stirred, a whisper of the giant clans, yet I was Yehudah's kin, bound by the same covenant these women claimed. Their dispute, though small, mirrored the greater war—truth against deceit, faith against doubt.

214

I lifted a hand, silencing the murmurs, "Describe the amulet's blessing," I said, my gaze shifting between them. "If it is yours, you will know its words."

The accuser hesitated, her eyes darting. "It speaks of... protection," she said, her voice faltering. "Of Yahweh's shield over His people."

The other woman stepped forward, her voice steady, though her hands trembled. "It reads, 'May Yahweh, the God of Israel, guard this house as He guarded the ark through the wilderness, a light in the shadow of His wings.' I learned it at my mother's knee, as she prayed for our kin."

A hush fell, the council's eyes on the amulet, its script too worn to read in the dim light, yet her words carried the cadence of truth. Phineas's staff stilled, his gaze softening, while Othniel nodded, his fingers tracing the air as if to etch her words.

Eleazar's eyes met Joshua's, a silent accord passing between them. Joshua rose, his presence a pillar, his voice resonant with the authority of Ebal's altar.

"The blessing is known to her who spoke it," he said. "Yet let us test further. Who among your kin can vouch for your claim?"

The accuser's veil fluttered, her voice thin. "My cousin, of Benjamin, knows my father's hand. He is in the camp, tending flocks."

The other woman straightened, her eyes bright with conviction. "My aunt, who crossed the Yarden with us, saw my mother place it in my hands. She is among the weavers, near the Levites' tents."

I glanced at Joshua, my heart stirred by the second woman's clarity, yet wary of haste. "Summon them," I said to the Levite, who nodded and hastened from the tent.

The council waited, the air thick with the scent of myrrh and the weight of judgment. I thought of Rachav, her scarlet cord, her faith that had woven her into Israel's story. This amulet, like her, was a sign of covenant, a thread of grace in a land of war. Yet Ai's first defeat, when Achan's greed brought death, lingered in my mind—a warning against trusting too swiftly.

The Levite returned, followed by two figures: a man of Benjamin, his face weathered, and an older woman, her hands stained with dye. The man spoke first, his voice halting. "I knew her father's work," he said of the accuser, "but I never saw the amulet in his hands. He spoke of it, but it was lost before Ai."

The woman stepped forward, her gaze steady on the second claimant. "I saw my sister give it to her daughter," she said, her voice firm. "Before Ai's fire, she prayed its blessing over her, a shield for our house."

Joshua's eyes met mine, a silent accord. "The amulet is hers who knows its words and whose kin bears witness," he said, his voice carrying the weight of justice. "Return it to her, and let no strife linger in Benjamin's tents."

The second woman took the amulet, her hands trembling, her veil hiding tears. The accuser's shoulders slumped, her rage spent, and she turned away, guided by an elder's hand. The council exhaled, the dispute resolved, yet the weight of judgment lingered, a reminder of the fragility of truth in a people poised for war.

I stepped back, my thoughts drifting to the Anakim, their altars defiled by blood, their shedim a shadow that tested our covenant. As the council prepared to move to matters of war, I felt the amulet's echo in my soul—a blessing of protection, a call to stand firm, as Yehudah's kin, against the darkness that awaited us in Kena'an's heart.

The council sighed as the women were led away, and Eleazar whispered a prayer for peace. I sheathed my blade, the cold weight of it resting again at my side, but my soul felt heavier still.

More came—arguments over disputed fields, water poisoned by runoff from careless flocks, a stolen garment that turned out to be traded twice and never returned, a boy wounded in play now limping and his father seeking silver.

On and on they came. We had crossed the Nehar ha-Yarden to tear down giants, yet now it was these smaller trials—petty wounds, jealous neighbors, bitter envy—that pressed hardest upon us.

The sun, cruel and relentless, was now dim and faded. Joshua, his shoulders stooped with each case, the joy of conquest replaced by the wear of governance.

Othniel's voice, young but grave, broke into my thoughts, "It is like shepherding goats with one staff and no dog." I turned toward him, the firelight catching the hard angles of his face—still more youth than man, yet already bearing the quiet determination of seasoned years. His dark eyes held little mirth, only the steady flame of one who had watched too many fall in battle to ever speak lightly. Broad-shouldered and lean, he wore his father's blade at his side though it was nearly as long as his leg. Among the sons of Kenaz, he had been first into the breach at Jericho, and I had seen him lift a wounded brother onto his back while still striking down an Amorite with the haft of his spear. There was no jest in him, no flourish—only a burning obedience to Yahweh and a loyalty to Joshua that clung like sinew to bone. He spoke little, but when he did, the elders listened.

Joshua offered a dry smile. "No fire from heaven for false witness. No earth to swallow deceit. Only us."

Though it was late, the line still wound like a dry serpent across the clearing, each petitioner a node of grievance, pride, or desperation. The sun sagged westward, casting a burnt-orange hue on the canopy above us. Joshua, his voice rough with fatigue, raised a hand. "Only one more today," he said. "Let the rest return tomorrow."

The people groaned, but none dared argue. We were all weary. Was it truly just three days ago that we were felling giants at Ai, fire and bronze flashing beneath Yahweh's thunder? Now here we sat, not with swords but with questions, not with warriors but with the endless, petty unraveling of life.

The final petitioners stepped forward—two men from the tribe of Benjamin, both sun-darkened and bruised, the kind of bruises not earned in battle. Their tunics still bore the grime of Ai's ash. One clutched a shattered helm; the other, a length of costly dyed linen, folded like an accusation.

"The spoils were divided unfairly," the first man spat before being asked. "He kept more than was his portion. The robe was taken from the eastern gate—it was marked for my tent."

"I bled for it as much as you," the second snapped. "And you took two shields and the silver weight besides."

Joshua did not rise, nor did he flinch. He had heard ten versions of this same quarrel today—land boundaries, lost sheep, failed betrothals. But something in his eyes flared with righteous exhaustion. "What says the record?" he asked.

A Levite stepped forward with the list—items taken, names tallied beside them in careful charcoal lines. "Both were granted share," he said, "but the robe was not clearly assigned."

I studied the robe. Fine weave. Dyed in Tyrian purple. It was the kind of spoil that once tempted Achan to sin and brought Israel to its knees. Joshua's gaze flicked to mine.

I rose and stepped down from the platform, standing between the two men. "You speak as if this cloth gives you honor," I said, holding the robe. "But it is stained already—with pride and quarrel."

The first man clenched his fists. "Then let it be burned."

"No," said the second, more softly now. "Let it be given to the tabernacle."

I turned to Joshua. "Let it be done."

Joshua nodded. "The robe shall go to the house of the Lord, and both of you shall return to your tents with what remains of your dignity. Should you quarrel again, you will answer not only to us, but to the assembly of Israel."

The two men bowed stiffly and departed in opposite directions, their feet dragging.

Silence followed, as it had so many times before. That silence —the one not of peace, but of drained spirits.

Joshua leaned back, closing his eyes for a moment, "Ai was simpler," he muttered.

I sank down beside him, shoulder to shoulder, our cloaks dusted with the day's grievances. "Giants fall easier than men's greed," I said. "At least giants fall only once."

He exhaled, slow and bitter. "These disputes—they don't end. The people dream of milk and honey but choke on envy and offense."

Outside the canopy, a child's laugh rang out, thin and far away, carried on the evening wind like a forgotten song.

"I slipped away this morning," I admitted, brushing grit from my knees. "I couldn't face it again. The noise. The bickering. You let me rest, but I used it to vanish."

Joshua didn't open his eyes. "You went to Rachav's house?"

I hesitated, then nodded. "Yes."

"She has peace in her walls," he said. "More than in the tents of many elders."

We were quiet a long time.

"And now," I said, "Yahweh has brought me back."

Joshua smiled faintly, a tired crescent etched beneath his beard. "To remind you that the real battle is not with fire or bronze— but with hearts we are sworn to shepherd."

I stared at the dust beneath our feet. "Sometimes I envy the stones of Hebron. They do not argue. They do not forget their place."

He turned to me then, eyes rimmed red with weariness, but still burning with that strange, holy fervor. "Would you return there, Kalev? To the land of Hebron, where you faced the caves?"

219

I thought of Azubah. Of the hush before Jericho's horns. Of the simple prayer before war, when hope was uncluttered by compromise.

"One day I will come to you, and ask my inheritance, and it will be Hebron; the place where the shedim and Nephilim lurk, I will redeem the land in the name of God," I said.

He smiled, just once, and then said "Your name will live on forever brother."

The stars had kindled high above, pale fires scattered across the deepening violet of heaven. The last of the petitioners had been sent away, leaving the judgment canopy creaking faintly in the breeze, empty as a molted shell. The dust beneath our feet felt heavy, like the very weight of decision had settled into the soil.

From the hill's edge, a scout approached with quick, eager steps. His hair was dust-laced, and the folds of his cloak fluttered like a tattered banner. He bowed low before Joshua.

"Men from the west," he said. "Cloaked in travel and mystery. They speak peace, bring dry bread, wineskins cracked with sun. Say they've come from afar."

Joshua did not answer at once. He looked to me, and I saw it in his face—the fatigue of a man who had measured too many lies in a single day.

"Let them pitch their camp beyond the outer fires," Joshua said at last, his voice low but steady. "Past the last banners of Reuven. They can shelter beneath the tamarisks near the southern road."

The scout nodded, already turning.

"And post two watches through the night," Joshua added. "Quiet men with clear eyes."

The scout's head bobbed again. Then he vanished into the descending dark like a jackal in dusk.

Beside me, Phineas stretched with a groan and tapped the butt of his staff against the ground, "I swear even Yahweh's signs have grown quiet—like He's giving us space to argue ourselves to death."

"You didn't ask Him," I said with a half-smile.

He grunted. "And neither did you."

Joshua reached for the wineskin hanging from a bronze hook near his seat,

"We've judged a hundred disputes today," he said. "The sort of grievances that grind the soul down like river stones. Tonight... we drink."

And so we did.

Not in excess, at least not at first—just a few draughts beneath the canopy, passed between us like a covenant older than Sinai. But the wine warmed us, dulled the aches in our joints, and stirred a fleeting laugh from each of us as the weight of our roles slipped, if only for a little while. Yet the night's laughter would soon turn to reckoning, its cost heavier than we dared imagine.

Chapter Thirteen
Laughter Before the Storm

The heat of the day had long passed, but the chieftain's tent still bore the scent of sweat, leather, and dust. Oil lamps flickered in copper sconces, casting long shadows on the hide walls, while woven rugs softened the packed earth beneath our feet. Outside, the sounds of children playing and the occasional call of a sentry floated in on the wind. Within, the world slowed. The day's judgments had ended, and the burdens of the people—for the moment—were pushed to the edge of the tent, like cloaks shrugged off.

Servants moved deftly between us, replenishing the platters of roasted lamb, lentils with cumin, and freshly torn barley bread. Copper pitchers of watered wine made slow rounds from hand to hand. Beautiful decorated clay jars and plates from Caphtor littered the table set before us. The scent of figs and sesame oil hung in the air. Clay vessels filled with almonds and pistachios were passed around.

Joshua reclined against a cushion of dark-dyed wool, his leather armor unbuckled and pushed aside. A young servant girl washed his feet in a shallow bronze basin, and another draped a light linen over his shoulders.

He raised his cup, half-laughing, half-weary, "There are near thirty thousand tents out there," he said, voice roughened by wine and judgment. "Maybe more, if you count the children. All of them looking to one man to judge between them, to lead them through wilderness and battle, to keep them fed, to keep them holy."

"Thirty thousand is conservative," muttered Phineas, picking at the charred ribs of a lamb shank. "Yehudah alone brought near six thousand men of fighting age. And none of them quiet."

"They make war like lions," I said, "but settle arguments like jackals snarling over bones."

A ripple of laughter moved around the cushions. These were men who'd once cut through the ranks of Kena'ani battle axes—now worn thin from hours arbitrating over grazing land, spilled grain, and wounded pride. The people had peace, but not rest.

Joshua turned to me, his face caught in the flickering lamplight. "And we—you and I—we were made for blood and stone, Kalev. You think I ever imagined I would sit beneath a canopy of goat-hide and argue over cooking fires and tent-ropes?"

"You led us in battle against Ai" I said

He grunted. "I did. And I still remember the weight of it. But this—this is heavier."

Othniel's voice cut through the hum of the gathering, "It is like leading blind lambs through thorn and bramble".

The men laughed again, and I turned to study him. He was young—his beard barely full, but his bearing steady. His eyes were too old for his face, and his words struck true more often than not. Already the other elders glanced his way in silence. He had the bearing of a judge and the heart of a warrior—Yahweh willing, he would carry on what we had begun.

Then, the tent flap stirred. In stepped Tirzah, Joshua's wife, her hair plaited in silver-threaded cords. Her cloak was dyed the deep blue of Ephraim's banners, but her face bore the warmth of a woman who had waited long to see her husband home. Beside her was my Azubah, wrapped in a crimson shawl from the spoils of Ai, her eyes finding mine as surely as if we were alone.

The room shifted subtly as the rhythm of the evening changed. The servants, attuned to the unspoken cues of their masters, bowed low and withdrew to the edges of the tent like the tide pulling back from shore. The light from the oil lamps caught in the bronze bangles on their wrists, flickering like stars along the hem of the night. Dishes were cleared, fresh dates and spiced almonds laid out, and more wine was brought—not quite as strong this time, yet still potent, poured from long-necked vessels cooled in damp cloth.

A space was made beside Joshua, and Tirzah entered with the poise of a queen returning to her court. Her headscarf, pinned in place with silver clasps was loosed, her hair fell back from her shoulders like a banner long loosed in the wind, revealing thick black hair bound in braids that gleamed with oil and perfume. She folded her legs beneath her with quiet ease, her hand reaching to rest on Joshua's, and the taut lines of his brow softened the moment their fingers met.

"You found us deep in folly," he murmured, his voice loosening with the warmth of wine and woman.

Tirzah smiled, eyes knowing and steady. "I found you among men pretending not to miss their wives."

He laughed, a full-throated, unguarded sound, free of judgment and command. "Guilty, then."

Across the low table, Azubah had entered like a flame drawn toward her hearth. Her dark eyes sparkled beneath the lamp-glow, her cheeks still warm from the day's sun, and she wore a robe of Ai silk, the color of deep wine. She settled beside me, and the touch of her thigh against mine was more grounding than the skin of wine I had drained.

"So even the mighty need comfort?" she teased, her voice low, brushing my arm with her fingers.

I kissed her hand, letting it rest against my beard, "Especially the mighty," I said.
"Today I would have traded Ai's stones and towers for one hour of peace."

"Even your stones weep without me," she murmured, and I laughed—not out of mirth, but relief. Azubah had always known how to say the truth plainly and make it feel like honey.

The wives joined the circle as naturally as flame joins wick. Fresh pitchers were brought, and the wine grew darker, richer, laced with dried figs. Bread passed from hand to hand, this time with sliced pomegranate, sweet melon, and a wheel of goat cheese so soft it nearly wept. The tension that had clung to our shoulders all day melted into something looser, more human. Our words turned toward familiar ground—children, old stories, the silly habits of tribesmen, the smell of the Yarden's edge in spring.

Joshua reclined, his arm slipping around Tirzah's waist, and rested his head against her temple. "This," he said softly, "this is what I miss in the thick of war."

Tirzah stroked his forearm with her fingers, and I saw the corners of his mouth twitch into a smile he would never show his captains, "You are too long among the tents of men," she said. "You forget what the heart fights for."

On my other side, Azubah took a jug from a servant and refilled my cup, then brushed a stray crumb from my lip with her thumb. She smiled, eyes glinting with mischief. "And the great Kalev, whose hair twists like the ancient roots of the cedars—few among all Israel bear such a crown. You should be grateful for the hours I spend weaving each strand with care."

I caught her wrist and kissed the inside of it, tasting the perfume she'd crushed from lilies, "I do," I said. "More than I dare admit." While others bore hair like the windswept strands of the desert—straight and fleeting—mine wove a story in every coil, a living testament to the sun scorched earth from which I came, stubborn as the ancient cedars that stand unbowed through centuries of storm.

Joshua raised his cup, its rim wet with pomegranate wine, and looked toward the edge of the tent where the servants lingered in silence.

"Bring the singer," he said, voice low but firm. "Let him come and remind us of the day."

A boy slipped away, and moments later returned with a man whose beard was streaked with red and gray, his garments plain, his sandals caked in dust. He carried no lyre. He needed none. His voice had once stirred battle lines. Now it stirred the hearts of the weary.

He bowed low before the elders, before the women, before the Lord's anointed.

"What shall I sing, my lord?" he asked, eyes lowered.

Joshua looked across the company, "Sing of Ai. Sing of the God who split stone and smoke. Of the fire that fell from behind. Sing of giants defeated and covenants remembered."

The singer nodded. He stepped into the center of the circle, where firelight carved his shadow across the rugs, and he raised his head. No instrument needed tuning. No throat needed clearing. His voice came like the breath of the hills at sunrise—rough, holy, filled with dust and wind,

Ai Nafla
(Ai Has Fallen)

"Ai, O Ai, be silent now—
For your gates have fallen like Rephaim!
Your zera is scattered to the four winds,
And your elohim lie broken beneath sandal and flame.
Your king is buried beneath a pile of stones.
El Elyon is our strength—
Yahweh Tzevaot is His Name!
He is a man of war,
His Ruach goes before the anashim of Israel.
From Shittim we rose like the morning mist,
Quiet as the fox, swift as the deer upon Eretz Kena'an.
Yehoshua, son of Nun, bore the rod,
And Kalev ben Yefunneh, the Kena'ani of Hebron,

His face dark as oiled bronze, eyes like sharpened flint—
He strode among us, his voice thunder, his arm sword.
Othniel, child of lion-hearted blood,
Ran like flame through the alleyways of Ai.
His spear struck true—
Not once, but sevenfold.
And Phineas, son of Eleazar the kohen,
Cast down the idols of Dagon and Ba'al.
He poured their stolen oil upon the ground
And anointed it with fire.
Hear, O Israel!
The giants of Anak fell like trees before the axe.
Not by strength of arm,
But by the outstretched hand of HaKadosh Baruch Hu.
Barukh atah, Adonai Eloheinu,
Who gives the land to His people.
We crossed the Yarden on dry ground.
We circled Yericho with ram's horns and faith.
And now Ai is ashes beneath our feet.
Let the elders rejoice.
The Spear of the Twelve Clans leads us,
Let the women strike the tof and sing!
Let the children remember this day,
For Yahweh has done wonders again in our sight.
Not for our righteousness—no,
But for the covenant of Avraham, Yitzhak, and Yaakov.
Ai boasted high walls and thick gates.
But Yahweh whispered once—and they were no more.
Blessed be the Name who cuts down the mighty,
Who lifts the humble from the dust!
So write this song on a scroll,
Teach it to your sons and daughters—

That they may never forget the fire,

Nor the mercy that walks with the sword."

Silence followed. Not because the song was done, but because it lingered. The fire crackled, the cups were stilled in hand, and I felt Azubah press closer, her breath shallow with awe.

Joshua did not move at first. Then he nodded, solemn as a priest.

"You have sung well," he said. "Go. Eat. Drink."

The singer bowed once more and backed into the shadows, and slowly—one by one—cups were raised again, bread was broken again, and laughter returned like a tide that had remembered its shore.

A chuckle came from the shadows—Othniel, seated further back, his cup in one hand, the other resting over the curve of his knee. "If I stay here much longer, I'll be ruined for the battlefield," he said, grinning. "They'll call me the Poet of Yehudah."

"Better that than the Bachelor of Yehudah," Azubah quipped, earning a burst of laughter from Tirzah and even Joshua.

"Don't tease him," I said, raising a brow. "He'll go find himself a wife just to spite you."

"Then may he find one with a tongue as sharp as mine," said Azubah, lifting her cup. "To keep him from drinking too deep."

"I heard that," came a voice from the side curtain. Tirzah's younger sister, Haggith, peeked in, balancing a tray with more cups and dried figs. Her laughter rang like a harp-string, and even Phineas grinned as she poured him a drink and bowed playfully low.

Phineas had been quiet most of the night, but now he leaned back, cradling his wine as if it were a sacred vessel. His eyes were bright and alive, softened just enough by the drink, "This is the table I defend," he said. "This. Not the altar alone. Not the scrolls or the flame. But this—bread, laughter, women, peace."

"Well spoken," said Joshua, raising his cup.

Tirzah nestled against him, "He remembers now."

We drank to peace—not as a theory, not as a covenant carved in stone, but as a moment. As a breath. As wives sitting close enough to catch the scent of your skin after battle, as the ache in your back that finally lifts when she presses a hand to it without asking.

Othniel sighed. "How does one go back to spear and sword after this?"

"Slowly," I said, finishing the last of my cup. "And with regret."

Azubah laid her head on my shoulder, her hair spilling like black silk down my tunic. Her headscarf having fallen off many drinks prior, "Then don't go yet."

"I won't," I whispered. "Not yet."

Azubah's fingers found mine and laced them together, her thumb brushing the scar across my knuckle—the one from the wilderness, where I'd split an Amalekites helm but lost a piece of myself in the process. "You keep that same look," she said.

"What look?"

"The one you had when you came down from the hills after your father died. Like you're half here, half somewhere far off."

I smiled against the rim of my cup. "That's because I am. Part of me never left the ridge where I first looked out over the land Yahweh promised."

"And the rest?"

I turned to her fully, letting the wine and her eyes blur out everything else. "The rest is here. Where your voice is."

Azubah was not a woman who blushed easily, nor did she waste words on flattery. She was the kind who noticed when a servant's hands were cracked from labor or when a horse limped slightly in its gait. She kept jars of oil steeped with myrrh and cedar, and she lit them only on nights when the old battles pressed too close to my bones. Her black hair, usually bound tight against the world like a guarded secret, tonight spilled free—dark as the desert's velvet night—offering a rare grace to those who watched in quiet wonder." There was a scar behind her left ear—she never told me how she got it —but tonight, the wine had made her soft, and I traced it with a touch.

"Don't," she said, though she didn't pull away. "You'll make me cry, and I told myself I wouldn't cry tonight."

"And why tonight?"

Because this is a rare night you haven't gone to sleep reeking of war and reckoning".

We laughed then, full-bodied and shameless, and Joshua raised his cup to us with a smirk. "If Kalev keeps pouring that fig wine, I'll be the one weeping."

"It's not the wine," Tirzah said, leaning across him to claim the next slice of melon. "It's the years catching up to you, my love."

"They caught me years ago," he said, laughing. "I've just been too stubborn to admit it."

The room had become something more than a feast now— something familial, ancient. A woman at the edge of the tent began to hum, a tune that felt older than any one tribe, and soon Haggith joined her, singing softly while she filled our cups yet again.

Othniel, still clinging to the edge of boyhood, leaned back with his arms folded behind his head, wine staining the hem of his sleeve. "If I ever take a wife," he said, grinning, "I hope she mocks me as well as yours mock you."

"You'll be lucky if she doesn't beat you with a broom," Azubah quipped.

"You say that like it hasn't happened already," Haggith said, tossing him a wink.

Even Phineas chuckled at that, though he'd been silent for nearly a quarter hour. He was nestled beside the flame, legs folded beneath him, his cup empty on the mat. He watched us with a kind of affection, as though we were younger siblings playing at life.

The wine thickened in our blood. Tirzah stood and returned with a clay jar of date liquor—a rare gift from a caravan that had passed near months ago—and poured it with care. We drank again, and again, and laughter began to stumble over itself, voices slurring in that way that made everything feel warmer than it should.

Joshua, cheeks ruddy now, leaned against a cushion and closed one eye. "Thirty thousand tents," he muttered. "And not one of them has a better night than this one."

"We should bottle this and ration it to the people," I said.

"Forget that," said Azubah. "We should bottle it and sell it to the Egyptians. Maybe then they'd stop building pyramids and try being happy for once."

I nearly choked on my wine. "You're terrible."

"And beautiful," she replied, resting her chin on my shoulder, her fingers playing with the frayed edge of my cloak. "And you're mine."

Somewhere near the back of the tent, someone dropped a plate and a servant apologized profusely, but none of us noticed much. Othniel had begun a ridiculous tale about a talking ox he'd met in Shiloh, and Haggith was trying—and failing—not to laugh into her cup. Tirzah leaned in to Joshua and began whispering, her voice low and sultry, and the look that passed between them was the kind of look no soldier could mistake.

Azubah watched them and whispered in my ear, "Are we staying long enough to stagger, or just long enough to be forgiven?"

I turned to her. "Which do you want?"

She smiled, slow and sure. "To be remembered."

"Then let's drink another."

We did. Two more, in fact. And by then Joshua's voice had lowered to a gravelly murmur, and Othniel was snoring softly in the corner. Phineas had slipped away without notice, as he often did, leaving only the gentle rustle of the tent flaps and the glow of a few dying coals.

Azubah said first. "Come," she said. "Before you start singing," her voice thick with wine.

"I never sing."

"You do. Badly. And only after your fourth cup." Everyone laughed.

We took leave from our brothers and sisters, and bid them peace into the night.

Arising first, she reached up for my hand with a grin—unsteady, yet certain—and I took it. Her other hand clasped to a clay pot of date wine given us by our hosts. The tent floor swayed beneath us both, but her grip held fast, perhaps firmer than mine, though the wine had softened her laughter and tangled her tongue. Tonight, she matched me cup for cup, cheeks aflame with a reckless fire, eyes bright with a wild abandon—no longer the woman who prized clarity, but one surrendered wholly to the tender warmth of the night.

As we stepped out into the night, the air met us cool and vast, the scent of earth and ash drifting on the wind. The fireflies had begun their low flickering, like little heralds of peace across the camps. We didn't speak for a while—only walked in silence, hands clasped, weaving between the rows of sleeping tents and quiet fires, until we reached our own.

The flap of our tent was fastened back.

"The children-" I began to ask,

"—are in the tent next to us with the servants and our family, tonight is for us" her eyes sparkled

The cushions inside were plumped, the blankets laid neatly. But we barely noticed. Azubah turned and pressed herself against me, her arms sliding beneath my cloak as she rested her forehead on my chest. I could feel her smile.

233

"You drank more than usual," I said, brushing a lock of hair from her brow.

She tilted her head up to meet my gaze. "I did."

"Why?"

Her voice was quiet, warm as coals under ash. "Because tonight, we are not in Hebron or Ai surrounded by enemies. Tonight, I am not waiting to hear that you've fallen beside a shattered gate. Tonight we have peace, Kalev. We have victory. You live. The camp is strong. Yahweh is near. And for once, I let myself feel it."

She leaned into me, her words softening further. "And because the wine was good."

We laughed again, that kind of laughter that lives in the belly and needs no reason. I held her face in both hands then, marveling—not for the first time—at the lines that had begun to settle at the corners of her eyes, carved there both by age any by watching too much, waiting too long, loving too fiercely. She was not a woman of timidity. She had followed me into Kena'an, into battles, into years of wandering. She was more wilderness than garden. But tonight, beneath this humble roof of goat-hide and starlight, she had let the wildness ease its hold upon her soul.

As we settled onto the woven mats, she reached for the last of the wine—only half full—and sipped it with a carelessness she rarely shown. She cradled it, turning it between her fingers, watching the way the last red drops clung to the rim.

"I used to imagine," she said, "that peace would come like thunder. That the enemies would be crushed, the land silent, and we'd sit beneath fig trees with crowns of olive leaves and never lift a hand again." She shook her head, smiling at her own foolishness. "But peace came like this instead—like laughter that won't stay in your throat. Like you beside me, not dead. And I'll take it. I'll drink it while it lasts."

I took the cup from her, drained it, and set it aside.

We fell into silence, a silence full of nearness and gratitude. There was no urgency, no fear, only the slow undoing of all the tension built from years on the edge of blades. Azubah curled beside me, head nestled against my chest, her arm draped across my ribs.

She was the stone beneath the tent peg, the weight that held me to the ground when everything else threatened to drift. But tonight—just for tonight—she had chosen celebration. She had chosen to lift the cup, to sing along with the laughter, to join the men at the fire as an equal, as a partner, as a soul unburdened.

I kissed her temple, felt the rise and fall of her breath as it slowed.

"Azubah," I whispered, the name tasting ancient and right in my mouth.

Her eyes opened a sliver. "Mmm?"

"You are the fiercest joy I've ever known."

She smiled without opening her eyes, her eyes heavy from drink. "And you, husband, are drunk."

"Only on you."

She laughed softly, and I let my hand rest against the small of her back, the rhythm of her breath anchoring me at last.

Then, later, just when I thought she'd drifted into sleep, her voice rose low beside me—gentle, unhurried, as if singing from a well carved long before our wandering:

"You drew me from the pit where no light dwelled,
From the depths where cords of death encircled.
You clothed me with strength like linen,
You anointed my head with mercy.
In the shadowed valleys, I called to You—
And You answered with fire and wind.
You set my feet on the height,
And made my name known among the tents of the living.

Your hand was a shield in the raging storm,
Your voice the song that calmed the sea.
When enemies gathered like wolves in the night,
You wrapped me in refuge, a fortress of grace.
The earth shook beneath their fury,
But You, O Lord, stood unshaken.
My heart rejoiced in the shelter of Your wings,
And my lips spoke praises beyond the dawn."

Her hand found mine again, fingers slipping between my own. "It's from my mother's songs," she said sleepily. "Before the Red Sea. Before Sinai."

I let the words settle in me like wine in the belly—slow and burning. They didn't need a priest's voice or a scroll's ink to be holy.

"You remember it well" I said.

She nodded against my chest, "What else is memory for, if not for songs of deliverance?"

We lay there, quiet, the heavy breaths of the camp fading into distant murmur. The warmth of her body against mine was a balm, a peace earned through sweat and battle. As the fire of wine and prayer dimmed, we found the silence between us ripe and full, and we gave ourselves over to it, over to each other, as two warriors who had earned their brief respite beneath the vastness of God's canopy.

Afterwards I stared at the dark canopy above us, where the goat-hide roof met the breath of the stars, and thought: perhaps the scribes will write of the kings we felled, the cities we burned, the land we claimed. But I hoped someone, someday, would write of this too— the song of a woman who drank deeply, laughed freely, and in the stillness between wars, gave thanks not with offerings of blood, but with words woven from the mercy of God.

And with that, we slept. Morning would come, unmercifully too soon.

236

Chapter Fourteen
Under the Veil of False Vows

The dawn did not come gently. It clawed its way through the thin goat-hair curtains of our tent, tearing at the edges of sleep with a cold and unforgiving hand. My head throbbed in rhythm with the slow beat of my heart, each pulse a dull drum of yesterday's wine and laughter now turned to ache.

Azubah lay beside me, her dark hair tangled on the pillow like spilled ink, a few loose strands brushed across her brow. Her breathing was steady, the peaceful rise and fall of her chest a quiet hymn amid the clamoring in my skull. I dared not move at first, afraid my stirring would shatter the fragile peace she still held.

A faint breeze slipped through the tent's flap, carrying the scent of dust and smoke from the campfires still burning beyond the ranks of tents. Somewhere close, a child cried—an ordinary sound, yet somehow sharp enough to pierce the haze. I blinked into the growing light and found my hand resting lightly on the curve of Azubah's waist, where the warmth still lingered, a tether to the world I was reluctant to face.

"Azubah," I murmured, my voice rough, a rasp from the dryness that clung to my throat. She stirred then, eyelids fluttering open, revealing eyes like deep wells of black glass, calm and steady despite the chaos I felt within.

"Good morning, husband," she whispered, a teasing softness in her tone that made me smile through the dullness.

"How long have I lain here?" I asked, trying to sound steady but failing.

"Since before the first light," she said, brushing a gentle finger across my forehead. "You look like a man who wrestled a lion and lost."

I groaned, rolling onto my side, my body heavy as lead. "The wine fought well."

She laughed, a sound like warm honey dripping over stones. "And yet you survived."

Her hand traced the line of my jaw, a tender balm to the pounding behind my eyes. "You drank hard as hard as the stones of Mount Ebal" she laughed.

I closed my eyes and remembered—the night of wine, the stories shared, the rare laughter echoing among the elders and their wives. Azubah had joined the revelry, her usual reserve softened by the warmth of wine and company. It was not often she drank, and never like last night. I remembered the way her cheeks had flushed like ripe pomegranates, the sparkle in her eyes as she dared to laugh louder than custom allowed.

"You drank too," I accused, one brow arched.

She smiled, eyes half-closed in that slow way that made my heart seize, "Only to be near you," she said simply.

A silence fell between us, thick and full, broken only by the distant sounds of camp stirring awake—the murmur of voices, the clatter of pottery, the low bleating of sheep. Outside, the great wilderness stretched endlessly, a reminder of the battles still to be fought and the fragile peace held in our hands.

"I wish these moments could last forever," I said, voice barely more than a breath.

Azubah shifted closer, resting her head against my shoulder, "So do I, my warrior."

Her words stirred something fierce and tender within me—a flame flickering through the fog of my hangover. This woman, my anchor and my joy, made the heavy weight of command lighter, if only for a time.

But duty called. I knew I could not remain here, wrapped in the fragile embrace of dawn and warmth. The council awaited—the ever-turning wheel of judgment and leadership that spun beneath the vast canopy of our wandering camp.

Slowly, painfully, I rose, wincing as the ache in my temples flared anew. Azubah watched me with quiet concern, her fingers tightening around mine for a moment before releasing.

"Be careful today," she said softly. "The camp feels... restless. The wind carries whispers I cannot yet understand."

I nodded, pulling my cloak about me, the rough wool scratchy against skin still tender from sleep and wine. "I will."

We stepped out into the pale light together. The camp was already alive, a sea of movement and sound. Azubah went off to gather the servants and our children, and to tend to the days work ahead. Men sharpened their swords, tended their flocks, and prepared for the day's duties. Children darted between tents, their laughter a sharp contrast to the heavy weight settling on the shoulders of their fathers.

The Tent of Meeting stood at the heart of the camp—a hub of decisions, debate, and sometimes, weary concession. As I approached, the flurry of voices drifted through the canvas walls, the low hum of men whose faces bore the strain of command as deeply as mine.

I hesitated at the flap, drawing a slow breath, the cool air a balm and a warning all at once. The memory of last night's revelry and the ache of this morning's reckoning mingled inside me—two halves of the same coin.

Stepping inside, I found Joshua seated, his eyes shadowed and red, Othniel looked barely awake, and Phineas too looked as if he had been awoken by his servants before he was ready. The council was gathering, barely. Yet the weight of the camp pressed down upon us like like the very stone that Mosheh struck.

My footsteps echoed softly on the packed earth as I took my place beside them, the dull throb in my head a reminder that even the fiercest warriors must sometimes face battles within themselves before facing those without.

Outside, the winds shifted, carrying with them a distant and unfamiliar sound—the first stirrings of a day that would test us far beyond the ordinary trials of camp and council.

The morning light slanted weakly through the rough tent flaps, casting pale stripes across the dust-strewn floor, a frail veil over the council tent's shadowed heart. The air was thick, heavy with the stale reek of smoke, spilled wine, and unwashed bodies—the remnants of last night's revelry clinging like a shroud to the worn goatskins. The tribes had feasted under Ebal's shadow, their songs of covenant and conquest rising with the myrrh-scented smoke, their cups brimming with the bounty of Kena'an's vines. Now, the cost of that joy pulsed in our temples, a dull throb that mirrored the ache in my bones.

My throat was dry, scratched raw, and the taste of wine soured my tongue. Around the low fire, Joshua stirred, a grimace carving deeper lines into his weathered face. His eyes, sharp even through the fog of indulgence, scanned the scattered parchments on the low table —tribal tallies, scout reports, disputes unresolved. Othniel slumped nearby, his arm across his chest, his quiet snores a soft rhythm against the camp's waking murmurs. Phineas, had finally fully awoke, ever the restless zealot, paced by the tent's edge, his hands clenched, his staff leaning against the pole, its tip glinting like his deeply restrained thoughts. Eleazar, the high priest, sat still, his ephod dulled by dust, his fingers tracing the Urim's pouch as if seeking clarity through the haze.

"We cannot hide behind drink forever," Joshua muttered, his voice raw as gravel, each word a labor against the weight of the night. "The people need justice. The tribes will not wait."

I rose unsteadily, swallowing past the scratch in my throat, my head swimming. "This day will test us more than Ai's fire," I said, my voice low, hoarse. "Battle was clear—sword and shield, light against shadow. Judging, governing—this wears the soul like sand on stone."

Othniel stirred awake, rubbing sleep and wine from his eyes, his youthful face creased with effort. "Our swords thirst for Kena'an's giants," he said, his voice thick, "but today we face tongues sharper than blades, disputes that cut deeper than bronze."

Phineas halted, his gaze fierce despite the shadows under his eyes. "Let us be done with petty quarrels," he growled. "The Anakim muster, their shedim stir. We waste breath on flocks and fences while altars burn with blood."

Eleazar lifted a hand, his voice a priest's cadence, though strained. "Yahweh's justice must prevail, even in weariness," he said. "No sin, no discord, can abide in our camp, lest we falter as at Ai."

Joshua nodded, his hand brushing his sword's hilt, the blade that had pierced Ai's heart. "We judge, then turn to war," he said. "But first, the tribes' grievances."

Before we could summon the next claimant, a sharp knock cut through the tent's heavy air. The guards at the entrance stood stern, their eyes alert despite the camp's lingering stupor. A Levite warrior stepped forward, his tunic dust-stained, his voice urgent. "My lords," he said, bowing low, "the strangers from last night, who approach from the west—they still await you, seeking audience."

"Bring them," Joshua said, his voice steady, his eyes looking less so.

The tent flap parted, and the guards led in a small company of travelers, cloaked and hooded, their faces half-hidden beneath scarves caked with dust. They moved cautiously, their steps faltering, their eyes flicking about like prey in a predator's den. Their cloaks were patched, frayed at the edges, their sandals split, their hands clutching wineskins that sagged, their contents sour. One bore a sack of bread, its crusts green with mold, while another, younger, held a scroll of cracked parchment, its edges curled, its surface etched with script faded by time. They knelt, their movements a practiced supplication, their forms hunched as if broken by a thousand leagues.

Joshua leaned forward, his gaze piercing through the fog of revelry. "Sit," he said, his voice a commander's probe, raw but unyielding. "State your business, strangers."

The tallest traveler lowered his hood, revealing a face weathered by sun and wind, pale with exhaustion, yet his eyes gleamed with a merchant's cunning. "Oh Spear of the Twelve Clans," he began, his voice cracked yet resonant, honed by years of barter, "we come from a far country, beyond the rivers, beyond the hills, drawn by the fame of your God, the Almighty who dries seas and shatters cities. We seek a covenant of peace, that we may live and not perish."

Voices rippled through the council, Phineas's his eyes narrowing, Othniel looked at the strangers, trying to assess their inner being, while Eleazar's gaze fixed on the scroll, his lips moving silently. The travelers' tale was too polished, their disarray too perfect, yet their fear trembled in their eyes, a truth beneath the guise.

"What land do you name?" Joshua asked, his voice steady, though the wine's haze dulled his usual edge. "And why seek us, knowing the God who topples walls?"

The leader bowed lower, his hands spreading in humility. "We are but humble folk, my lord, from a place beyond the Euphrates, where your God's name is a thunder. Our provisions—bread warm when we departed, wineskins new, cloaks whole—bear witness to our journey's length."

He gestured to the scroll-bearer, who stepped forward, his hands trembling as he unrolled the parchment. "This scroll, passed through generations, tells of our kin, the Nahorim, a tribe spared by your God when He judged the earth. We claim that bond, seeking to renew it, to live under His mercy."

The scroll's script—angular, faded, etched in a foreign tongue, like the Torah's ancient forms—caught the light, its words unreadable in the dim tent, yet its presence stirred us. Phineas's staff shifted, his zeal warring with curiosity, while Othniel leaned closer, his eyes tracing the parchment's lines. Eleazar's fingers brushed his ephod, but he hesitated, the scroll's claim clouding his thoughts.

"Read the scroll," I said, my voice hoarse, the wine's fog blurring my thoughts.

"Let its words speak."

The younger traveler cleared his throat, his voice soft, almost reverent, "It tells of the Nahorim, wanderers who honored your God in ages past, spared when He drowned the nephilim's seed. 'By the hand of the Almighty,' it says, 'we were set apart, to dwell beyond the rivers, to seek His people when the time was fulfilled.' We are their heirs, come to bind our fate to yours."

The council was restless, elders exchanging glances. The scroll's tale, though strange, echoed the covenant at Ebal, where mercy and justice had been sworn and fulfilled. My heart tugged—Rachav's faith, my own grafting into Yehudah—The travelers' provisions, their tattered cloaks, their trembling hands, painted a picture of distance, of desperation, and the scroll's script seemed to seal their plea.

Phineas spoke, his voice a blade. "Their words are honey, their scroll a riddle. Let us test this parchment, lest it be a serpent's lie."

Othniel countered, his tone cautious. "Yet if they speak true, to reject them may defy Yahweh's heart. Rachav was spared, as was Kalev's kin."

Eleazar's eyes narrowed, his hand on the Urim's pouch. "We must seek Yahweh's voice," he said, but his voice wavered, the wine's haze and the scroll's weight dulling his clarity. "Yet Ebal's covenant bids us consider mercy."

Joshua's gaze held mine, a storm of doubt and compassion, his judgment softened by the night's excess and Ebal's vows. "The scroll speaks of mercy," he murmured, "as Rachav's cord did. Our hearts are heavy, our minds clouded. Could we turn away a remnant spared by Yahweh?"

He turned to the leader, his voice firm, though strained, "Your tale moves us, but our God sees all. Show us your provisions, share your bread, and we will weigh your words."

The leader nodded, his eyes flickering—relief, or guile? His men opened their sacks, offering the moldy bread, its crusts crumbling, and poured wine from cracked skins, its scent sour as vinegar. The council tasted it, the act a gesture of trust, yet my stomach churned, not from the wine's bite but from a stirring in my spirit. Phineas grimaced, his hand on his staff, while Othniel broke the bread, his eyes on the scroll, as if seeking truth in its lines, foreign letters he could not understand.

The leader spoke again, his voice a supplicant's plea. "We ask only a covenant, lord of the Twelve Clans, to live under your God's shadow. Our kin, the Nahorim, honored Him, and we seek the same. Bind us to you, and we will serve faithfully."

The council's voices grew, clashing like bronze in a forge. The scroll's tale, the travelers' provisions, their trembling fear—it wove a beautiful spell, exploiting our weariness, our hangover's fog, our hearts softened by Ebal's altar and Rachav's redemption. I felt the weight of my Kenizzite blood, a whisper of the Anakim's shadow, yet I was Yehudah's kin, bound by covenant. Could we reject a plea that echoed my own salvation?

Joshua raised a hand, silencing the council, "We will make peace with you," he said, his voice heavy, the words falling like stones. "A covenant, sworn by Yahweh, that you may live among us. But know this: our God's fire consumes deceit."

The leader bowed low, his eyes veiled. "We thank you oh Spear of the Twelve Clans," he said, his voice smooth as oil. "We will serve your God and your people."

The travelers withdrew, their steps slow, their cloaks trailing dust like a shroud. The council exhaled, the tent's air lighter, yet a shadow lingered in my heart. We had not sought the Urim, had not waited for Yahweh's voice, swayed by wine, weariness, and a scroll's cunning lie. As Joshua's eyes met mine, I saw his doubt, a mirror of my own—a covenant sworn too swiftly, a mercy that might yet prove a snare, echoing the scarlet cord of a woman who had once been Kena'an's own.

The travelers withdrew, their steps slow, their cloaks trailing dust like a shroud.   The council exhaled. The air inside the tent grew thinner, less heavy somehow, as if a storm had passed — but it had not passed, not really. It had merely shifted.

We sat in that stillness like men who had run a race before the course was laid.

The smell of old parchment clung to the air, mingled with the acrid remnants of wine and sweat and weariness. Someone let out a grunt, another man muttered under his breath, but none dared speak what we all felt.

Joshua's shoulders dropped, the scroll still in his hands, the wax seal broken but intact enough to remind us of the far-off council who had "sent" the men — he gave it to Eleazar to study in more detail, he who could read the foreign tongues—whoever they were. The writing was clever. Too clever, I thought. It said everything and nothing. It invoked no gods by name, asked no true favor, but praised our deeds in elegant flourishes, as if trying to buy our pride.

Finally, Joshua spoke again, "Let it stand," he said simply. "It is done."

No one challenged him.

We were the elders, the princes of tribes, the war-proven and the covenant-bound. And still, not one of us had asked to wait. Not one had dared say aloud, "Let us seek the Lord first." Perhaps we were afraid. Or perhaps we were tired — bone-tired, soul-tired, the kind of weariness that no sleep can touch.

And so the messengers were welcomed.

That evening they returned, as was expected. And we, who had sworn by Yahweh's name, received them. This was how covenants were made — with shared bread, with shared cup. Even bitter bread, even soured wine. We drank it all the same.

The light in the tent dimmed as the sun fell away. Torches were lit but their glow was sullen, casting long shadows. No wives came to sit beside us. No laughter stirred the corners. We drank in silence, watched them eat in silence, and when they bowed again and took their leave, the silence remained.

The fire in the center of the tent crackled and sighed. I looked around at the others — Othniel, glassy-eyed, arms crossed tight. Phineas, grim and silent, his face unreadable. Joshua, still seated at the head, his gaze now on the floor, his hands limp at his sides.

No songs were sung. No prayers were offered.

There were no white stones set, no holy markers for this covenant. No bulls sacrificed, no altars built. The covenant had been forged not in joy, but in fatigue. Not by prophetic utterance, but by exhaustion. We had fought two cities and judged a thousand quarrels since Jericho. The weight of leadership had crept into our bones.

We had wanted peace.

And peace, it seemed, had found us.

I rose slowly, joints stiff. Azubah would be waiting. My tent would be warm. My head would not.

I passed beneath the flap and stepped into the night. Behind me, I heard Othniel groan as he stood. I caught Joshua's eye, and there

— just for a moment — I saw it: not regret, not anger, but something colder.

Doubt.

It mirrored my own.

Still, we said nothing. Some oaths echo longer in silence than they ever would in words.

That night, the wind was sharp against the tents, whispering secrets in tongues older than any scroll. Azubah pressed against me beneath our blankets, her breath warm, her body curved like a prayer I dared not voice. But my thoughts would not be still.

I closed my eyes. The bread was eaten, the wine drunk, the words sworn. We had taken them into our fold. There was no undoing it now. Only waiting.

Only time.

No one challenged the story of the travelers. Perhaps because Rachav and I had had both once been strangers, and perhaps—just perhaps—these tattered men were a third miracle. We shared their bread, dry as ash. Their wine, bitter as old leather. The covenant, when it came, was not sealed with joy, but with the deep exhale of men too tired to suspect more betrayal.

Not until the third day did we learn the truth.

Chapter Fifteen

A Treaty Forged in Fog

The third night after the covenant with the foreigners found the camp restless and quiet all at once. It was the hour of second sleep, that fragile time between midnight and dawn when most would have returned to their dreams—but my eyes remained wide open. I wasn't simply heavy with last night's wine, which had become a necessity for all of us elders on the council, burdened by a week's weight of judgment and dispute. The council had not ceased since the trumpets fell silent over Ai. Each day brought petitions and quarrels from the thousands who now looked to us—not only for victory, but for law, for order, for justice. The spoils of war were only the first step; what followed was a tangle of human need and unrest, the Twelve Clans carried on the weary shoulders if its elders.

Azubah stirred beside me, her breath deep and even. "Still awake?" she murmured, her hand reaching to brush the sweat from my brow.

"I think I have grown older in these few days," I answered, voice rough. "The battles tested our strength, but the council tests our souls."

She sighed softly, nestling closer. "And yet, you rise still, a pillar among men."

"I wonder if pillars can bend without breaking," I said. "The people's voices—cries for fairness, for mercy—have no end. Joshua leads them with fire, but even fire can burn low."

Azubah's fingers traced a slow pattern along my arm. "You carry what others cannot see, the weight of a thousand needs pressed into one man's chest. Sometimes I fear you will forget to breathe beneath it."

I looked into the shadows where her eyes flickered awake. "How do you bear watching? You are not bound by council duties. You have your own burdens, yet you stay—steadfast beside me."

Her smile was a faint flame, steady and sure. "Because it is not just your burden. It is ours. You do not fight alone, Kalev, even when the night grows long and dark."

I pulled the worn blanket closer about her, "Sometimes I fear my strength will fail before this task is done. The people want law, yes —but justice demands more. Mercy, patience, and at times, harshness. How does one balance these scales when every judgment strikes deeper than a sword?"

Azubah's voice dropped to a whisper, filled with quiet conviction. "The scales do not rest on one hand alone. Joshua's voice is fierce and steady, and you—your wisdom is the calm in his storm. Together you are the sword and the shield. And when you falter, you return to this—this hearth, this home, this love that holds you whole."

I felt the weight in my chest ease a fraction, warmed by her words. "You make it sound easier than it is."

She chuckled softly, the sound like water over stones. "It is not easy, nor should it be. To lead a people chosen by Yahweh is to walk the razor's edge every day. But I have seen the fire in your eyes. I know you would walk through shadow and flame before letting them fall to ruin."

Her hand clasped mine, steadying me, "Remember—no man is meant to carry the burden alone. Even the strongest pillar leans on the earth beneath."

I nodded slowly, grateful for her presence, the quiet strength she offered in a world of turmoil, "And you, Azubah—you are that earth beneath my feet."

Her breath caught, a flicker of something tender in her gaze. "If I am the earth, then you are the sky that gives me shape."

Her eyes closed slowly, and the soft timbre of her voice rose, carrying the ancient rhythm of our people—words like stones laid carefully into a song, binding hope and strength beneath the morning light,

> "Asharim stand, the righteous strong,
> Am echad, hearts bound in song,
> Lo yipol even, stone shall not fall,
> Adonai oz, strength of us all.
> The mayim flow, a whispered prayer,
> B'rakha sweet, fills desert air,
> Gedulah shines where shadows part,
> Emet in heart, Yahweh's art.
> Kol echad, one voice, one breath,
> Chesed flows beyond the death,
> Together strong, we rise and stand,
> Shalom reigns across the land."

For a long moment, I lay still, the echo of her song lingering in the quiet shadows of the tent. Her voice—woven from the very breath of our ancestors—held a fierce grace that stirred something deep within me. Azubah loved the old prose, the sacred rhythms that spoke of Yahweh's mercy and the strength of our people. It was a love that reached beyond words, anchoring her soul in a time when faith was both sword and shield.

Slowly, her breathing softened as she laid her head upon my chest, the steady rise and fall a quiet hymn of peace in the dim light. Nearby, our two boys slept with the servants,, their chests rising gently with the soft murmur of dreams, the faint rustle of linen and whispered sighs filling the stillness. The weight of the day, the unyielding cares of the council, all seemed momentarily distant, held at bay by the fragile sanctuary of family and song.

But as the night wore on, sleep eluded me. The weight of counsel, the endless disputes and the restless hearts of our people, pressed heavy upon my chest. I had lain awake, turning over judgments and prayers alike, knowing that the dawn would not bring rest but another day burdened with decisions that could shape the fate of Israel.

Now, as the first light crept beneath the canvas, I willed myself to rise. The council tent awaited—its shadows long and filled with voices seeking guidance. The land might have been won in battle, but the true war was in the hearts and laws of the people we were called to lead.

The dawn broke and was slow and pale over our camp, the first faint light slipping beneath the council tent's edges. The day was heavy with expectation, as if the earth itself held its breath, waiting.

It had been three days since the strangers had come—men wrapped in worn cloaks, their eyes watchful and guarded. They came as weary travelers, pleading for peace and protection, claiming to be from lands far beyond our sight. The council, weary from war but eager to cement peace, had granted them a covenant—a promise sealed by oath and the blood of Yahweh.

But now, the air inside the tent was thick with suspicion, the easy hope of those days beginning to curdle into doubt. Our minds were less clouded with stiff drink.

I took my place to the right of Joshua wrapped in his mantle of decisive command. His storm-gray eyes, carved deeper by each passing season, scanned the tent. His eyes had a look of anger, he held a strip of parchment in one hand, but it was not the scroll that carried the weight—it was the stillness in his frame, the tension that drew every gaze toward him.

Zadok, ever alert and taut as a bowstring, stepped forward first. His dark eyes flicked toward Joshua before landing on us. He bowed his head briefly. "Elders," he began, his voice like a scout's whisper before a charge, "the men who came to us three days past...

those who wore the garb of far-off lands, with cracked wineskins and molded bread…"

Joshua raised a hand, "I will speak it, Zadok."

The silence thickened. Joshua's voice was low, but every word landed like flint against stone, "They are not from distant lands." He turned, meeting each of our eyes in turn. "They come from Gibeon."

A breath escaped Othniel beside me—a sharp hiss through his teeth. His young shoulders, bronzed and broad, stiffened beneath the leather strap of his cloak. "That's not possible," he said. "Gibeon lies two days north. We have been called by God to destroy their city."

Eliab, older, grayer, hunched like a hawk from years of scouting, grunted. "Their vineyards nearly brush our camp's edge."

"They came in rags," I said aloud, feeling the bitterness stir in my chest. "Their bread was moldy—"

"They made it moldy," said Zadok grimly. "They laid it in damp cloths for two days before setting out."

Phineas, wiry and blazing with unrelenting energy, slapped his staff against the ground. "Then they came not in peace—but in cunning. They dressed their lie in dust and shadows." And then as though an afterthought, he added, "They feared the sword. Can we blame them?"

"Yes," Othniel snapped, stepping forward, his frame coiled with intensity. "Yes, we can. They lied to Yahweh's anointed. The lied to the Spear of the Twelve Clans in this very tent! This covenant was forged with our clean hands—but theirs were stained. It is a pact made in deception. It cannot stand."

The tent trembled beneath the tension.

Joshua said nothing for a moment. He looked not at us, but at the parchment he held. Not a scroll of command, but a letter from one of the Levite scribes who had questioned the men the night before after finding out the deceit.

He let the silence stretch like a drawn bow.

"They feared death," he said at last. "But they chose not to cast themselves at our feet in truth. Had they come openly—had they laid down their arms and said, 'We are Gibeon, and we fear your God'— then Yahweh's mercy might have been poured out like water."

"But instead," I said quietly, "they feared man more than God."

Eliab spat onto the floor, "Then we should finish what was started. Curse or no curse, our oath was drawn from a poisoned well."

Othniel lifted his spear, "Let me go. I will strike the chiefs through the heart and spill their blood on the altar of deceit."

"No." Joshua's voice, though calm, cut through the tumult like a sudden wind.
Othniel froze, his jaw tight.

Joshua stepped forward. "We swore an oath by the name of Yahweh. Even if it was made in ignorance, it was not made in vanity. If we break it now, we bring the curse upon ourselves. Not them."

Othniel's voice was low. "Then what justice remains for Israel?"

Joshua's eyes, silver-rimmed with grief, turned to him. "Justice is not always the sword. Sometimes it is the yoke."

He turned then to me. "Kalev, you walked the valleys of Anak. You've seen what becomes of nations who hold their pride tighter than the truth. What would you do?"

I held his gaze for a long moment. I thought of the caves near Hebron, where the bones of the Rephaim still lay. I thought of the Gibeonites, whose blood carried that same shadow. But I also thought of my people—slaves once, strangers once, liars even—yet redeemed.

"They must live," I said. "But not as brothers. Let them be hewers of wood, drawers of water. Let their backs remember the weight of their lie."

Othniel turned away, his knuckles white on the shaft of his spear.

Joshua lifted his hands. "So let it be written. The covenant will stand—but they will serve. Not because they are holy, but because Yahweh is. Forever to be the slaves of our people"

Phineas slowly nodded. "Mercy... wrapped in fire."

Joshua's voice grew louder, hard now, like sun-baked stone, not sorrow, "From this day forward, the Gibeonites shall be bound to the sanctuary of the Lord—not as priests, but as servants. Their lives will remind Israel what happens when fear triumphs over faith, when guile is chosen over repentance."

Zadok rolled the parchment back up, his hands steady once more.

Outside the tent, the camp stirred as the sun crowned the eastern ridge.

Within, the fire had spoken.

Chapter Sixteen
The Angel of the LORD

The sun stood high, a white fire overhead, flattening every shadow and silencing even the more restless children in the southern quarter of the camp. The dust was hot underfoot, and the steady rhythm of daily life beat around us like the soft echo of war drums. Tents rustled in the breeze. Oxen groaned. Somewhere nearby, a copper-smith hammered at a cracked blade, sending a ringing clatter through the open square where

Othniel and I sat beneath the meager shade of a fig-draped awning.

Our midday meal was humble—lentils, barley cakes, a wedge of goat cheese gone soft in the heat—but I welcomed the silence that came with it. Othniel, on the other hand, did not eat so much as attack his food, as if the bread might confess Gibeonite treachery if pressed hard enough.

His body had grown much in recent time—more stocky—like that of a warrior, his frame pulled taut like a bow kept strung too long. His copper-toned skin shone with sweat, and his beard was beginning to finally fill out, threads of it curling like smoke. His eyes —always his eyes—never rested. Even now, they flicked from the crowd that passed us to the guards at the council tent, to a pair of young boys pretending to spar with sticks near the water carts.

"You're grinding that cheese into paste," I said.

He grunted but didn't answer. The scrape of wood on clay rang between us as he pressed his thumb into his bowl.

I let the silence stretch. There was no rush.

All around us, the camp hummed with a weary kind of purpose. Women wove flax into cords beneath a scaffold of drying hides. Traders bartered over salted fish and dyed cloth—half the goods still smelt of Ai's rubble. A line of goats bleated impatiently near the priests' tents. Smoke curled from the ovens where unleavened bread was baked in great round stones. Beyond them, the Levites' ram-horn trumpets sat cooling beside a basin, waiting for their next call.

We were a city on the move, a nation packed into canvas and rope, and somehow still standing. I often marveled that we hadn't torn each other apart from within.

Othniel finally spoke. "You know it isn't right."

I looked over at him. "What part?"

He scowled. "That they breathe. That they eat the same food as our children.   That they walk among us with skin unbroken."

"Joshua judged wisely," I said, though even I could hear the fatigue in my voice.

"Wisely?" His eyes snapped to mine, sharp as flint. "You call it wisdom to let the enemies of God drink from our wells?"

"They were clever," I said. "But they feared us for good reason. For the fear of Yahweh was upon them, even if it came through lies."

"They feared *us*, not *Him*," Othniel spat. "They chose deceit over repentance."

I took a slow bite of barley cake and chewed, watching the crowd shift before us.

"Perhaps. But what would you have done?"

"I told Joshua already. Kill them. Let their blood water the dry places."

His passion didn't shock me. Not from Othniel.

A shadow shifted, and I looked up—Phineas had joined us, silent as ever. He bore the fire of his father Eleazar, and his grandfather Aaron before him—but it was tempered less by patience, more by a hunger for purity.

Phineas and Othniel were close, rarely far from each other.

"What say you brother," I asked him as he sat down. Amongst our clans Phineas always bore his staff, and he placed it beside him.

He didn't answer at first. His eyes wandered to the edge of the square, where the Gibeonite water-carriers—newly branded with their servitude—hauled buckets from the well under Levi supervision.

"Would you sit so calmly," he asked at last, "if they had tricked *you* into covenant? Would your mercy stretch so far if the city of Rephaim blood stood mocking you just across the plain?"

His words struck deeper than he knew. My jaw tensed, remembering the slopes near Hebron where Anak's children had once made their dwellings. The memory of giants wasn't poetic for me—it was flesh and bone, the taste of fear in the back of my throat. Gibeon wasn't so far from that shadow.

"I would not sit calmly," I said. "But I would still hold my sword."

Phineas stared at me, trying to read my meaning.

"They are slaves now," I continued. "Every time they draw water for the altar, every time they stack wood for sacrifice, they will remember. And their children will remember. The weight of their lie will be the rhythm of their days. That is no small punishment."

He and Othniel scoffed but said nothing more.

We fell into silence again. The heat pressed down like a hand from above. A pair of doves fluttered down near by and pecked at crumbs. A Levite boy passed carrying a scroll twice his length, one end dragging behind him like a trailing vine.

I studied Othniel more closely. He sat like a man wound too tightly for comfort. Even in stillness, something within him vibrated. His hands—scarred and calloused from training and sacrifice—trembled now and then, as if holding back what they longed to unleash.

"You see too clearly to be content with easy peace," I said. "But you must learn what justice looks like when there's no blood on the ground. You must learn when mercy strengthens, not weakens."

Othniel looked away. "I am not made for mercy."

"No," I agreed. "But you are made for holiness. And holiness demands more than wrath."

The words settled between us. Somewhere across the square, a horn called out—a summons to the elders. Another dispute. Another voice crying for fairness in a world that no longer made sense.

I stood and brushed the dust from my knees. "Come. Let us see what justice demands today."

They rose beside me, and for just a moment, the fire in Othniel's eyes dimmed, replaced by something quieter. Not peace. Not yet. But the beginning of wisdom.

The sound reached us before the men did—like thunder muffled in the belly of the earth, like feet pounding against parched dust. Phineas had just slung his water skin across his shoulder when the shouting began.

"Kalev! Son of Jephunneh!"

Heads turned. From the edge of the merchant tents, three young men ran toward us—dust-smeared, wide-eyed, and breathless, their tunics clinging with sweat. Behind them, the life of the camp seemed to pause, traders lowering their voices, children stilled in play. Even the goats fell into silence.

The lead runner—one of the scouts from Benjamin, perhaps sixteen summers old—stumbled to a halt before us, chest heaving. "My lord," he gasped, bowing with a fist pressed to his heart. "Urgent word—from the hills."

I stepped forward, the weight of command tightening across my shoulders like a familiar mantle. "What news?"

"It's the cities, my lord," he said, struggling to speak quickly through gulps of air. "The southern kings. Five of them. They've broken from their own lands—Jerusalem, Lachish, Hebron, all—marching together."

My jaw clenched. "Where?"

He looked up, dread etched into the sweat-lined creases of his face. "Not toward us, my lord. They march on Gibeon."

Beside me, Othniel made a sound like a hiss through clenched teeth. His hand was already at the leather loop on his belt where his spear usually rested. "Cowards turning on the ones who sought peace," he growled.

I narrowed my eyes, the wind suddenly feeling sharp against my skin. "You're certain?"

"All five kings," another of the runners added—this one broader, from the tribe of Naphtali. "Adoni-Zedek leads them. Their vanguard was seen at the pass of Beth-Horon, moving fast with chariots and footmen."

I nodded once. "Come. We take this to Joshua."

Othniel was already striding ahead, his long legs cutting through the crowd with the urgency of a man born to battle. I followed, my own pace quickening, the runners falling in behind. Around us, the camp awakened to the stirrings of war: elders rising from shade, sentries whispering, mothers calling their children close. Even the smell changed—less of lentils and smoke, more of leather and dust and bronze being drawn.

As we approached the Tent of Meeting—the guards stepped aside without question. The flap was open, and Joshua stood just within, already meeting with Eleazar and Eliab. He turned as we entered, his gray eyes catching mine.

"You heard," I said simply.

He nodded. "Word came from a Gibeonite rider—he collapsed at the altar stones. Cried out for help with his dying breath."

"Then it's true," Phineas muttered. "The five kings have risen together."

Othniel stood tall beside Joshua, his brow furrowed. "The men of Gibeon plead for protection. They used lies to bind us, and yet now —they ask our shield?"

"The oath binds more than words," Joshua said, his voice low but steady. "We swore before Yahweh. To break it now would be to bring judgment on our heads."

"Let them burn," Othniel said, though not with his usual fire. "They deceived us. Let their new masters take what they deserve."

Joshua turned to him, and in that look—stern and sorrowful both—I saw the burden we all carried. "Would you have our covenant mean nothing? Would you let men fall to the sword because they feared us enough to grasp at life?"

Othniel folded his arms, his face darkening. But he said no more.

I stepped forward. "We must move before the kings reach their walls."

Eliab nodded. "They'll strike by nightfall. They've gathered chariots from Lachish, and slingers from Hebron. Their numbers are more than twice the Gibeonite guard."

"And what of Israel's numbers?" Joshua asked.

Eliab grinned grimly. "Enough to remind them who they march against."

Joshua's eyes swept the room. "We march from Gilgal tonight. By dusk, I want every man armed and fed. Phineas, sound the horns and gather the captains. Kalev, you'll lead the scouts ahead of our vanguard. I want reports from the hills before sunrise."

I nodded, already calculating the distance. "We'll need to take the ascent at night. The pass is narrow—good for defense, bad for haste."

"I'll take my men and scout from the west," Eliab said. "We'll harass their flanks if they camp."

Joshua looked to Othniel. "Will you march with me?"

Othniel hesitated, then nodded. "I will not let them face the wrath of Yahweh alone."

Joshua's voice dropped into the cadence that had stirred hearts since Mosheh laid hands upon him. "Then let every sword be sharpened. Let the hosts of Israel move not in anger, but in faith. For Yahweh goes with us, and the lies of men will not undo the promises of God."

A solemn hush followed.

Outside, the first notes of the trumpet call broke the midday heat. Not the blasts of alarm, but the rhythmic rise that summoned warriors to assemble—the beginning of battle not yet seen.

I stepped out with Othniel the heat hitting us like a wall.

Already, movement stirred at the edges of camp. Men strapping on leather armor. Slingers stringing their cords and gathering together fist sized stones. Spears lifted from racks and tested in the sun. Women handed waterskins to sons, mothers pressed kisses to foreheads. A great city rising from dust, ready once more to make war in the name of the covenant.

Othniel said nothing for a while, watching a group of Levites chalking sacred names onto the leather straps that would bind the Ark's poles. His eyes lingered on the holy vessel,

"Why does faith so often come after passion?" he asked softly.

I looked at him.

"Because it's harder," I said. "But it's the only thing that lasts."

He nodded, then turned, his copper skin bright beneath the sun, his shadow stretching long behind him.

The wind shifted.

I turned toward the north, where the cloud line of dust shimmered in the sunlight like a specter—armies of the South stirring, gathering, preparing to descend. The noise of the camp surged louder now: the clatter of shields being lifted from posts, the hiss of sharpening blades, the barked orders of captains wrangling their men into readiness. Othniel had already vanished into the swell of bodies, likely preparing his unit, his eyes still burning from our conversation.

Then, a hush—thin at first, like a frayed thread pulled taut—began to wind through the crowd. The air turned still, unnaturally so. The men stiffened, some falling silent mid-sentence, others instinctively lowering their voices. The sound of sand and sandal grew clearer. Even the children, playing near the cooking pits, paused and looked toward the north entrance of the camp.

Eleazar son of Aaron stepped into the light.

He walked with no fanfare, no trumpet or herald, but the silence that followed him was more commanding than a king's decree. His robe—deep linen dyed in the hues of pomegranate and sand—swayed lightly with his movement. He bore the ephod across his chest, the twelve stones glinting faintly under the midday sun, each one seeming to pulse as if lit from within. His beard was long and silvered, falling like a river of ash upon his chest. But it was his eyes that made the men draw back and bow their heads—eyes dark as olive wood and yet clear, seeing through men as if their hearts had no walls.

Eleazar carried the presence of the Tent with him. Wherever he walked, it felt as though the veil between heaven and earth grew thinner, as if Yahweh's breath brushed the back of one's neck.

He did not shout. He raised a single hand, his fingers marked with the oil of anointing, and spoke.

"Brothers of the covenant," he said, his voice low and smooth as flowing water, "before your hands draw the sword again, let the hands of the priest draw down the fire of heaven."

The men shifted. Others straightened their backs, caught between awe and confusion. A few of the younger ones glanced toward Joshua, uncertain if orders were being countermanded.

Eleazar did not wait for their understanding. He continued, stepping now into the center of the open square.

"We failed not in strength," he said, "but in silence. When the strangers from Gibeon came, did we pray? Did we seek the Voice behind the veil?" His hand rose again, this time gesturing westward toward the Tent of Meeting. "No. We relied on eyes, on words, on the dust-stained garments and cracked wineskins of men—and we forgot the Voice that speaks from flame and cloud."

I felt the words stab deep, even in my own chest. He was not wrong. We had been so drunk on the victory of Ai, so weary from the endless rulings and disputes, that when the strangers came with their flattery and crumbs, we saw in them only relief. Peace, or at least a delay from war. We had taken the burden from our own shoulders, but we had not laid it at the feet of Yahweh.

Joshua stepped forward now, slow and deliberate. The lines around his eyes seemed deeper than before. He had not spoken since the scouts' warning had arrived, had not issued a single command. But now he bowed his head to Eleazar, and all the men followed.

"Speak, priest of Yahweh," Joshua said quietly. "Show us the path."

Eleazar nodded. "Bring water," he said, and a few servants ran to obey. "And bring the horn."

A boy approached, cradling the ram's horn like a newborn. It was thick and worn smooth by use, its spiral shape flecked with lines of oil and ash from a hundred campfires.

Eleazar took it in his hands as the water arrived. He poured the water into a bronze basin, then lifted it high so the light caught its surface, making it flash like molten silver.

"From the Rock," he intoned, "water flowed in the desert. Not by our might. From the heavens, manna fell, not by our wisdom. From the mountain, the voice of Yahweh thundered, not by our choosing."

He raised the horn now to his lips. The sound that followed shook the air—not harsh, but deep, ancient, like something older than

265

the camp, older even than Sinai. It was the sound of fire on the mountain, the breath of God across the wilderness.

We raised our arms to the heavens. Even the warriors among us who feared nothing in battle now trembled—not with fear of men, but with awe.

Eleazar looked upward, arms spread wide. "You who called us from Egypt," he said, "You who made covenant with Avraham and showed mercy to Ya'akov, hear now your servants."

He dipped his fingers in the basin and sprinkled the water in four directions, speaking words that were old before our fathers were born. I did not know them all, though some sounded like the chants of the elders in the days of Sinai, the way Mosheh used to sing in the twilight.

"Cleanse us of presumption," he said. "Cleanse us of the sin of certainty. Restore our ears to hear, our hearts to bow, our steps to wait upon You."

He turned now to Joshua. "You carry the Spear, my brother," he said. "But even Mosheh climbed Sinai only when Yahweh called. So we now wait—for fire, for cloud, for peace or for war, but we wait not without the covering of prayer."

Joshua stepped forward and stood beside Eleazar, shoulder to shoulder. "Let none raise a blade until the priest has raised his hands to heaven," he said to the assembly. "Let none speak of marching until we have heard from the One who speaks in silence."

A long breath moved through the camp.

And then, slowly, with deliberate care, Eleazar began a chant —not loud, but steady. A litany of Yahweh's names, one after another, many I had not heard since the night Mosheh died: **El Elyon, El Roi, Adonai Sabaoth, Yahweh Yireh...**

The names filled the air like incense, curling through our bones, kindling something old and wild and holy within us. Men wept openly. I saw hardened warriors fall prostrate. The sound of swords and shields quieted. Even the animals seemed hushed.

For the first time in days, no man spoke of war.

Only Yahweh was named.

And as Eleazar's chant rose, the wind returned, rushing through the camp from the east—like the breath of the Red Sea once more being parted.

And as Eleazar's chant rose, the wind returned, rushing through the camp from the east—like the breath of the Red Sea once more being parted.

The banners of the tribes rippled, and dust lifted in swirls about our feet as if the very ground bore witness. The Angel of the LORD was among us. He would fight alongside His people. The priest's voice did not falter; if anything, it deepened. The sacred names fell from his lips like drops of oil, setting flame to hearts that had grown cold with the wear of command.

When the final syllable faded, Eleazar lowered his arms. His chest heaved slightly, not with weariness, but with the stillness of completion. Then he turned, his eyes searching, settling on Joshua and then on me. The crowd around us held its breath.   A   p a t h parted between the men, and without a word, Joshua stepped forward. I followed.

Eleazar dipped his hand again into the bronze basin, now holding the water cupped between his palms. It shimmered faintly—not merely from sun, but from something more ancient than firelight. He held it high. "This water was drawn and carried here from afar, from the edge of the Nehar Ha-Yarden, where your feet once parted its flow," he said. "It is not common. The river remembers. And Yahweh has made it holy."

He turned to Joshua first. "Joshua, son of Nun, servant of Mosheh, servant now of the Most High," Eleazar said, and his voice carried through the camp like a proclamation. "You lead not by sword alone, but by covenant. This water is upon you not for conquest, but for purity, for remembrance, and for endurance."

He let the water fall upon Joshua's head. The droplets scattered into his hair, down his face, and into his beard. Joshua did not flinch. His storm-gray eyes closed, and the wind caught his cloak, lifting it like wings.

Then Eleazar turned to me.

"Kalev, son of Jephunneh, grafted to Yehudah, faithful spy and fearless elder—" he paused, looking directly into my eyes, "—you stood firm when others trembled. You believed when others doubted. May Yahweh remember your loyalty, and may this water guard the fire in your bones."

He poured the water over my head.

It was cold—startlingly so—and yet it burned. Not like flame, but like truth. It ran down my neck and along my shoulders like unseen fingers pressing their seal upon me.

Eleazar raised both hands once more, and his voice thundered across the camp,

"Let these men be set apart—not just for war, but for the will of Yahweh. Let every step they take be taken beneath His gaze. Let not victory make them proud, nor hardship make them falter."

The wind answered, swirling around us, pulling robes and banners and hair into its dance.

In the silence that followed, no man spoke. Not even Othniel.

Only the sound of breath and wind and the distant call of a horn far beyond the hills reminded us that time still moved.

But we had been marked. Not for vengeance.

For holiness.

The fire of heaven had not yet fallen. The enemy still gathered. But for a moment, time bent under the weight of prayer, and the camp of Israel remembered who we were: not conquerors, but chosen. Not lords, but sons.

We were now ready.

We were no longer blind.

The Angel of the LORD was among us.

Chapter Seventeen
March of the Storm Bearers

The night clung to us, a moonless veil thick with dust and divine weight. Our sandals stirred the wilderness earth, each step a pulse in the silent march from Gilgal to Gibeon. I strode near the front, my tightly wound locks of hair swaying, carefully bound anew by Azubah earlier, my eyes sharp despite the ache in my bones. The covenant burned in me, urging my feet through the dark, though years of war pressed heavy on my frame.

The column stretched behind, a shadowed river winding through jagged hills. Joshua led, his tall frame cutting the gloom, silver streaks in his beard catching faint torchlight. His silence held us, a tether to the promise we carried, though I saw the sorrow etched in his jaw, the weight of Mosheh' mantle. The men followed, their steps hushed at first, but as hours bled into the night, a chorus rose— prayers half-spoken, chants of Egypt's chains, promises of Yahweh's fire. Young warriors gripped spears too tightly, eyes darting to ridges where shadows lay still. I felt their fear, heavier than the dust on my cloak.

Othniel kept pace beside me, his bronze skin slick with sweat, his young beard full but his eyes heavy with thought. "This march feels like the wilderness again," he said, voice low. "Like we're chasing a shadow we can't name." I adjusted my cloak, the grit rough against my fingers. "Shadows have names, Othniel," I said. "This one's duty. Gibeon calls, and we answer." He nodded, jaw tight, wrestling with the weight of it.

Ahead, Uri stalked, his blondish hair unkept and becoming more wild with each new battle, his spear glinting in his grip. His mutters carried on the wind, sharp with zeal, "Gibeon deserves judgment, not our blood." An echo I had heard many of the young men say during the march that night.

I glanced at him, his copper-toned skin taut with frustration, but held my tongue. The treaty bound us, and we marched for Yahweh's name, not man's worth. My hand brushed my blade's hilt, and the east wind stirred, sharp and alive, a breath of the Almighty's presence.

The terrain grew harsh, stones slipping underfoot as we climbed. Eleazar's voice, like wind through stone, rose behind, chanting Avraham's promise, Sinai's flame. The air stilled when he prayed, as though the heavens leaned closer, and the men's murmurs faded into awe. His white robes glinted in the dark, his stride slow but unyielding, a bridge to the unseen. I caught Phineas's glance at his father, Eleazar, his zeal tempered by the ancient faith.

Joshua had sent Zadok and Eliab ahead of our army, each with a contingent of men, their forms barely visible for awhile before disappearing entirely into the shadows. Earlier, Zadok, had whispered of Amorites watching the hills, his cynicism cutting through the dark. Eliab, younger, twitched toward his dagger, his prayers louder than his steps. I trusted Zadok's edge and Eliab's loyalty, though his nerves frayed with each gust. They'd return soon with word of Gibeon's fate.

As we drew closer to the city of Gibeon, our men's chants grew ragged, their prayers faltering into grunts. Yet none stopped. The covenant was fire in our bones, forged in manna, quail, and parted seas. I remembered Ai's giants, their towers crumbling under my blade. My blood was hotter then, my strength raw. Now, it was quieter, tempered by scars and wisdom, but no less fierce. The east wind roared, carrying dust and something ancient, like creation's first breath. I gripped my blade, and the air pulsed, alive with divine tension.

Joshua raised a hand, and we slowed. He turned, eyes sweeping over us, "We march for Gibeon," he said, voice low thunder. "Not for their worth, but for Yahweh's name. The treaty holds."

Othniel snorted, spear shifting, but Joshua's glance silenced him. Eleazar's chant rose, and the men joined, their hum shaking the earth. I felt it in my chest, more than sound—a stirring of the Almighty's nearness.

Phineas leaned closer, voice barely a whisper. "Do you feel it, Kalev? The air—it's different." I nodded, hand on my blade. "Yahweh is in the wind," I said. "The Angel of the LORD goes before us."

The path twisted through a narrow defile, stones clattering beneath hurried feet as the line pressed forward. Then a figure slipped from the shadows—silent as mist. It was Shammah, son of Uri, eyes sharp beneath the hood of his wolf-hide cloak. His breath came steady, though he had run.

"Commander," he said, voice low, "the hills are empty. No sign of movement—but the air's turned. Still as a held breath. Something's waiting."

I narrowed my eyes, listening to the silence behind his words. "Keep watch. And pray."

A wry smile tugged at the corner of his mouth. "Doing more praying than much else these days—but I'm steady."

I gave a grunt that might have been a laugh. "Keep praying. It keeps your senses sharp."

Without another word, Shammah melted back into the dark, as if the rocks had opened to receive him.

The hours stretched, the night unyielding. My legs burned, but my spirit blazed. Othniel brooded, his spear a shadow. Phineas prayed, and the heavens listened. Joshua led, and we followed, bound by a promise older than the hills. Leadership is weary, a mantle heavier with each step. I thought of the wilderness, the caves of Hebron, the giants' blood on my hands. I couldn't help but think of what Phineas had said, it truly felt as though the Angel of the LORD strode with us, His presence a storm held in check.

The wind tugged at our cloaks as we marched—eastward, always eastward—toward Gibeon's trembling walls. Dust rose in soft clouds at our heels, muffling the creak of leather and clink of bronze. No one spoke. The weight of covenant hung thicker than armor. Joshua's eyes burned forward, unblinking. And then—just before the ridge broke into view—Eleazar suddenly slowed his pace. The silver fringe of his robe caught the dawn, and with a voice that seemed pulled from the tabernacle itself, he lifted his arms. The line of warriors behind him halted as if struck by an unseen hand. In that breathless hush, between step and sword, the high priest began to sing,

"Oh Flame that walked with Father Avraham ,
Smoke and torch 'twixt blood and stone,
You split the sea with breath of thunder,
You made the mountain groan.
Yahweh Tsevaot, flame in the whirlwind,
Speak once more through dust and tread.
Lead Your people with sword of mercy,
Tread Your enemies with dread.
You are the fire upon the mountain,
You are the hush within the tent,
You are the cry in Midian's darkness,
And the rock the hammer rent.
Pour Your fear upon the mighty,
Break the bones of kings in pride.
Remember Gibeon though they fooled us,
You are justice, not denied.
Bind the sun until we finish,
Hold the moon till vengeance sings.
Let no one stand against Your chosen,
Till the earth forgets their kings."

The song fell into silence like coals into ash—still burning, still alive. No one clapped, no one spoke. Some closed their eyes, others clutched their weapons more tightly, as though the sacred words had been etched onto the blade. I glanced at Joshua. His brow furrowed in reverence, lips moving in quiet prayer. Even Othniel stood motionless, eyes bright with something deeper than battle-readiness. The march resumed without command, our feet now steady with more than determination—with remembrance. I felt the weight of Yahweh's mercy like a mantle across my shoulders. The hills ahead waited for us, but it was not only swords we carried—it was a promise, forged in fire, sealed in blood, and now stirred anew by song.

Then, torchlight flickered in the distance—two figures running. Zadok and Eliab, faces pale in the glow. Zadok's voice was a hiss,

"Gibeon is under attack, the city burns."

I looked to Joshua, his eyes blazing like storm clouds. The wind roared, and the covenant pulsed in my blood. The battle was near.

The horizon bled fire, Gibeon's walls wreathed in flame beneath the siege of the five Amorite kings. From our ridge above the valley, the Israelite host stood in shadowed silence, a sea of slings and spears and shields glinting faintly in the pre-dawn glow. I gripped my blade, its weight familiar yet heavy with the promise of blood. The air thrummed, alive with divine tension, and I felt the covenant pulse in my veins, a fire older than the hills.

Zadok and Eliab's words—"*Gibeon still burns*"—hung like a curse. Smoke curled upward behind them, and the scent of scorched grain and cedar clung to their cloaks. Joshua stood before us, the Spear of the Twelve Clans, as though the Almighty's own fire coursed through him. I watched my old friend, and a shiver traced my spine—

not from fear of the enemy, but of him, of what he was becoming under Yahweh's hand.

He did not speak long, nor loud. With a glance toward the western ridge, he turned to Zadok and Eliab, "Take your men," he said, "run west and circle the ridge unseen. Cut off the retreat. When the Amorite line breaks—and it will—you will strike from the rear." Zadok gave a short nod, already turning. Eliab paused just a moment longer, eyes scanning the horizon. Analytical, cautious—he was reading the terrain like a scroll. Then he followed.

They vanished into the veil of dust, their departure swift and silent. We would not see them again until the field turned red, and their blades found the backs of men who thought they had escaped.

Joshua raised his arms, and the host stilled. His voice, raw and resonant, broke the silence,

"Yahweh, God of Avraham, Yitzhak, and Ya'akov, You have bound us to Gibeon by covenant. Fight for Your people! Let Your enemies scatter!" The words were a thunderclap, and the wind roared, sharp with the scent of dust and flame. Eleazar, behind the lines, took up a chant, his voice like Sinai's echoes, and the air seemed to bend, heavy with the Almighty's nearness. I felt it in my bones, a weight that was both terror and awe.

Joshua turned, his gaze sweeping the host. "To the valley!" he cried, and we surged forward, his spear raised to heaven, a tide of flint and faith. My sandals pounded the earth, Othniel at my side, his bronze skin taut with purpose, shield in one hand, spear in the other, his battle axe tucked tight into his leather belt. The warrior's eyes burned, no longer questioning but ready to descend upon the seed of the Anakim. Uri ran ahead, his wiry frame a blur, his spear already raised, along with thousands of others beside him. Their zeal was a flame, bright and dangerous, and I wondered if it would consume them before the day was done.

The Amorites filled the valley like a living wound across the land. From ridge to ridge they stretched—hordes uncountable, warriors shoulder to shoulder, their armor clattering like a plague of locusts. Smoke curled around their standards, and the wind carried the scent of ash, blood, and burnt meat. I had seen war. I had bled on high places and trampled the dead beneath my sandals—but never had I seen anything like the hosts that gathered beneath the banners of five kings, a force bred not for conquest, but for desecration.

They came from the cities of fire and black stone—Jerusalem, Hebron, Jarmuth, Lachish, and Eglon—each king bringing his own breed of devils. Men who carved the bones of their enemies into whistles, who drank blood and called it worship, who lit their own children on stone altars and danced as they burned. This was no army of mortals alone. These were the seed of giants—not all of them towering, but all marked by the old corruption. Twisted men, unnaturally broad of shoulder and pale of eye, their veins thick with cursed blood. Their faces were painted in the style of the Rephaim— jagged lines of red and black that bled into their hairlines and ran like rivers down their necks. Some wore armor, if it could be called that— patchwork scales of bronze stitched into hide and human skin. Others went shirtless, their torsos scarred with ritual lashings and brands of forgotten gods.

The war drums began—a relentless rhythm like the beating of the earth's own heart. Their voices rose with it, high and shrill, not like the cries of men but the keening of jackals. One of their priests, a black-robed creature half mad with his own sorcery, began to shriek a curse from the center of their line. His voice warped the air around him, and several of our own men flinched. I watched Joshua step forward. He raised his Spear to the heavens—and the priest fell silent, gasping, clutching his head as though it would split. He collapsed to the ground and did not rise again.

This was the Angel of the LORD doing it, He had already descended on the armies of our enemy.

As our ranks formed—twelve thousand strong, drawn from every tribe save Levi—we stood beneath the shadow of Gibeon's smoldering walls. The city still burned, but the people were safe. That was what mattered. We had made covenant with them in the Name, and now we would keep it with blood. I looked to my elef—a thousand men of Yehudah, the heart of the left flank. Behind me stood Avidan, banner raised high, cords snapping in the wind like whips. The warriors around me were gibborim, mighty men, tested and tempered by fire. My voice rose, not in command, but in prayer,

"O Elohei Avraham, Yitzchak, v'Yaakov—strike the mind of our enemy. Let their sins return upon their heads."

And then we charged.

The valley shook with our rage. Dust flew like mist, and our sandals thundered across the broken earth. But as we closed the gap, something—shifted.

The Amorites began to shudder. It wasn't our swords that unmade them. It was something deeper. I saw men drop their weapons mid-run, hands trembling, eyes wide with terror not of flesh but of spirit. Some clutched their ears, howling as if the Angel of the LORD Himself had whispered damnation into their skulls. Others spun in place, striking out at unseen foes, their mouths frothing with confusion.

One Amorite captain stood in my path. He was tall, muscled, body painted in black spirals. He held a spiked mace and swung it wide with a howl—but it was a howl of panic, not rage. I caught the blow on my shield, stepped inward, and drove my blade beneath his ribs. He gasped, blood erupting from his mouth, and collapsed in the dust. I did not stop.

To my left, I saw an Amorite man fall to his knees and begin clawing at his own face, as if to tear out whatever horror had taken root in his soul.

The Angel of the LORD was among them—not in fire, not in flood, but in madness. He was turning their own minds into dust.

Still, they were many. Countless. And though they were unraveling, they could still fight. Most did. They fought like cornered beasts, snarling, flailing, bleeding. One bore down on Avidan, swinging a crude blade of volcanic glass. Avidan caught the blow with his staff, the banner twisting in the air, and drove his knee into the man's chest.

The Amorite stumbled, and Avidan smashed the staff across his temple. The banner never fell.

And then—I saw him.

The giant.

He stood head and shoulders above the others, a grotesque colossus clad in bronze plates too large for any forge I knew. Chains hung from his belt, some ending in broken jawbones. His skin was the color of ash, and his head was bald save for a single braid that reached to his waist. His eyes were black—no sclera, no soul. He did not scream like the others. He did not flinch at the Presence. He walked through the chaos as if born for it, crushing friend and foe alike.

I watched him backhand two of our men into the dirt with a blow like a hammer. Another he kicked square in the chest, sending him flying through the air. But none of them died. Yahweh had promised.

We would not lose a man.

"Shield wall!" I roared, and my gibborim formed at once, the clatter of bronze and leather like thunder made flesh.

Still the giant came.

I met his gaze. He raised his weapon—a pole arm jagged with teeth and bone—and pointed it at me. The unspoken challenge was clear. Not yet. Soon.

"Let him wait, corner him and keep him busy" I yelled, then turned back to the ranks. Fifty of my men circled around him, their long spears keeping the giant at bay, unable to storm their fence.

To my right, Othniel shouted, "Flank right!" and a score of men followed, his voice already seasoned with command. A smile broke across my face, grim and proud. Behind us, Naphtali and Ephraim lifted their horns, their war cries echoing across the field like the shouts of angels.

Othniel and his men bound toward the giant, his anger and fury growing with each moment he could't escape my men who had surrounded him. Othniel grasped his battle axe out from his belt, and with the bronze tip glistening in the light, he threw it which such force it swung over and over through the air and landed directly into the forehead of the beast. Instantly it crashed to the ground, and our soldiers had to dash out of the way or else get crushed by its sickening size.

Our men let out a huge battle cry of joy, but there was no time to relish in the defeat of this spawn of the Watchers, too many Amorites still fought with wild abandon.

Uri was a terror, his spear a blur as he carved through the foe, his voice rising in a psalm of vengeance,

"The Lord is a warrior; Yahweh is His name!" His skin glistened with sweat and blood, his eyes alight with a fire that bordered on madness. An Amorite charged him, but Uri sidestepped and thrust, the man crumpling with a scream. I saw the zeal in him, sharp as a blade, and feared it might cut too deep, sparing neither friend nor foe.

The ground was slick with the mingling of blood and flesh, and each step became a contest of will and balance. I pressed forward through the mire, my sword swinging wide, cutting down a warrior with skin the hue of clay and muscles thick as cedar branches. He roared as he fell, a sound more beast than man, and his bulk crashed into the mud like a fallen pillar of some foreign temple.

To my right, Othniel and his men surged ahead, his spear an extension of his rage. He was not a large man—though wiry and compact—but in the midst of battle, he burned like a lamp of judgment. His voice never stopped—half battle cry, half prayer, he chanted the sacred psalms between gasps of blood-soaked breath.

"Yahweh, scatter the bones of the wicked!" he bellowed, and with a swift thrust, he drove the bronze tip of his spear beneath the ribs of a fleeing Amorite. The man stumbled and coughed out a black gout of blood, collapsing in the churned soil. "Let the righteous rejoice in vengeance!"

I caught sight of Serach, son of Asher, young and silent, his arms painted red with the day's work. His shield arm hung low from the weight of countless blocks, but his stance remained steady, centered, as if forged to the earth itself. He faced down a foe nearly twice his size—an Amorite bearing a curved blade of foreign bronze, likely looted from a fallen Hittite or Egyptian. The giant moved like a toppled column but struck with the panic-born speed of a man who knows the gods have turned from him.

Serach parried once, his buckler ringing like struck bronze. Twice, his blade caught sparks. Then he dipped low—not with desperation, but calculation—and swept behind the man's knee with surgical precision. The Amorite buckled, letting out a groan that sounded more animal than man, and Serach ended him with a single stroke across the throat, clean and sure.

His chest heaved. I saw no terror in his eyes. No awe. Only fire, contained and directed. The boy I had seen just moons ago at the battle of Ai was gone. In his place stood something honed—

something Yahweh had shaped in silence. Not just a warrior. A witness. A judge.

As my spear found one cursed piece of flesh after another, near the hill's bend, I spotted Abihud of Dan, his ash-blond hair clinging to his temples, dark streaks of war-paint bleeding with sweat. He was locked in close combat with a pair of Amorite twins—enormous, snarling men whose faces bore matching tattoos like ancient runes. Their attacks were brutal, uncoordinated but thunderous. Abihud wove between them like wind through reeds, blades flashing. He slashed one across the thigh and then vaulted into a roll beneath the hammer-fist of the other, coming up behind them like a wraith.

I reached him just as the second raised a war axe overhead.

"Down!" I shouted.

Abihud dropped to a crouch, and I slammed into the Amorite's side, blade-first. He screamed and grabbed at me, his hand crushing my shoulder like a bear's jaw. I gritted my teeth and drove the hilt of my sword into his temple. He reeled, releasing me, and Abihud rose with a cry, plunging one of his curved blades deep into the man's chest. The twin collapsed, and the other fled, limping. I did not pursue. There were others still fighting.

From above, Shammah of Reuven held the line alone. He had mounted the broken ridge at first light and stood like a pillar among falling men. His round shield shone with blood and dust, and he swung his short spear in wide, measured arcs. I watched as he caught an Amorite under the chin with a backhand blow of his shield, then crushed the man's skull beneath his foot. Calm and unmoved, he turned to face the next warrior. His voice rang out across the chaos—deep, commanding, fearless.

We had stopped briefly to reorient the advance—Joshua and I needed to confirm the direction of the march, the ground having twisted with hills and broken ravines as if the land itself sought to mislead us. I stood at the head of my elef—one thousand warriors from Yehudah, arrayed in disciplined order. The banners of our clans moved like flames in the wind, their shields catching the light of the rising sun, glinting like copper. Around me, my immediate contingent of three hundred—the gibborim, my chosen warriors—tightened their ranks. These were men who would follow me into fire if I asked it.

Alongside me stood Othniel, son of Kenaz—my blood, my shadow, my future. He shouted commands with a voice that had grown steadier in the last days, a man ripening quickly under the strain of war. His eyes flicked from ridge to gulch, reading the signs of movement, of terrain, of threat. His spear gleamed with use, and his shield arm never lowered. He had become what Yahweh had whispered in his bones.

Then we saw him.

Another giant.

He rose from the smoke like a nightmare remembered—a remnant of the Rephaim, a beast of living bone and sinew, standing a full head and shoulders above any man. His skin was gray and scarred, his chest painted with the blood of animals and men alike. He wore no armor, for his flesh was like stone. In one hand he wielded a massive flanged mace—black stone bound in leather straps—and in the other, a chain bound with hooks, still dripping with flesh.

He roared once, and the sound shivered the air. Our men staggered, though none fled. Not a one. The terror he brought was real, but it found no root in us. Not here. Not today.

I had seen giants fall. Othniel had just smashed a brutal beast with his axe. I had cut them down with my own blade at Ai, in the mountain passes that drank blood by the gallon. This one was no different. His size did not make him a god.

Only taller.

I raised my sword and pointed toward the beast. "Surround him," I ordered. "Yehudah presses from the south, Dan from the east, Reuven from the rocks. Net him in."

The commands were not shouted—they were roared. And the captains obeyed like wheels turning beneath a chariot. Trumpets answered across the slopes. Dust rose like smoke from the feet of our men as they moved, a thousand voices humming the name of Yahweh. Banners dipped. Formations shifted.

And the trap closed.

Still, the giant did not run.

He swung that chain like a threshing tool, knocking warriors from their feet. But no one fell to death. Bruised, bloodied, perhaps—but not broken. I saw Abihud take a blow to the chest that would've split a horse. He rolled, spit blood, and rose laughing. Another man—Danite, his name I did not know—caught the edge of the mace on his shield, was thrown back a dozen paces, but staggered upright with a grin and threw a rock into the giant's face.

That got his attention.

The giant bellowed again and turned—but the world had shifted. The fire was no longer his.

It was ours.

I broke from the line, Othniel at my side, and together we closed the final span of earth. The giant saw us coming and grinned, those filed teeth blackened with rot. He raised his chain to strike, but I was already moving.

I dove left. The hook-laced chain whistled past my shoulder, missing by inches, striking a boulder and carving into it like butter.

Othniel was on him from the right—his battle axe flashing like lightning. He struck low, behind the knee.

Thunk—the sound of bronze in flesh.

The giant screamed and staggered, but did not fall.

I rolled beneath his guard and sliced at his thigh, the edge of my blade biting deep. Blood burst in a hot jet, dark and reeking.

Still, he fought.

He raised the mace and brought it down like a falling star. I threw myself to the side, felt the ground quake as it struck. Pebbles danced in the shockwave. I rose, panting, and met Othniel's eye.

"Now," I said.

Together we charged.

The giant tried to bring his chain around, but it caught on a dead tree root. His weapon snarled in the earth for one fatal heartbeat —and that was all we needed.

I went high. Othniel went low.

I plunged my sword into the giant's chest just below the collarbone. Bone split. Blood poured. I held on with both hands as he staggered backward.

At the same instant, Othniel's axe drove upward beneath the ribcage, through gut and lung and into the heart from below.

The giant screamed.

It was not a battle-cry, but a death-wail.

He dropped to one knee.

I climbed his body, tore my sword free, and drove it a second time into his throat. His hands clawed the air once, then fell limp. His body crashed to the earth like a falling tower.

Dust choked the sky. Silence followed.

Then—

A cheer.

It began as a murmur, then a roar. Yehudah shouted it first, then Reuven, then Dan.

Men beat their shields and howled like wolves. Shofars blared from the ridge.

The valley shook with joy.

The giant was dead.

And Yahweh's name was sung above the ruins of fear.

Othniel stood beside me, breathing hard, blood on his face and arms. He said nothing. He didn't need to. We had done what we came to do. He wiped his battle axe upon the ground, the black blood of the giant was thick and heavy,.

And still—there were more Amorites to drive into the jaws of judgment.

I lifted my sword.

"Forward," I said.

And the clan of Yehudah moved like fire.

"Zadok and Eliab have not returned," Othniel muttered to me, "But I saw a glint up high—Zadok's position. He is marking their path ready for blood."

I nodded, scanning the horizon. "Eliab will follow," I said. "He is Yitzhakhar. He calculates before he leaps."

Then the ground itself began to tremble—a low rumble that at first I mistook for thunder. But it was not thunder. It had weight. It had rhythm. Another Amorite reserve had entered the field, emerging from behind a boulder-strewn rise: massive men, their bodies thick with scar tissue and ritual paint, some wielding dual axes, others clubs made from petrified tree roots dark with time. These were not Rephaim, but they bore the blood of giants—kin to the Anakim, bred in defiance of heaven. Their chieftain wore a helmet made from a lion's skull, its teeth yellowed, its eye sockets hollow with dread. When he lifted his blade—a jagged obsidian thing that caught the sun like fire—the warriors behind him roared as one.

I looked to my elef, to the commanders of the hundreds and fifties. Each stood ready. My banner-bearer, Avidan, raised the staff high, its cords snapping in the wind. Around me, the gibborim tightened formation. We were the heart of Yehudah's strength. No man would pass us unless it was through blood.

286

But even before I gave the command, movement caught my eye.

Uri, son of Hur broke from the line. He charged like a desert hawk, spear spinning in a deadly arc, his face bore the stillness of an altar. He struck the Amorite chieftain high in the chest—but the blow glanced off bone and hide. The beast-man roared, swinging his tree-root weapon with an arc so wide it cleaved the air itself. It clipped Uri's shoulder and spun him to the ground like a doll.

"Uri!" I shouted, breaking rank.

But before I could reach him, Joshua was already there.

He moved like judgment descending—a swirl of cloak and bronze, his blade already red, his footsteps sure upon blood-slick stone. With one hand, he pulled Uri to his feet; with the other, he blocked a blow from the chieftain's axe that would have cracked a chariot wheel. Their blades clashed, sparks flying like stars struck from heaven's anvil.

Joshua's face was unreadable—stoic, focused. But in his eyes was that same unrelenting fire I had seen once on Sinai's slopes. Not anger. Authority.

He struck three times—shoulder, thigh, chest—and on the third, the Amorite chieftain dropped to his knees, the lion skull slipping sideways on his head. Blood frothed from the man's mouth. His weapon fell with a thud, and then his body toppled, the lion's helm cracking against the rocks like the ending of a curse.

The Amorites hesitated, their line faltering.

I seized the moment.

"To me!" I shouted, raising my blade high. "Yehudah—press the line! For The Name, the God of Avraham, Yitzhak, and Ya'akov!"

My elef surged forward, the rhythm of war mounting like waves on a shore.

Around me, my hundreds of gibborim formed a wedge like sharpened flint, our shields locked, our spears and swords bristling.

We were a storm bound in flesh. Behind us, the war horns of Naphtali and Ephraim blared from the hills, echoing across the valley like the shout of angels. The sound turned the heads of dying men and gave strength to the legs of the living. Zadok reappeared atop the ridge, silhouette sharp against the morning haze, loosing another arrow. The shaft vanished into a clamor of bronze and flesh—his presence a quiet benediction of death, each arrow a final prayer over a soul that had stood against the Living God.

Then, to our right, movement like smoke breaking from stone —Eliab, along with Reuel and our most skilled stone slingers. Reuel could hit the eye of a sparrow at three field's length.

Eliab and his men rose from the cover of shattered rock, not with haste, but with gravity. His cloak bore the mud and frost of hours in waiting. His face was smeared with ash. Yet his eyes—those sharp, storm-lit eyes—were untouched by time or weariness. In his right hand, he lifted a curved ram's horn and blew a single, piercing note. I motioned to Avidan to sound the ram's horn to unleash our stone slingers.

The sound rolled like thunder across the flank. It was not a call for courage—it was the pronouncement of judgment. At the sound of the call, Reuel and the slingers let out volley after volley of stones, the size of a grown man's fist, they came raining down like a hurricane upon the waves of Amorite soldiers.

Eliab and his men fell upon the Amorites with the precision of a hawk breaking a serpent's spine. One by one the enemy of the ridge turned to meet them, and one by one they fell, necks split or bellies opened. Eliab himself fought in near silence. His curved blade danced with cruel grace, snatching light with every turn. I saw him lock blades with a war-chief twice his size, sidestep a killing stroke, and open the man's throat with a reverse cut so clean it looked like water spilled.

I stood for a moment, unmoving—awed, not by the slaughter, but by the weight of timing. Eliab had not hesitated, but neither had he rushed. His men had trusted him with their stillness, and now they reaped the reward of fire unleashed. It was what it meant to lead.

Around me, my own gibborim roared their approval and lifted their spears to the sky. Yehudah would not be outdone. We surged forward, drawn into the chaos by the certainty that the battle had shifted. Not by strength alone—but by vision.

Uri, bloodied but upright, stood behind Joshua, leaning on his spear like a prophet come down from the mountain. Othniel grinned beside me, teeth bared, his sword lifted.

"Today," he said, "the sun will not set on these men."

And I believed him.

Because Yehudah was moving, and the wrath of heaven marched with us.

The remaining warriors faltered.

Our men surged forward like a tide unbound. Othniel led a charge down the slope, driving the enemy into disarray. Ten the arrows of Zadok's an his men rained down. Eliab, limping but unbroken, took up a fallen axe and hurled it into the back of a fleeing warrior. The tide had turned.

I moved among the men, cutting where I must, shouting encouragement, striking down those too slow to flee. It was not beauty—it was not even heroism—it was survival, and it was covenant. These were the seed of ancient evil, and the land would know no peace while they yet drew breath.

But as I paused atop a slope slick with blood and ice, a knot began to form in my gut. The ranks of the Amorites were deeper than we'd seen in the valley below. Their lines, though ruptured, spread wide across the horizon, cresting hills like waves. I saw banners still waving near the tree line of Reuel, more flanking out toward Makkedah, where the road wound into hill-country thick with brush and caves. This was no minor host. These were not just five kings and their city-levies. These were old alliances awakened—clan after clan of giant-blooded Amorites, drawn by fear and rage into one final stand.

Their confusion still held, a madness sewn by the hand of the Name, but even madness had legs. And legs could run.

"Commander!" a voice called behind me—young, breathless. One of the men from Yehudah, I didn't catch his name. His left hand was soaked in blood, but it dangled limp at his side. "There are more of them, sir, past the hill. We routed three lines, but they're reforming near the pass! They are like locusts that never end"

I nodded, shoved him toward the medics, and turned back to the fray.

Our pursuit had begun to scatter. Some men, hungry for vengeance, chased too far. Others paused, exhausted, stunned by the endless tide of enemies. Phineas's chants of prayer still rang—somewhere ahead of me—and Othniel's band pressed hard on the right flank, pushing a group of armored warriors back toward the ravine. But it would not be enough. We were thinning, and the sun was climbing high. I squinted into its light.

Midday. At best, we had three or four hours of full sun. Maybe less, if the haze returned. And there were too many. Too many hills. Too many paths of retreat. Too many giant-kin with blood oaths in their mouths and blades in their hands. If the sun set, they would vanish into terrain they knew better than any of us.

They would crawl into caves and shadowed woods, heal their wounds, sharpen their hatred—and strike again. Not in force, but in whispers: raiding our herds, burning our storehouses, killing our children in the dark. Guerilla war. Ghost war. A serpent that could never be found, only felt by its bite.

I spat into the dirt and turned, pushing downhill toward where I last saw Joshua. The chaos thickened around me. Men cried out—some from pain, others from victory. Swords clashed like hammers, and the ground groaned under the weight of broken bodies. I hacked through one fleeing Amorite, caught another across the knee, and shouldered past a dying horse sprawled across the road.

"Make way!" I shouted. My foot soldiers cleared a path for me, yelling, "Make clear the field for the Elder of Yehudah!"

An Ephraimite recognized me and pulled two spearmen aside. "Joshua is ahead, near the eastern rise!"

I pressed on. Somewhere behind me, the thundering voice of Eleazar still rose, reciting from the ancient chants, breathing into the bones of the men. His was a voice forged in fire, cooled in blood. And still, it would not be enough if night fell.

Another knot of Amorites—this one not fleeing, but crouched in ambush. One threw a spear. I turned my shoulder, felt it scrape past my ribs. Pain burst, but not deep—flesh wound. I didn't slow. My blade caught the first in the gut, shoved him backward into the second, whose eyes were still wide with fear. They fell, and I leapt over them, lungs heaving.

When I finally spotted Joshua, he stood—his face streaked with ash and blood, eyes like twin embers. He was directing the men from the rock ledge, his sword lifted high, rallying where formations were breaking. He looked like something carved from the mountain.

"Joshua!" I called out as I neared.

He turned, recognized me, and stepped down from the ledge, pushing through two guards.

"Kalev," he said, voice hoarse but firm.

I grasped his arm in greeting, but there was no time for pleasantries.

"There are too many," I said, keeping my voice low. "Even with the confusion Yahweh has cast, they're still slipping away. North, east, west—every escape path is bleeding them. If the sun falls before we finish them—"

"They'll return," he said, finishing my thought.

"Yes. In shadows. In threes and fours. They'll strike caravans, slit throats in the dark. We will never know peace."

Joshua nodded slowly, gaze drifting skyward. The sun was still above us, a burning eye in the pale blue, but it had already begun its arc downward.

"We've no time to set snares or chase them across every hill," I said. "We must finish this now. All of it. Here."

He said nothing for a long breath.

Around us, the battle churned. The cries of war continued— raw, ragged, righteous.

Then Joshua looked back to me, and something flared behind his eyes. Not despair. Not frustration. But the same fire I had seen once before—when we crossed the Nehar Ha-Yarden, when the priests' feet touched the riverbed and the water fled.

"The sun," he said, quiet but certain. "It must not set."

I blinked. "You would ask that of Yahweh?"

He didn't answer with words. He only turned from me and climbed back onto the rise, lifting his sword again.

The men fell silent. They knew something was coming. They could feel it—the breathless hush before thunder.

Joshua raised both arms.

"Men of Israel," he called, his voice stronger than I had heard all day. "This day does not belong to us—it belongs to the Living God! And the hour is not yet full!"

He turned his eyes heavenward, and in that moment, time seemed to fold in upon itself. The blood on his face glistened like oil. The wind stilled.

"Sun," he cried, "stand still over Gibeon! And moon, over the Valley of Aijalon!"

A silence swept across the valley—long and eerie. Even the Amorites seemed to freeze. Even the birds stilled.

And then... the light changed.

It did not dim. It did not move.

It paused.

The sun held its place in the sky as if gripped by an invisible hand. The air grew dense, full of unseen fire. And every man who stood beneath that burning eye knew: the day had been claimed, not by man, but by the command of Heaven.

From the ridge, Eleazar's chant grew louder, a cadence of fire and promise. The wind howled, carrying the scent of ash and earth, and the sky darkened, not with clouds but with something heavier, as though the heavens themselves leaned low. Then it came—a crack like the splitting of the world, and hailstones fell, massive and unnatural, each the size of a man's fist. Reuel and his stone slingers struck the Amorites ranks with merciless precision, crushing skulls, shattering shields, sparing our ranks as though guided by an unseen hand. Off in the distance, entire regiments of Amorites were being engulfed by massive hailstones pounding down upon with no mercy.

The Amorites broke, their confusion now panic, their cries swallowed by the hail's roar. We pursued, our blades relentless, but the storm did greater work than our swords. Bodies littered the valley, blood mixing with ice, and I saw Joshua ahead, his cloak billowing, his sword raised as he drove through the fleeing ranks. His face was alight, not with joy but with divine fire, and I wondered if he was still the man I knew or something more, a vessel for the Almighty's wrath.

Othniel rallied his men, leading them to cut off a knot of Amorites fleeing toward the hills. His commands were sharp, his battle axe crashing left and right, smashing the bodies of one Amorite after another, and I saw the leader he would become, forged in this crucible of blood and covenant. "Hold the line!" he called, and his unit moved as one, their trust in him absolute. I fought on, my breath ragged, my blade heavy with the weight of lives taken.

The battle stretched, the sun burned bright, its light harsh against the valley's carnage. My muscles burned, my scars ached, but the covenant drove me forward. Phineas's voice still rang, his psalms now hoarse but unbroken, his staff raised, Eleazar's chant pulsed behind, a heartbeat of faith, and the hail ceased, leaving the valley a field of ruin.

The sun burned overhead, fixed like a gold coin hammered into the sky. The shadow it cast never moved, and time—whatever it once was—had fled before Y Yahweh's command. We gave no quarter.

The battlefield was not a field at all, but a torn and muddied wasteland strewn with broken spears, shattered shields, and limbs that no longer knew the men they had once served. And the storm— oh, the storm still lashed out like a living spirit, chasing the cowards who turned their backs. Hail crashed down on fleeing Amorites, piercing helms, cracking bone, burying itself into the flesh of giants' sons. The Angel of the LORD rained down upon wave after wave of Amorite legions.

But those who stayed to fight? They met us.

And we met them with fire in our eyes.

I lunged beneath the swing of a tall warrior with ochre-painted skin and cleaved him from knee to groin. The cry he gave was brief, gurgled, as blood poured like wine over the earth. He staggered forward, dead before he fell, and I turned to find another.

There was always another.

To my left, Uri fought as though the Ark itself was behind him. His spear moved with speed that defied flesh, striking with precision honed not by years but by calling. His lips never stopped moving— chanting psalms, roaring curses, whispering the Name. One Amorite tried to catch him from behind, but Uri wheeled and drove his spear through the man's throat so cleanly that it whistled coming out.

Ahead, Othniel led a wedge of of our clan into a knot of retreating soldiers. They did not break formation; they became the blade of Yahweh's judgment. I watched as Othniel's axe was tossed in a perfect arc and took a man through the shoulder so forcefully that the corpse spun backward. Then he was among them—picking up a spear off the ground he heaved it into the gut of beast of a man, his face wearing the scull of a jackal, the force of the spear knocking him back, yet still he came at Othniel. Wrenching his battle axe out of the shoulder of the fallen enemy, Othniel turned just in time to strike it into the jackal face Amorite who instantly stopped, and fell to the ground with a thud.

Everywhere I looked, my brothers were aflame with purpose.

We became the judgment of God.

One of their champions—a hulking man in lion pelts—rushed toward me with twin axes, his mouth frothing with curses in the tongue of the hill clans. I met him head-on. His first axe caught my leather bracer and rang like a bell. The second missed. I drove my elbow into his nose, shattering it, then stepped inside his next swing and rammed my blade up under his chin. His body twitched as the bronze found his brain, and I yanked the sword free with a cry that was more breath than voice.

All around us, the earth ran red.

And yet—they kept coming.

The Amorites were not like other Kena'ani kings. These were not soft men of walls and feasts. These were wild men—sons of desert and cliff and ancient blood. Their ancestors had warred against us in the wilderness, had preyed on our stragglers, had tried to poison our journey before we even reached this land. And their seed had grown savage in the dark. Many were half-giants, tall and broad, with sinews like rope and eyes that held no mercy.

One such brute barreled toward me, wielding a club the size of a tree branch. He bellowed something in a tongue I did not know. I ducked beneath his first swing and drove my shoulder into his gut. He didn't move. The second swing grazed my shoulder, sent lightning up my arm, but I clung to him, drawing my dagger and driving it again and again into his side. He roared, backhanded me into the dirt, but I rolled with it and came up beside him, slicing the back of his knee. He collapsed, and I drove my sword through the base of his neck, severing spine and soul.

My breath burned like smoke in my chest.

Still the fighting raged—bronze against flesh, shouts swallowed by wind and the hiss of hail striking bodies already broken. Yet even as the field turned red beneath our feet, a gnawing unease took hold of me: no word of the Five Kings. Not a whisper from my men, no sight of royal garb among the heaps of dying. I had scanned the carnage again and again, and nowhere did I see the proud standards or jeweled cloaks that should have marked their presence. Only the shattered ranks of the Amorite host, dying by sword, by stone, by storm.

I knelt beside a man gasping on the edge of death, his leg crushed beneath a fallen shield, his chest cleaved but not yet still. He looked at me—his eyes wide with the terror of a defeated world.

"Where are your kings?" I asked, low and hard, my hand tightening around the hilt of my sword.

His lips quivered. Blood spilled from the corner of his mouth, thick and dark, bubbling with each labored breath. He coughed, a sound like gravel stirred in the throat of the earth.

"They… fled," he rasped, voice barely more than wind. "Before… before the hail… they knew it was lost. They ran—east… east of Makkedah. A cave. They hide… in a cave…"

His words trailed off into a final rattle. I rose, the weight of his last breath clinging to me like ash.

The kings had fled the battlefield while their men died by the thousands.

Cowards.

But worse—strategists.

I turned, scanning the eastern hills for a cave. The light had not faded yet, and

Joshua had prayed for more.

We would have time.

And we would find them.

The sun refused to fall. The light remained sharp, as though the day itself held its blade to the throat of night and would not let it pass. I lost track of time—was it one hour? Two? How many men had I cut down? Ten? Twenty? I could no longer feel my fingers. I could not hear my own heartbeat. I was bone and muscle and breath—and the covenant that guided us.

Joshua had disappeared into the thick of it. I caught glimpses of him only now and again—his cloak flaring as he descended upon the enemy like a tempest, sword blazing. Men fled at his approach. And rightly so. He did not fight like a man defending a cause; he fought like one possessed—by purpose, by prophecy, by the Spirit of Yahweh. No arrow found him. No blade slowed him.

He was war incarnate.

At one point I passed Eleazar. He stood atop a high stone, arms raised, his priestly garments made him stand out, his voice still carried, deep and strange, half a prayer and half a song. I did not know the tongue. It was older than Ivrim—older than Sinai, perhaps. The ground beneath him seemed to tremble as he prayed.

The storm of hail grew fiercer whenever he spoke.

Men fell by dozens.

Some tried to run, but the hail hit them, the Angel of the LORD felled them. Others turned to fight, but we met them with the fire of generations. One warrior, mad with fear, tried to throw himself at my feet in surrender. I hesitated only a moment—then ran him through. This was not the day for mercy. Mercy had its time. This was a day of reckoning.

There were no songs now.

Only the ring of bronze, the sound of lungs gasping, the wet splash of blood hitting dirt.

I stood in the red slush of churned mud and blood, scanning the battlefield one final time. The storm was thinning now, the sky above still locked in that strange stillness—the sun arrested in its path. We had hours yet, perhaps more, if Yahweh willed it. I turned and caught the eye of Hanoch, a swift-footed Ephraimite barely into his manhood, his sword notched and dripping.

"You—Hanoch," I called. "Run like thunder to Joshua. Tell him the kings fled before the hailstones fell. They're hiding in a cave, east of Makkedah. Go!"

He nodded, fear and purpose mingling in his face, and took off through the chaos, ducking between corpses and struggling wounded, vanishing into the storm's edge like a wraith. Around me, the last pockets of Amorite resistance collapsed, their lines broken beyond repair, their men surrendering only to death.

Moments later, as I drove my blade through the ribs of a limping spearman, I saw Hanoch return, breathless and wide-eyed, with blood from another man splashed across his chest. "Commander!" he called. "Joshua ordered the cave to be sealed. He's sent men already. Says let no king slip away, but the battle must end before judgment comes. He will deal with them in full when the field is ours."

I nodded once, grimly. The Lord's anointed knew what he was doing. The kings would not escape their fate. Not this day. Not after what we'd seen.

By the time we cleared the last ravine, the battlefield behind us looked like something out of an ancient tale—red, broken, silent but for the wind. I saw bodies heaped in mounds, men still twitching as blood pooled beneath them. There were none of the Twelve Tribes among the fallen. Not one. I saw bruises, cracked shields, bloodied faces—but no corpses with the mark of the covenant.

The sun still held its throne above the sky—burning, unmoving, eternal. The blood of the enemy cooled, darkened, and began to crust in the valleys where they fell. My sword arm trembled —not from fear, nor fatigue—but from the weight of having survived.

Around me, the men moved like ghosts. No one cheered. No songs rose. This was not a victory we danced for. This was a reckoning fulfilled.

I knelt beside one of the fallen, placing my hand upon the broad chest of a warrior who had once screamed defiance into the storm. He was still now, mouth agape, eyes empty to the sky that had refused to set. His brow bore the mark of his tribe—a burned glyph from the high cliffs of Debir. The brands had not faded, even in death.

I scanned the field, the groans rising like smoke from smoldering wreckage. The storm had ceased, but the work was not done. These were not mere men strewn across the valley—they were the brood of defilement, the remnant of giants who had once mocked heaven and consumed the innocent. I raised my voice, steady and cold,

"Leave none breathing," I said. "Their blood is curse enough. They must not rise again to poison the land."

Othniel nodded and relayed the command. Young men, warriors in many ways still boys, began the somber work of moving through the mounds of flesh and bone. Their spears were steady—not to defend, but to finish. The dying were given no reprieve. The wounded gasped, some begged in languages we did not speak. But they were of the seed of Rephaim, and mercy for them was not kindness—it was foolishness.

One of the younger men hesitated, holding back as a bloodied Amorite reached toward him, whispering something in a cracked, foreign tongue.

I walked over.

"Finish it," I said.

"But he's—"

"He is not a man like you or me. He is a vessel of defilement."

The youth looked into the eyes of the fallen and saw not remorse, but hunger—still. And then he obeyed. His spear pierced cleanly, and the creature stilled.

These were not giants—but they had the taste of giants in them. You could see it in their unnatural height, the gray tint of their flesh, the thickness of their bone. They were not made for peace. These were the last offshoots of the darkness that had once covered the land in the time of the Watchers. They did not build cities—they took them. They did not grow crops—they consumed flesh. These were the people who offered their own infants to the fire, whose priests drowned the cries of children beneath the drums of sacrifice. Their end had long been written. We were only the ink.

The last cries of the battlefield had faded into silence, a silence not of peace, but of completion. The sun hung, impossibly unmoved, casting long shadows that should not yet have been. It lit the carnage in gold and fire, as if Heaven itself refused to let the day close before justice had run its full course. Amid the wreckage, I saw Joshua again —no longer in the thick of the charge, but standing among the wounded, his cloak stiff with blood, his gaze unflinching.

He gave no smile when I approached, no clasp to my shoulder. Only a nod—the kind only warriors give when they've both seen the same horror and known it to be righteous. He was overseeing the last phase of cleansing: each Amorite body checked, none left half-alive to rise again. The men followed his commands without question, reverent in their grim labor. There was no joy in this harvest—only obedience to the covenant, to Yahweh, and to the leader who had become more than a man.

Joshua turned to me, his voice rough from command and prayer. "It is finished here," he said, though his eyes swept the field once more, ensuring that no corruption clung to the soil. "But the heads of this snake yet breathe." He meant the kings. "Take your strongest, Kalev. Go to the cave near Makkedah. Unseal it. Bring them to me. Their time comes with the setting sun."

There were no cheers. Only movement—measured, sharp, dutiful.

As we gathered to march, I looked once more at the field. The enemy lay in heaps, their banners soaked and shredded. The earth groaned under the weight of what had been poured into it. And the sun—it had not moved. The heavens still watched.

"Let it be written," I muttered, more to the bones and wind than to any man, "that when Yahweh stood for His people, no evil escaped."

And then we turned east, toward Makkedah, where judgment waited, sealed in stone but not yet complete. I did not take the full strength of my *elef*—this was not a march of conquest but a procession of reckoning. I chose only a handful, the men whose loyalty had been proven in fire and blood, the ones I would trust beside me at the mouth of Sheol. These were my brothers, not by birth but by covenant, and it was right that they should share in the honor of dragging kings from darkness into light. Let others recount the storm and slaughter—this task, this final act of justice, would be ours.

The east wind howled, carrying the stench of blood and ash as we marched toward Makkedah. The sun, now that the battle was over had slowly begun its descent in the West, the clenched fist of Yahweh finally beginning to lessen as the day would come to a close….but not until we found these cowardly kings.

I walked ahead with Othniel at my right, his bronze skin taut with calculation, his battle axe balanced. Uri, to my left, muttered psalms under his breath, his body tense, his spear-tip stained red from the valley's carnage. Zadok and Eliab were at the rear, their eyes scanning the ridges, Zadok's cynicism a quiet blade, Eliab's nervous loyalty a flickering flame.

We arrived at the edge of a rocky defile. The cave's entrance loomed, a dark scar in the hillside, sealed with great stones piled high, their edges jagged, blocking the mouth as Joshua had commanded after the battle. A handful of our guards stood watch, their spears planted, their faces grim under helms splattered with dust and blood. They straightened as we approached, their leader—a lean warrior from Yehudah—stepping forward.

"Commander," he said, his voice rough with the day's weight, "the kings are within, as Joshua ordered. None have entered or left. The cave is secure."

"Unseal it," I commanded, my voice blunt as stone. "We bring the kings to Joshua."

The guards heaved at the stones, their muscles straining, dust rising as the boulders shifted. The cave's mouth yawned open, its darkness swallowing the light, the air thick with damp and fear. Othniel stepped closer, his axe ready, his eyes meeting mine with a silent vow. Uri's lips curled, his zeal a live flame, his spear hefted like an extension of his soul. Zadok and Eliab drew their daggers, Zadok's movements sharp, Eliab's hands trembling but steady.

We stepped into the cave, having lit torches, their flames spitting against the damp air. The passage was narrow, the walls slick with moisture, their surfaces scarred by desperate scratches—marks of men fleeing Yahweh's judgment. My sandals scraped the uneven floor, the sound swallowed by the oppressive weight of the earth above. The air grew colder, clinging to my skin, and the flickering torchlight cast wild shadows, twisting like specters of the slain.

A sound broke the silence—a low clatter, bronze on stone, followed by a hissed curse. I raised my torch, its light revealing a bend in the passage. Othniel tensed, his axe ready, and Uri's psalm grew sharper, a cadence of vengeance.

The passage opened into a wider chamber, and there they were—seven Amorite soldiers, their bronze armor dented, their faces pale but defiant. They guarded the path to the kings, their swords and axes raised, their eyes wild with the desperation of cornered beasts. Torchlight glinted off their blades, and the air thrummed with the promise of blood.

I charged first, my blade arcing as I met the nearest warrior. His sword swung high, but I ducked, feeling the air hiss above me, and drove my blade into his side. Blood sprayed, hot and thick, coating my arm as he screamed, his body crumpling. I yanked the sword free, the wet snap of sinew echoing in the chamber.

Othniel was a blur beside me, his battle axe hacking with lethal precision. An Amorite lunged, his axe aimed at Othniel's chest, but the young warrior sidestepped, driving his axe into the man's throat. Blood fountained, splattering the cave floor, and the soldier gurgled, clutching the shaft as he fell, his eyes rolling back in a mask of agony.

From afar, Uri roared, his psalm a snarl of divine truth, "The Lord is a warrior!" he cried, he faced a towering Amorite wielding a double-headed axe. The warrior swung, the blade whistling, but Uri dove beneath it, his spear piercing the man's belly. Blood and entrails spilled, the stench sharp, and the Amorite bellowed, swinging wildly even as Uri twisted the spear, tearing flesh. The warrior collapsed, his axe clattering, his body a ruin of gore.

Zadok and Eliab fought with cold efficiency, Zadok's dagger flashing as he faced a lean swordsman. The Amorite's blade slashed, grazing Zadok's arm, but he didn't flinch. Beside him Eliab lunged, driving his dagger into the man's eye. The soldier screamed, blood and fluid bursting, and Eliab twisted the blade, silencing him. The body slumped, the dagger pulling free with a wet suck, blood dripping from Zadok's hand.

As I gathered my strength another warrior came crashing at me in my side, I blocked his sword thrust, but I fell backwards under his weight and fell to the ground.

Eliab came running over, the Amorite's switched his attention and swung with a strike that twas brutal, forcing Eliab back, but he parried with his dagger, the clash ringing in the cave. The warrior overreached, and Eliab stabbed upward, the blade sinking into the man's armpit. Blood poured, staining Eliab's tunic, and the Amorite staggered, swinging weakly. Eliab struck again, slashing the man's throat, blood arcing as the body fell, twitching in the torchlight.

Two soldiers remained, their courage faltering but their blades still raised. Back on my feet, I faced one, his sword trembling, his face streaked with sweat and dirt. He lunged, but I parried, and countered with a slash across his chest. Blood welled, soaking his leather armor, and he gasped, stumbling. I drove my blade through his heart, the bronze grinding against bone, and he collapsed, blood pooling beneath him, his final breath a wet rattle.

Othniel and Uri took the last, their movements a deadly dance. Othniel's axe grazed the warrior's thigh, blood spurting, slowing him. Uri struck from the side, his spear piercing the man's shoulder, pinning him to the cave wall. The Amorite screamed, blood streaming, and Othniel finished him, crashing his axe through the man's chest. The body sagged, held upright by Uri's spear, blood dripping to the stone below.

The chamber was a slaughterhouse, the air thick with the coppery tang of blood and the stench of death. Bodies lay sprawled, their armor shattered, their blood painting the walls and floor. My chest heaved, my blade dripping, the torchlight casting my shadow over the carnage. Othniel wiped his axe, his face grim but steady, the leader within him forged in this crucible. Uri's eyes burned, his zeal a flame that seemed to feed on the blood, and I feared its hunger. Zadok sheathed his dagger, his arm bleeding but his smirk returning, a mask for the weight of what we'd done. Eliab clutched his bloodied hands, his prayers louder now, a shield against the horror.

We moved deeper, the passage narrowing again, the walls closing in. The torchlight flickered, revealing more scratches—frantic, clawing marks of men who knew their end was near. A faint sound reached us, a whimper, and I raised my torch, my heart thudding with the certainty of judgment. The kings were close.

The passage opened into another chamber, and there they were—five figures huddled in the shadows, dressed in various skins of animals, some I'd never seen, their faces pale with terror. The kings of Jerusalem, Hebron, Jarmuth, Lachish, and Eglon, their gold rings glinting uselessly, their swords discarded. Their eyes reflected the torchlight, wide with dread, their breaths ragged gasps.

I stepped forward, my shadow falling over them. "Your armies are dust," I said, my voice blunt as stone. "Your gods are silent. Where is your strength now?"

The king of Jerusalem spat, his beard matted with blood. "You are nothing," he hissed. "Your God is a desert phantom."

Othniel surged, his axe raised, but I caught his arm. "Not here," I said, my eyes locked on the kings. "They face the Spear of the Twelve Tribes."

So our men bound them in leather straps. The king of Lachish alone struggled, but Othniel's fist silenced him, blood trickling from his jaw. Zadok and Eliab stood guard, their daggers ready. Nearby Uri's lips moved in silent prayers of thanksgiving. The kings' defiance crumbled, their curses fading into whimpers as we dragged them from the chamber, their feet scraping the blood-slick stone.

We emerged into the cool of the evening, the sun finally spent after a day of miracles. The wind howled, carrying the scent of blood and earth, and I knew the covenant's blade was not yet sheathed.

We marched, the kings stumbling, their wrists bound, their royal trappings mocked by the dust. The host had gathered, thousands strong, their faces grim, their spears planted in the earth. The valley was a slaughterhouse, littered with the broken bodies of

Amorite warriors, their blood pooling in the cracked earth, their banners trampled into the mire. The hailstones lay scattered, some still glistening, as though the heavens had wept ice and fire.

We brought the kings bound and beaten before our lord— in that hour, none dared call him merely a warrior. None dared think of him as just a chieftain. He was Yahweh's chosen, the one who could speak to the sun and be answered, the one through whom heaven made war. He was the Spear of the Twelve Tribes.

He urned to me,

"Kalev, bring them to the hill beside the valley. Let the people see."

At Joshua's command, we led the captured kings up a low rise overlooking the field, so that all the sons of Israel might witness the judgment of the LORD. A blast from the ram's horn split the air— clear, solemn—and the men gathered like a tide, forming a great host upon the hillside. We forced the kings to their knees, their heads bowed before the assembly. The crowd parted, and Joshua stepped forward, his cloak catching the wind like a banner, his sword gleaming in the unmoving light.

"This day," he proclaimed, his voice like thunder over dry stone, "The Angel of the LORD has fought for Israel. These kings, who raised their hands against the people of the covenant, shall fall as a sign to all nations."

Joshua knelt, his voice a low growl. "Did you think you could defy Yahweh's covenant? Did you think your walls, your armies, and your false gods would stand?" He rose, his sword drawn, its edge catching the eternal noon. "You will know the God of Israel."

He nodded to me, and I drew my blade, its edge still crusted with the valley's gore. The king of Jerusalem was first, his eyes wild, his lips trembling as he muttered prayers to a god who would not answer. I seized his hair, yanking his head back, and drove my sword through his throat. Blood sprayed, hot and thick, soaking the earth, and his body convulsed, a gurgling scream fading into silence. The crowd watched, silent, their breaths held as the life drained from him.

Othniel took the king of Hebron, his axe swift as he split it through the man's neck. The king's bulk shuddered, blood bubbling from his mouth, his eyes rolling back as he collapsed, his royal cloak pooling crimson. Uri, his zeal a live flame, approached the king of Jarmuth. His psalm was a snarl now, and he drove his spear into the man's belly, twisting it with a ferocity that made even me flinch. The king screamed, his entrails spilling as he fell, his hands clawing at the dirt in vain.

Zadok and Eliab stepped forward, their daggers flashing. Zadok's strike was precise, severing the king of Lachish's throat in a single motion, blood arcing like a fountain as the man choked and fell. Eliab, his hands shaking, stabbed the king of Eglon in the heart, the blade sinking deep. The king gasped, his body jerking, and Eliab yanked the dagger free, blood dripping from his trembling fingers.

The earth drank deep, the valley a charnel house of royal blood. The kings' bodies lay in a heap, their gold and bronze trappings dulled by gore, their faces frozen in terror. But Joshua was not done. He turned to the host, his voice a thunderclap,

"Bring them to the trees. Let them hang as a sign to all who defy Yahweh."

We dragged the corpses to a grove of oaks, their branches gnarled and stark against the unmoving sun. Ropes were tied, and the kings' bodies were hoisted, their lifeless forms swaying in the wind. The king of Jerusalem's head lolled, his throat a gaping wound, blood dripping to the roots below. Hebron's bulk strained the rope, his chest a ruin of torn flesh. Jarmuth's entrails hung loose, swaying like grotesque pendants. Lachish's face was a mask of blood, his eyes staring blindly. Eglon's body twitched once, a final spasm, then stilled, his heart's wound a dark stain.

The host watched, their silence a weight heavier than the blood-soaked earth. Eleazar's chant rose, a hymn of covenant and justice, and the wind carried it, sharp with the scent of death. Uri stood, his spear planted, his eyes alight with a zeal that chilled me. Othniel knelt cleaning his axe one last time, his face grim but steady, the leader he was becoming forged in this moment. Zadok sheathed his dagger, his smirk gone, his cynicism silenced by the weight of what we'd done. Eliab clutched his bloodied hands, his prayers a whisper now, his loyalty unshaken.

Eleazar the high priest raised his arms, the wind catching his mantle as though heaven breathed through him, and he sang:

"O Flame of Sinai, speak again!
O Breath who stirred the deep!
From Avraham's bones to Mosheh's staff,
Thy covenant do we keep.
Giants have fallen, O LORD Most High,
Seed of the Nephilim cast to dust.
Thy name is a hammer, Thy will a blade,
In Thee alone we trust.
Let kings who curse Thee bow and break,
Let altars of blood be torn.
For children cried in fire and ash—
But now the day is born.
Not by the might of arm or sword,
Nor by the hail that fell,
But by Thy Word, eternal, sure,
Thou hast cast down the hells.
So let it be sung from Makkedah's cave
To the far hills of the sea:
'The LORD is God! The LORD alone!'
Forever shall it be."

Joshua stood before the hanging kings, his sword lowered, his eyes fixed on the horizon. The fire in him burned still, but I saw the cost—the lines deeper in his face, the sorrow beneath the divine wrath. I wondered if he, too, felt the fear of a God who could still the sun and shatter kings. The covenant bound us, but its justice was a blade, cutting both ways.

I stepped beside him, my blade heavy in my hand, the blood of Jerusalem's king still warm on my skin. "It is done," I said, my voice rough. "Let it be written."

He nodded, his gaze distant. "Let it be written," he echoed, "that Yahweh's hand spared no evil this day."

The kings swayed, their bodies a grim testament to the Almighty's wrath. The heavens watched, and the earth groaned, heavy with the weight of covenant fulfilled. I stood, breathless, my scars aching, and felt the fear of Yahweh—a God who fought for His people, and left no enemy standing.

Chapter Eighteen
The Quiet Hour of Kindred Spirits

The evening air hung thick with dust and the lingering scents of sweat, woodsmoke, and roasted meat. Five years had passed since the day the five kings fell beneath our feet, yet the echoes of that battle hummed in the quiet moments amid the camp's clamor. Beyond my tent, the encampment thrummed with life—a low murmur of men cleaning armor, trading tales, and stoking the last cookfires of the day. Their voices mingled with the clink of pottery as servants wove between tents, bearing pitchers of wine and baskets of barley loaves. Some had stood with me when Jericho's walls crumbled, their shouts swallowed by the thunder of stone. Others, once captives, were now kin by oath and covenant, their eyes bright with the fire of a shared calling.

I gazed upon my children, my beloved wife, and the sprawl of our people beneath the deepening sky. The stars began to pierce the dusk, sharp as the spearpoints we had carried through the valleys of Ayalon. Memory stirred, unbidden, and drew me back to that day at Makkedah, when the sun hung still and the air was choked with the cries of the vanquished. Five kings—lords of Jerusalem, Hebron, Jarmuth, Lachish, and Eglon—had fled like shadows before the flame, cowering in a cave's dark mouth. We dragged them forth, their crowns humbled, their eyes wide with the terror of men who glimpsed their doom. Joshua, our sword and shield, bade us set our feet upon their necks, a sign to all the earth that the Lord's anointed would not falter.

Then, by his command, their lifeless bodies swaying in the hot wind, silhouettes against the amber sky. The ropes creaked, and the branches groaned under their weight, as if the earth itself mourned the folly of their defiance. Until night they hung, a warning to the nations, until Joshua spoke, and we cut them down, casting their forms into the cave that had been their refuge. Great stones sealed their tomb, and the dust of our victory settled over Makkedah.

Five years of fire and sword had followed. From the Yarden's parted waters to the heights of Har HaGadol, we pursued the sons of the Anakim, those towering shades who once ruled the highlands. Their strongholds fell, their altars shattered, and their names faded like smoke. Yet, as I sat in the camp's fading glow, the weight of those days pressed upon me. Not all was triumph. The sting of Ai's first defeat lingered, where thirty-six of our brothers fell for one man's hidden sin. But the Lord had turned our shame to strength, and the land opened before us, hill by hill, promise by promise.

Now, in the stillness, the names of those battles rumbled through the soul like thunder—Jericho, Ai, Gibeon, Makkedah. The faces of the fallen, the laughter of the living, the prayers woven into every step of this long march. I rose, my cloak heavy with the night's chill, and stepped toward the firelight. The camp's songs swelled, songs of hope and memory, and I knew the Lord's hand still guided us, through the dust of yesterday and into the dawn of tomorrow. The names of those days rumbled through the soul like thunder.

Horma. Lachish. Eglon. Hebron. Debir.

Ruins now. Ash heaps. Cities of ancient evil, once proud fortresses where the Rephaim drank blood and mocked the heavens.

We did not weep for them.

For it was not men we warred against, but monsters— offspring of defiled kings and the watchers, the shedim, the fallen ones who were neither wholly of heaven nor wholly of earth. The giants did not teach their children righteousness. They consumed the land like fire devours dry wheat. They drank from skulls and named themselves gods. And they bled the ground with the cries of the innocent.

But El Elyon, the Most High, had set His face against them. And we were His sword.

We fought under the mantle of Joshua, servant of Moshe, the Spear of the Twelve Clans. I have seen his hand cleave the sky. I have heard his voice still a thousand men in a breath. The Spirit of God was with him. He carried not just the rod of command, but the burden of covenant. It was he who first stood beside me in the hill country of Hebron and said, "This shall be your inheritance, Kalev—though the giants dwell there still."

And I believed him.

The hill country had been the seat of the Anakim, sons of Arba, a people whose heights scraped the clouds. Their chieftains had names older than memory—Talmai, Sheshai, Achiman—and they stood clad in bronze like beasts from before the flood. Men said they could not be killed, that their blood ran with fire. But we slew them. We brought down their towers. We salted their temples and burned their sacred groves. We shattered their carved idols of ash and obsidian—grinning monsters that wore the faces of fallen watchers.

We purged the land with holy flame.

There were losses, yes—more than I care to count. Men I loved. Brothers who laughed beside me beneath the terebinths, who bled beside me beneath the walls of cities now gone to ash. I can still see their faces, though they sleep beneath standing stones. A few fell in battle over these five years, too often because they were moments we did not listen. Like Achan, who buried his theft beneath his tent and brought ruin upon our ranks. Like the covenant we made with the Gibeonites, cloaked strangers with stale bread and lying tongues —because we did not inquire of the LORD. Such moments left cracks in our shield wall, and into those cracks, death found its way. The land itself groaned beneath the weight of these ancient abominations. What we waged was no conquest of nations, but a cleansing—a sacred fire to purge the poison of the watchers.

I remember the scrolls we uncovered in the ruins of Qiryat Sefer, blackened by fire yet legible still, echoing the madness of their kings. Words in tongues older than Bavel, scripts carved in dread and shadow. One of the elders said they were prayers—not to the True God—but to rouse the Nephilim once more, to wake the watchers in the deep.

But we burned them.

We dug the scrolls into the earth and set fire to them with cedar and hyssop, and as the smoke rose, I remember the silence. A silence that did not feel empty, but watchful.

Not all of them were gone.

The Rephaim had sons still—fragments and remnants scattered across the hills and lowlands. In the Valley of the Rephaim south of Yerushalayim, we fought their cousins. In Bashan, under the shadow of Mount Hermon, we faced giants that bore the mark of Og, last king of the iron bed.

Yes, I saw it with my own eyes—Og's bed, forged of hammered iron and inlaid with serpent sigils, as long as two men laid head to foot. A monument to blasphemy.

But now Bashan too was quiet.

The ziggurat still stood near Ugarit, though the city stank of ghosts. I had once crept close to its base, years before the conquest, when I was young and foolish. The wind there sang with strange voices, and even the goats refused to graze nearby. Now, word came from the north that its steps were cracked and blackened, the fires long gone cold. Whether by war or by divine hand, I did not know.

But I felt it. The land was changing.

And not only the land. The people.

We were no longer the children of the wilderness, those wanderers born between Egypt and Kena'an. We were becoming a people of promise, a nation forged in fire and held by covenant. The tribes were settling—Reuven by the Yarden, Ephraim in the fertile lowlands, Zevulun near the sea. And Yehudah—my tribe—had taken the mountains.

314

Not without cost.

The war did not end in a single blow. Cities had to be retaken. Outposts rebuilt.

The Clan of Dan, though granted land by covenant, found their grasp slipping like water through fingers. The Amorites and their kin held fast to the plains, and Dan's foothold grew narrow and uncertain. Time and again, they wrestled with shadows in the lowlands, their strength tested by foes who refused to yield. At last, weary and pressed, the Danites looked northward, to a new horizon beyond their given portion, seeking a place where their swords could find purchase and their families take root. Their journey was a testament—not of defeat—but of the restless will to claim a promised inheritance, no matter the cost.

I sighed and leaned back on my elbows, feeling the ache of years settle into my bones. The voices outside the tent had begun to soften. Night had gathered its cloak around the camp. Fires burned lower. Somewhere a flute played, thin and sweet, its song threading through the hush like a memory.

I stood near the tent flap, the weight of command still pressing against my shoulders despite the quiet. Dust clung to the hem of my cloak, and the scar along my jaw caught the last slant of sunlight like a thread of silver. Azubah moved nearby, gently admonishing Mihlat —now grown, sixteen years old and married—who'd nearly stumbled carrying a basket of figs. Her voice was steady and kind, tempered by years of knowing how to lead without raising it. Iru and Elah tussled just beyond the fire pit, their laughter booming over the crackle of the dying flames. They'd argued again over who should carry my shield —both bigger now, but still stubborn enough to try, and proud enough not to admit they needed help.

A small company made their way up the rise toward our tent. The woman at the front I recognized even from afar: Rachav. Her walk was quiet, measured, like someone who'd spent her whole life listening for doors to close behind her. Beside her walked Salmon her husband—broad-shouldered, with wind-scoured skin and a heavy beard. He carried himself like a man who'd lived on the edge of war, never quite certain which banner to kneel beneath. But his eyes held a steady loyalty, one I already knew could weather great trials.

Behind them came their children and servants, each growing into their own shape beneath the sun's unyielding gaze. Lirah, now ten, moved with the quiet grace of her mother, her dark braids swinging against a modest dress. Aram, twelve years old, brimming with restless energy and the spark of a dreamer. Close at Salmon's side toddled Boaz, the child of promise, their youngest, only three, his chubby legs stumbling over the rocky ground as he strained to keep pace. The family's presence stirred a strange warmth in the camp, a living testament to redemption and new beginnings amid the dust and blood of conquest.

I stepped from the tent's shadow to meet them, raising a hand in greeting. "You made it," I said, a smile tugging at my lips. "I was starting to think the road's dust had claimed you."

Rachav's faint smile carried the weight of their journey. "The road is crueler than the battlefield some days. Yet the promise of Yehudah bore us onward."

Salmon clasped my forearm, his grip steady as stone and we kissed, "We've been made welcome where once we were warned away. That counts for something."

One by one, they approached the tent's entrance, where the Shema, inscribed on its small scroll, rested upon the doorpost, a silent sentinel of covenant. Lirah paused, her small fingers brushing the mezuzah with reverence, then touching her lips in quiet devotion. Aram followed, his touch brisk but earnest, a boy's haste tempered by awe as he kissed his fingertips. Salmon, broad-shouldered and sure, pressed his hand to the sacred words, his lips grazing his fingers with the ease of long habit. Even young Boaz, hoisted by a servant's gentle hands, reached out, his tiny palm grazing the mezuzah before a clumsy kiss to his chubby fingers, a gesture more mimicry than understanding, yet no less holy.

Rachav came last, her steps deliberate. She rose slightly on her tiptoes, her frame stretched toward the doorpost as if drawn by an unseen tide. Her lips met the doorpost of the tent directly, a tender act of veneration, her eyes closed for a fleeting moment as the words of the Shema—Hear, O Israel—whispered through her soul. In that gesture, I glimpsed the woman who had once hung a scarlet cord in a window, binding her fate to ours, now sealed anew by faith each time she crossed the threshold of God's people.

The camp thrummed beyond us, its fires casting long shadows as the evening deepened. Five years had passed since the five kings dangled from Makkedah's trees, their silhouettes swaying against a blood-red sky, a warning to the nations. Yet here, in the simple act of touching the Shema, the weight of those victories found their truest echo—not in the clash of swords, but in the quiet fidelity of families redeemed. I ushered them inside, where the warmth of the tent's glow awaited, a haven woven from covenant and memory.

The children's laughter spilled into the air, mingling with the low chant of prayers from nearby tents. Servants moved among us, their own hands still dusted with the road's grit, yet each had paused to honor the mezuzah, their fingertips kissed in solemn rite. This was our strength, I thought—not only in the spear or the shield, but in these small, sacred acts that bound us to the Eternal. As Rachav settled beside the fire, her face softened by its light, I saw the promise of the land taking root, not merely in the earth we had claimed, but in the hearts of those who carried its hope.

Azubah stepped forward, brushing flour from her sleeves. "You've traveled far enough to earn your bread tonight. Sit. Eat. Rest your bones. There's time yet before the next storm finds us."

Iru paused his game that he and Elah had been playing, the pebble still balanced between his dusty fingers as he looked up at Rachav, eyes wide with that restless hunger for stories only a young man, but still a boy could have, "Ima K'tanah, will you tell us again about the city whose walls came down?"

Rachav was already crouching to gather the empty bowls, but at his words, she turned with a wry smile, her gaze softening. "Haven't I told you that story enough times?"

Iru's eyes gleamed with quiet insistence. "But were you really there? Did you ever see a giant there? Were they really so tall they could reach the tops of the walls?"

She knelt beside him, her hand brushing back the mop of curls that perpetually fell across his brow—an effortless gesture of a mother's love and patience.

"Giants from Jericho, yes. But remember, not everything in a city is what it seems. Stories grow taller than the men who tell them."

Iru's grin didn't waver. "But there were giants, weren't there?"

Rachav sighed, a softness in her eyes as she nodded slowly. "Some came, yes, to demand tribute. But most were just cruel men. And cruelty can make a man seem bigger than he truly is when you stand alone."

He squinted, wrestling with the weight of those words, stitching them into the patchwork of stories he'd gathered in his young life. "But you weren't afraid?"

"I was afraid," she said honestly. "But Yahweh found me in that fear."

Iru tilted his head, the earnestness of a boy growing into a man. "And the spies? Did you really hide our father on the roof?"

"That part is true." Her eyes twinkled as she tugged gently at his ear. "But if I tell the story too often, I fear it will weigh heavy on my tongue."

She glanced over at me, exchanging a look filled with remembrance and gratitude—for the past she'd left behind, and the hope she carried forward. It seemed like another lifetime since Othniel and I met her in the square of Jericho, when God used her as an angel of mercy to hide us from the city guard.

"You never tell the same story twice," Iru protested with a half-smile. "Last time you told me about father blessing the red cord you hung on your window."

She smiled warmly. "He did. He prayed over it, and I will keep that sacred cord with me until the day I die, then pass it to my children."

She touched her arm reverently, hidden beneath the sleeve of her robe—the crimson cord never leaving it except for bathing, she once told Azubah.

Iru dropped down beside her on the rug, his voice softer now. "And the time before, you told me about the goat that climbed in your window."

"That was a real goat. It got stuck and bleated like a trumpet until half the neighborhood came to watch me chase it out."

He laughed quietly. "But you never tell me the hard parts. About the mean men, the false gods, or the babies you said were—" He stopped abruptly, eyes flicking to the adults across the tent.

Rachav's expression sobered. She reached out and held his hand, just for a moment. "Some stories wait for later," she said gently. "When the heart is old enough to hold them without breaking."

Azubah nodded at her, she placed her hand upon Rachav's hand and gently squeezed it in sisterly love, letting her know she carried the burden of her past alongside her in prayer.

Iru's expression changed, sensing something weighty behind her words. Taller now, he leaned into her side not like a child clinging for comfort, but like a son drawing strength from someone he trusted deeply.

"You like it here?" he asked, his voice quieter, more reflective than it had once been.

"I love it here," she answered without pause, a quiet conviction in her tone. "Yehudah gave me a name. A family. A people who know how to weep—and still stand tall."

She looked past the firelight, her gaze momentarily distant. "It's been five years now. And not a day goes by that I don't thank Yahweh for bringing me here."

Iru considered that, lips twitching in thought. "I'm glad you're in our clan."

She smiled and kissed the crown of his head. "So am I."

He nodded once, the way boys do when they're on the edge of becoming men but still need the quiet touch of affection. Then he slipped back to his pebbles, his focus already shifting as boys' minds often do.

Rachav watched him a moment longer, her hand lingering on the rim of a bowl, and then turned back to her work, letting the shadows of Jericho fade again into memory.

Elah tugged on my belt, his eyes wide with anticipation. "Tell them about the day the sun stood still."

I laughed, tousling his thick dark hair. "That story needs the right kind of fire," I said, nodding toward the western sky, "and it needs night to fall fully. You'll spoil it rushing the telling."

Othniel came up beside me then, dusting off dirt from the edge of his sandals, his brow dark with the weight of fresh news. "It's Merom," he said, low and steady. "The scouts say Jabin of Hazor is gathering the northern kings. Chariots, bronze, the works. Word is they're rallying by the waters—more men than we saw at Lachish and Eglon combined."

I turned slightly, the evening light catching the line of his jaw, leaner now than in the days when we first fought side by side, "So it begins again."

"They never stop," he muttered. "We just pushed them back far enough to catch our breath."

I nodded, eyes scanning the horizon where smoke curled soft against the blue. Five years of hard-won ground, and now the north stirred like a wounded lion. The peace we had was always a sharp-edged thing—never sheathed, only waiting.

"There's no peace yet—not for men like us. But tonight is for family. Five long years of war, we've earned a night I should think." I invited him to join us for a meal.

The sun faded slowly, and the shadows grew longer. Servants laid out the meal—roasted lamb, barley with herbs, sliced figs, soft cheese wrapped in leaves, and pitchers of wine the color of blood. We sat cross-legged around low tables. The children gathered close to their mothers, content for now, ears bent toward the older men who shared half-whispered stories of things they'd seen and couldn't forget.

Across the fire, I watched Rachav and Azubah speaking quietly. Azubah nodded toward Salmon once and gave Rachav a knowing smile. "He's not the first of giant seed to find a new tribe" she said.

Rachav's reply was soft, but I caught the shape of it, "We carry that past, yes. But we carry something greater now—a name, a covenant, a hope."

Iru settled down beside me, worn from play and food, but still trying not to look it, and leaned his shoulder against mine. I rested a hand lightly on his back, eyes fixed on the flames.

"This land isn't only for the strong," I said. "It's for the faithful. The ones who stay. The ones who build. The ones who believe."

Iru looked up, the firelight casting solemn shadows across his face. "Will the giants come back?"

The question fell like a stone into still water. Among the young sons of Israel, tales of giants stirred both fear and fascination. They had grown up hearing the songs of conquest, the stories of their fathers and grandfathers — men who had faced down monsters as the Hand of Thunder. There was pride in that lineage, a fierce sense of identity shaped by blood and victory. For boys like Iru, the giants were not just shadows of the past; they were symbols of the strength they hoped to become.

I thought of the caves near Ai, of bones larger than any man should bear, and finally I spoke, "Their bones are buried, but their shadow still walks. Not in size. In pride. In cruelty. But that's why we need men like Salmon. And like you, one day."

Othniel took a drink, then set his cup down hard. "I've seen signs of them in the hills. Stragglers. Not as many as before we arrived. But more than none."

Salmon nodded. "I've seen them too. Far south. Keeping to caves, avoiding the roads. Some still bear arms."

"We'll find them," I said. "But not tonight."

There was a pause then, the kind that settles over people who have seen too much and still feel too little time left to make peace with it. Azubah busied herself near the tents, her voice warm as she gave quiet instructions to our two blessed servant girls—now grown, married, but still devoted to the rhythm of our camp.

Rachav's daughter Lirah darted past the fire pit, her laughter chasing after Elah, who was now looking ever more like a man, though he still loved to provoke a race. Not far off, Aram sat cross-legged, watching the fire like a map, eyes narrowed, his thoughts distant. There was always something older than his years behind those eyes. The boy born in Jericho, now of the family of Yehudah. I could only image the thoughts that darted through his mind.

Salmon leaned toward me, he gave a quiet nod, then lifted his cup. "You are a testament to the giant clans who repent Kalev—of the redemption the one true God offers to all. An elder of Yehudah now, the LORD's anointed, the blessed friend of the Spear of the Twelve Clans. Truly He blesses those whom He will bless."

"And truly He will curse those He will curse," added Othniel, raising his own cup. His young face was half in shadow, but the lines of command were already forming in his expression, "A toast," he said, rising to his feet, "To Kalev the giant killer, the righteous judge, and elder of the clan of Yehudah!"

Iru stood suddenly, nearly toppling the clay bowls in front of him. His shoulders were still narrow, but already he carried himself like one born to the hills—wind-burnished and steady. He raised his cup with both hands, the firelight catching the sheen of oil and dust across his brow.

"To my father, Kalev the Giant-Killer!" he declared, voice bright with untempered reverence, "He who stood when others faltered, who saw the sons of Anak and did not flinch. Who did not merely chase shadows—but drove them into the earth."

A hush held for the space of a breath, then burst into a chorus of voices and lifted cups. The name echoed through the tent like the ring of sword on stone—Kalev. Giant-Killer. Friend of God.

Azubah rose with him, her frame slight but fierce, the fire of festival days alive in her eyes. Her voice rang out like a song too long held in the throat, "To Kalev the dark, the anointed, the warrior, the gracious father, the kind husband, and friend!"

She drained her cup in a single draught and set it down with the sharp thud of joy fulfilled. Laughter rippled around her like banners snapping in the wind. Someone began to clap in rhythm; another stomped once, twice. Even Aram, ever watchful, smiled behind his hands.

Across the fire, Rachav caught my eye and gave a single nod— one of remembrance, of deep waters passed through, of blessings still to come. Salmon lifted his cup toward me in silent agreement, the

323

kind of man who knew the weight of history and the hush of holy things.

I said nothing at first. My hand rested on Iru's shoulder, the same boy who had once slept curled beneath my cloak on mountain marches, now standing upright and proud.

"I killed giants," I said at last, voice low, steady. "But only after the LORD made me small enough to know the difference between my strength and His."

The hush returned, not heavy, but holy—like the stillness just before the shofar sounds on the day of gathering.

Iru leaned closer, his voice barely above a whisper, yet lit with boyish awe, "Still... it's no small thing, Abba. To strike down a monster and still be kind."

I turned and looked into his face—the dust-smudged brow, the eyes too old for his years—and felt something rise in me. Not pride. Not even joy. But the solemn ache of legacy, passed not through blood alone, but through the quiet, daily acts of mercy, of courage, of remembering who we are before God.

I reached for my cup, and drank. Not to myself—but to the One who makes boys brave, who turns spies into saints, and who teaches us to plant vineyards in lands once ruled by fear.

The campfire crackled. For a moment, I thought that was the end of it. But then Rachav rose—slowly, with the kind of grace that knows its own scars. Her hair had been braided in the older ways, drawn back from her face and bound in cloth the color of desert stone. Her hands, once used to haggling in Jericho's streets, now bore the calm steadiness of one who tended children.

She held her cup before her, the clay glinting in the light, and her eyes swept across us before settling on me.

"If I may," she said, and all fell quiet.

"I met him first," Rachav said. "Before the walls fell, before the trumpets sounded, when faith had not yet shown itself in flint and fire. He was one of two men who walked into my home with the scent of judgment on their garments, and yet he brought me mercy instead. That night, I chose Yahweh's people. That night, I yielded the scarlet cord because he looked at me—not as harlot, but as daughter."

Her voice softened. "I saw who he was. Not just a spy. A man unshaken by fear. And now I see it fulfilled: the warrior who did not lose his tenderness. The judge who did not forget mercy. The elder who has not cast out the lowly, nor closed his table to the stranger."

She lifted her cup higher. "To Kalev son of Jephunneh. May your strength never dim, and your heart never harden. May your sons walk in your courage, and your name be spoken in honor long after your bones rest in the earth."

There was no shouting after her words—only the hush of reverence. We raised our cups in silence this time, the firelight flickering in the tears that shimmered in more than one pair of eyes.

Azubah reached for my hand. Her grip was firm. "She speaks true," she whispered. "You do not even know half of what you've carried for us all."

I swallowed the lump rising in my throat and managed a nod. Rarely did I shed a tear, but being here, with my family, my clan. Once an outsider like Rachav, yet brought into covenant with the one true God who forgives. It was overwhelming to think upon how great His mercy was to me all these years.

Othniel had been quiet for some time, content to drink and listen. But now, ever the loyal soldier and ever watchful of me, he saw the silence growing too long and chose his moment to speak.

"The food of your tent is good, Kalev," he said with a half-smile, "but all of Yehudah knows it is not for bread alone that we come." His gaze shifted toward Azubah, warm and imploring. "You are husband to a songstress whose voice the angels would pause to hear, one worthy of the name of Saint Miriam herself."

Then, lifting his cup slightly, he turned to Azubah and bowed his head. "Gracious one," he said gently, "sing us a song, that we might drink deeper and rejoice the more."

Azubah set down her cup, her fingers brushing the rim as if the clay remembered something her lips had not yet spoken. The fire crackled low, a hush spreading again among us like breath before a storm.

She began to hum, almost to herself, a tune old as cracked desert stone. Her voice, gentle but sure, rose in song — the cadence like wind through papyrus, like water over the reeds of the Nile.

When the towers fell and the ships burned,
In the days when the traders vanished,
We were slaves in a foreign land,
But Yahweh had not forgotten.
Sea kings trembled in their harbors,
Horses lay still in the dust.
No rider came, no message flew—
The gods of the nations were sleeping.
Hatti's thrones broken,
Mizraim's stars dimmed,
Even mighty Keftiu turned to ash,
But Yahweh heard our cries.
Ugarit's scrolls smoldered in silence,
Her scribes cut down mid-letter,
The harps of Byblos wept in vain,
And Tyre sealed her gates in fear.
Ashkelon wept behind her walls,
Gaza's markets lay bare,
The high towers of Hazor fell,
And the chariots of Megiddo grew rust.
In Alashiya the copper ran dry,
In Sidon the ships were adrift,

The firebrands of the sea-men came—
The gods of the coastlands fled.
The mighty fell not by spear alone,
But by the rot of pride and lies,
And all the works of kings and scribes
Were scattered like chaff on the wind.
But Yahweh raised a cry in Goshen,
A flame where none had looked,
He called forth a nation from dust and clay,
From brick and lash and cry.
So we crossed while empires crumbled,
We sang as temples sank,
The stars that ruled the heavens fell,
But the cloud led us on by day.
Let the bones of Ra and Baal lie cold,
Let Marduk sleep beneath his stone,
Yahweh alone stood in the fire,
And He is still our song."

When the last note faded into the cool stillness of the tent, no one spoke. The children were still. Even the wind outside seemed to hold its breath.

Then Salmon leaned forward, brows drawn low. "We heard songs like that, when I was younger, in the wilderness," he said. "Travelers and traders would bring stories from old men who remembered the sea peoples. The night the ports fell. The gods didn't answer. Everything crumbled, and the old order with it."

I nodded. "My father told me tales—of traders from Crete who stopped coming, of weapons harder to find, bronze turning scarce. And of the silence that came afterward."

Iru, eyes wide again, leaned close to Azubah. "Was it like the flood?"

327

"No," she said, brushing his cheek. "Not water this time. It was like the world itself ran out of breath."

"The world was dying," said Rachav softly. "And Yahweh was beginning something new."

I looked around the circle. "The giants ruled during that dying. They rose when the nations weakened. They fed on the chaos. And Yahweh brought them low."

Mihlat, the servant girl stirred at that, her voice quiet. "And now the land is quiet. For now."

"For now," I agreed. "But the peace of the land is not like the silence after a storm. It must be guarded."

Azubah turned toward me. "We are the ones who walked through the wreckage," she said. "We are the song He brought out of the ashes."

"Mosheh spoke of a world that perished in Egypt's shadow, when he was a child" I murmured, "its death preparing the Promised Land for our rebirth. Great cities once crowned these hills, but now their stones lie scattered, their names lost to the dust."

"Even Jericho, where I was born, the elders said was a mere shadow of the ancient cities that dotted the clouds" said Rachav.

The fire burned steady between us, the past smoldering in its embers—but the future beginning to glow in the eyes of our children. Rachav reached across to place her hand over her husband's, her fingers curling into his with the gentle gravity of years borne together,

"The shadows of the past don't vanish," she said softly, "but they don't have to rule the present."

Azubah looked up from her cup and gave the faintest smile. "The past may follow us, but it's the steps we take now that set the road for our children."

As if summoned by her words, Boaz toddled into the ring of firelight, his eyes heavy with sleep and cheeks smudged with ash from the bread ovens. He made no announcement—only rubbed one fist against his eye and padded toward his mother on unsteady feet. Rachav opened her arms without a word, and he climbed into her lap with the unthinking trust of the very young, folding into her embrace like a prayer returned home.

"Some things," I said, "should be remembered. Others, only carried."

Azubah nodded slowly, her eyes drifting across the fire to the two servant girls sitting near the tent wall. Tirata was busy twisting a length of thread between her fingers, pretending not to listen. But the servant girl Mihlat's gaze was serious.

She was still. Too still.

Iru noticed as well. He turned, brow furrowing slightly, "Mihlat?"

The girl blinked, startled. Her eyes darted to me, then downward. Her shoulders tightened as if to fold inward, though a new grace had settled into her posture since last I saw her.

"It's all right," I said softly, "you may share your tale".

Her sister Tirata cast her a warning glance, and Mihlat hesitated no longer.

"My people feared the Rephaim," she said, voice quiet but steady—carrying the weight of memory and a newfound strength.
The words fell like stones into the stillness.
Azubah and Rachav's eyes softened with quiet affection, their gaze full of the tender knowing reserved for a story they had heard many times over. Among all of us, the tale was no stranger—woven into the fabric of our years, having raised Mihlat and her sister. Now, at last, the boys—still unburdened by such memories—were hearing it for the first time.

"I was born among a wandering band, south of Arad. My mother called us sons of Anak, but we had no cities, no altars—only tents and the endless flight," she said.

Iru's brow furrowed. "You were Amalekite?"

Azubah answered gently before Mihlat could: "We found her before Jericho—before we crossed into this land. She and her sister, and a handful of others—what remained of their clan."

Iru's curiosity flared. "Did you ever see a giant?"

Mihlat's eyes flickered toward me uncertainly.

"You may continue, he is old enough to hear now," I said quietly, though I caught Azubah's cautious glance.

Mihlat drew a deep breath, her gaze distant but firm. "I was but a child—three years old. Yet I remember the sound."

"What sound?" Iru asked.

Her fingers tightened around her ankle, as if anchoring herself,

"Screaming. Stones falling. My father's voice calling for my mother to run. My sister's cries. Then only firelight and one towering shape—taller than any man—standing over us all."

Tirata laid a gentle hand on her sister's arm, but Mihlat's eyes remained fixed on some unseen flame within the fire's glow.

"I don't recall the face," she whispered. "Only how it had to turn sideways to enter our tent... and its feet—so vast, they cracked the basin where we washed."

Iru opened his mouth to speak, but Azubah placed a firm hand on his shoulder.

"She was three," Azubah said quietly. "And still those memories hold."

"It was the Rephaim—the one they named Mavzur," Mihlat said, voice low as a shadow. "The men of the camp, before his coming, laughed and said his arms could carry two oxen at once. But when he found us, no one laughed."

She fell silent.

The crackle of fire filled the pause. The distant murmur of voices outside the tent softened.

"How did you survive?" Asked Iru.

Mihlat blinked, as if rousing from a dark dream, "I ran. Or was carried. I cannot say. But when Mosheh still walked the earth, your people found what remained of our camp. I remember little after that, only that someone brought me to the tents of Yehudah."

"And you have remained with us ever since," Azubah said, voice tender, and abruptly ending Mihlat's tale. Leaving more of the horrors of that night for another day, always protective of our boys.

Mihlat nodded slowly toward Azubah, a faint glow of gratitude shining through the shadow of her past.

"I am married now," she added quietly— speaking more to herself than anyone else— "to a man of Yehudah, good and kind. This household has been my home, and Kalev, a father to me in all but blood."

Turning to Iru she spoke,

"I no longer fear the giants, I no longer fear the shedim that lurk in the shadows. The clan of Yehudah has wrapped its arms around me, like a hen with its chicks, and the fear I once had is now gone. Peace I have found in the joy of the covenant that has claimed me".

I met her eyes. "No child should bear such memories alone," I said. "But I am glad you are here, Mihlat—that you are safe."

She blinked quickly, then nodded and lowered her gaze. Tirata drew her closer, protective as ever.

"Do you believe they'll return" said Iru, turning back to me, the subject of giants rarely gone long from his mind, "How many are left in this land father?" He asked.   "I think the land grows weary of them child. And I think Yahweh has judged what they built."

I looked again at my friends and family, thankful to the God that had bestowed so much good upon my life.

"The giants once ruled with fear," I said, "but they never loved the land. They only consumed it. They built no covenant. Only ruins."

"And now?" Salmon asked.

"Now," I said, reaching for the last of the bread and tearing it in half, "we build something they never understood. A home. A people. A faith that doesn't shrink from giants, or from memories."

Iru stirred again, sitting up straighter despite the heavy weight of sleep. His eyes, clear and earnest, searched mine. "Father," he said softly, "where did the giants come from? Were they made by God, or... something else?"

I looked toward the flickering shadows cast by the fire, between the dancing flames and the faces around the tent.

Azubah's hand slid into mine, a soft but firm pressure. She met my eyes and whispered, "Kalev, there are young ears near."

Elah and Iru were ever curious, their young minds restless with questions about the giants that haunted whispered tales. Yet, we —parents and protectors—spoke of them sparingly, for the stories carried a darkness that could too easily root itself in youthful hearts. The evil entwined with those ancient beings was not mere legend but a shadow cast long and deep, one we guarded against with measured words and careful silence. To feed fear was to invite it in; to plant dread was to watch it grow. So we tended their innocence as a flame in the wind—vulnerable, precious, and not yet ready to face the full weight of those cursed memories.

Her gaze drifted to our youngest son, Elah, his innocence a fragile flame not to be snuffed out too soon.

I nodded, swallowing the heavier truths that pressed at my tongue.

Othniel shifted beside me, his voice low and steady. "We walk a fine line, old friend. These tales... they can chill the heart if told without care. Yet the truth must be faced, for ignorance is a poison too."

I met his eyes with a grateful nod. "Yes. We owe our children the truth, but not the terror."

Elah more restless than his older brother simply blurted out, "Abba, Were they made by the hand of God, or are they born of something evil?"

I turned to him, the firelight flickering across his curious eyes, feeling the weight of the question settle like a solemn hush upon the tent. "Giants did not rise from the earth alone," I began, voice slow and deliberate as one turning the pages of a holy scroll. "Long before our tents crowned these hills, mighty kings ruled faraway lands—men who sought power not by sword, but through secret rites hidden beneath the gaze of common folk."

Azubah's hand which had never left mine, squeezed it once again. Her eyes flicked toward Boaz, curled like a lamb in Rachav's lap, his lashes heavy with sleep but his heart still listening. Then her gaze shifted to Elah and Aram, their faces upturned to the firelight, eyes wide, too young yet to carry the weight of such truths. "Their souls are tender flames," she said. "Let us not snuff their light too soon. And some of these tales come from the secret scrolls, that are read by the Elders and not by the people"

Azubah had always guarded the mysteries, not from cruelty, but out of reverence. She, like all wise women of our people, knew that some fires must be kindled slowly lest they burn too bright and blind the soul. She spoke not only as a mother, but as one who had sat beside the elders when the scrolls were unrolled in secret—those ancient parchments never read aloud to the multitude, but kept within the circle of the aged and discerning. Azubah was among a small group of women and men who had heard the reading of the secret scrolls, and mysteries of God reserved for the wisest of our people.

We elders, even when we gathered to read the scroll of Mosheh, took care in what we spoke before the tents of Israel. From Bere'shith, the scroll of beginnings, we never read the first day of creation aloud to the people. It was tradition, older than even the stones of Avraham's altar, that the mystery of that first divine utterance—when the world was formless and the deep teemed with hidden things—should be veiled. The people heard only from the second day, when the firmament was stretched and the heavens were named. The first day was for the elders alone, and the people privately, lest the minds of the simple stumble in wonder over what cannot yet be grasped.

Likewise, the scroll of Ḥanokh, righteous son of Yered and great-grandfather to Noach, was held in great esteem, though never brought forth in public reading. Ḥanokh walked with Elohim, and he did not taste death. His words, written before the floodwaters came upon the earth, are like thunder caught in a jar—holy, but terrible. We read them in the quiet hours, by the flicker of oil lamps and the weight of silence. For within those lines are names not spoken, deeds not told to children, and histories of the Nefilim and the Watchers that bend the mind like fire bends bronze.

Azubah understood this well, and so did I. Not all knowledge is given in one day. Truth, like wine, must age, and be poured with care. So I let her words settle in me like dew on dry grass. And I turned my voice aside from the shadows.

Softening my tone, my words now a careful weaving of truth and mercy,

"These kings did more than command armies or carve their names in stone. They performed dark ceremonies in places like Ugarit, where the ziggurats still reach skyward—great towers built to scrape the heavens, monuments of power and dread. I have seen the smoke rise from those high towers, heard whispers of sorcery that twists the soul itself."

Salmon's brow furrowed, voice low. "The kings who climbed those steps left behind their own flesh and mind. They became vessels for the Watchers—spirits neither wholly man nor angel, but something far stranger."

334

Iru's breath caught. "Watchers? What are they?"

"Fallen ones," I said, "gods cast out from the heavens, bound to the earth by their own rebellion. They did not come to father children by their own hand. Instead, they entered the bodies of kings —vessels of flesh and blood—and through these men, the giants were born. The Rephaim, shadows of ancient pride and sin."

Iru frowned, struggling to grasp it all. "But if the watchers were once gods, why did they choose to fall? Why would they turn against the Maker?"

Rachav's hand rested gently on Iru's shoulder, calm and steady. "Because even the highest can be tempted by pride, my son. The watchers, though mighty, sought to claim worship that was not theirs to hold. Their rebellion brought ruin—not only upon themselves but upon the earth and all who dwell in it. That is why they were cast down, and why their legacy is one of sorrow and shadow. The Watchers are older than men and giants. They sat on the divine council of the Most High. Their spirit is that of the giants."

Mihlat, who had listened silently, spoke at last—her voice low, but steady. "I was too young to name it then, but even in my bones, I felt it when the giant destroyed my home. As if the earth itself remembered his footsteps from the beginning of time. A heaviness that sank into the stones... and into us."

Azubah nodded, pulling her cloak tighter. "That fear touches us still, but it does not bind us. We build with faith, not fear. Our covenant is a light in the darkness."

I took a breath and then spoke softly of something sacred, known only to those with the wisdom of years and authority. "The Sefer Ha'Irin—the Scroll of the Watchers—is a scroll carried by Noach, the righteous man who walked through the floodwaters to save creation. Noach, son of Lamech, son of Methuselah, son of Ḥanokh, whom some call Enoch — the seventh from the first man — bore this scroll with him into the ark. He was a man set apart, chosen by the

Maker to survive the cleansing waters, to carry not only life, but knowledge preserved from the ruin of the old world."

Iru's eyes grew wide with wonder. "Noach carried the scroll on the Ark?"

"Yes," I said. "When the waters rose to cover the earth, when the old world was judged and cleansed, Noach took with him more than beasts and kin—he bore the knowledge of things hidden and terrible. The scroll tells of those Watchers, how they fell and how their children, the giants, came to walk the earth. It is a solemn reminder that power wrested from the heavens by pride brings ruin."

Azubah added, "This scroll teaches us the cost of rebellion, the shadow cast by those who seek to rule beyond the will of Yahweh."

Othniel, who had been quiet until now, spoke with a grave voice. "I have seen signs of that dark power in the places beyond our borders. The ziggurats are not mere towers but altars to things best left unnamed. The sorcery there twists men's hearts and poisons the land."

Salmon nodded in agreement. "We fight not just flesh and blood, but shadows born of that ancient rebellion."

I looked at Iru and then at the younger boys, their faces a mix of wonder and fear. "We speak these things not to frighten, but to prepare. The giants are part of a story older than our tribe, a warning etched in scripture and memory."

Iru swallowed hard. "But how do we fight what is half spirit, half man?"

"With faith," Rachav said softly. "With courage born of covenant. The Maker who saved Noach and his family from the flood will guide us still. His hand is mighty, and His justice sure."

Mihlat's voice, small yet unyielding, whispered, "We walk in the light, even when shadows press close."

Azubah's eyes shone. "And so must we. The fear lingers, yes, but it will not rule us. We are the children of promise, not despair."

I reached for a piece of bread, breaking it slowly, "The giants once ruled with terror, but they did not love the land. They consumed and left ruins. We build anew—homes, faith, and a people who stand unafraid."

Iru yawned, but murmured, "I'm not afraid."

I smiled, "That's because you have not yet met one."

Before the fire's glow faded, my thoughts turned to Hanokh — the righteous one, the scribe who walked with God and was taken from us, who long ago transcribed the secrets of the Watchers in the heavens and the reckoning to come. It was Hanokh who first bore witness to their fall, who chronicled the darkness that would stain the earth in generations to come. His name, whispered in reverence, calls us back to the path of obedience, reminding us that even amid shadow, the light of the Maker endures.

Othniel, ever the warrior looked around the circle, his voice grave but steady, "Each giant felled is a blow against the dark powers that seek to consume the land. But remember—our greatest strength lies not in the sword, but in the faith that binds us to Yahweh's promise."

Azubah rose and gathered the last of the plates. "The night calls us to sleep"

Rachav helped her, moving with a quiet grace that made even the fire seem to settle.

Salmon stood slowly, his eyes still thoughtful.

"I'll send word," he said. "When we are more settled, Rachav wants to build near a spring by fig trees."

"We'll visit," I said. "We will bring wine next time. Not the kind from the hill country. Something better."

He gave a rare smile. "Agreed."

He turned to Mihlat then, and nodded with quiet respect. "You speak with courage."

She looked startled. But said nothing, lowering her gaze. Her fingers twisted in the fringe of her tunic.

Rachav rose and gently lifted Boaz into her arms. The boy had gone soft with sleep, his brow against her shoulder, a small trail of hair clinging to her cheek. She turned toward the tent's edge.

But as her foot crossed the threshold, Mihlat suddenly gasped. Her head lifted—not by will, it seemed, but by wind. A stillness swept over the tent like a cloak thrown across the night. The fire crackled once, then dimmed.

Mihlat's voice came out low, layered—strange, and not entirely her own,

> "From the field of the just
> shall rise the hope of the broken.
> She shall come from Moab,
> cloaked in the dust of sorrow,
> her hands empty, her heart steadfast.
> This child shall give her grain,
> And the Lord shall give them a son.
> And from their house,
> the Shepherd of Israel shall come,
> born not in gold,
> but in the gleaning of grace.."

Silence.

Not a breath stirred. Even the stars beyond the tent seemed to pause.

Boaz stirred lightly in his sleep, shifting his hand against his mother's shoulder. Rachav did not move. Her eyes had widened, and she looked down at the servant girl as though seeing her for the first time.

Mihlat blinked, breathless, then turned crimson and stumbled back a step. "Forgive me," she whispered, clasping her hands and bowing her head low. "I—I don't know what came over me."

Azubah reached for my arm. Her voice was quiet, but sure. "I've long said there was something different about this girl. Now I am certain."

Mihlat turned away quickly, drawing her cloak around herself and slipping toward the darker edge of the tent readying her things to return to her husband, her eyes on the ground and her mind deep in thought.

Rachav finally breathed, clutching Boaz just a little tighter. "Your tent is full of wonders tonight, Kalev son of Jephunneh."

I nodded slowly. My gaze followed Mihlat's retreating form, lit faintly by the fire's last flickers. "Wonders," I said, still watching. "And signs."

Outside, the night deepened. The stars watched. Silent. Waiting.

Chapter Nineteen
Footfalls in the Valley of Farewell

The clang of iron rang across the sun-dried earth, sharp and rhythmic as a smith's forge tolling the hours. Beneath the sprawling shade of a terebinth tree, I sat, my eyes tracing the dance of blades. Iru, my eldest, twisted on the balls of his feet, his sword held low, bright eyes locked on his foe. His shoulders, once narrow as a boy's, now bore the sinew of manhood, dark skin gleaming with sweat. Beside him, Elah darted forward, reckless and laughing, as was his way when he thought to best his brother. Their swords met in a clash older than Sinai—iron to iron, foot to foot, neither yielding though the dust curled in clouds about their ankles.

Othniel, my kinsman and truest friend, sat near, arms crossed, his bronze skin catching the sun's fire. His eyes, narrow beneath the wiry fringe of his hair, missed nothing. "Elah spends his strength too soon," he murmured, voice low as the hum of a bowstring. "He will learn patience, or it will learn him."

I grunted, not in dissent. "He carries his mother's fire."

"And Iru bears yours," Othniel replied, a half-smile softening his words.

I nodded, my gaze lingering on my eldest. Iru, now twenty, was ever slow to speak, slow to strike—but when he moved, it was with purpose, as if the weight of remembrance rested upon him. Like me, he had seen too much too young—the blood of Anakim, the fire of altars broken, the shedim fleeing before the Name.

A sudden lunge from Elah broke my thoughts. Iru parried deftly, and the younger sprawled into the dust, his laughter rising like a spark. Othniel tossed a water skin toward them, his chuckle deep. "Enough, you cubs! You fight as if the Rephaim still haunt these hills."

"Perhaps they do," Iru said, sheathing his blade.

I rose, my cloak stirring the dust. "Enough," I called. "The sun climbs, and the table waits."

Aram, who had been circling the sparring ground also, joined us, his olive skin dusted with earth, his robe with a small swath of cloth from Jericho, something he wore proudly, reminding all the men of Yehudah that he had survived the destruction, when the walls of the city fell within themselves. At twenty-five, he bore the lively eyes of his mother, Rachav, and a heart that wandered to distant horizons. "They fight well," Aram said, clapping Iru's shoulder. "But I'd wager a merchant's coin I could outlast Elah's fire."

Elah grinned, brushing dirt from his knees. "Name the day, wanderer."

We walked back through the hills of Hebron, the gold of midday gilding the slopes like a scribe's ink on parchment. My steps were slower now, not from weariness, but from the hush that settles when one begins to count more memories than ambitions. My hair, once dark as the cedars, now bore the ash of years, silvering in the sun like the first frost on the barley. Our home was no longer the camp of wanderers. Groves of olive and fig wove between the tents, their leaves whispering secrets to the breeze. Goat pens lined the southern slope, their bleats mingling with the chatter of children. Azubah's grapevines, heavy with fruit, crawled along woven trellises, and the grinding stones sang with women's voices, a melody of flour and memory.

The main tent stood at the heart of our dwelling, its canvas thick with age, scented with myrrh and new-baked bread. Within, the air was cool and dim, a sanctuary from the sun's unyielding gaze. Azubah sat crosslegged at the low table, her petite frame radiant in deep red and purple fabrics, her black hair braided beneath a crimson scarf. Bangles chimed at her wrists as she worked, her fingers nimble among bowls of almonds and pistachios, their shells piling at her side like sun-bleached relics of the wilderness years.

Mihlat moved quietly near the hearth, her slender frame steady as she set baskets of barley loaves. Now in her twenties, her almond eyes held a quiet warmth, her braid tucked beneath a plain headscarf. She was a pillar of our household, loyal to Azubah, fond of my sons, and now a mother herself. Tirata, her sister, older and nimble, also married, she to a man of Benjamin, with her newest child cradled to her hip, her bronze skin freckled, her curly hair tied with a cord. Her large eyes darted with curiosity, though they softened in Azubah's presence. The older of the sisters, she was still learning the rhythms of service, and her joy bound her to us like kin. Azubah carried herself with such grace that the many male and female slaves of our household under her care were not merely servants, but woven into the life of our household—no less kin to us than our own children.

Boaz, now thirteen, sat cross-legged, reciting from the scrolls of Mosheh. His voice, steady as a shepherd's call, as recalled the sacred words he had memorized from the lessons with the Levites earlier in the day, though he paused to glance at Aram, who sharpened a blade nearby. Aram spoke softly to Iru of trade routes from the coastlands, his voice alight with dreams of distant ports and adventures that await.

"There's barley in the outer field ready to thresh," Azubah said, her hands never still.

"I saw," I replied, bending to kiss her brow, the scent of myrrh clinging to her.

She glanced at Iru and Elah, sweat-streaked and sun-burned. "And those two will soak their feet before treading my rug."

"I heard that," Elah muttered, but his grin betrayed him.

We gathered at the table, the tent filling with the hum of voices. Tirata brought figs and wine, her steps light, while Mihlat passed bowls of lentils and oil. Bread was broken, and the meal unfolded in the easy rhythm of years layered like wine in jars. It was not the peace of idle men, but it was good—a foretaste of the land's promise.

Azubah's eyes met mine across the table. "The vines are heavy this year," she said. "The LORD has remembered us."

"Or tested us," I said, half in jest. "A full harvest means full labor."

Iru leaned forward, his voice thoughtful. "The labor is worth it, if the land yields. But I wonder—does the earth still carry the stain of the shedim? The altars we broke, the high places we burned... do they linger?"

Othniel, our ever present friend seated nearby, stirred. "The shedim flee before the Name, Iru. But the heart of man is another matter. That is the battle now."

Aram nodded, his fingers tracing the edge of his blade. "In Jericho, they spoke of spirits in the hills. Even now, traders whisper of shadows in the north. But I say the fire of the LORD is stronger."

Azubah let out a sigh as she passed a loaf, "Speak not of such things. For once may we have a meal without mention of giants and spirits!"

Mihlat, ever Azubah's shadow in love and loyalty, tilted her head with a conspirator's smile, the flicker of candlelight dancing in her eyes. "Even saints," she said, "must yield one day a year to silence, so their women may feast in peace.'"

He bowed his head, chastened but unbowed. "As you say, mother of the house."

Elah, ever impatient, broke the silence. "I'd rather fight a giant than thresh barley. At least a sword feels alive."

Laughter rippled through the tent, and even Boaz giggled, his scroll forgotten. Mihlat smiled quietly, her eyes on Elah. "A sword may sing, young master, but barley feeds the heart."

Tirata, setting a pitcher of wine, glanced at Mihlat with admiration. "And the heart feeds the soul," she added, her voice soft but clear. Azubah's nod was her reward.

The meal stretched on, woven with talk of harvests, memories of good times, and the small joys of the day. Iru spoke of a new well dug near the groves, Aram of a ship he'd seen at the coast, its sails like wings. Othniel listened, his silence a steady anchor, while B o a z peppered Aram with questions about the sea.

"You ever sail, Aram?" Iru asked, elbowing his friend.

Aram chuckled, breaking a barley cake in two. "I stepped onto a boat once. It rocked like a drunken ox and smelled of fish guts. That was enough adventure for me at the time, but one day, one day I will."

Boaz wrinkled his nose. "I want to sail! I want to see the big waters."

"You'll first learn to walk the ridges of Yehudah before chasing waves," Azubah said firmly, though her eyes twinkled.

Iru leaned forward. "But it wouldn't be the worst thing— trading in spices from Ophir, copper from Kittim, silk from beyond the rivers."

"Silk tears too easy," Elah said with a grunt, his fingers toying with the leather strap of his sword belt. "Better a garment that can take a blade."

"You speak as if you expect war," Othniel said, his voice low. "But peace walks among us now. Do not wish away the breath of quiet."

Elah bristled slightly, but Mihlat, sensing it, spoke gently. "Peace is a sword turned inward, young lord. Harder to master, but far more lasting."

"I don't trust peace," Elah muttered. "It dulls us."

Azubah gave him a look that stilled the air, "It reveals us."

Boaz, eyes bright with curiosity, suddenly turned toward Mihlat, "Mihlat, why do you follow the threshers each day? What are you doing?"

Mihlat smiled softly, wiping her hands on her apron. "I gather the grain they leave behind, the bits that fall when the barley is cut."

Boaz blinked, his forehead furrowing. "But why do you need to do that? You are a servant in the house of Kalev, and you, your husband, and your children are in want of nothing."

Mihlat's smile deepened, touched by a distant memory. "I do it for the poor, young master. For those who have no fields of their own, no kin to bring in harvests. I remember well when the tribe of Yehudah took me in as a child, small and alone, with nothing but the clothes on my back. They gave me a home, and so I give what I can."

Boaz's eyes widened, the weight of her words settling on him.

She reached for a fig from the bowl and held it up, turning it gently. "Once, when I was very small, I followed a woman into the fields at dusk. Her hands were thin, her cloak too large. She walked behind the reapers, gathering only what fell. She never took more than the law allowed. I watched her pray over each handful. It was not just food. It was mercy."

Boaz looked down at his barley cake, then at his hands. "Did she have children?"

"One," Mihlat said. "A girl, silent and fierce-eyed. She carried the basket for her mother and never dropped a single grain."

Boaz was quiet a moment. "If I owned a field, I'd let them take what they needed."

Iru laughed softly. "You'll say that until the goats eat your barley heads."

"I mean it," Boaz said, frowning. "If Yahweh gives you more than you need, why guard it with a sword?"

Othniel nodded toward Boaz, eyes glinting. "That's a thought worth keeping, lad. Many elders forget it."

Elah shifted uncomfortably. "It's not so simple. Some of those gleaners... not all of them are honest."

"True," Azubah said. "But the law isn't built on exceptions. It's built on trust."

"And on mercy," Mihlat added.

Aram leaned forward, "There's a woman near the lower fields —Naamah. Her husband died in Lachish. Her boys are too young to reap. Mihlat brings her a bundle every Sabbath eve."

Boaz' eyes widened. "You do?"

"I do what I can," Mihlat said, a little flushed.

Boaz looked between them all, "Maybe... I could help her."

Azubah raised an eyebrow, "Help how?"

"I could carry a sack. Or leave the edge of the rows fuller. Next season. So they don't have to pick stones."

There was a silence then—not an awkward one, but the kind that settles when something rare is said aloud. Something holy.

Azubah's eyes softened. "Boaz... the field is not just for feeding bellies. It is where Yahweh watches the hearts of men."

Boaz nodded solemnly, then turned back to Mihlat, "Next time you go to Naamah, will you let me carry something for her?"

"I will," she said. "But only if you don't drop it."

"I won't," he promised.

Tirata giggled, and even Iru smiled, ruffling his younger cousin's curls.

"I hope you keep your heart like this," Azubah said, "The world needs more field-keepers than sword-bearers."

"But sometimes it needs both," Elah muttered.

"True," said Othniel. "But a field can feed a thousand. A sword? It only silences."

Azubah stood then, brushing her hands on her skirt. "That's enough talk for one meal. Tirata, bring the basin. We'll wash before prayers."

As the women moved, Boaz lingered by the doorway, looking toward the far slope where the olive trees met the barley. The wind stirred the stalks in soft waves, and somewhere out there, Naamah would be tying her cloak tight against the dusk, waiting for a mercy she hadn't earned but was given just the same.

And Boaz, son of Rachav, quietly vowed to leave his corners uncut.

I sat in stillness, having spoken little throughout the meal. There was a quiet gladness in it—in simply watching, listening, bearing witness. Now, in the autumn of my years, it was enough to behold the laughter, the clatter of shared bread, the faces shaped by time and covenant. This was the family God had given me, and it was very good.

Then the tent flap stirred, a breath from nowhere, and a shadow darkened the threshold.

A messenger stood tall and lean, dust thick on his sandals, his robe torn from haste. His eyes met mine, and the air grew heavy with knowing.

"Elder of Yehudah," the messenger's voice came, hoarse as a desert wind. "Joshua, son of Nun, lies stricken. He calls for you."

The tent fell into silence, sharp as the edge of a blade drawn swift and sure. Even the babe at Tirata's breast stilled, as if the child's breath held the weight of those words.

Azubah rose first, her hands pressed to her heart. Her dark eyes met mine with unyielding strength.

Othniel shifted beside me, a steadfast shadow. Iru bowed his head, his bright eyes now dimmed beneath heavy lids. Elah's fingers clenched, the fire within him banked tight. Aram's sword rested forgotten by his side, and Boaz looked up with a child's wide eyes, confusion and fear tangled in his gaze.

For long moments no one dared to breathe.

Finally, Mihlat stepped forward, offering the messenger a cup of water. He drank with reverence, as if the vessel contained more than spring's gift—memory, oath, the weight of a broken world.

I rose slowly, the weight of years pressing heavy beneath a calm surface,

"Where?" The word was little more than a breath.

"Timnat-Serach," came the reply. "His house lies quiet. One by one, he named the tribes in his prayers—but your name, yours he saved for the last."

I closed my eyes and saw him clearly—the man who stood with Mosheh on the mountaintop, who led us through desert dust and fire lit nights. Joshua , son of Nun: warrior, prophet, the flame in the gathering shadow.

"When did his voice falter?" I asked.

"He speaks still," the messenger said, "but only in whispers. The priests say he will not see the dawn, though it may come any day."

A sudden gust rattled the tent flap. Goats bleated from the ridge above, and far off, a lone hawk cried once before silence claimed the hills again.

Azubah's eyes met mine with quiet understanding. Her voice, steady and sure, cut through the silence: "Iru, saddle the ass. She will carry your father faster than he can walk on foot."

Iru nodded without question, the weight of her meaning settling like dust in the air. I was no longer swift on my feet—none needed to say it aloud.

Iru moved with practiced grace. "Will Father go alone?"

"No," Othniel answered before I could. He wrapped his cloak tight about his shoulders like a shield. "We go as one."

Azubah stepped closer, resting her hand lightly on my arm. "We shall all go," she said, the words steady as the earth beneath our feet.

Elah's jaw tightened and turning to one of the young male servants standing outside our tent he said, "Run and tell the elders. We all leave tonight."

Boaz, small but fierce with a fire only youth can carry spoke, "I must tell my mother. She will want to come."

Azubah's eyes softened, then sharpened, "Go swiftly, then."

Boaz slipped away through the shadows, weaving between servants and tents to find his mother in the next valley over. The name Rachav carried weight here—a story older than the dust beneath our feet, a story of shelter and courage, of a city fallen but not forgotten.

Aram, Boaz's brother—born among the stones of Jericho and marked by its ruin—stood at my side. "We go as one?"

"Yes," I said. "All who bear this burden, all who carry this hope."

To the servant girls, Azubah addressed them softly. "Tend the hearth and the children. Guard this place as we guard our hearts."

Mihlat nodded, eyes reflecting the firelight's flicker, "The fields can wait. We will hold the home."

Tirata cradled the babe once more, whispering, "We wait for your return."

Boaz returned soon, breathless with news, "Mother and Salmon will come with us."

Aram's hand came down hard on Boaz's shoulder. "Together, then."

The tents shifted as voices rose in a soft hymn—a prayer woven through the night air, a call for strength and protection.

Outside, the olive trees whispered their ancient secrets, and the barley bowed beneath watchful stars. I mounted the ass, the quiet weight of years settling on me like a mantle. Once I marched at the front of armies, sword in hand, leading the charge—now I rode as the elder, while my family walked beside me. My sons, strong men shaped by years and faith—Iru and Elah, my legacy would live on in them. Rachav's children, Aram, a warrior forged in Jericho's shadow, and Boaz, still a boy balanced on the cusp of manhood. Beside me, Azubah walked, her fingers entwined with mine, steady and warm, a tether in the uncertain night.

Rachav and Salmon joined us in silence, their steps measured and sure. Rachav's eyes held the memory of city walls and crimson cords. Boaz glanced up at his mother, his young face lit with pride and quiet awe, his whole life he observed that everywhere she walked people bowed. Her faith in the One True God was forever a testimony to the Twelve Clans.

The air grew hushed as the earth beneath us shifted toward holy ground.

Then Azubah, her voice like wind through the terebinth, began to sing—a song not loud, but clear enough that it seemed even the stars bent low to hear:

He walked with Mosheh through fire and cloud,
The servant whose hands did not falter.
The Spear of the Twelve Clans,
The mountain trembled at his obedience.
At his word, the sun stood still in the heavens,
And hail fell like judgment upon the wicked.
He led the tribes into the land of promise.
The faithful remember his courage,
And they follow the path his sandals broke.

The song slipped into the hush again, settling like dew upon us all. No one spoke for some time. The way before us stretched long —but the hearts around me beat with one rhythm, and the old stories rose once more to guide our steps.

Behind us, the tents stood silent, the hearth's embers glowing faint in the dark—a promise made in shadows, waiting for our return.

And in the quiet night, that promise beat steady and sure, like the pulse of a faithful heart.

The hills of Yehudah stretched before us, their slopes silvered by moonlight, the terebinth trees whispering ancient secrets. Azubah's song lingered in the air, its echo a thread binding us to the covenant. "He walked with Mosheh through fire and cloud," she had sung, and now those words wove through my soul, conjuring Joshua 's face— the warrior who parted the Yarden, who stilled the sun, who led us into the land of promise. His whispers now faded, the messenger had said, yet they called me still, a summons I could not refuse.

Iru's voice broke the silence, low and thoughtful. "Father, did Joshua ever speak of the end? Of what waits when the torch dims?"

I turned to him, his face half-shadowed. "He spoke of the Name," I said. "Of a fire that burns beyond the flesh. He said the land was ours not by sword alone, but by the promise that outlasts all kings. That the righteous shall live by faith and fear, and repentance, and that we will one day dine in the bosom of Avraham"

Elah, ever restless, kicked a stone from the path. "I wish I'd seen him in battle.   The stories—Gibeon, Makkedah—they say he was a storm."

"He was," Othniel said, his voice steady as stone. "But it was his faith that parted rivers, not his blade. Remember that, Elah."

Aram glanced at Boaz, who walked wide-eyed beside Rachav. "Tell him, Mother," Aram said. "Tell Boaz again how Joshua spared us in Jericho. We never tire of this story"

Rachav's voice was soft, yet it carried the weight of memory. "He was mercy clad in iron," she said. "When the walls fell, he saw the scarlet cord and honored it. He gave us life when death was our due."

Boaz's young face lit with awe. "Did he speak to you?"

"He did," Rachav said at length, her gaze slipping past the firelight into memory. "He said, 'The Lord has given you to us, and us to you.' I have borne those words ever since."

And then she told the tale—again. The fall of Jericho. As we had heard it before, as I had spoken it more times than I could count, in tents and courts, to children wide-eyed and elders nodding slow with wonder. It is a story that will not die. Not while time yet turns. For on that day, the Lord of Hosts remembered His people. And by His breath alone, the stones of a mighty city crumbled, and the proud walls fell like sheaves before the harvest wind.

Salmon, silent until now, placed a hand on Boaz's shoulder. "That is why we go," he said. "To honor the man who bound our fates."

The path wound northward, through valleys where the air grew sharp with the scent of cedar and wild thyme. Torches flickered in our hands, their flames dancing like the spirits of the wilderness. The stars wheeled above, a canopy of light that seemed to bend low, as if to witness our pilgrimage. I thought of the shedim, those shadows we had driven from the high places, their altars shattered beneath our feet. The land was cleansed, yet the heart of man remained a battleground, as Othniel had said. Joshua had fought that war with every breath, and now his final battle called us to his side.

Hours passed, and the night deepened. Azubah's hand found mine, her fingers warm against the chill. "Do you fear for him?" she whispered.

"Not for him," I said. "Joshua walks with the Name. He will lie in the bosom of Avraham. But for us—without his voice, who will guide the tribes?"

She squeezed my hand, "The same fire that guided him. It does not die."

Her words were a balm, yet the weight of them settled like dust. Joshua was the last of Mosheh's hand, the bridge between wilderness and promise. His passing would leave a void no elder could fill.

Chapter Twenty
The Final Breath

Dawn touched the horizon, painting the hills with gold as we neared Timnat-Serach. The village lay nestled in Ephraim's embrace, its tents and few stone buildings clustered like sheep beneath the oaks. A multitude had gathered at the outskirts of the city, their faces marked by grief, their voices a low tide of mourning. Yet as we approached, the crowd stirred and parted before us—slowly, reverently—as though the very earth remembered the days of Mosheh and made way once more. A hush fell like dew over the people when they saw who walked among us.

"It is Rachav the holy," I heard them whisper, bowing as she passed, their hands to their hearts as if a queen had come down to die among them.

"Kalev, slayer of the giants!" others cried, wonder mingling with sorrow.

And from still others came the amazement to see my beloved wife for the first time, "Azubah, the songstress of the Twelve Tribes— the voice so beautiful it silences the shedim!" they whispered.

Each name passed like incense through the air, bittersweet, weighty with remembrance. They had come not merely to witness a death—but to honor the final breath of an age.

The boys, seldom straying beyond the hills of Hebron, looked on with wide-eyed wonder at the welcome that met us. It puzzled them, this hero's reverence offered to those they simply called mother and father. For children rarely see the weight their parents carry—nor the stories others tell in their name.

Eventually, as we drew closer we found Phineas, son of Eleazar, now high priest in his father's stead. His body more seasoned with age, his copper-toned skin gleamed, his priestly tassels swaying.

His piercing eyes met mine, and in them burned the zeal for God I had see all those years ago.

"Kalev," Phineas said, his voice sharp as flint. "The Elder of Yehudah comes at last."

I dismounted, the ass snorting softly. "Phineas, son of Eleazar. How does he fare?" He grabbed my arm, and we kissed as brothers.

"He clings to life," Phineas said, "His breath is a whisper, but his spirit is a flame. Come quickly."

Azubah and the others gathered behind me, their presence a steady anchor. Phineas led us through the crowd, his steps swift, his tassels snapping in the breeze.

The people parted, their eyes tracing us—Iru's steady gait, Elah's restless energy, Othniel's quiet strength, Aram's thoughtful gaze, Rachav and Salmon's measured grace, Boaz's youthful fire. We were a remnant of the war, a family forged in the crucible of covenant.

The tent of Joshua stood at the village's heart, its canvas weathered by years, its entrance flanked by elders, priests and guards. A low chant rose from within, the Shema woven with prayers for mercy. Phineas lifted the flap, and we entered, the air thick with the scent of oil and myrrh.

Joshua lay on a pallet, his frame frail beneath a woven blanket, his face etched with the lines of a life spent in service. His eyes, once bright as a prophet's, were dim, yet they found mine with unerring clarity. His lips moved, a whisper barely heard.

"Kalev," he breathed. "Brother… you came."

Iru and Elah held both my arms and helped me kneel beside him, my heart a stone in my chest. "Joshua , son of Nun. The tribes are with you."

Azubah kneeling at my side, her eyes glistening and red, tears beginning to flow. Othniel's hand rested on my shoulder, a silent vow. Aram, Rachav, Salmon, and Boaz gathered near, their presence a tapestry of memory and hope.

Joshua's hand trembled as it reached for mine, "The land... is yours," he whispered. "Guard it... from the shedim... from the heart that forgets."

I clasped his hand, its warmth fading. "We will guard it," I said. "As you did."

Phineas stood at the tent's head, his staff a sentinel, "The Name is his shield," he said, his voice fierce, "The Spear of the Twelve Clans will feast in the bosom of Avraham, but the covenant endures."

Othniel stepped forward, his voice steady. "What would you have us do, servant of Yahweh?"

Joshua's eyes flickered to him, a spark of the old fire. "Remember... the Yarden. The stones we set... they speak. Teach the children... the Name."

Elah, his impulsiveness softened, spoke. "We will teach them. Your voice will not fade."

Aram knelt, and bowed before his lord, his Jericho-born heart open, "You spared my mother, my kin. Your mercy is our strength."

Rachav's now prostrating herself before him, her voice was barely a whisper. "We owe you our lives my lord, we will never forget."

Boaz, small but fierce, stepped closer, and hesitantly and unsure, he got on his knees and bowed before the great man, "I'll tell the stories," he said as he looked up, his voice trembling. "Of the sun that stood still, of the walls that fell. I will show mercy on those who need mercy."

Joshua's lips curved, a faint smile. "Good... boy. Tell them... all."

The chants grew louder, the Shema a river of sound that swelled beyond the tent walls. Joshua's breath had slowed, each exhale a tether loosening from the earth, his chest rising with effort, but steady still. I leaned close, my voice low, "You led us through fire and cloud. Rest now, brother. The Name is with you."

His gaze met mine—clear, unwavering—and then shifted upward, toward the roof of the tent, as though the canvas itself had faded and he looked upon the stars. "The mountain... trembles," he whispered. "The promise... lives."

Then his hand moved, a slow lift of command. "Enough," he said, louder than before, voice like dry wind over stone. "Let them go."

The high priest Phineas stepped forward, brows knit. "My lord Joshua—"

But Joshua raised his hand again, firmer now. "All of you. Even you, Phineas. Leave us."

The servants froze, glancing at one another, unsure.

He didn't repeat himself. Only turned his eyes back to me.

"Let him stay," Joshua said. "Just Kalev."

Silence fell like a curtain, the murmurs outside fading. One by one they filed out—the priests, the elders, even the sons of Nun's house, and mine as well—until only I remained beside him, the lamp's flame between us casting long shadows, two old warriors, brothers in dust and covenant.

Joshua's breath rasped like wind through the reeds, but his eyes remained sharp, fixed on mine with a clarity that cut deeper than any sword. He lay back against the cushions, arms crossed over his chest, the weight of years etched into the furrows of his brow and the silver of his beard. "You remember Hebron, Kalev?"

I nodded, though no words rose to meet his.

"So do I," he said, eyes narrowing as if peering across the years. "It lives in my bones more than any other place. Not Sinai. Not Jericho. Hebron." He smiled faintly, the memory warming his face. "We walked into the shade of Anakim towers, with sandals full of dust and mouths dry from silence. Do you recall the stillness of that land? Like the breath of God had paused there. Even the jackals kept their distance."

I smiled, a breath of laughter rising in my chest. "And the vineyards."

"Yes," he whispered. "The grapes the size of a man's fist. And the silence of the hills, broken only by the creak of our ropes as we cut the clusters down. The land did not resist us, not then. It welcomed us —us, of all men—like sons who had wandered too long."

His eyes darkened. "And yet, when we returned... they would not listen. Ten voices sowed dread like weeds in the soul of Israel. They spoke of giants and cursed their birthright before the whole assembly. But you stood up, blazing like the altar fire, and I with you. I thought we would be stoned that night. I remember gripping the hilt of my blade, not to strike, but to fall with honor beside you. Then the cloud came. The fire. The Voice."

A hush settled in the tent, his voice, with each new sentence became a struggle, the candle flame bending as if drawn into the weight of what had been spoken.

"We saw wonders, Kalev," Joshua said, quieter now, I had to lean close to hear, "The sea split like linen torn in two. Manna on the stones, water from the rock, the earth itself opening its mouth to swallow rebellion. We were boys when we crossed the Sea... but warriors when we crossed the Nehar Ha-Yarden."

He reached for my hand, his grip frail but still bearing the memory of strength. "I've killed kings. I've seen cities fall with a trumpet's blast. But no moment was greater than when Mosheh turned and laid his hands upon me. I felt the fire run down my spine like oil set aflame, and I knew—I would lead them where he could not."

He turned his gaze away, toward the canvas wall. "But now the pillar moves without me. My feet have grown heavy. It is for you, old friend, to speak when I am silent. The land is not finished. Nor is the covenant."

He looked at me once more, and though the warrior faded, the prophet remained. "Finish the work, Kalev. Take the heights. Crush the sons of Anak beneath your heel. And tell them... tell them I was not perfect, but I always repented. I always believed."

Joshua's voice dropped, hoarse as wind through dead leaves. "They are a stiff-necked people, Kalev. They always have been. Too quick to grumble, too slow to give thanks. They forget in days what took years to deliver. Even now, in their peace, they are restless. One clan envies another. The Levite gripes about the oxen. The Reuvenite broods over borders. And the sons of Ephraim—" he exhaled, a slow, bitter breath—"they boast as if their right was born before Avraham himself."

He turned his face toward me, his brow furrowed in warning. "Guard your children, Kalev. Teach them. Bind the Word upon their hearts, as Mosheh commanded us. Tell them the stories—the fire, the sea, the blood on the lintel. Tell them until their bones remember it. The day is coming when every man will do what is right in his own eyes, and the land will groan under the weight of its freedom."

He reached for his staff, fingertips grazing it. "But Mosheh— he prophesied this, even before we crossed into the land. He said the time would come when Yahweh would raise a king—not like the nations, but a ruler chosen by God, not by men. A shepherd of hearts. A sword of justice. And from that king, from the seed of Yehudah, would rise a greater King still."

His voice trembled, not with fear, but with awe. "A ruler of all the earth. The King of kings. The mountain of His reign will not be shaken, and the nations will come to His light. You and I, we will not see that day. But your children might. And their children after them. So teach them, Kalev. Carve it into their souls."

He closed his eyes. "Prepare the way."

The tent was still, save the hush of Joshua's breath—the last ember of a life that had burned like fire through the wilderness. I knelt beside him, my hand clasping his, once strong as stone, now fragile as wind-scoured bark. We were two old men, who had lived a lifetime that few would know. His eyes, clouded yet steady, found mine once more, and a faint smile touched his lips. Then, with a final exhale—soft, steady, like the closing of a scroll—he was gone.

I bowed my head over him, I kissed him one last time, my tears falling into the folds of his cloak. "Rest, brother," I whispered, the words catching in my throat. "May the bosom of Avraham envelope you, may your sins be forgiven." I prayed.

The grief rose in me like a flood, fierce and unrelenting. I, the warrior of Yehudah, wept openly. For my friend. My captain. The Spear of the Twelve Clans. My brother in arms. The man who stood with me when all others faltered. His battle was done, but mine would go on without him.

The tent felt hollow now, like a vessel poured out.

I rose and stepped outside.

The air was thick with waiting. All had gathered beyond the circle of the tent—priests, family, servants, warriors—eyes watching the entrance, hearts straining toward what they feared to know.

I walked carefully, more a shuffle than a walk, my boys immediately came to me and let me put my arms around them. I met Phineas's gaze across the hush. No words passed between us. I gave a single nod.

Phineas straightened, raising his staff to the sky. His voice rang out like a trumpet at dawn: "The Spear of the Twelve Clans returns to the fathers!"

A groan passed through the assembly. Azubah gripped my arm, her tears falling freely. Iru and Elah bowed their heads. Aram leaned into Rachav's side. Boaz clung to Salmon, and Othniel stood still, eyes shining.

The elders began a lament, their voices weaving through the tent like smoke. Phineas led the rites, his zeal tempered by reverence, his spear lowered as he anointed Joshua 's brow with oil. The crowd outside joined the lament, their song rising to the hills, a tide of sorrow and gratitude.

We stepped from the tent, the dawn now full, its light gilding the oaks of Timnat-Serach. The people looked to us, their eyes seeking strength. I raised my hand, my voice steady though my heart trembled. "Joshua has gone to the fathers, but the Name endures. The land is ours, by covenant and fire. Let us guard it."

Phineas stood beside me, his piercing eyes sweeping the crowd. "The tribes will not falter," he said. "The Shema is our shield, the promise our sword."

Azubah's voice rose, soft but clear, a song of hope: "The faithful remember his courage, and they follow the path his sandals broke."

The hills of Ephraim cradled the dawn, their limestone ridges gilded by light, the terebinth groves whispering secrets older than the stars. We buried Joshua, son of Nun, according to our fathers' custom, with mourning that pierced the heavens. I, the elder of Yehudah, stood among the tents of Timnath-Serah—also called Timnath-heres— his inheritance nestled on the northern slope of Gaash's mountain. No cities rose here, only a sea of weathered canvas, pulsing with the breath of a people forged in covenant, their camp alive with servants grinding barley, tending goats, and bearing baskets of figs through the dust.

In that week of mourning, my family stood as my rock, unshaken amidst the sorrow that cloaked Timnath-Serah. Azubah, my wife, held me with her steadfast heart. Othniel, my kinsman, anchored me with quiet wisdom. Phineas, high priest, burned with zealous faith. Iru and Elah, my sons, stood silent, their reverence a strength. I myself am now old and weathered, and I see with piercing clarity: the legacy of Joshua and I would live through our lineage, a covenant woven in their blood, through my boys, and through their children's children.

Rachav's redemption, woven through the scarlet cord, would live on in her sons, Aram and Boaz, bearers of the twelve tribes' hope. The mercy of Jericho, a weight upon their hearts, binds them to the covenant, their lineage a flame for Israel's future.

Eventually, the cave was readied, hewn into the ridge, its mouth agape like a silent prayer. Before the stone was rolled, I laid beside Joshua the spear he raised at Ai, its bronze tip gleaming with the memory of victory. The Spear of the Twelve Tribes finally lay down, in a darkened cave.

Then, with Phineas's blessing upon them, his hand in prayer touching them: I placed twelve iron nails—one for each tribe—consecrated to shield his body from the shedim that linger near the dead, a covenantal sign that his spirit might rest in Avraham's bosom until the Judge of all the earth tears open death's gates. "The Name guards him," Phineas intoned, his voice sharp as flint, "a flame against the shadows."

The elders say the spirit hovers three days, reluctant to part, so we watched in reverent silence. Servants lit clay lamps near the tomb, their flames dancing like stars, and poured oil upon the stone, a sign of remembrance. Each night, under a canopy of stars, Azubah's voice rose, deep as the wilderness wells, in the tradition of Miryam, sister of Mosheh. Her hymns, neither loud nor proud, wove lament and hope —songs of the Yarden parting, of Jericho's walls falling, of the sun stilled in Gibeon's sky, of the Spear of the Twelve Tribes. The camp joined, thousands of people, their voices a tide, while servants moved among us, bearing water and bread, their hands trembling with awe.

"Kalev," Azubah whispered on the third night, her black hair bound tightly under her veil, "his spirit feels the Name. Do you sense it?"

I nodded, my heart heavy. "He walks with the fathers now, yet his fire lingers, a charge to us."

Othniel, his eyes on the tomb, spoke low. "The tribes waver without him. We, the elders, must hold the Shema fast, lest the shedim creep back."

Phineas, his priest's scepter planted, joined us. "The Lord has given the land, and Joshua kept it holy. Kalev, you saw the great work. Speak it, lest the generation rising forgets."

"I will," I vowed, my voice steady. "The Yarden's stones, the Nephilim's fall, the covenant's fire—these will not fade."

The seven days of mourning bound all Israel. We tore our garments, dusted our heads, and sat upon the ground. No music played save dirges and psalms. Men from distant tribes—Dan, Asher, Benjamin—passed through, their hands on my shoulder or Phineas's robe, saying, "Peace be upon the servant of Yahweh." Servants tended fires, their smoke curling like prayers, while children, hushed, carried olives to the mourners.

On the fifth day, Azubah gathered the women, her voice a balm. "Sisters, sing of the manna, the tents, the Name above the Ark. Let the children hear."

Othniel spoke to the elders, his voice a rock. "Joshua bore our burdens, even when we turned. Let us bear the tribes now, as he did."

I walked among the tents, my heart tracing Joshua's deeds— not only the victories, but the quiet judgments, the faithful steps, the weight of a stiff-necked people. "He was our brother," I said to Phineas, "a flame in the wilderness."

Phineas's eyes burned. "And we are his heirs, Kalev. The Shema is our spear."

Iru and Elah, silent, tended the lamps, their reverence a vow. Aram and Boaz, with Rachav and Salmon, sat near the tomb, their quiet presence a testament to Joshua's mercy. "He spared us," Rachav whispered more than once that week, her voice breaking, always tears would follow.

On the seventh day, we sealed the tomb. A great stone was rolled before the cave, and twelve men pressed their hands to it as we cried the Shema: "Hear, O Israel…" Silence followed, the hills of Ephraim bearing witness, the cedars mourning with us. Phineas raised his staff, his voice a cry. "Here lies Joshua, son of Nun, the Spear of the Twelve Clans!"

Azubah's final hymn rose, soft as dew: "The faithful remember his courage, and they follow the path his sandals broke." The camp echoed, a chorus of hope.

We returned to the tents, hearts heavy yet anchored. Joshua slept with the fathers, but the promise lived. I looked to Azubah, her eyes a well of faith. "The stars guide us home," she said.

"And the Name lights our path," I replied.

Othniel's hand rested on my shoulder. "The generation rises, Kalev. We must teach them, or the land will forget."

"We will," I said, my gaze on the hills. "Hebron will sing of Joshua, and the covenant will endure."

Thus we departed, the camp's hum fading—servants tending goats, women carrying water, life stirring despite death. Mihlat and Tirata and their families awaited in Hebron, their hearth a beacon. Joshua's legacy wove into our steps, a fire no darkness could quench.

Epilogue

Beneath the ancient terebinth, its gnarled branches weaving a canopy against the Hebron sun, I sat, my bones aching with the weight of years, my mind sharp as a flint. The dust of Yehudah swirled at my feet, stirred by the tread of servants and elders who came from every tribe—Yehudah, Ephraim, Benjamin—seeking counsel. Their voices carried reverence, for I was the last living thread to Egypt's chains, to the wilderness manna, to Mosheh's fire and Joshua 's sword. The terebinth's shade was cool, its leaves whispering secrets of the covenant, and I listened, my heart tethered to the Name.

My grandchildren played in the dust, their laughter ringing like distant bells across the groves. Azubah, white-haired now, her beauty deepened by wisdom's grace, approached, her crimson scarf catching the breeze. She bore a basket of dates and a clay cup of wine, her bangles chiming softly, a psalm of fidelity. Her hand brushed my shoulder, and for a moment, the years fell away, the wilderness nights alive again in her dark eyes. "Rest, my heart," she said, her voice a well of Beersheba, "The tribes lean on you, but the Lord sustains."

I took the wine, its warmth a quiet fire, "They come as if I hold Mosheh's staff," I murmured. "Yet I am but a man, Azubah, clinging to the promise."

She smiled, fierce and tender. "A man who walked with giants. That is enough."

Beyond the tents, Boaz strode among his vineyards, a landholder now, his quiet strength a mirror of a steadfast heart. His servants moved with purpose, pruning vines heavy with fruit, their voices mingling with the hum of bees. Rachav, once the harlot of Jericho, now a matriarch wrapped in fine linen, leaned on a cane, her tongue still sharp, her heart tender as the dawn. She gathered the women and grandchildren beneath an olive tree, her voice weaving tales of the scarlet cord and the God of Israel who spared her. "The

Name saw me," she said, her eyes bright with memory. "And through His mercy, you stand here."

The women nodded, their hands busy with spindles, while the children listened, wide-eyed. Azubah joined them, her white hair gleaming, and sang a hymn of deliverance, her voice deep as the wells of Hebron. Rachav's eyes met hers, and they shared a quiet smile, bound by years and songs. Salmon, Rachav's husband, rested now with the fathers, buried with honor beneath a terebinth. Each week, Azubah and Rachav visited his tomb, their voices rising in the old songs of the Yarden's parting, of walls falling, of mercy woven in crimson. They sang for him, that he would be found faithful in the bosom of Avraham. Boaz, ever the guardian, stood nearby, his stylus scratching papyrus, preserving the hymns for the generations yet to come.

Othniel was away at his tents, tending to his family, a husband now and no longer the young kinsman of my youth. His broad shoulders bore the weight of a mature man, his wisdom deepened by years, and his grown children, a new strength in Yehudah, thrived under his steady hand.

Our family had grown vast, a tapestry of tents stretching along Hebron's ridges, alive with laughter, arguments, and the pulse of the clan. Besides Iru and Elah, who were both married, now great men of Yehudah in their own right, we had a third son, Naam, a skilled builder whose hands shaped stone with the precision of a psalm. Our six daughters, each a flame of the covenant, had married into the twelve clans—one to a Levite, her prayers rising with incense; another to a man of Issachar, her fields abundant. I walked among their tents daily, when my legs would provide, staff in hand, offering blessings, guidance, and the occasional correction. "Honor the Shema," I told a bickering son-in-law, my voice firm. "The Name binds us, not our quarrels."

Naam approached, his hands dusted with limestone. "Father, the new well is finished," he said, his voice steady. "The children already draw from it."

I nodded, my heart warmed. "Good, my son. Let it be a sign— the land yields when we walk with the Name."

Azubah's eyes gleamed. "And let the children sing of it, as they sing of Joshua ."

That evening, messengers, my servants, arrived, their cloaks stained with dust, their faces drawn. They knelt before me, voices low, "many of the Twelve Clans keep wandering away from their land. Reuven and Gad have crossed into Moab, seeking pasture and grain. The Danites have conquered cities with no abandon."

Another spoke, hesitant. "In Yehudah, households wander— names like Elimelech, Naomi—seeking bread among the Moabites. The Edomites offer trade, even land....and even daughters in marriage."

I stroked my beard, the weight of memory heavy. Lot's daughters, Esau's line—the old stories stirred, their echoes troubling yet intriguing. "If brothers quarrel," I said, my voice a low hum, "hunger may bind them or break them forever."

Azubah's hand rested on mine, "The Lord has brought us through hunger before," she said. "He will not forsake the promise."

I nodded, but my heart was a stone. The shedim were gone from Hebron, their altars broken, yet the heart of man remained a battleground. Would the tribes hold fast, or scatter like chaff?

That night, by the fire's glow, I sat with Azubah, the embers casting shadows on her white hair. The air was thick with cedar and memory, the tents quiet save for the distant bleat of goats. I spoke of Joshua , of Mosheh, of manna falling like dew, of fire guarding our path. "Will they remember, Azubah?" I asked, my voice a whisper. "The Yarden's stones, the sun's stillness—will the children know?"

Her hand pressed my heart, her eyes a flame. "Your children remember. And they will teach their own. The Name is written in their blood."

I drew her close, her warmth a covenant. "You are my rock, as you were when Joshua slept. The tribes lean, but you hold me."

She smiled, soft as dawn. "And you hold them, my heart. As Joshua did, as Mosheh before him."

The next day, Boaz came to me, his vineyard cloak dusted with earth. We walked among the tents, the sun warm on my shoulders. I spoke of Mosheh's prophecy, words etched in my soul. "One day, when every man does what is right in his own eyes, Yahweh will raise a king, Boaz. A scepter from Yehudah, to bind the tribes."

He listened, his quiet strength a mirror of the past. "A king?" he asked, his voice low. "Will he be like Joshua?"

"Greater still," I said, placing my hand on his head, my fingers tracing the weight of years. "Watch the hills of Bethlehem, child. From Yehudah shall come the scepter, perhaps even through you, or your son's son."

Boaz's eyes gleamed, a spark of the covenant. "I will watch, and teach my house to do the same."

I nodded, my heart stirred. The promise lived, not in my sword, but in the hands of those who followed.

Days later, my strength waning, I took a final walk, staff in hand, memory my guide. The hill was familiar, its slope worn by my steps, the terebinth groves stretching below like a song. I climbed, my breath heavy, the land unfolding before me—Hebron's ridges, the vineyards, the tents alive with my clan's pulse. The sun hung low, gilding the hills, and I stood, a silhouette against the sky, the weight of an age upon me.

I thought of Egypt's chains, the wilderness fire, the shedim's fall. I thought of Joshua, his whispers at Timnath-Serah, his grave north of Gaash. I thought of my family—Azubah's hymns, Iru's steadiness, Elah's fire, my daughters' laughter, Boaz's vineyards, Rachav's cord. They were the covenant's flame, burning beyond my years.

Suddenly, a shadow leaned upon me. It was Rachav, my old friend, her cane tapping the earth like a quiet drum, each step a testament to years unyielding. Her linen cloak, frayed at the hem, swayed in the Hebron breeze, its folds clinging to a frame bent by time, frail as a reed yet defiant. Her face was that of an old woman, her hair, white as the cliffs of the Salt Sea, caught the fading light, a crown of age woven by decades. Only in her eyes—sharp, fierce, alight with the fire of that young spark who hid us in Jericho's shadow—did I glimpse the Rachav of old, undimmed by the weight of years.

We walked quietly, without saying a word, the air was thick with the scent of olives and memory, heavy with the covenant's promise.

Finally, she spoke, "You climb still," her voice sharp yet warm, a blade softened by the forge of time, "The hills know your name."

"As they know yours," I replied, leaning on my staff, its wood worn smooth by decades. "Our God's mercy lives in your sons."

She nodded, her eyes distant, tracing the ridges where the tents of Yehudah glowed with firelight. "Aram carries it to the coastlands, Boaz in the vines. The Name is faithful."

I turned to her, the weight of years a cloak upon us both. "Rachav, do you ever see it still? The walls of Jericho, trembling before the shofar, the scarlet cord in your window?"

Her lips curved, a spark of the woman who once defied a city, out of sacred habit she traced her aging fingers around each of the weaves of the scarlet cord around her arm, "Every night, in dreams. The dust rose like a storm, the shouts of Israel a thunder. I stand at the window, my heart pounding, the cord a lifeline to the God of

Avraham. I was of the Anakim's shadow, a daughter of giants, yet He saw me."

"As He saw me," I said, my voice a murmur. "A Kenizzite, born of the Nephilim's kin, my blood tied to the clans we broke. Yet the Name called me from the desert, bound me to Yehudah, wrapped me in the covenant."

Rachav's cane paused, her gaze piercing. "We were outcasts, you and I, children of the tall ones, feared by men. The Kena'anim whispered of our strength, our curse. But Avraham's God redeemed us, wove us into His people. I stood in Jericho's ruin, you in Egypt's chains, and He made us whole."

I nodded, the memory a fire in my chest. "I walked with Mosheh, I stood with Joshua, the Yarden dry beneath our feet, the shedim fleeing before the Ark. We were not merely spared, Rachav. We were chosen, grafted into Yehudah's vine, our names etched in the covenant."

She leaned closer, her voice a well of Beersheba. "Chosen, yes. I hung the scarlet cord, just as you commanded, not knowing if Israel would honor it. I came to your clan, and when Joshua's eyes met mine, and he spoke of the Name's mercy, I was no longer Jericho's daughter, but a child of the Most High. My sons, Aram and Boaz, carry that mercy now, a flame for the twelve tribes."

"And my sons," I said, my heart stirred. "Iru, steady as the hills, Elah, fierce as a storm, Naam, building with stone and faith— they bear the promise, as your sons do. The God of Avraham has woven our blood into His story, our children the threads of His vow."

"Even Othniel," I said, almost to myself. "He was once all fire —young, intense, too quick to raise his voice or his blade. But time tempers iron. Now he sits as judge in the hill country of Ephraim, discerning between right and wrong with a steadier hand. The same zeal still burns in him, but it's been refined. Like the bronze in the furnace, he has learned to endure the heat without cracking."

Rachav's eyes gleamed, wet with memory. "Do you remember Makkedah? The five kings, hanging from the trees, their shadows long against the sky? I heard the tale in the camp, newly spared, my heart still trembling. You stood there, a giant among men, yet your eyes were on the Name, not the victory."

Memories flooded my mind, soft as the breeze, my heart stirred by the weight of that day, "A giant, perhaps, but humbled. When those kings—sons of the Anakim—fell,   I saw the shedim flee their bodies, dark wisps rising like smoke to the heavens. I thought all saw it, Rachav, the air thick with their departure, but the Lord granted me sight into the invisible, it was a mantle that Mosheh placed around my neck, a glimpse of His war against the shadows. Their altars crumbled, but it was Joshua's faith that broke them. I was but a sword in the Lord's hand, as you were a cord in His plan. We, of giant clans, became His instruments."

She gripped her cane, her voice fierce. "Instruments, yes, but family now. Yehudah's tents are ours, its covenant our shield. I teach the women, the grandchildren, of the Name who saw a harlot and called her kin. You counsel the tribes, your voice a rock. We are no longer outcasts."

The wind stirred, carrying Azubah's hymn from the tents below, a thread of hope. I closed my eyes, seeing Egypt's dust, the wilderness fire, the Yarden's stones.

"Our people have seen wonders, Rachav. The sea parted, the sun stilled, the Nephilim fallen. Yet the greatest wonder is this: you and I born of giants, stand as Yehudah's own, our children the hope of Israel."

Rachav's hand touched mine, her fingers frail but warm. "They will carry the stories—Jericho's fall, Makkedah's judgment, the Shema's call. The Name has bound our children, as it bound us."

"And my children," I said, my voice a prayer. "Iru will teach, Elah will fight, Naam will build. The famine may scatter the tribes, but the covenant holds. The God of Avraham will not forsake His own".

She nodded, her cloak catching the fading light. "The other cities trouble me, Moab, Edom—they call to our kin. Yet I trust the Name. He brought me from Jericho's walls, you from Egypt's shadow. He will bring them home."

I looked to the horizon, where the hills of Bethlehem gleamed, I thought of the servant girl Mihlat's prophecy, "Mosheh spoke of a king, Rachav, a scepter from Yehudah. I told Boaz to watch those hills. Perhaps his son, or his son's son, will see it rise."

Her eyes followed mine, a spark of prophecy. "A king of mercy, to gather the scattered. I pray we see his shadow."

I raised my staff, my voice a prayer, soft yet piercing the heavens. "Avinu Malkeinu, guard this land. When the tribes scatter, when faithlessness drives them to Moab or Edom, hold them in Your hand. And when the time comes, bring the King of Mercy, to gather what has been scattered."

The wind answered, stirring the terebinth, and I felt the Name, a fire no darkness could quench. The hill held me, its stones bearing witness, and I knew the promise would endure—not in my breath, but in the blood of those who followed. The tents below glowed with firelight, a constellation of covenant, and I turned back, my heart anchored, the closing of an age a whisper of the dawn to come.

Acknowledgments

This book would not have been possible without Jessica. Her deep knowledge of ancient pagan religions and antiquity proved instrumental at every stage. Time and again, she illuminated details I had never considered—each one adding richness and depth to the world I sought to bring to life.

I am also indebted to the late Dr. Michael Heiser. Though I encountered his work later in my journey, his rigorous scholarship, meticulous citations, and breadth of references inspired a greater standard for my own research. His influence helped sharpen both the scope and substance of this project—To Dr. Heiser, I pray that our Lord may count him among the righteous on the Day of Judgment and grant him rest in the eternal embrace of Abraham. Memory eternal

www.ingramcontent.com/pod-product-compliance
Lightning Source LLC
Chambersburg PA
CBHW061512020726
47502CB00006B/2039